WITNESS
TO EVIL

By Janet Dawson

WITNESS TO EVIL

JANET
DAWSON

Fawcett Columbine • New York

To Gus

A Fawcett Columbine Book
Published by Ballantine Books

http://www.randomhouse.com

Library of Congress Cataloging-in-Publication Data
Dawson, Janet.
    Witness to evil / Janet Dawson. — 1st ed.
      p.   cm.
    ISBN 0-449-00042-7
    I. Title
PS3554.A949W58   1997
813'.54—dc21   97-20594
                                                                                 CIP

Text design by Jie Yang

Manufactured in the United States of America
First Edition: October 1997
10   9   8   7   6   5   4   3   2   1

ACKNOWLEDGMENTS

Merci beaucoup à Bonnie Odiorne, *ma chère compagnon de voyage.*

Thanks also to Nina Koepke; Dawn Church; Fay Gaul; Jerry Kennealy; Barbara Littwin; Sunny Frazier; Sergeant Ed Bowen, Bakersfield Police Department; Commander Donny Youngblood, Kern County Sheriff's Department; Sergeant Ron Adolph, Fresno County Sheriff's Department; Paul Bishop, LAPD; and the staff at the Simon Wiesenthal Center and Museum of Tolerance, Los Angeles.

PROLOGUE
JULY

I KNEW DARCY WAS IN TROUBLE EVEN BEFORE I FOUND OUT about the murder.

The tremble in her voice told me as I listened to the answering machine tape, once, twice, three times. Teenaged bravado only went so far. It didn't disguise outright fear.

"Jeri, it's Darcy. Are you there? If you are, please pick up the phone. Damn."

She sighed. For a few seconds the answering machine cassette played background noises. I leaned forward, my auditory filters picking up voices in the distance, indistinct, each overlaying the others. I heard the tinkling of a bell, the whir of wheels on pavement, the impatient bleat of a horn.

"Jeri, I called because . . . you said any time I needed help, just call. Well, I need it now." There was another pause, with the same background sounds as before, with one addition, the slam of a car door. When she spoke again, Darcy's voice sounded hurried, stretched with anxiety. "I gotta go now, Jeri. I'll call you again. Remember, we'll always have Paris."

I'd heard enough to be seriously disturbed. This time when I rewound the tape, I removed the cassette from the machine for safekeeping, for . . . what? I reached for my car keys, thinking about Darcy and how our beautiful friendship began, nearly three months earlier, when I went to Paris on someone else's franc.

PART ONE
APRIL

C H A P T E R 1

I T WAS THE MONEY.

I admit that, quite readily. I could use the money. The Stefanos were willing to part with it. In fact, they had more money than they had sense. They also had a problem.

When I was working as a paralegal, before I'd been recruited to join the Errol Seville Agency as an investigator, one of my colleagues told me that people who go to lawyers are sick and want to be healed. People go to private investigators for similar reasons. We get hired to solve other people's problems, the ones they can't—or won't—solve themselves.

Dan Stefano phoned me on a Monday morning in late April. After hearing him out, I agreed to meet him and his wife, Elaine, that afternoon, at The House.

The ostentatious edifice the Stefanos were building was located just off Sea View Parkway, on what the developers call Harbor Bay Isle and I call Bay Farm Island. It's a section of Alameda that used to be marshland and is now landfill, located north of the Oakland airport. Once it really was an island, where farmers grew produce, at the end of a causeway that became Island Drive. Now developers grow condos and huge houses that crowd small lots. A good many of them are stucco palaces that look as though they belong in Miami Beach, not the Alameda I grew up in, with its stately Victorians, wood-framed and decorated with gingerbread trim.

When I first saw the place Monday afternoon, all I could think of was the Winchester Mystery House down in San Jose, the project that just kept getting bigger and bigger. Sarah Winchester, heir to the Winchester arms fortune, gave new meaning to the term eccentric. Haunted by evil spirits known only to her, she designed a house built to outwit them and spent thirty-eight years remodeling. The place has a hundred and sixty rooms, thirteen of them bathrooms. There are two thousand doors, ten thousand windows, and forty-seven fireplaces, as well as secret passageways and doors and staircases that lead nowhere. The place is such a rabbit warren that Sarah and her servants needed maps to find their way around.

Elaine Stefano wasn't aiming for a hundred and sixty rooms, but the structure that rose from the shoreline lot resembled an office building rather than a home. It was three stories high, blocking the view of the house behind it. Terra-cotta-colored stucco and a brown tile roof contributed to a vaguely Spanish-Italian-Mediterranean look. A three-car garage with a short driveway presented its face to Sea View Parkway. I parked my Toyota here, alongside a contractor's truck and a late-model Mercedes. Then I followed a path that snaked around to the left, where a few steps led up to a porch and the double front doors, one of them ajar.

As I stepped into a spacious foyer, I heard the whine of a power saw coming from somewhere above me, accompanied by a radio playing country music. Several voices conversed in Spanish. A wide uncarpeted staircase curved up to my right, while ahead of me I saw an open airy space that looked as though it were going to be an enormous kitchen when it grew up.

On my immediate left was an area probably intended as a formal dining room, but as yet there was no table beneath the spiky modern chandelier. Beyond this, a foot lower and anchored by a massive stone fireplace, was a living room, also uncarpeted. It was bigger than my one-bedroom apartment over in the Adams Point section of Oakland. I walked slowly toward a wall of glass, windows and a sliding door looking out onto the water, with a sweeping view of the Bay Bridge and San Francisco beyond. The water reflected the glare of the afternoon sun.

I turned from the Bay and looked back the way I'd come, seeing several paint cans arrayed against the dining room wall. Carpet samples and books of fabric swatches were piled in the corner. The huge kitchen featured lots of blinding white tile and bleached pine cabinets, with a rectangular work island in the middle. There was a big gap on one wall, next to the window over the white porcelain sink, where the refrigerator would go. On the counter between this and the sink, someone had set up a white Braun coffeemaker, its carafe half-full of strong black coffee, and, next to it, a motley collection of plastic mugs.

I was alone, save for the workers upstairs. Then a woman with straight, shoulder-length brown hair came through the sliding glass door that led from the living room to the small rectangle of dirt that was the yard, fronting on the Shoreline Trail. She wore loose-fitting blue slacks with a matching jacket over an ivory blouse, and sandals with low heels. A slim leather shoulder bag completed this ensemble.

She had a cordless phone glued to her left ear and was gesturing with her right hand. "I don't want to listen to any more excuses," she barked into the mouthpiece. "It's the last week in April. You're three weeks behind, anyway."

A couple of runners jogged by on the trail, followed by a cyclist and an elderly woman walking a frisky golden retriever. The woman with the phone listened impatiently to the other person's half of the conversation. She walked into the kitchen, poured some coffee into a mug, and swallowed a mouthful. Then she started talking again. Her abrupt tone made me guess she'd cut off the other voice. I didn't think she'd seen me. Certainly she hadn't acknowledged my presence.

She was still talking when a man wearing a short-sleeved yellow knit shirt, faded jeans, and a pair of loafers without socks came through the front door and looked at me. "Jeri Howard?"

"Yes." I held out my hand. "Dan Stefano?"

He nodded distractedly as he shook my hand, his brown eyes on the woman I assumed was his wife, Elaine. I'm five-eight, and he was perhaps an inch taller, with an incipient paunch rounding his stomach and a computer-nerd slouch. He was losing what used to be a headful of curly black hair.

When he'd called me earlier, Dan Stefano had told me he was in the computer game business. I'd checked him out. He was being modest. He'd started StefanoWorks two years ago and was considered a hot entrepreneur in a highly competitive business. He and his small staff of employees created innovative interactive CD-ROM

games in a suite of offices located not far from here at the Harbor
Bay business park. His most recent release had won a prize and was
selling like the proverbial hotcakes. StefanoWorks was worth serious
big bucks.

I'd checked out Elaine Stefano as well. She was a real estate agent
at a big firm in Alameda. When she wasn't selling houses, I guessed
she supervised construction of The House.

"Elaine, get off the phone already," Dan said in a voice that told
me he was from back east someplace, Jersey maybe. "I need to get
back to work."

"This conversation isn't over," Elaine snapped into the phone, the
chill in her voice designed to strike fear into the heart of whoever
was on the other end. "I'll call you back." She punched a button and
set the cordless on the kitchen counter. "Damned decorators."

Then she looked at me as though seeing me for the first time, and
put on her company face. It smoothed the scowl that drew lines between her eyebrows and at the corners of her hazel eyes. Her full
mouth segued from a frown to a polite and businesslike smile. She
was taller than Dan, with sleek athletic curves that made me speculate she was into jogging or aerobics when she wasn't terrorizing
decorators.

"Hello, I'm Elaine." She held out her hand. "You must be Jeri
Howard. Thank you so much for meeting us here. Would you like
some coffee?"

"No, thanks." I shook the proffered hand. "I gather Mr. Stefano
has to get back to the office. Let's get right to it."

"Call me Dan," he said. "I'd offer you a seat, but . . ." He
shrugged and looked at the disarray around him.

"Never mind," I said, leaning against the kitchen work island.
"Dan, you said on the phone you want me to look for your daughter.
You were very brief. Now I'd like a more detailed picture. When did
you realize Darcy was missing?"

CHAPTER 2

"IF WE'D SENT HER TO BOARDING SCHOOL, AS I SUG-
gested, none of this would have happened."

Elaine's cool exterior cracked, just enough for me to see the anger
crackling underneath. She ran one hand through her glossy brown
hair and skewered her husband with her gaze.

Dan wasn't the source of her fury, however. Elaine Stefano was
royally pissed at her daughter.

"We already had this conversation," he said wearily. "Several
times."

I interrupted. I was here to get information, not watch a domestic
squabble. "Darcy went missing . . . when?"

"It was Wednesday, last week," Elaine said.

Dan shook his head, brow furrowed. "No, it was Thursday."

"She left Wednesday, okay?" Elaine's voice grew argumentative.
"We didn't notice until Thursday."

And why was that? I'd have thought the parents of a seventeen-
year-old girl would notice if their daughter didn't come home that
night. Of course, I'd met a lot of parents who didn't give a damn. At
least the Stefanos wanted me to find the girl.

"We thought she was spending the night with her friend Heather."
Elaine gave me another company smile. "That was on Darcy's calendar, but obviously she planned it as a diversion. We didn't know
she was gone until Sister Bernardine called us from St. Joseph's
Thursday morning, wanting to know why Darcy wasn't in class."

"Catholic school instead of boarding school." I scribbled the information in my notebook. St. Joseph's was over on the main island on Chestnut Street, near the old Victorian that had belonged to my grandmother Jerusha Howard.

"Both the kids go to St. Joe's," Dan said. "They started last fall." This was the first I'd heard of another child in the Stefano household. I must have looked curious, because Dan enlightened me. "Darren. He turned thirteen this past weekend. He's in the eighth grade."

"A well-behaved kid," Elaine declared. "Darren's never given us a moment of trouble. Unlike his sister. Suspended for fighting in the halls . . ."

As I digested this last comment, the power saw stopped. The workers' voices, full of laughter, splashed down the stairwell. Elaine sniffed the air like a bird dog. "Excuse me," she said, heading for the stairs. She went halfway up, to the landing, and spoke a few sharp words in Spanish. The laughter stopped abruptly.

As Elaine marched down the stairs and back to the white-tiled kitchen, I steered the conversation back to Darcy. "So the Sister told you Darcy had cut class, and you checked with her friend Heather. What's Heather's last name?"

"Heather McRae. She goes to school at Alameda High. But Heather said she hadn't seen Darcy since the weekend before last," Elaine finished. "Then I checked my wallet and saw that my American Express card was gone. Her name's Darcy Elaine, you see. She's gotten damned good at forging my signature." She scowled again. "I figured she'd pulled another stunt like New York."

"She's done this before?" I raised an eyebrow. His daughter had run away, Dan Stefano had told me on the phone this morning. He hadn't mentioned that this was a repeat performance.

"Yeah," Dan said. "She . . . ah . . . lifted her mom's credit card last October and headed for the Big Apple. Bought a shitload of stuff and went to a bunch of shows. I caught up with her four days later. At the Plaza, no less."

The lyrics and tune of "Autumn in New York" suddenly sauntered through my mind, as Darcy must have sauntered down Fifth Avenue, purloined credit card in hand. "How many other times has she run away? Before New York?" I wasn't sure I wanted to get into this. What Dan had told me on the phone this morning sounded simple. It was getting more complicated as the Stefanos talked. Was Darcy a habitual runaway?

"Well, there was Carmel," Elaine said, even as Dan muttered something about last summer up at Lake Tahoe.

Great . . . They couldn't even get their stories straight.

Dan assured me that Lake Tahoe was merely a misunderstanding about Darcy staying at someone's summer cabin. But Carmel pre-dated Lake Tahoe. That one happened over Memorial Day week-end, nearly a year ago, at the end of Darcy's junior year at Alameda High School. Darcy helped herself to Mom's Mercedes and tootled on down to Carmel with a carload of classmates, including the afore-mentioned Heather.

It was this incident, I gathered, that led the Stefanos to discuss boarding school. Instead they transferred their errant daughter, and her paragon of a younger brother, from public to parochial school. I had the distinct feeling the Stefanos had hoped the nuns would wave a magic wand and make Darcy behave. She'd gone to New York instead.

I held up my hand. "Let's get back to the current incident. What did you do when you discovered the credit card was missing?"

"I called the credit card company," Elaine said, with a shrug. "Same as I did before. I didn't cancel the card, I just explained the situation and told them I needed to know what she'd charged on it and when." She rolled her eyes upward. "I certainly wasn't expect-ing a plane ticket to Paris."

"Paris?" I repeated. "Your daughter ran away to Paris?"

"She's got her own passport," Dan said. "We went to Mexico a couple of years ago."

"She flew Air France out of SFO Wednesday evening, arrived at Charles de Gaulle Thursday afternoon." Elaine unfastened the clasp of her shoulder bag and pulled out a slip of paper. "She got a cash advance at an airport ATM right before she took off. She used an-other ATM in Paris on Saturday. The American Express people told me that particular ATM is in the Latin Quarter, on the Left Bank."

"How did she get your personal identification number?" I asked, marveling at just how far this particular runaway had gone. I cer-tainly gave her points for originality.

"I never can remember it." Elaine looked exasperated. "So I'd written it in the margin of my checkbook."

"Am I to understand that you want me to go to Paris," I asked slowly, "to locate your daughter and bring her back?"

"Of course," Elaine said. "I'll have my travel agent make the arrangements. How soon can you leave?"

I looked at the Stefanos, wondering if I should pick up this can of worms, let alone open it. One of my fellow PIs never takes cases involving juveniles. Too much potential for trouble, he says.

"If you know Darcy's in Paris, why don't you go after her yourselves?"

This question netted me a long silence. Dan looked glum. Elaine didn't meet my eyes. Instead she tucked the paper into her bag and shut it.

"I can't get away," Dan said finally. "We're about to release a new game. It's just impossible."

"I can't leave The House." Elaine's voice capitalized the words as she swept a hand around her. "Or my work. It's a busy time right now. And Darren, of course. He needs his mother."

I'll bet, I thought. When she has time between showing listings, supervising contractors, and haranguing decorators.

"Besides," Elaine continued, "Dan and I wouldn't have the slightest idea where to look. That's where you come in. I'm sure that you, a trained investigator, can locate her much more quickly than we could."

"Paris is a very large city," I pointed out. "Even if I only look on the Left Bank."

The Stefanos, sensing my reluctance, proceeded to throw money at me. Figuratively, of course. With the kind of money they were talking for this retrieval job, I realized, I could combine it with what I had in savings and put a down payment on something larger than my one-bedroom apartment. Something, of course, decidedly smaller than The House.

That kind of money was tempting. It always is. I've got a business to run as well as bills to pay.

I leveled a gaze at both Stefanos. "Are you sure you want me to do this?"

I thought Dan hesitated for a second. After all, it was he who had gone to New York to fetch Darcy the last time.

"Of course we're sure," Elaine said, a bit more forcefully than was warranted, forestalling any argument from her husband.

Still I hesitated. Kids usually run away for a reason, whether it's a fight with the folks or something more serious. I questioned Dan and Elaine Stefano closely, trying to determine if there were indications that Darcy was using drugs, if there were hints of emotional or physical abuse. Was the girl sexually active? They didn't know. Any boyfriends? Dan and Elaine couldn't come up with any specific names. I needed to talk with Darcy's friend Heather McRae, who, I was quite sure, knew more about Darcy's social life than did Darcy's parents.

Something told me this wasn't going to be as simple as just flying to Paris to fetch Darcy from her adventure in the City of Lights. I smelled a strong scent of dysfunctional family, upscale division.

Even if I took the case, how was I going to find the girl? Darcy's use of the ATM on the Left Bank didn't do much to narrow the search. Unless the girl's personal belongings would provide some clues.

Finally I let myself be seduced by the money. "All right. I'll take the case. But I can't leave right away. I have to make some arrangements and tie up some loose ends first." Even as I spoke I was ticking off a mental checklist. My passport was in order. I'd need to board my cats, Abigail and Black Bart, reschedule several appointments, cancel a dinner date with my father. "Before we go any further, there are a few things I need."

The first of these was my standard contract, which I discussed with the Stefanos. This was followed by a very large retainer check, written and signed with a flourish by Elaine. These details out of the way, I asked more questions about Darcy, writing the answers in my notebook as I tried to decide how I was going to retrieve the girl as expeditiously as possible.

"I'll need a recent photograph. And just to be safe, I'd like a notarized statement from you, saying I'm authorized to act on your behalf."

"I've got some snapshots at the condo," Elaine said. I sensed her desire to stay at The House and continue her telephone battle with the decorators. Dan had already told us he needed to get back to StefanoWorks.

But I was calling the shots now, at least some of them. "I want to search Darcy's room," I told them. "And I'd like both of you to be there when I do it."

W HILE THE HOUSE EVOLVED, THE STEFANOS WERE LIV-
ing in a three-bedroom condo. It was located in one of the
complexes clustered along the lagoon, just off Mecartney Road near
the Landing, the shopping center anchored by a grocery store and
several smaller businesses. Once inside the second-floor unit, I could
see why the family needed more space. The rooms seemed small
and cramped, full of furniture, belongings, the everyday clutter of
life. One end of the dining area adjacent to the kitchen had been
turned into an office, with a desk shoved up against the wall.

While Elaine dug through a box of snapshots, Dan showed me
to the girl's bedroom. He stood awkwardly in the doorway as I
surveyed what seemed to be an orderly space, atypical for a teenaged girl. My own room at age seventeen was a hell of a lot messier
than this.

The double bed was covered with a quilted comforter in a deep
blue that complemented the framed poster hanging above the bed.
It was from a recent exhibit of Monet paintings at San Francisco's
de Young Museum, a print of delicate pink and yellow water lilies
floating on the artist's blue and green water garden.

Next to Darcy's white laminate student desk was a matching
bookcase. I pulled up the desk chair and sat down, sifting through
the volumes that filled the three shelves. The bottom shelf held
school books and supplies. On the middle shelf I found an assortment of paperback novels—mysteries, science fiction, and historical
romances—and a book about Rodgers and Hammerstein. There

was a trade paperback on the making of the movie *Casablanca*. Next to this I found a videotape of the movie itself, along with two other Bogart films, *The Maltese Falcon* and *The African Queen*. I smiled. Darcy and I had the same taste when it came to old movies.

The top shelf held a number of books. Two were overdue library books: William L. Shirer's *The Rise and Fall of the Third Reich*, and *The War Against the Jews* by Lucy S. Dawidowicz. The rest of the books had something to do with art. Three dealt with Impressionism in general, and one was about Claude Monet. I also found a copy of an art appreciation book, Strickland's *The Annotated Mona Lisa*. All of these were large trade paperbacks. There was also a hardback copy of *Monet's Passion* by Elizabeth Murray, a study of the artist's gardens at Giverny, north of Paris.

"Darcy's interested in art," I said, looking up at Dan.

He shrugged. "For now. She has phases. She went to see that Monet show three times. Before that it was Broadway musicals."

I leaned back in the chair. "You said when she went to New York, she saw a lot of shows. Do you think she went to Paris to see the Impressionists?"

"Hell, I don't know. That makes about as much sense as anything else."

The phone rang. Dan excused himself and went to answer it. From what I heard of his end of the conversation, the caller was from his office and there was a crisis in progress. Dan dealt with it, then rejoined me in the bedroom. By that time I'd searched the desk drawers, coming up with more bits and pieces of Darcy's life, including a research paper about the American musical theater. She'd gotten an A.

No sign of a diary or a journal. If she kept one, she'd taken it with her. The calendar Elaine had mentioned earlier was on Darcy's desk, but it didn't offer much insight. I found nothing useful in the closet. Now I knelt on the floor, poking my hand between the mattress and box springs.

"Finding anything?" Dan asked.

"I hope so." My hand had encountered something and now I pulled it out. It was a recent edition of a guidebook called *Cheap Sleeps in Paris*. I sat down on the bed and leafed through the pages.

Here and there I saw splotches of yellow highlighter and notes scribbled in pencil. It appeared she had been doing some research on hotels prior to her departure.

I finished searching Darcy's room, rifling through her underwear and socks, then headed back to the living room. "Have there been any calls to Paris on your phone bill?"

Dan scrunched his face into a frown. "I don't think so. But I'll call the phone company and check." He walked to the desk in the dining area and picked up the receiver.

I heard a key turning in a lock and looked up, into the hazel eyes of a skinny kid with unruly dark brown hair. His narrow frame was dwarfed by the dark pants and white shirt he wore. He looked as though he'd slept in them. Slung over one shoulder was a neon-green nylon backpack.

"Hi," he said, in a squeaky voice, removing the pack. "Who're you?"

"I'm Jeri Howard. You must be Darren."

"Yeah." His eyes raked over me with avid curiosity. "You must be the private detective." He noted my expression. "Oh, yeah, I heard Mom and Dad talking about it last night. Are you gonna go to Paris to get Darcy?"

"I guess I am."

A woman came through the doorway behind Darren. "I would have thought that your parents would go after Darcy." The words were tart, as though the speaker was aware she was expressing a minority opinion. She was in her sixties, I guessed, of compact build and medium height, with a stylishly coifed head of silvery hair and piercing brown eyes. She wore a simple navy-blue dress. Pearls clustered at her ears and around her throat.

"Good afternoon, Jeri Howard." She walked toward me and held out her elegant beringed hand, speaking in a precise, clipped voice. "I'm Adele Gregory, Elaine's mother."

I returned her greeting as Elaine walked briskly into the living room, carrying a handful of four-by-six-inch snapshots. She stopped and stared past me at the older woman, looking surprised. "Hello, Mother. I wasn't expecting you."

"You should be," Mrs. Gregory said, tight around the mouth.

"We discussed this last week. I thought you'd written it on one of your many social calendars. I picked up Darren at school, as planned. And I'm taking him out for a belated birthday dinner."

"I'm sorry, Mother." Elaine's voice was placating. "With all of this business about Darcy . . . well, it just went out of my mind."

Dan returned to the living room, acknowledging his mother-in-law with a quick peck on the cheek. "Hi, Adele. Have you met Jeri?" He didn't wait for an answer. Instead he turned to me. "Phone company says, no calls to Paris. Guess the next thing is to call my lawyer, so we can get that document you wanted."

"Here are the pictures you asked for," Elaine said, shoving the snapshots into my hand with the air of someone who wanted to get rid of a burden.

I sat down on the sofa, setting the Paris book on the end of the dusty glass-topped coffee table in front of me, pushing a stack of computer magazines to one side. I arranged the photos, seven in all, in a semicircle, and took a gander at Darcy Elaine Stefano.

Seventeen, going on forty. That was the way Dan had described Darcy on the phone that morning. She looked like hell on wheels for sure, I thought.

Darcy was a beauty, with her father's big dark eyes and her mother's glossy chestnut hair, which she sometimes wore cascading down past her shoulders, other times piled artlessly onto her head. She had a figure that was slender and curvaceous in all the places where that was required. In most of the photos she was laughing or smiling with a full-lipped, sensual mouth and a lot of straight white teeth. I saw intelligence and humor in her face. And trouble.

Darcy would be eighteen in a couple of months, but she looked older and could easily pass for twenty-two. Evidently she hadn't prompted any inquiries from the immigration authorities at Charles de Gaulle as to what she was planning to do in France.

"I don't think I'll have any trouble identifying her." I gathered the photos like playing cards and tucked them into my purse. Then I picked up the copy of *Cheap Sleeps in Paris*. "Darcy's highlighted several hotels in this book. I'll make some phone calls and see if I can narrow down her whereabouts. In the meantime, I'd like to talk with Sister Bernardine over at St. Joseph's. And with Heather McRae and some of Darcy's other friends. Maybe I can get a sense of why Darcy left. And why Paris."

Something flickered across Adele Gregory's face as she sat down next to me on the sofa. But if Darcy's grandmother knew anything about her granddaughter's plans, she wasn't saying, at least not now.

"Do whatever you need to do," Dan said, heading for the door as he checked his watch. It was four-thirty. "I'm really sorry, but I have got to get back to my office."

"I thought perhaps you could join Darren and me for dinner," Adele said, pointedly looking from her son-in-law to her daughter. "We're going to Lalime's in Berkeley."

"No can do." Dan shook his head. "Got a meeting at five."

"And I've got to get back to The House," Elaine said. "To make sure those damn workmen didn't knock off the minute I left. I've got to solve this decorator situation. And I'm showing a house at six." She looked at her mother as though she knew exactly what was going on in the older woman's head. "I know, Mother, I know. You and Darren go ahead, maybe I can get there in time for dessert."

"She won't, of course," Adele said, when her daughter had disappeared out the condo's front door. "It will be just the two of us." She smiled at Darren.

He grinned back at her, leaning over the arm of the sofa. "That's okay, Grandma. That means I get a sip of your wine. And two desserts."

"Bottomless pit." She ruffled his dark curls affectionately. "Two desserts, then. If you have room after you eat an enormous dinner. And I expect you will. Now run and clean up. Put on that lovely suit I bought you for your birthday."

He screwed up his face. "Aw, Grandma. Do I hafta?"

"Yes, you have to."

"Just a minute," I said, as he got up to leave. "Darren, do you know why your sister went to Paris?"

D ARREN ROLLED HIS EYES, THEN HE SHRUGGED. "I dunno. It's not like she told me she was going. She doesn't tell me a whole lot. I'm just the bratty kid brother."

I smiled, recalling my own bratty kid brother. Then I looked at Adele Gregory. Her response to my question was subtle, but noticeable. Her brown eyes lost some of the sparkle they'd had during her earlier banter with her grandson. The elegant older woman now looked guarded and troubled.

On the surface, I supposed that was because she thought her daughter and son-in-law should go after Darcy, not some hired gun in the person of Jeri Howard, private investigator. Yet I couldn't shake the feeling that Darcy's jaunt to Paris was no surprise to Darcy's grandmother.

Adele seemed to be avoiding any response to my question. So I took my inquiry in a different direction.

"How do you and Darcy get along?" I asked Darren.

"Okay, I guess." He shrugged again. "We don't beat up on each other, not much anyway. I help her with her homework sometimes. And she helps me. We're both good in different subjects. I'm better at math and science, stuff like that. Darcy's more . . . artistic. That's a good word, artistic."

"Creative." Adele nodded as she spoke.

It sounded as though Darcy got along better with her kid brother than I had with mine. Brian and I had fought some epic battles over the years. He used to throw tomato worms at me because he knew I couldn't stand the ugly things. I'd once retaliated by paddling him with a tennis racquet. This led to a knock-down fight. We were rolling in the grass in the backyard of our Victorian house in Alameda when my mother turned the hose on us. As for helping Brian with his homework, he was such a little wiseass know-it-all, I'd never once volunteered.

It's amazing my kid brother turned out to be such a responsible adult. I'm sure he thinks the same about me.

As I talked with Darren, he seemed to be the stereotypical nerdy kid who was quite happy playing with his computer or his video games, or riding his bike along the Shoreline Trail. He had friends, both at his old school here on Harbor Bay Island and at St. Joseph's. It appeared that one of his best friends was his grandmother, however.

"I taught Grandma all about computers," he said proudly.

"It's true." Adele smiled and looked at him with affection. "I didn't know a thing about them. In fact, I was a bit leery of them. Darren insisted I should have one, so the whole family gave me one for my birthday last year. Now Darren and I e-mail each other every day. It's like talking over the back fence."

"Where do you live, Mrs. Gregory?"

"In San Francisco. The Richmond district, between the Presidio and Golden Gate Park. I've lived there most of my life."

"And Mr. Gregory?"

Her smile dimmed. "My husband died, eighteen months ago. But a friend has moved in with me. It's not so lonely that way."

"Darcy and Darren come visit you frequently, I take it."

"Oh, yes. They love to visit the city, with the shows and the museums. Darren's favorite is the Exploratorium, of course." She ruffled her grandson's dark hair. "Darcy likes the de Young and the Palace of the Legion of Honor."

"I noticed a poster in Darcy's room, from the Monet exhibit at the de Young."

"She went to that one several times," Adele said. "I went with her the first time, then she kept going back on her own. She developed such a passion for Monet, wanted to know everything about him."

"Might that be why she went to Paris?"

"I don't know." Adele's face closed up again. "It seems like such an extravagant response."

"It appears, from some of Darcy's previous behavior, that she's made some extravagant responses in the past."

"I suppose you're right." She looked at her watch. "Darren, you must change, or we'll be late for our dinner at Lalime's."

"Just one more thing," I asked. "Did Darcy ever give any indication of how she felt about being transferred from Alameda High to St. Joseph's?"

"Not in words," Adele said. "But I'm sure she was unhappy. She had gone through junior high and most of high school with the same friends."

"She hates it," Darren said succinctly. "She hates everything about it, from the uniforms to the teachers."

"Did you know she was in a fight at school?"

I could tell from the look on Adele's face that she hadn't known, but the altercation was old news to Darren. "Yeah. She got suspended. Mom and Dad were really pissed . . . er, upset about that. But I don't know what it was about."

I left them to their dinner plans and went home to mine, considerably less elegant than Lalime's in Berkeley. I live near Lake Merritt in downtown Oakland, in a U-shaped stucco building that surrounds a courtyard.

I'd lived in this one-bedroom apartment since my breakup with my ex-husband, Sid Vernon, a homicide sergeant over at the Oakland Police Department. I was comfortable here, until lately when I began feeling the urge to buy a place of my own, perhaps a condo or a cottage.

That's what led me to the admittedly mercenary decision to take the Stefano case. But my savings needed a little sweetening before I could scrape up the necessary funds for a down payment and closing costs. The condo market had been a bit slow recently but California real estate was still astronomical compared with other parts of the country. Not that I'd ever considered moving to the Back of Beyond, simply for a lower cost of living. I'd lived in the Bay Area my whole life and couldn't imagine living anywhere else.

My fat tabby cat Abigail was sprawled in one of her favorite snoozing spots, the back of my sofa. From this vantage point she could look out at the newly planted rhododendron in the flower bed under my front window, or at the fountain in the center of the courtyard where birds sometimes congregated. She'd been asleep until my key turned in the lock. Now she gave me a languid look, stretched and meowed as I scratched her behind the ears.

The elusive Black Bart, a kitten who still retained his feral roots, was in the linen closet. The latch didn't hold the door shut properly so he'd taken to sleeping on the second shelf, out of the reach of that other, larger cat who either played with him or jumped on him. Today I saw yellow eyes gazing from the white mask on his face. The rest of him was an inky spot of black fur wedged between a couple of red towels.

I reached in to stroke his back. He permitted my touch with wary resignation. He tolerates me because I rescued him from a cold December rain. I provide food on a regular basis and a warm place to sleep. Now and then he lurks under the bed and leaps out to bat at my feet with his paws. Over the past month he's warmed up enough to decide that I might be okay when I'm in a horizontal position. In the evening, when I read in bed, or in the mornings, just before I get up, he snuggles next to me and allows me to run my hand over his silky fur. At such times he musters a purr. Any other time, however, he shies away from my approach, or looks at me as though certain I plan to make kitty stew out of him.

I changed clothes, from my businesslike slacks and shirt to a pair of sweatpants and a T-shirt, then I padded barefoot from bedroom to kitchen and put a pot of water onto the burner. While I waited for it to boil I reached for the phone and punched in a number.

Kaz was in his office at Children's Hospital. That's Kazimir Pelligrino, the gorgeous workaholic doctor I met last December. We've been dating since then, at first just friendly companionship. But lately there's been more, including sharing a bed.

"What was the name of that hotel you stayed in while you were in Paris?" I asked him. "It's on the Left Bank, right?"

"I always stay on the Left Bank. The Hôtel Solférino, near the Musée d'Orsay. Great location, seventh arrondissement. It's quiet and close to the Seine. The hotel is a couple of blocks from the Métro. What are you planning to do, accompany Cassie and Eric on their honeymoon?"

"It's a case. Believe it or not, someone's paying me to go. Client with more money than sense. 'April in Paris, chestnuts in blossom . . .' " I sang.

"Beats serving subpoenas, I'm sure. That must be some case."

"It is. Listen, if you were young and going to Paris for the first time, where would you stay?"

"Latin Quarter," he said without hesitation. "Fifth arrondissement, on the Left Bank, close to the Sorbonne and a lot of other schools. Students, nightlife, close to everything. It's noisy, plenty of cheap hotels and restaurants."

That jibed with Darcy's use of an ATM in the Latin Quarter. I didn't tell Kaz anything more, nor did he ask. As a doctor, he understood the need for confidentiality.

"When are you leaving?" he asked.

"Maybe Wednesday. I've got to do a little research first. And I don't know how long I'll be gone. If it goes well, only a few days."

I rang off and tossed a couple of handfuls of pasta into boiling water. While it cooked I pulled a few greens together for a salad and opened a jar of sauce, heating a cupful in the microwave before I spooned it over the pasta and decorated the lot with some grated parmesan.

Not as elegant as Lalime's, I thought as I sat down to dinner, but quicker.

Darcy had evidently come to the same conclusion as Kaz about the Latin Quarter. When I read through *Cheap Sleeps in Paris* and made a list of the hotels Darcy had highlighted, fully half were in the 5th arrondissement. The rest were in the 6th, with a couple, including the Solférino, in the 7th. The Stefanos had told me that there had been no Paris phone calls on their bill. Nor did it appear that Darcy had torn any pages from the book. She must have made a list to take with her. It was a long shot that she might be at one of the hotels in the book, but maybe the long shot would pay off.

It did.

I arrived at my office early Tuesday and began making calls to Paris, where it was the middle of the afternoon. The Hôtel Belloc was midway down the list, at an address on rue Thénard, just below the boulevard Saint-Germain, and probably not far from where Darcy had used the ATM on Saturday.

I asked questions in my college French. The voice on the other side of the Atlantic told me that Mademoiselle Stefano had checked in five days earlier. She had gone out. Did I wish to leave a message?

No, I didn't. I wanted Darcy still to be registered at the Hôtel Belloc when I got to Paris.

CHAPTER 5

"DARCY DIDN'T LIKE IT HERE. SHE MISSED HER FRIENDS at Alameda High."

Sister Bernardine put it much the same way Darcy's kid brother had. But the nun's voice was deeper and she spoke with authority from behind her desk at the administrative office of St. Joseph's Notre Dame High School.

The basilica itself fronted on Chestnut Street in central Alameda, with the stucco buildings of its various schools grouped around it. The high school was located on the tree-shaded corner of Chestnut and San Jose Avenue, full of students wearing uniforms. Both sexes wore white shirts, with the boys in dark trousers and the girls in skirts of dark blue and green plaid.

I'd arrived at the school just before eleven Tuesday morning, having arranged the appointment over the phone. Through the Sister's window I saw a group of youngsters gathered in front of St. Joseph's elementary school. They looked as though they were getting ready to leave on a field trip. Somewhere out of sight, I heard a band practicing, ragged, uneven music floating on the spring air.

I'd gone to public schools here in Alameda, not parochial. Somewhere in the back of my mind I expected Sister Bernardine to look like Audrey Hepburn in *The Nun's Story*. She didn't. She was in her forties, a sturdy woman with short black hair and creamy brown skin. She wasn't wearing a habit and she looked tough and capable, useful attributes when dealing with teenagers.

"That's to be expected," I said. "Since Darcy went through junior high and high school with the same kids." I shifted on the hard wooden seat of the chair just in front of Sister Bernardine's desk. "Why did the Stefanos transfer Darcy?"

I'd already heard the Stefano version. I wanted to see if the Sister's take jibed with theirs.

"I'd like to think it's because we provide an excellent education," the nun said wryly, with a smile to match. "But I have a feeling it was also because we're stricter about discipline."

"Did you know the Stefanos had considered sending her to boarding school?"

She shook her head. "No, they didn't mention it. As I recall, Mrs. Stefano seemed quite concerned about Darcy's behavior. She used the term 'out of control' several times. Mr. Stefano is Catholic, and he said he attended Catholic schools when he was growing up in New Jersey. He also said he felt we could provide more direction and guidance for Darcy."

"But it didn't work out."

The nun shook her head. "Not really. Darcy rebelled by cutting class and going down to Alameda High to hang out with her friends. Then she pulled the New York escapade. Her father went after her. She seemed to settle down for a while. Then at the end of March she was suspended for three days, for fighting with another student. As a matter of fact, we suspended both of them."

"What was this fight about?"

"Neither one of them would say. Nor would any of their classmates." The nun rubbed one sturdy finger across her chin as she described the incident. "Evidently they exchanged words just as a history class was ending. They began shouting at one another in the hall during the class break. From there, it escalated into what my father used to call fisticuffs. I'm not sure who threw the first punch, but the teacher had to wade in and break up the fight."

"The history teacher broke up the fight?" She nodded. "Did the teacher have any idea what triggered the argument?"

"I don't recall," she said. "I can certainly ask him."

"May I talk with the other student?"

Sister Bernardine frowned and thought about it for a moment.

"I'm not sure what bearing it has on Darcy's disappearance. But . . . I suppose it wouldn't do any harm."

Sister Bernardine left her office. I waited for about ten minutes. When she returned, she had the other student in tow. Again I was surprised, expecting the person Darcy had fought with to be another teenaged girl. Instead I found myself looking at Peter Avon, a gangly boy of seventeen, with a bad case of acne scarring both cheeks.

Peter wasn't much help. He remained closemouthed, even sullen, despite the incentive provided by sharp-eyed Sister Bernardine and her pointed questions. Peter said he didn't remember the subject of the quarrel. Either that, or he had no intention of talking about it, especially to a couple of adults. All he would say was that he and Darcy had been arguing and it was her fault, because she slapped him.

"I spoke with the history teacher when I went to fetch Peter," Sister Bernardine said when the boy left the office. "The week the fight occurred his class was talking about twentieth-century European history, World War I, World War II. As he remembers it, he was answering a question from another student when he heard Peter and Darcy arguing. He told them to keep it down, and then the bell rang. The students left the classroom, and next thing he knew, there was a commotion in the hall. He went out to break up the fight."

I thought about this for a moment, staring past the nun at the world outside the window. World War II, I thought, recalling those overdue library books I'd found in Darcy's room.

I turned my attention back to the Sister. "Any guesses as to why Darcy would take off for Paris?"

She shook her head. "For the fun of it? That's evidently why she went to Carmel, and later to New York City. From what I've seen of Darcy she operates on impulse, without thinking of the consequences of her actions. She suddenly wanted to see Paris, so she went. That's my best guess. It means, of course, that she won't graduate with her class. That's one of the consequences she didn't consider before she left."

"Couldn't she make up the work?" Assuming I found her quickly and got her back to the States with minimal fuss.

Sister Bernardine frowned. "Her grades have been mediocre, and this escapade . . ."

She didn't finish her thought. She didn't have to. I figured the powers that be at St. Joseph's had reached the limit with Darcy Stefano's disruptive behavior.

CHAPTER 6

I LEFT THE PAROCHIAL SCHOOL BEHIND AND HEADED FOR
the public one. Alameda High was several blocks away, its campus bordered by Encinal and Central avenues, and Oak and Walnut streets. I was meeting Darcy's best friend, Heather McRae, on her lunch break. The meeting had been scheduled after a phone call from Elaine Stefano to her mother. Heather herself had chosen the site, the produce market on the corner of Central and Oak.

I snagged a parking space on Central and walked down to the corner. I was a few minutes early, so I strolled through the market, gazing at the panoply of color, from the dark green heads of broccoli to the shiny red bell peppers and the soft red-gold fuzz on the early apricots. I was tempted to fill up one of the red hand-baskets, but since I was leaving for Paris the next day there was no point in replenishing my stores of fruits and vegetables. Instead, I watched an enterprising squirrel make its way across Oak Street, pausing its jerky progression to look out for traffic. It jumped onto the nearest fixture, singling out a display of unshelled nuts, tucked a large walnut into its mouth, and made its escape back across the street to the bushes bordering the old high school.

Shortly after noon students swarmed off the campus headed for downtown Alameda and whatever lunch awaited them in the food establishments that lined nearby Park Street, the city's main drag. As I watched them walk past on this bright spring day, I contrasted the kids' colorful grab-bag attire with the uniforms worn by the parochial school's students.

Elaine had told me Heather was a tall blonde, so I scanned the students as they passed the produce market. Then I spotted a tall, slender girl with long cornsilk hair, wearing red tights and a short-sleeved cotton dress striped with blue and yellow. She was walking with a group of girls, black, white, Asian, Hispanic, all of them talking at once. They all had packs on their backs, similar to the one Darren Stefano had worn yesterday. That seemed to be a fashion requirement these days. They crossed the street and headed toward the market. The tall girl angled away from the rest and approached me.

"Are you Jeri Howard?" she asked. Her friends hovered behind her, whispering and watching. When I answered in the affirmative, she hesitated. "My mom says I'm supposed to ask to see some identification."

"Fair enough." I pulled out my wallet and showed her my license.

"Cool," she said. "I've never talked to a private eye before." She turned and waggled her fingers at her friends, whose whispers had turned into a buzz. "Catch up with you guys later." Reluctantly they continued their progress along Central.

"You want something to drink?" I asked, indicating the frozen yogurt shop next to the produce market.

"Could we go to this coffee place on Park Street? I'd love a mocha."

We cut through a nearby parking lot and headed for the espresso place, a block away on Park Street. It had become a popular hangout for teenagers and twentysomethings. This noon hour it was crowded, customers spilling out onto the sidewalk. It looked as though I was the oldest person in the joint. I ordered a mocha for Heather and a caffè latte for myself. While I waited for our coffees, Heather snagged a tiny table near the back, just as its previous occupant vacated it.

Once we were seated, Heather stuck an exploratory tongue into the whipped cream atop her mocha. "So what do you want to ask me?"

"About Darcy." I sipped my latte.

"What about Darcy?" When my silence indicated I wasn't going to play word games, Heather shrugged. "I don't know why she went off to Paris, if that's what you mean."

"She didn't tell you she was going?"

Heather rolled her big blue eyes. "No, I swear it, honest to God. Mrs. Stefano accused me of knowing all about it. But I didn't. You coulda knocked me over. I thought she had balls when she ran off to New York. But Paris . . . wow! It's just like Darcy."

"Why is it just like Darcy?"

"She's always willing to go out there, on the edge, out on a limb." Heather sighed in admiration of Darcy's bravura performance and swallowed a mouthful of her coffee.

"What about that weekend in Carmel last year?" I asked.

"What about it?" Heather gave me a sidelong glance and sighed. "It was sort of spontaneous, y'know. Darcy showed up at my place in her mom's Merc and said, let's go to Carmel. It just sounded so cool a bunch of us piled into the car and went."

"I take it the Carmel trip is one reason Darcy's parents transferred her to St. Joseph's."

"She hates it there. Who wouldn't? I mean, it's so unfair. We went to school together since junior high. And just because Darcy's high-spirited, her parents send her into exile over at that Catholic school."

The two long blocks between Walnut Street and Chestnut Street didn't seem like exile to me, but I suppose to Darcy and her friends, it must have felt that way.

"High-spirited," I repeated. "Tell me, Heather, did Darcy ever experiment with drugs?"

Dan and Elaine Stefano had vigorously denied that their daughter had ever done such a thing, but these days the stuff was everywhere, from a simple toke on a joint to the really bad stuff that could kill you. Darcy's getting into drugs was a very real possibility that had to be considered.

Heather didn't meet my eyes. Instead, she seemed to be awfully interested in the long spoon she was using to stir her mocha.

"Come on, Heather. Level with me. If I'm going to find Darcy I need to know who she is, why she did this."

"She's just herself," Heather protested. "And maybe she doesn't want to be found."

"That's not realistic," I told her. "Darcy's seventeen years old. She's got no business roaming around Paris on her own, even on a lark. She's already in serious trouble. Is she involved with drugs?"

Heather shook her head. "No. Well, we . . . she's smoked a little pot, okay? Just now and then. It's not like she was using crack or crank or any of that stuff."

"But it's out there," I said.

"Yeah." Heather ducked her blond head and sipped her coffee. "There was this guy named John, a couple of classes ahead of us. He got into this really bad crowd over in Oakland. They were all into crank. I think some of his friends were dealing."

Crank, or methamphetamine, is known as "the poor man's cocaine." Easy to manufacture, it makes big bucks for the dealers.

"He got caught, got sent away," Heather continued. "To some treatment program. Some of his buddies got busted. They're at CYA, y'know, the California Youth Authority."

"Were Darcy and John friends?" I asked, wondering where this was leading.

"Yeah, they were dating for a while, but it was over when John got sent away. But when Darcy heard what happened to him, she swore she'd never use that stuff. That it wasn't worth it. So you see, she wasn't into drugs. That proves it."

That might prove it for Heather, but it didn't necessarily cinch it for me. "When was this?"

"Two years ago," Heather said. "We were sophomores and John was a senior."

"Long before Darcy went off to New York," I said. "Can you think of anything that might have prompted that trip?"

"Darcy doesn't need a reason." Heather shrugged. "She just does things. Darcy says life's short, you better do what you want to do while there's time. She went to New York because she wanted to go. She said she had a great time, going to all those Broadway shows. She loves the theater."

Somehow I wasn't surprised. Darcy struck me as quite theatrical.

"And old movies," Heather added. "She's forever dragging me to the U.C. Theatre in Berkeley to see some old Humphrey Bogart flick. She just loves Bogart." She shook her head as though she were unable to understand this obsession with an actor who'd been dead since before she was born.

I laughed. "I'm with Darcy when it comes to Bogie. Broadway shows might explain New York. Why Paris?"

Heather looked thoughtful as she drank some more coffee. She started to shake her head, then brightened as though something had just occurred to her. "Well . . . I don't know if it means anything, but there was that Monet thing at the de Young Museum over in San Francisco. She went a bunch of times. Darcy said those paintings just blew her away. She said she'd love to go see all the Impressionists at the museums in Paris. And the place where Monet lived, to see if the water in that lily pond was really that color."

"It really is," I said, thinking of my own visit to Giverny a couple of years ago. "You think she went to Paris to see the art?"

"I don't know why she went," Heather said. "It was just something she said when we came out of that Monet thing. I never gave it another thought until Mrs. Stefano called and started interrogating me."

"Did Darcy ever say anything about a fight at school in March, with a guy named Peter Avon?"

Heather's eyes widened. "No. She got into a hair-pulling thing with a girl in our junior year at Alameda High, but it wasn't during school hours."

"Know what it was about?"

"It was about a guy, and he wasn't worth fighting over. Darcy kicked her butt, though." She looked at her watch. "I really have to grab a sandwich and get back to school."

"One more question. Does Darcy get along with her folks and her brother?"

Heather seemed hesitant as she finished her coffee. "Well, I think she likes her dad more than her mother." A not uncommon pattern, I thought, considering my own relationship with my parents. "Her brother's okay. Nicer than mine, for sure. But Darcy thinks they pay more attention to Darren than they do to her."

Acting out in order to attract her parents' attention? I considered this after Heather had gone. Darcy Stefano certainly acted where others might hesitate. She was an impulsive seventeen-year-old who had acquired a reputation as a troublemaker.

But I hadn't signed on to straighten out Darcy, just to find her. Once I had her with me on a plane back to the Bay Area, that would end my involvement.

I finished my latte and headed back to my car. I was almost ready to leave for Paris. Before meeting Sister Bernardine, I'd been to Dan Stefano's office at the Harbor Bay Island business park, to pick up the notarized legal document I'd requested. Tonight I'd pack, and tomorrow morning I'd corral my cats and take them to my vet to be boarded during my absence. One of my neighbors would keep an eye on the apartment, while my friend Cassie would check my mail and messages at the office. I had a reservation for Paris tomorrow evening, on the same regularly scheduled Air France flight Darcy had taken, and a week reserved at the Hôtel Solférino on the Left Bank, all of it courtesy of the Stefanos' credit card, the one their daughter hadn't stolen.

I wondered if I'd have time to revisit the Impressionists at the Musée d'Orsay.

CHAPTER 7

'D CHECKED WITH SEVERAL COLLEAGUES BEFORE LEAVING
for Paris. All of them said I didn't need to advise the Paris police
that I was in town, working on a case. So I told the young man at
Immigration that I was in France on vacation. I must have looked
trustworthy, as well as relentlessly American. He barely glanced at
my passport and ticket before waving me through.

It was the middle of the afternoon on Thursday, more than twelve
long hours since I'd left San Francisco. I hadn't managed much
sleep on the big Air France jet. I never do. Now I hauled my roll-
aboard suitcase through the terminal toward the exit, dodging an
elegantly clad woman who looked unconcerned as her black poodle
squatted and urinated, leaving a spreading yellow puddle on the
floor. She puffed away on a cigarette, as did most of the people
around her.

Oh, California . . . I stifled a cough. The French smoked. All
the time. Everywhere. It took some getting used to. So did the sight
of armed troopers in bérets and boots with automatic weapons
slung over their shoulders, France's response to a recent spate of
bombings.

I found the Air France bus from Charles de Gaulle Airport into
Paris. The driver stashed my suitcase in the baggage compartment. I
climbed aboard, paid the fare, then sat back as the driver circled
around the rest of the terminals, which sprouted like mushrooms in
the fields northwest of Paris. When he'd collected passengers from
several locations, he headed for the freeway. I sat back and watched

the scenery change from open fields to the suburbs, then to the crowded streets of Paris itself.

Forty minutes later the bus pulled to the curb at place Charles de Gaulle. The Arc de Triomphe loomed in the middle, looking far larger in real life than it ever did in photographs. The Arc was surrounded by the most chaotic traffic I'd ever seen. I flagged a cab and told the driver, a tough-looking woman puffing on a cigarette, that my destination was the Hôtel Solférino, on the rue de Lille. She inhaled a final lungful of nicotine before tossing the butt onto the pavement. Then she heaved my bag into the trunk of her Citroën and took off, making me queasy as she plunged into the fray, muttering, gesturing, and leaning into the taxi's horn.

The driver brazened across place Charles de Gaulle unscathed, then hurtled down the Champs-Elysées. I saw the place de la Concorde in the distance and thought about my first and, until now, only trip to Paris. It was in the fall, two and a half years ago, when I decided my marriage to Sid Vernon was over. I'd just moved out of the apartment he and I had shared but I needed to get farther away than that.

My father understood. He matched the money I took from savings, and I flew off to Paris. Once there, I concentrated on seeing how many museums and monuments I could cram into nine glorious days, including day trips to Giverny and the cathedral at Chartres. I prowled the *fromageries*, wolfing down exquisite cheese with fresh baguettes, and at dinner I sampled France's fabled cuisine and wonderful wines, topping it off with all the *crème brulée* and *mousse au chocolat* my stomach could tolerate. If it hadn't been for all the walking I'd done in those nine days, I'd have gained twenty pounds on the trip.

That time I'd stayed at a little dump on the Left Bank, just off the rue Mouffetard. It met three basic tourist requirements: cheap, clean, and close to a Métro stop. From what Kaz had told me, the Solférino wasn't the Georges V, but it was slightly higher on the amenity scale than my previous Paris accommodations.

The cab driver crossed the Seine on the Pont Alexandre III. She continued along the quay, angled onto boulevard Saint-Germain, which headed southeast from the river, then quickly made a left onto the narrower rue de Lille. The cab stopped abruptly just before reaching the next cross street, rue Solférino.

I peered out the window to my right. The hotel looked okay from the outside, definitely nicer than my last Paris digs. The driver turned toward the entrance and rattled off the amount in francs, waiting while I mentally translated her words into English. I kept my passport and other valuables in a security wallet around my waist. Now I unzipped it and pulled out some of the franc notes I'd received when I changed my dollars back in San Francisco.

Check-in was easy. Dan and Elaine Stefano were paying for the room as well as the airfare, having made the arrangements with their own travel agent. I filled out the usual paperwork at the front counter, and Madame showed me the room at the back of the ground floor where breakfast was served each morning. Then she indicated the small oval lift, metal openwork mesh looking out on the hotel's red-carpeted stairs spiraling upward. It was just big enough for me and my suitcase.

My accommodations were on the third floor, a pleasant room with a double bed and a tiny bathroom that held a toilet, sink, and shower. Windows looked out on a courtyard. I quickly unpacked, stashing my clothes in the wardrobe and the chest of drawers. Then I washed my face in cold water, feeling the jet lag call me toward the bed. Instead I went back downstairs, leaving my key at the front desk as the sign requested.

I walked along rue de Lille to the Musée d'Orsay, the railway station that had been turned into a museum housing a vast collection of nineteenth-century art. The courtyard in front of the museum was crowded with people. A young boy on a skateboard, looking no different from his counterparts in Alameda, skimmed toward me, jostling my elbow. He stopped and inclined his head as he apologized.

"Pardon, Madame. Je suis très désolé."

I guess I'm not in California anymore.

I smiled at him. He grinned back, hopped onto his skateboard, and took off toward the massive bronze statues, each woman representing a continent.

Back to work, I told myself. Walking was the best therapy for my jet lag. Besides, I had a destination—the Hôtel Belloc, on rue Thénard in the 5th arrondissement.

I'd checked my folding map of Paris several times on the plane and now I glanced at it again. Rue Thénard was two blocks east of the Maubert Mutualité Métro stop. But after spending half a day on a jet, I felt the need to walk.

I left the museum courtyard and headed up rue de Bellechasse to boulevard Saint-Germain, where I turned left and walked briskly along the broad sidewalks. This end of the boulevard was home to a lot of government buildings, since the Assemblée Nationale was nearby. The character of the neighborhood changed as I crossed rue du Bac, headed toward the church of Saint Germain-des-Prés. It was busier, with more shops and restaurants. Farther along I approached the University of Paris and the Sorbonne, just two of the many colleges and *lycées* in the Latin Quarter.

I crossed boulevard Saint-Michel and rue Saint-Jacques and turned onto rue Thénard. Hôtel Belloc was on my right, distinguished only by a small sign over the front door. I pushed it open and found myself in a narrow lobby that was a shabbier version of the one in my hotel. There was a low sofa and a few chairs in the front, where a talking head was reading the evening news on a small color television set. The counter at the back was staffed by a slender young man with round glasses and a thin mustache, a phone receiver propped between his ear and shoulder. He looked vaguely Middle Eastern but his French certainly sounded better than mine.

My French could be a problem, I realized. It was one thing to ask a person on the street for directions to the Louvre. It was quite another to dig for information in a strange language. But I'd done all right on my long-distance phone calls two days ago, I told myself.

I waited until the clerk finished talking on the phone, then I stepped up to the counter. *"Parlez-vous anglais?"*

"Yes, I do," he said, his English accented but quite good. "How may I help you?"

"I'm looking for one of your guests, Mademoiselle Stefano."

Something about his downturned mouth and the way his brown eyes suddenly looked over my shoulder alerted me. "Mademoiselle Stefano is not here," he said slowly.

"She's gone out?"

He shook his head and glanced down at the hotel register on the counter in front of him. "Mademoiselle Stefano has checked out. This morning."

CHAPTER 8

I MIGHT HAVE KNOWN IT WOULDN'T BE THAT EASY.
I'd missed my quarry by just a few hours. Had Darcy been alerted by my phone call to the hotel two days ago? The clerk looked alarmed as I fired questions at him.

"Did she say where she was going? To catch a plane or a train? Did you call a cab for her?"

The clerk favored me with a classic Gallic shrug and some obfuscation. He clearly didn't want to talk about the American mademoiselle. I wondered why.

Our exchange attracted the attention of the proprietor, a short, gruff man with a paunch and a receding hairline. *"Qu'est-ce ce problème, Khalid?"* he barked.

"Non, Monsieur Belloc." Khalid looked from his boss to me and continued in English. "Madame is looking for a guest who has checked out. Mademoiselle Stefano."

"The American girl? A college student, yes?" Monsieur Belloc rubbed his chin and looked me up and down with a pair of appraising blue eyes. "Are you her mother?"

"No." I didn't know whether to be insulted or wonder if I did indeed look old enough to be Darcy's mother. "But it's important that I find her. I know that she checked in last Thursday. Was there anyone with her?"

"Non, non, non." Belloc shook his head. "She was alone. We gave her . . ." He elbowed Khalid aside and checked his register. "The

small room on the fourth floor, at the back. She ate breakfast alone, she went out alone. To the museums, yes. I have seen her with the books, the cards from the Louvre, the Orsay. She stayed a week and has paid with the American Express. Nothing out of the ordinary with the card. You see, we have the authorization here."

"I thought perhaps Khalid could tell me where she had gone." I fixed the clerk with a stare. So did Monsieur Belloc. He questioned the young man in rough, rapid French. Khalid shook his head vigorously. I understood enough of his answer to know that he denied having anything more than a professional relationship with the American mademoiselle. And *non, Monsieur,* he could not say where she had gone.

But he could say. I saw it in the way his eyes shifted from me to his boss to a point somewhere out the front door. Finally Monsieur Belloc turned to me. Despite his earlier tone of voice when addressing Khalid, he assured me that his employee, a young man of the finest character, whom he trusted implicitly, knew nothing of Mademoiselle Stefano's whereabouts.

Fine. I'd get answers on my own. I traded *merci*s with Monsieur and left the hotel. There was a café on the corner, on the same side of the street as the hotel. I sat down at one of the small tables on the sidewalk. I ordered Perrier, fearful that a glass of wine would send my jet lag over the line into comatose.

The café closed at six, as is the evening custom in Paris. If you want dinner you must wait until the restaurants open up again at seven-thirty or eight in the evening. That, like the constant miasma of cigarette smoke, also requires some adjustment for those of us who are used to eating earlier.

Fortunately six was when Khalid got off work. I watched him exit the Hôtel Belloc, shouldering a brown backpack. He walked the other direction down rue Thénard and I followed. He turned left at a cross street, rue des Ecoles, heading in the direction of the university. I caught up with him before he reached the campus.

"Let's talk, Khalid." He turned, startled, and his eyes widened with alarm when he saw me.

"Madame, I must be somewhere. I have a class."

"Maybe you do. But I need information."

"I know nothing."

I shook my head. "You might be able to fool Monsieur but not me. You know more than you're telling me."

He evaded my eyes and stared instead into the display of clothing at a nearby shop. "Why do you want to know where she is?"

"She's only seventeen. I've been sent to bring her home."

"I thought she was older. Twenty, *certainement.*" He sighed. There was that Gallic shrug again. "A young man, a friend of mine. I do not know how they met. At a museum, perhaps. I know that is where she spent her days. The Impressionists, she particularly talked of seeing the Impressionists. And this friend of mine, he also loves them. He is at the Orsay every chance he gets. He called at the hotel for her, on Tuesday. I recognized him. We said hello, but didn't have much chance to talk before she came downstairs."

"Was Darcy alone when she checked out this morning?"

"No. She was with him. They left together. He carried her bag." Khalid said the words reluctantly. He paused. "He is a friend. Not close, but I know him. He would not harm her."

"I'll be the judge of that."

It sounded as though Darcy had graduated from visiting the museums to checking out the local male talent. I blinked my tired eyes. The jet lag was catching up with me. I needed sleep. "Look, I just want to find the girl and take her home. There's no reason to involve your friend any more than he is already. What's his name? And where can I find him?"

"If I tell you . . ." Khalid thought about it for a moment. "All right. His name is Claude Rousset." He pointed back in the direction of boulevard Saint-Germain. "He lives near the Odéon Métro, on rue des Quatre-Vents."

"What does he look like?"

"About my height, perhaps a bit taller." When pressed for a more detailed description, Khalid added that Claude Rousset was slender, with dark, curly hair and brown eyes, a long, straight nose, and pierced ears.

I let Khalid resume his journey toward the university. I consulted my Paris map and doubled back in the direction I'd come. Rue des Quatre-Vents was just off rue de l'Odéon. The address Khalid had given me was a four-story apartment building with a plain yellow-brick facade, its main attributes, no doubt, cheap rent and proximity to the university.

There was no concierge and I didn't have a key to the outer door. I waited, fighting fatigue and frustration, for about fifteen minutes, hoping one of the residents would come home so I could get into the building. One did.

She was tall and slender, with ebony skin and eyes, and a fountain of black hair piled on top of her head that made her seem to tower over me. With her sleek figure draped in an umber dress that ended just below her knees, she looked like a fashion model, but she was carrying a pack like most of the students I'd seen. I followed her into the black-and-white-tiled entry hall, and saw her sideways glance as I examined the row of mailboxes, looking for Claude Rousset's name.

"*Pardonnez-moi,*" I said. "*Claude Rousset, habite-il ici?*"

"*Oui. Je le connais.*" She looked at me with curiosity. "*Vous êtes Américaine, n'est-ce pas?*"

I nodded. "*Oui. Parlez-vous anglais?*"

She switched to English, her words heavily accented. "I do, but not very well. My name is Senaya."

"My name's Jeri," I said with relief. "Do you know where I can find Claude Rousset?"

She smiled and moved her head in the direction of the stairs. "Top floor, at the back. His flat is down the hall from mine."

"And if he's not there?"

"Perhaps the Orsay. Today is Thursday. The museum is open late."

I looked at my watch. It was past seven. "Have you seen a girl with him? An American girl, with brown hair and eyes. They were seen together earlier today."

I tugged open the zipper of my waist-pack and slipped out one of Darcy's photos. She took the snapshot, examined it, then shook her head. "*Non.*"

"Thanks." I tucked the photo into my bag.

I followed her up the narrow staircase. When we reached the top floor Senaya pointed me in the direction of Claude's door. I knocked, but there was no response.

It looked as though I'd be revisiting the Impressionists after all.

CHAPTER 9

THE MUSÉE D'ORSAY BEGAN LIFE IN 1900 AS A RAILWAY station, designed by Victor Laloux in the Ecole des Beaux-Arts style, and commissioned by the Orleans Railway Company to be its terminus in the heart of Paris. The Gare d'Orsay closed in 1939, right before World War II, and stood neglected until the threat of demolition loomed. An outcry ensued. Instead, the station and its adjoining hotel were converted into a showcase for the arts of the period from 1848 to 1914.

The museum is one of my favorite places in Paris. Ordinarily I'd be happy to spend hours roaming through the collection, but not tonight, with my bed at the nearby Hôtel Solférino calling to me. Still, there was a chance—a very slim one, I admitted—that Darcy and her newfound friend Claude Rousset were inside. Khalid claimed Claude Rousset was crazy about the Impressionist painters. So was Darcy Stefano.

I paused in the courtyard outside the main entrance, looking across the Seine at the City of Lights in its evening illumination. Then I went through the door and let the guard search my bag. It was just past eight, and the sign said the last admission on Thursday night was nine-fifteen. Once I'd paid the fee, I went straight up the museum's central aisle, heading for the escalators at the other end of the long building, the ones that led to the upper level.

In this gallery of connected rooms the Impressionists were all around me, a wealth of beauty by Monet, Manet, Sisley, Pissarro, Cézanne, Renoir, and Van Gogh. I moved quickly through each room, scanning the people around me, my eyes drawn, in spite of my purpose, to the paintings that beckoned. When I'd made my way through the Impressionists, the Postimpressionists, and the Neo-impressionists, I doubled back to one of the gallery's middle rooms. Fatigue propelled me to a bench near Claude Monet's huge canvas depicting the Gare Saint-Lazare. I sat and gazed at it until the blues and browns ran together.

Suddenly someone was shaking my shoulder. *"Madame?"* a museum guard said gently. *"Madame?"*

The guard tapped her watch. Groggily I looked down at my own. Twenty minutes to ten. I'd fallen asleep. I shook myself into semi-alertness and got to my feet. So much for this evening's labors, I thought ruefully. I might as well have skipped the museum and gone straight to bed.

Outside, the evening breeze restored me to enough consciousness to walk the block and a half along rue de Lille to my hotel. As I reached rue Solférino, it began to rain, a soft caress of drops that felt cool on my face. I passed a short, dark-haired woman lingering in front of a shop window and crossed the street. Collecting my key from the night clerk at the desk, I went upstairs.

Paris noises woke me at eight-thirty the next morning, horns honking and tires whirring on pavement, accompanied by French voices. I'd been so tired the night before, I'd simply undressed and fallen into bed, not bothering to insert the foam earplugs I'd brought with me. My stomach growled, reminding me that, for all my chasing around the Left Bank last night in search of Darcy, I hadn't bothered to eat.

I scrambled out of bed and opened the window, peering out into the little interior courtyard. All I could see besides the exterior walls of buildings was a glimpse of a gray morning sky. It looked as though it had rained steadily during the night but it wasn't raining now. I headed for the tiny bathroom and the shower. Once dressed, I went downstairs to the hotel's breakfast room.

I took a seat at one of the small, round tables, across from two men in business suits. One was reading this morning's edition of *Le Figaro* and the other held the *International Herald Tribune*. We acknowledged one another with polite smiles.

"Café au lait, s'il vous plaît," I told the woman who emerged from

the kitchen and looked at me inquiringly. She nodded, disappeared, and returned a few minutes later with a tray holding my *petit déjeuner*. Pots held coffee and hot milk, which I poured together into the china cup she'd provided. A matching plate held a croissant and a hard roll, with butter and packets of jam in another small bowl. I broke the roll into several pieces and buttered one.

There were four Americans at the next table, two men and two women, all of them gray-haired and perhaps my father's age. As I sipped my coffee I eavesdropped on enough of their conversation to figure out that they hailed from Lawrence, Kansas, and they were debating whether to spend the day at the Louvre or the Pompidou.

Refreshed, I returned to my room to gather the items I'd need for my day, including my umbrella, just in case it decided to rain again. I left my key at the hotel desk and headed back to the Latin Quarter, to Claude Rousset's building on rue des Quatre-Vents. It was just after ten. This time I entered the foyer as a young man left, carrying a canvas shopping bag over one arm. I climbed the stairs to the top floor and once again knocked on the door of Claude Rousset's flat.

Still no answer. But the door opposite his opened. I found myself being scrutinized by a young man in his twenties, short and thick-chested, with dirty blond hair brushing his collar and a pair of bold blue eyes that looked me up and down.

"Claude n'est pas là," he said.

"Savez-vous . . . ?" I began, trying to frame my question in proper French.

The young man cocked his head to one side. *"Américaine,"* he said. How could they tell? Was my accent that bad?

He switched to English, his accent considerably rougher than mine. "What is your name?"

"Jeri. And yours?"

"Jeri," he repeated. "Sounds like mine. I am Thierry." He stuck out a callused hand, a laborer's hand, and I shook it. "Why you look for Claude?" Before I could answer he spoke again. "Ah, the young girl. She is American, too. You look for her. Has she run away?"

At least he hadn't assumed I was Darcy's mother. I didn't acknowledge the accuracy of his speculation. "Has Claude gone to class?"

He shook his head. "He has gone, but not to class. He visit his parents. The girl, she has gone with him."

"Where?" I asked impatiently.

I got my first Gallic shrug of the day. "Claude is from Vernon. You know Vernon?"

I nodded. The town was on the Seine about an hour northwest of Paris, where the landscape gives way to Normandy. "Near Giverny," I said.

"Exactement." Thierry grinned. "You catch the train from the Gare Saint-Lazare."

CHAPTER 10

THE GARE SAINT-LAZARE WAS THE SAME TRAIN STATION Monet had captured on the canvas I'd been gazing at last night in the Orsay when I fell asleep. The station didn't look the way it had when Monet painted it. The locomotives in the painting were obscured by clouds of blue and white steam. Now the trains were sleek, silvery tubes powered by diesel. Monet's passengers, barely glimpsed in the haze, wore Victorian-era top hats and long skirts. I saw a hodgepodge that included chic Frenchwomen in couture dresses, men in business suits, tourists of both sexes clad like me in pants, a soupçon of native dress from Africa and Asia, and the ever-present paratroopers with bérets and automatic weapons.

I found the ticket booths and purchased a ticket to Vernon. With thirty minutes to wait before the next train, I bought a bottle of Evian and an onion tart to occupy me on the journey.

There was a weird logic to it, when I considered what I'd found in Darcy's room back in Alameda. The poster of Monet's water lilies, the copy of *Monet's Passion*, the book about the gardens the painter had created in Giverny, the little village on the Seine about a mile from Vernon. This was sounding more and more as though Darcy's escapade to Paris was for the sake of art, much as her jaunt to the Big Apple last October had been to immerse herself in Broadway shows.

Before leaving Claude's building I'd pressed Thierry for more information, asking where in Vernon the Roussets lived. It sounded like a fairly common name, and Vernon was a good-sized town, as I recalled from my day trip two and a half years ago. Thierry wasn't sure, but finally told me Claude's father worked for the railway. Maybe the family lived near the station.

As I queued with the other passengers to board the train, I felt something bang into my hip. *"Pardon,"* said the dark-haired woman who'd been hoisting the navy-blue nylon pack onto her shoulder. She got into the same car and took a seat at the other end.

The train began to move out of the dark enclosed station and through Paris. My eyes were drawn to the view outside the streaked glass window. I always enjoy seeing the backsides of cities one glimpses from trains. When I'm on the street I'm looking at the face the town wants me to see. There's something fascinating about viewing alleys and backyards with laundry hanging from the line.

The train was not one of the *Trains à Grande Vitesse*, the high-speed trains known by their initials, TGV. It was one of the *Grandes Lignes*, or long-distance services, operated by the SNCF, the *Société Nationale des Chemins de Fer*, France's state railways. This train's destination was Rouen. Vernon was just one of several stops along the way as the train headed northwest, following the route of the Seine into Normandy, though the track was a lot straighter than the river's meandering path.

The trip took about an hour. Most of those getting off the train at Vernon headed straight for the buses that went back and forth between the station and Giverny, which was on the other side of the river. I stayed inside the station, approaching the man at the ticket counter. I asked about a man named Rousset who worked for the SNCF, hoping that Thierry's information was correct.

"Rousset?" The man thought for a moment, then shook his head. He turned from the counter and repeated my question to another railway employee, a woman, who in turn conferred with someone in the office. Conscious of the fact that there was a queue behind me, I stepped to one side while the ticket seller waited on customers. My question having made the rounds of the Vernon station, I finally learned that Georges Rousset worked as a brakeman on this line. When I asked where he lived, I was directed to a neighborhood south of the station.

The Roussets apparently were Jewish. How else to explain the mezuzah fastened to the wooden-framed doorway of their two-story stone house? The house itself was on the corner of a winding street full of similar houses, across from a store that sold fruit and vegetables. It had taken me about ten minutes to walk here from the station. But my knock went unanswered. It didn't look like anyone was home.

By now it was the middle of the day. I knocked on a few nearby doors but didn't gain much information. Finally I retraced my steps to the produce shop across from the Rousset house. The proprietor was a short woman whose gray hair was caught up in an untidy bun. Over her white blouse and black skirt she wore a cream-colored apron stained with spots of dark red, as though it had absorbed the juice of some berries or currants.

She spoke no English, but we communicated well enough in French. The family who lived in the corner house was indeed that of Georges and Sabine Rousset. They'd lived there as long as she'd owned the shop, which was more than twenty years. They had three children. The eldest son was called Alain, and he lived in Rouen. The daughter, Yvette, lived with her parents. And the youngest was Claude, in school in Paris.

At least I'd found the right Roussets. But where were they?

Madame shook her head and told me she hadn't seen the Roussets since she closed the shop the previous evening. She certainly hadn't seen Claude arrive from Paris with an American girl.

Did she have any idea where the family had gone?

She thought for a moment. *"Synagogue? C'est vendredi,"* she said, then shook her head again. *"Non, non, c'est le midi. Synagogue ce soir."* She paused again. *"Le grand-père . . . c'est possible."* But Madame didn't know exactly where Grandfather Rousset lived, only that it was in one of the smaller villages outside of Vernon.

I tried a different tack. Did Yvette Rousset work here in Vernon?

Madame brightened. *"Giverny. Musée Claude Monet."*

MONET PAINTED IN PARIS AS WELL AS TWO TOWNS ON THE SEINE, Argenteuil and Vetheuil, before finding his way to Giverny in 1883. He lived in a pink stucco house and planted a garden.

But oh, what a garden.

On my first visit it had been autumn. The *Grande Allée* had been overgrown with nasturtiums, and rambling roses covered the arches over the path and filled the air with their perfume. Now, on this Friday in late April, the pathways were lined with lavender-purple bearded iris, pink and mauve tulips, and plenty of tourists, the buzz of their voices drowning out the buzzing bees that swam lazily through the air from blossom to blossom. People sat on the benches or made their way through the two-story house that was still furnished as it had been when Monet lived there, its shutters the same dark green as the benches, contrasting with the rough pink stucco.

As I'd entered the museum that now encompassed Monet's house and gardens, I asked where I could find Yvette Rousset. The man who sold me my ticket directed me to the gift shop in an adjoining building, selling everything from postcards to silk scarves, all featuring Monet reproductions. I waited until the rush subsided, then worked my way to the counter. There were four women there, of varying ages.

"Yvette Rousset?" I asked the youngest.

She shook her head. *"Non, je suis Marie."* Yvette worked out in the garden, she added, one of the museum employees who strolled the pathways to make sure no one trampled the flowers. No doubt I would find her near the water garden.

Outside again in the early afternoon sunshine, I headed down the *Grande Allée*, walking under the arches to the bottom of the garden. I turned right and made my way to the passage that led under a nearby road to Monet's water garden. Here were the lily pond and the weeping willow, the Japanese footbridge with its wisteria arbor, and the water lilies he painted over and over, exploring light and color with a brush and palette.

I stopped on the bridge to drink in the scene. Yes, the water really was that color. I hadn't believed that it was when I saw the huge panels on the walls of that room on the lower level of L'Orangerie, the palace turned museum on the Right Bank in Paris. But when I came to Giverny, then and now, I think I saw what Monet saw. At least I hoped so.

A nearby couple asked if I'd take their photograph with the footbridge as backdrop. I complied with their request, then continued on my search. I found a middle-aged woman who appeared to be a museum employee and asked about Yvette Rousset. She wasn't at work, I learned to my dismay. Yvette had taken the day off.

She rattled off something about Yvette's grandfather. The old man was ill. Had he died? That might explain why Claude had come to Vernon. But why would he have brought Darcy with him? According to Thierry, he had. But Thierry could be wrong. Darcy and Claude may have gone separate ways after leaving Claude's apartment.

I consulted my watch. While on the bus out I'd noted the times of the return buses, and I had an hour or so to wait. So I wandered the paths of Monet's garden a while longer, then joined the rest of the tourists walking through the pink house. I admired the extensive collection of Japanese woodblocks hanging on the walls. When I realized I was hungry I left the museum in search of food. I found a small café near the modern white structure that housed the Musée d'Art Américain, which featured the work of American Impressionists such as Mary Cassatt and Winslow Homer. After consuming an omelette, I walked back to the Musée Claude Monet. There was a bus due to arrive in ten minutes. I sat down on a bench to wait, considering my plan of action when I got back to Vernon.

"Mind if I sit down?"

The voice had a middle-American flavor that was welcome to my ear after a day spent querying people in French. I looked up into a pair of brown eyes in a face that looked vaguely familiar. It belonged to a short woman whose dark brown hair was streaked with gray and worn in a loose ponytail that fell onto the top of the backpack she carried on one shoulder. She wore a red T-shirt and blue jeans and I guessed she was in her mid-forties.

"You were on the train from Paris," I said, scooting over on the bench so she could sit down.

"Yes. I bumped you with my pack." The laugh lines in her face crinkled as she smiled. She sat down, setting the pack near her feet. "I'm Lindsey Page."

"Jeri Howard."

"I know someone named Howard." She pulled a bottle of Evian from her pack and tilted it back for a long swallow, then she offered it to me. I shook my head; I still had the bottle I'd bought at the Gare Saint-Lazare.

"Who might that be?" My last name is fairly common.

"He's a history professor from California."

Well, maybe not that common. "Where in California?"

"California State University, at Hayward. That's in Northern California."

"I know. I'm from the Bay Area. You must be talking about my father, Timothy Howard."

Lindsey Page chuckled. "Tim Howard is your father? I've known him for years. I got my Ph.D. at Berkeley and so did he. We share a passion for cowboys, Indians, and outlaws. He's such an expert in Western Americana. We're both members of the California Council for the Promotion of History. I see him at conferences from time to time."

"Then you're a history professor, too."

"Well . . ." She took another swallow of water, then stowed the bottle in her pack. "I'm on the lam."

I laughed. "On the lam from what?"

She counted the reasons on her fingers. "Academic politics, committee meetings, tenure squabbles, publish-or-perish, survey classes for freshmen who can't understand why they have to take history." She shook her head and drew an imaginary horizontal line about two inches above her dark head. "I've had it up to here. I'm on sabbatical from Cal Poly in San Luis Obispo, and I'm seriously thinking of not going back. I've been teaching for fifteen years and I just don't think I can do it anymore."

"My father complains about the same things. So does my cousin Angie, who teaches at Cuesta College in SLO. Dad's been at it for nearly thirty years and shows no sign of retiring. What would you do if you gave up teaching?"

"I have a few ideas." Dr. Page snapped her fingers as though something had just occurred to her. "You must be the private investigator."

I laughed. "I can see my father talks about his children."

"With great pride, of course. And since I devour every mystery I get my hands on, I'm just fascinated by the fact that you're a private eye. Are you on vacation? Or is the game afoot?"

"Believe it or not, someone is paying me to be here. I'm on a case."

"Such a deal. Me, I'm doing research. Funded by me. Good thing I found a reasonable hotel. It's on the Left Bank, just a block from the Orsay."

"The Hôtel Solférino?"

She confirmed this with a laugh. Our world was getting smaller by the minute.

Diesel fumes heralded the approach of the bus to Vernon. Dr. Page and I joined the rest of the tourists waiting to board. "I've found this great little restaurant not far from the hotel," she said, as we found seats. "Want to have dinner when we get back to Paris?"

"I've got to make a stop in Vernon," I told her. "So I'll have to take a later train, and I'm not sure when I'll get back to the city. Tomorrow night, maybe."

When we got back to Vernon I went inside to check on the times of trains to Paris. Then I set out on foot, heading for the Rousset house. There was still no one at home and the proprietor of the produce market hadn't seen anyone coming or going. I waited as long as I could, until the market closed, and still didn't see any Roussets. Finally I walked back to the station and took the last train to Paris.

CHAPTER *11*

I SPENT THE NEXT TWO DAYS IN A FRUITLESS AND FRUSTRAT-
ing stakeout of Claude Rousset's apartment building on the rue
des Quatre-Vents.

There was a small café opposite, near the corner where the street
intersected rue de l'Odéon. It had a clear view of the entrance to
Rousset's building and, like cafés all over Paris, had tables on the
sidewalk. I became a regular, sipping glass after glass of Perrier as
the hours slipped by. I saw Senaya, Thierry, and other occupants of
the building come and go. But I didn't see any sign of Darcy or
Claude.

On Saturday night, the day after we met at Giverny, Lindsey
Page and I had dinner at the restaurant she'd mentioned. Le Petit
Oignon, on rue Bellechasse, was small, with tables crowded together
and a second story reached by a spiral staircase. Lounging in the
doorway between the dining room and the kitchen was a big yellow Labrador who occasionally roused himself and barked at the
customers.

I worked my way through a sublime appetizer consisting of *chèvre*—
goat cheese—which had been wrapped in grape leaves and baked.
Lindsey and I traded histories. She was unmarried, forty-seven, and
had grown up in the San Luis Obispo County town of Paso Robles,
at the southern end of the Salinas Valley, where her parents, both
retired, still lived. She'd attended U.C. Santa Barbara, then acquired her M.A. and Ph.D. at U.C. Berkeley before moving into a

professorship at California Polytechnic State University in San Luis Obispo.

Right now she was tired of teaching. We talked about her options as she spooned up her *aubergine* caviar, which had sounded interesting and proved to be eggplant. I poured us each a refill from the carafe of Bordeaux.

"I've heard of public history," I said. "Dad talks about it all the time. History outside the classroom, more accessible to the public, through museums and other programs. But I've never heard of a consulting historian."

"They do exist. I know several. One of them is a professor at Brigham Young who does business history. Corporate genealogies, that sort of thing. A consulting historian is someone you'd hire to write your family history or research a building to see if it qualifies for landmark status." She finished her eggplant and pushed the dish aside. "I've been doing projects like this on the side for the past eighteen months, as well as some writing. I'm not sure I can make a living at it. But if I don't get out of the classroom soon I'm going to be a basket case. I'd like to try this for a while. Maybe extend my sabbatical for another unpaid year. I know it's a risk, but I just have me to support. And two cats."

"I've got two cats of my own," I said. "I wish I could declare them as dependents."

The waiter appeared with our entrées, chicken for her and fish for me. He whisked away the plates that had held our appetizers and headed for the kitchen, stepping over the dog in the doorway.

I sampled my fish. "Try some of this, it's wonderful," I said, cutting off a section and placing it on my bread plate.

"Mine's great, too." Lindsey slid the fish onto her own plate and replaced it with a morsel of her chicken. We sampled each other's choices and nodded our heads in unison.

"What brought you to Paris?"

Lindsey answered my question with one of her own. "How would you like to go with me to an art show? I've got two tickets to an opening. It's Monday evening, starts at six."

"So your research has something to do with art history."

"Local history. And World War II." Lindsey leaned back, sipping her wine. "I'm researching an artist named Pierre Vauchon."

"Vauchon," I repeated. "I've never heard of him."

"He was a Surrealist, like Magritte and Miró. Some of his work is at the Musée National d'Art Moderne, over at Pompidou Center."

The dog in the kitchen doorway barked at a couple of newly arrived diners, who were accompanied by a fluffy white terrier on a leash. The woman who presided over the restaurant greeted them as friends and seated them next to us. The terrier settled under the table, an old hand at dining out. The Labrador, having defended his status as restaurant dog, settled down in the doorway once again.

"I found out about Pierre when I was working on an article about San Luis Obispo County history, and I was hooked." Lindsey's brown eyes took on a sparkle as she warmed to her subject. I'd seen that look on my father's face when he was talking about a subject that fascinated him. "Pierre's mother was American, a rancher's daughter from San Luis Obispo. She did the Grand Tour in the summer of 1911 and fell in love with Pierre's father. He was handsome, wealthy, from a good family. They were married in 1912 and Pierre was their first child, born in 1914."

"The year World War I began. Where does World War II figure into the story?"

Lindsey finished a mouthful of chicken before going on. "Pierre began to make a name for himself as an artist in the late 1930s. He had his studio in a house not far from here. In fact, that's where the show will be held Monday. It's been turned into a gallery featuring his work. I'm very anxious to see that house. You see, when the Germans occupied Paris, Pierre hid French Jews in his house. He used it as a transit point, sending them out of Paris to the family estate near Chartres where his sister Céline lived. She made arrangements for people to hide in villages all over the countryside."

"I can see why you're fascinated. What happened to Pierre?"

"The Gestapo caught up with him in 1944," Lindsey said, "right before D-Day. They sent him to Auschwitz. He died there in the winter of 1945. Céline is still alive, though. She's eighty years old. She's corresponded with her mother's family in California all these years, which is how I found out about it. I've been writing to her as well. She lives in Chartres, with her son. I'm taking the train down there tomorrow, and I'm so excited about actually having the opportunity to meet her."

"It's intriguing," I said. "I'd love to go with you to the opening. But it depends on how well Monday goes. I'm looking for someone I haven't found yet."

Lindsey looked curious but didn't press me for information about my case. "I'm going to spend Monday in the Marais, the fourth ar-rondissement. Near rue des Rosiers, the old Jewish section of Paris. Then I'm going to the Museum of Jewish Art in Montmartre. A woman who works there has information on someone Vauchon hid." She unzipped one of the compartments on her backpack and took out a pen and a small spiral notebook. She tore out a blank sheet and scribbled an address. "If you can make it, meet me in front, around six. It's on rue de Sèvres, not far from the Vanneau Métro station."

The waiter appeared at our table to relieve us of our now empty dinner plates. He proffered a couple of menus and inquired as to whether we had considered dessert.

Lindsey had. She flashed me a wicked grin. "I don't know about you, but as far as I'm concerned, this is the *crème brulée* tour of Paris. I'm doing a taste comparison."

I laughed. "I'll keep up with you, as long as it's *mousse au chocolat*."

CHAPTER *12*

I PICKED UP DARCY STEFANO'S TRAIL MONDAY MORNING. She took me on quite a hike.

I'd been sitting in the café near Claude Rousset's building since eight that morning. I was nursing my second *café au lait* when the front door opened. A young man I hadn't seen before stepped onto the sidewalk. He was slender, with curly dark hair, clad in black jeans and a black ribbed knit shirt. From my vantage point his eyes looked brown and I could see gold studs glinting in his pierced ears. He looked close enough to Khalid's description to make me push back my chair and toss a few francs onto the table to cover my bill.

By the time I'd gotten to my feet Darcy herself walked into view. Her glossy chestnut hair had been braided and fell midway down her back. She wore sensible shoes made for walking, low-heeled and thick-soled, black leggings that molded to her shapely legs, and a loose-fitting shirt made of shiny red material that fell to her hips.

She put her arm around the young man and leaned into him, an intimate embrace as though they were the only ones on the sidewalk this morning. Claude kissed her, then the two of them set out at a brisk pace, walking up rue des Quatre-Vents. They turned left, heading for boulevard Saint-Germain, and turned right on that thoroughfare. I followed, keeping a distance of about twenty to thirty feet.

Once they stopped to look into a shop window. I got close enough to hear the tune Darcy was humming, "As Time Goes By," from *Casablanca*. Then they began walking again, with no indication that they had spotted me.

At rue Saint-Jacques they turned left again, walking toward the Seine. They crossed the Petit Pont onto the Ile de la Cité and veered off to the right, skirting the wide tourist-filled plaza in front of Notre-Dame. Instead, they hugged the perimeter of the island, walking past the great Gothic cathedral with its flying buttresses and rose windows, past the square behind it. They crossed the next street, dodging tourist buses. Their destination, I realized as they started down the stone staircase, was the Square de l'Ile-de-France and the Mémorial des Martyrs et de la Déportation.

The simple modern structure at the southeastern tip of the island memorializes the 200,000 French men, women, and children deported to Nazi concentration camps during World War II. Inside is a tomb dedicated to the Unknown Deportee, and the walls are covered with the names of the people and the camps in which they died. I stepped out of the sunlight and into the gloom.

The names of the death camps were excised into the stone walls above me. Dachau, Ravensbrück, Sobibor, Mauthausen, Birkenau, Bergen-Belsen, Auschwitz. Darcy and Claude stood in front of the barred gate leading to a long crypt that held the roll call of victims, whispering quietly. It didn't seem like the right time to approach them.

I looked at the walls, like any other tourist, then I followed them outside into the sunlight. Now they headed for the bridge that separated this island from the smaller and quieter Ile St.-Louis. A few blocks later they crossed yet another bridge, the Pont Louis Philippe, and we were on the Right Bank, in the 4th arrondissement, Le Marais.

Tailing them was easy, thanks to Darcy's red shirt. They hadn't noticed me, even when I'd gotten close, so I edged nearer and followed them up a side street and into another monument. I stopped short at the sight of an eternal flame and a large cylinder engraved with the same names I'd seen earlier, the names of the Nazi concentration camps. This was a memorial dedicated to the unknown Jewish martyr of the Holocaust.

What was going on here? The memorial was on a side street in an unremarkable neighborhood. I was sure it was in the guidebooks, but I guessed one either came across it by accident or looked for it on purpose. Darcy and Claude looked as though they'd intended this visit.

They left the memorial and crossed rue de Rivoli, heading up rue Vieille-du-Temple. This was the kind of Paris street I loved to explore, lined with pâtisseries, cafés, and shops. But I couldn't linger. I stuck close to the pair as they reached rue des Rosiers. Now we were in the heart of Jewish Paris, a narrow street lined with bakeries, kosher restaurants, and synagogues.

They didn't turn at rue des Rosiers but continued on to the next intersection. The building looked like some sort of exhibition hall. Claude held the door open for Darcy. I followed them, stepping up behind them as they paid the admission charge. I glanced quickly around me as I pulled out a five-franc note. It was a photographic exhibit about the deportation of the French Jews. Suddenly I recalled those library books, the ones I'd found when I searched Darcy's bedroom: *The War Against the Jews* and *The Rise and Fall of the Third Reich.*

Whatever Darcy's reason for her trip, this was not Paris on a lark, but Paris with a purpose. The question was, what purpose?

The hall was cavernous and dark, making it difficult for me to keep an eye on Darcy and Claude. Partitions and display cases formed a counterclockwise path through the exhibit. Here and there were areas where rows of chairs lined up in front of television sets showing videotapes. Former deportees spoke directly into the camera. I realized I was listening to personal testimony, individual accounts of what it had been like to be rounded up and sent to a transit camp, a way station on the journey to the death camps.

I watched Darcy and Claude as they moved through the hall, pausing to examine each display. Here were uniforms and other articles of clothing, with yellow Stars of David and triangles of several colors designating the status of the victims—Jews, political prisoners, Jehovah's Witnesses, homosexuals. And here were photographs, some small, others blown up nearly to life-size, all in stark black and white, testifying to the horrors of genocide.

As I passed one of the video sections I came face to face with Dr. Lindsey Page, whom I hadn't seen since our dinner Saturday night. She had told me she was spending part of the day in the

Marais. Now she looked as startled as I felt. Before she could speak I raised my hand to my lips and shook my head. She nodded quickly and stepped away from me.

Darcy and Claude had stopped in the middle of the exhibit, where a huge montage showed enlarged reproductions of hundreds of flyers, many with black-and-white photographs of adults and children, of both sexes, photographs of people on holiday in the mountains or at the beach, at weddings and parties, at home. They looked as though they'd been culled from family albums.

I leaned closer and stared at a picture of Thérèse Birnbaum. It showed a lively young woman in her twenties, with a pretty oval face, a wide smile, and dark hair sculpted in a style I associated with the forties. I translated the text of the flyer. Thérèse had been born in Tours in 1918. She was deported to the transit camp at Drancy, northeast of Paris, in 1943. From there she'd been sent to Ravensbrück. Anyone with information about Thérèse's whereabouts was urged to contact her brother Etienne, at a Paris address.

Had he ever found out what happened to his sister?

Flyer after flyer told the same story. Old men and women, those in middle age, adolescence, and youth, smiled innocently at those long-ago cameras. What they had in common was that they'd been deported from France, never to return. Their families, friends, or whoever was left had searched for them, or for whatever answers they could find.

From the corner of my eye I saw Darcy lift the hem of her oversized red shirt to reveal a small black waist-pack. She opened it and pulled out a tissue, which she used to mop the tears from her eyes. Claude put his arm around her shoulder and squeezed it. They lingered a while longer, examining more of the heartrending flyers on that wall of disappeared people, then they moved slowly through the rest of the exhibit.

To my great relief, Darcy detoured into a toilet before they left the building, one with two stalls. I dodged into the second stall and was out of the restroom before she was. Claude was waiting for her in the foyer. They backtracked to the rue des Rosiers and went into a deli for lunch. I contented myself with takeout and a bottle of Evian while I lingered on the nearby square that fronted on a synagogue.

I kept one eye on the two young people as they sat at a table near the window. With the other I translated the plaque on the synagogue walls, commemorating the Jewish children from the Hebrew school who'd been deported during the war. I recalled a French film I'd seen several years ago that dealt with the same subject, Louis Malle's *Au Revoir, Les Enfants*.

Finally Darcy and Claude left the deli and headed back toward the river. I followed them along rue de Rivoli to the St. Paul Métro stop. They took a train on the line heading west toward La Défense. I stayed in the same car and stuck to them as they changed trains at place de la Concorde, heading north toward Porte de la Chapelle. They got off at the Lamarck-Caulaincourt stop, in the heart of Montmartre.

Back to art, I thought as I trailed them. The village on La Butte, the steep hill crowned by the white basilica of Sacré-Coeur, has been associated with artists for two hundred years. It was here that Renoir painted *Le Bal du Moulin de la Galette*, his study of revelers at the windmill-turned-dance hall. At the Moulin Rouge, Henri de Toulouse-Lautrec had immortalized dancers La Goulue and Jane Avril.

But now Darcy and Claude made their way down a staircase to a narrow side street called rue des Saules. They entered a building. I came abreast of the structure and looked up, spying the Star of David. I waited outside, wary of entering for fear I'd tip them off. I'd been lucky so far, in not being spotted. But I had no idea what was inside and why they'd gone there.

"What in the world are you doing here?"

I must have jumped a foot. I whirled and saw Lindsey Page staring at me.

"I'm sorry, I didn't mean to startle you."

"I'm following someone," I said, moving away from the entrance.

"That young couple at the deportation exhibit?"

I nodded. "Why are you here?"

"This is the Museum of Jewish Art I told you about," she said. "Remember, I told you I had a lead on someone Vauchon hid. A relative of that person works here."

"If I go in I might be spotted," I said. "I'll just have to wait until they come out."

If they came out this exit, and not another. By now it was past three. After more than five hours of wandering all over Paris, I hoped I hadn't lost them.

"I'll get out of your way," Lindsey said, seeing the tension on my face. She crossed to the Jewish Center and went inside.

I waited nearly an hour. At a quarter after four Darcy and Claude left the building, walking arm in arm back up the stairs to the rue Caulaincourt. Now they climbed one of Montmartre's steep hills toward place du Tertre, the colorful square where street artists hawk their oils and watercolors to the tourists. The young couple lingered at one of the cafés, drinking wine and talking.

After a visit to the nearby basilica of Sacré-Coeur they stood on the edge of the bluff and looked down at central Paris. Then they boarded the *funiculaire*, a cable railway with cars simultaneously ascending and descending the steep hill. Once they reached the park below Sacré-Coeur, they wandered through the busy streets to place des Abbesses, site of one of the city's few remaining Art Nouveau Métro stations, all green wrought iron and amber lights.

I boarded the same car they did. We were traveling on the same line we'd taken earlier, but now headed south, toward Mairie d'Issy. The Métro hurtled under the streets and under the Seine, past the Solférino stop that was just two blocks from my hotel. Darcy and Claude left the train two stops later, at Sèvres-Babylone.

Now we were back on the Left Bank, but they didn't head toward the Latin Quarter, where Claude lived. Instead they walked in the other direction, strolling along rue de Sèvres, past a hospital and then another Métro stop, Vanneau. They were almost to boulevard des Invalides when they opened a black-painted door and stepped out of sight.

I quickly moved to the door and stared at it, then at the number on the wall to my right. Then I dug into my pocket for the slip of paper Lindsey Page had given me at dinner Saturday night. This was the same address, the gallery showing the work of the artist Pierre Vauchon.

"I CAN'T STAND IT ANY LONGER," LINDSEY PAGE WHISpered as we stood in the foyer of Pierre Vauchon's house, holding elegant flutes full of very good French champagne. "Tell me what's going on."

"I'd be happy to," I said. "Once I figure it out myself."

Twenty minutes earlier, I'd pushed open the shiny black door on rue de Sèvres and found myself in the narrow end of a triangular courtyard, a garden oasis in the middle of Paris. A flagstone path led to a three-story, gray stucco house wedged between two taller buildings, its walls covered with ivy and wisteria. I stopped and looked around me, getting my bearings. Then I saw Lindsey walk out onto the porch, just as Darcy and Claude entered the house.

I headed up the moss-covered stone path, past a fountain where water tinkled musically over stones, past a trellis covered with fragrant pink roses. Lindsey explained that she'd arrived at six. When she didn't see me, she'd assumed I wasn't coming. She'd been poking around the house that had been used as a hiding place for French Jews, then she'd spotted me from an upstairs window as I entered the garden.

Lindsey led the way into the foyer, where she snagged a couple of glasses of champagne from a passing waiter and asked her question. No sooner than I'd replied, we were greeted by an elegant white-haired woman in a blue silk dress, who wore ropes of what I was sure were real pearls. Lindsey introduced her as Madame Fontenoy, head of the Foundation Vauchon. While the two of them chatted in

French, I looked around for Darcy and Claude but didn't see them. Then Madame steered us into the room to our right.

It was full of people, all talking at once. They crowded around a long table that held a huge repast—bowls of fruit, artfully carved and arranged vegetables, little toasts holding miniature displays of everything from caviar to smoked salmon, a groaning board of France's superb cheese. Two smiling waiters poured Perrier and champagne. I glimpsed Darcy and Claude in the far corner of the room, drinking champagne and helping themselves to canapés.

Then I lost sight of them. Blocking my view was a tall, skinny woman all in black, including her hair, which looked as though it had come out of a bottle of ink. That and the blood-red lipstick accentuated her unhealthy pallor. She was puffing on a cigarette when she wasn't using it to punctuate her exchange with another woman, this one in *haute couture*, a yellow Sonia Rykiel scarf draped around her shoulder and a white toy poodle draped over one arm, the dog as much an accessory as the scarf.

I edged toward the table, the better to see Darcy and Claude. Lindsey had left Madame and was now sticking to me like Velcro. She followed the direction of my eyes as Darcy held out her empty champagne glass and smiled at the young waiter who filled it.

"That's them." Lindsey's eyes sparkled with excitement. "The couple at the Museum of Jewish Art. You've been tailing them. Who are they?"

I popped one of the caviar toasts into my mouth and washed it down with champagne before answering. "The girl is Darcy Stefano. I'm supposed to find her and take her back to California. She checked out of her hotel Thursday, the day I got here, in the company of the boy. Since then I've had a hell of a time locating them, until this morning. His name is Claude Rousset and his family lives in Vernon."

"Rousset? The woman I went to see at the museum is named Rousset."

I shook my head. "This case is getting curiouser and curiouser by the hour."

We grazed for a while at the sumptuous spread. More and more people arrived, crowding the foyer and the room with the food. I started to feel claustrophobic. There was only one way out. Darcy and Claude took it, squeezing past me without a glance and back into the foyer. Lindsey and I left our champagne glasses on a nearby tray and followed them, in time to see them go around a corner to my right and down a short hallway where several pen-and-ink sketches hung in their frames. I assumed they were by Vauchon, but I didn't have time to examine them. The two young people headed up a staircase to the second floor, pausing at the landing to look out an open window. When I reached the landing, I glanced out and saw that it looked down on another courtyard surrounded by houses, more little islands of tranquillity in the great surging sea of Paris.

I wondered how many exits and escape routes the house contained. Probably quite a few, since Pierre Vauchon hid Jews here during the Second World War. The building must be full of nooks and crannies, secret staircases, hidden closets and passageways.

Lindsey was at my heels, propelled by avid curiosity about my case. We went through a doorway and I glanced to my left. This was the large second-floor room with wide windows looking out at the garden where Lindsey had been standing when she'd seen me. Darcy and Claude were near a corner, examining one of Vauchon's canvases, holding hands as they gazed at splashes of blue and green on a pale yellow background. Claude was closest, between me and Darcy.

"I'm going to need your help," I told Lindsey. "I need to approach the girl—"

"Without the boy," she finished eagerly. "I can handle that."

Lindsey walked toward them, giving several paintings a cursory examination as she closed in on the pair. She moved up behind them, then brought her hand up between them, pointing at the painting in front of them. She tilted her head in Claude's direction and asked him a question in French, something about Vauchon's brush style. Claude released Darcy's hand and responded, then Lindsey asked another question.

Now Darcy wandered toward the center of the room, where a table was spread with more of the artist's pen-and-ink sketches. She studied them, sipping her champagne. Then she walked a few steps farther, toward another narrow staircase that led to the third floor. She glanced over her shoulder at Claude, who was still deep in conversation with Lindsey. With a shrug, she started up the stairs.

As soon as I saw her black leggings disappear from view I followed her up the stairs. We were the only two people in this small upper room, its walls hung with more of Vauchon's paintings. Here was a low bench in front of a window that looked down on the garden. Darcy sat down and stretched out her long legs. She sipped her champagne, then set the glass on the bench.

She sang to herself in a high, clear voice. Once again I heard the lyrics of "As Time Goes By." Her hands moved to her chestnut hair and she loosened it from the braid she'd worn all day, then shook her head so that the hair tumbled around her shoulders. As I walked up to her I could smell the perfume of the pale purple wisteria dangling at the edge of the window.

"Hello, Darcy," I said.

She picked up the champagne glass and took another fortifying swallow. Then she sighed and rolled her big brown eyes.

"It was just a matter of time, I suppose. Did my parents send you?"

"Yes. My name's Jeri Howard. I'm a private investigator."

"A PI? Cool." She frowned. "I was hoping my dad would come."

"He couldn't get away."

"Yeah, I'll bet. He's probably close to the release date on some game. And Mom wouldn't dare leave The House."

I smiled at the emphasis her voice put on those last two words. Evidently Darcy shared my opinion of The House.

"I'm curious, Darcy. Why Paris?"

"Why Paris?" Darcy took another hit of champagne. With her other hand she gestured out the window, at the rooftops visible beyond the garden. "*Chérie,* you have only to look around you."

I'd forgotten how dramatic a seventeen-year-old girl can be. That was a lapse, since I'd been one myself, seventeen years ago.

"People who come to Paris for the first time don't usually wind up at photo exhibits about the deportations."

"You've been following me all day." Her brown eyes twinkled. "You must be good. I didn't have an inkling."

"You seemed preoccupied."

She tilted her head to one side. "I thought once I checked out of that hotel . . . I mean, other than the plane ticket, I didn't use the credit card except to get a cash advance. But I suppose a skilled private detective such as yourself . . ."

"Found out where Claude lived by the end of the day I arrived. The same day you checked out of the hotel. I must say, you did sidetrack me when you went to Vernon. But I figured you'd be back in Paris sooner or later. You still haven't answered my question. Why Paris?"

"Darcy?" The young male voice floated up the stairs, followed a few seconds later by Claude Rousset himself. He looked at me, then at Darcy, who still sat artfully arranged on the bench in front of the window.

Another pair of shoes sounded on the stairs and now Lindsey's dark head came into view. She made a show of looking at a painting on the wall, but Darcy wasn't having any of that now. She narrowed her eyes and gazed at Lindsey's face, then she waved her nearly empty champagne glass at me.

"You have an accomplice." Then she fired at Lindsey, "You were at the Museum of Jewish Art this afternoon. I saw you lurking around that Lithuanian display while Claude was talking to his aunt. Are you a private investigator, too?"

"Actually, no." Lindsey looked nonplussed now that the game was up. "I'm a history professor from San Luis Obispo."

"What is going on?" Claude asked in plaintive English. He looked confused.

"She's been sent to drag me home." Darcy waved one hand at me. She downed the rest of her champagne, set the glass on the floor, and placed her open palm on her chest in a gesture worthy of Bernhardt. "But I'm not going yet. I'm not finished with what I started."

"Which is?" At the rate this was going I'd need another glass of bubbly myself.

Darcy stood up, a little unsteady on her feet. "I'm on a quest for my roots."

"You're Italian," I said.

"On my father's side. But on my mother's, I'm Jewish. My grandma is a French Jew. She was here, during World War II."

Darcy pointed emphatically at the polished floorboards beneath her feet. "Right here in this house."

"I want to hear all about it." By now Lindsey had the keen-eyed look of a historian on the trail of a heretofore-undiscovered primary source. She took Darcy's arm and steered her toward the stairs. "Let's talk over dinner. I know this wonderful little café over on the rue du Cherche Midi."

CHAPTER 14

THE CAFÉ WAS A CHEERY-LOOKING PLACE WITH RED-checked tablecloths. We sat at a corner table and ordered a carafe of Bordeaux. I scanned the menu as Lindsey recommended the house specialties: *cassoulet,* a casserole of white beans with a variety of meats, or *la poule au pot,* chicken-in-a-pot. I opted for the chicken. As soon as the waiter brought us the wine we'd ordered, Darcy reached for the carafe.

"You've had two glasses of champagne already," I told her, my hand covering hers. I sounded like my mother and I didn't like it. But still . . . "Besides, you're only seventeen."

"Three glasses of champagne," she informed me, defiance in her voice. I'd counted two while at the gallery. She must have downed her first before I'd gone into Vauchon's house.

"No wonder you're so unsteady on your feet."

"I'm sitting down now. What's the big deal? French kids drink wine all the time." She batted her long eyelashes at me. "Besides, you're not my mother."

Not that it mattered. I was here in Paris, not Darcy's mother. Or father. I fixed her with a firm look. "No, but I'm responsible for you until I get you home. I've got a signed and notarized legal document that says so."

"I didn't know she was only seventeen," Claude said disconsolately. "I thought she was much older. At least twenty."

Darcy sighed and slumped into her chair. Her mouth turned down in a sulky pout.

"She is older," I said. "In her mind." I turned to Darcy. "One glass." She brightened immediately. "One glass. That's all. I want you to keep your story straight."

"My story? It's the truth." Darcy filled her glass to the rim, then raised it in a salute. "My grandmother told me and she wouldn't lie."

"Then tell us." Lindsey leaned forward eagerly. "Is it okay if I take notes? I'm doing research on Vauchon."

"Yes, you may." Darcy enjoyed being the center of attention. She took a tiny sip of her wine, planning, no doubt, to make it last. She set the glass on the table and wrapped a strand of hair around her index finger.

"Grandma's name was Adele Levy. She had a sister and two brothers. Her father's family left Germany more than a hundred years ago after some revolution."

"The Revolutions of 1848," Lindsey said, more to herself than to any of us.

"They came to Paris," Darcy continued. "Grandma says her father was in the French army in World War I, and they always thought of themselves as French."

"This is a typical background for many French Jews," Claude interjected. "For my family as well."

I nodded, remembering the mezuzah on the door of his parents' home in Vernon. "When was your grandmother born?" I asked Darcy. When I'd met Adele Gregory last week, she looked as though she were in her sixties.

"In 1934. They lived right over there in the Marais." Darcy waved an arm in the general direction of the Seine and the 4th arrondissement, where I'd trailed her and Claude this morning. "Her father was a tailor. He had a shop on the rue de Rivoli and they lived in a flat on rue du Roi de Sicile."

"How did Pierre Vauchon figure into all of this?" Lindsey asked.

"He was a customer. At the tailor shop." Darcy stopped as the waiter brought our appetizers. When he'd set the plates on the table and disappeared again, she continued her story. "Grandma says the first thing she remembers is the grownups—her parents, aunts, and uncles—talking about *Kristallnacht.*"

Night of the broken glass.

Adele would have been only four years old during the events

of November 10 and 11, 1938, her recollections filtered through adult sensibilities. *Kristallnacht* had been precipitated by the shooting death of German diplomat Ernst vom Rath several days earlier, right here in Paris, at the German embassy on rue de Lille. Vom Rath's attacker was a German-born Jew of Polish extraction. The German response to vom Rath's death was a long night orchestrated by brownshirted thugs, in which synagogues burned all over Germany, and the windows of Jewish businesses became shards of shattered glass in the streets.

"Grandma says her parents were worried," Darcy said. "And the relatives who'd left Germany and Poland in the thirties were frightened."

"They had reason to be frightened," Claude added. "There was much anti-Semitism in France then. Because of the Depression and the influx of immigrants, fleeing all parts of Europe."

Lindsey nodded. "When the Republicans lost Spain in 1939, nearly half a million refugees came over the Pyrenees. The French put them into internment camps. The same camps were used later when they started rounding up Jews during the deportations."

I steered the conversation back toward Darcy's grandmother as the waiter appeared again to deliver the entrées. "Adele would have been eight years old when the roundups began in 1942."

"Grandma's father started looking for ways to get out of Paris," Darcy said, "down to the part of France that wasn't occupied."

Vichy France was no haven, I recalled from my own reading. Marshal Pétain's government rounded up Jews as well, sending them to the transit camps I'd seen in the photographs at the exhibit. I could guess at the next turn of events. "Adele's father found out that his customer, this artist, was hiding Jews."

"So he sent all four of the children out of Paris that way," Darcy continued. "To different places. Grandma went to live with a family in a little village near Chartres. She was there until the war was over. Then she was a displaced person. That's how she found out she didn't have any more family. They were all gone."

Darcy stopped, her young face troubled. She reached for her wine glass. As she took a sip I remembered those reproductions of flyers at the exhibit, and thought of all the survivors who never again saw their families.

"How did your grandmother get to the States?" I asked.

"She came to live with this family in San Francisco, when she was twelve years old. That's why I was so blown away when Grandma told me all this, because my mom says her grandparents were named Wise. But they weren't Grandma's birth parents. They adopted her. My granddad Malcolm Gregory, who died last year, he grew up in San Francisco and lived near the Wises. That's how Grandma met him."

"I'd sure like to talk to your grandmother," Lindsey said.

"So would I." I recalled Adele Gregory's reluctance to answer my questions when I'd asked if she had any idea why her granddaughter had flown off to Paris on a whim. Now it appeared that the whim was due to Mrs. Gregory herself. Telling her granddaughter about her past had certainly fired Darcy's imagination.

"You didn't know any of this until recently," I said. "Why did your grandmother suddenly decide to tell you?"

"I get the feeling she doesn't like to remember." Darcy frowned. "I don't even think my mother knows much about it. But after my grandfather died, Grandma was really lonely. She started going to temple again. Grandpa was a Methodist, so she'd gotten away from being Jewish. And she didn't want to live alone. So she met this woman at temple who didn't want to live alone either, and Shoshanna moved in with Grandma, about six months ago. Shoshanna's a survivor. She was at Bergen-Belsen."

"Shoshanna encouraged your grandmother to talk about her experiences?" Lindsey asked.

Darcy nodded. "She did more than that. She told Grandma that she should come back to Paris and visit all these places again. But Grandma didn't want to. So I decided to do it for her."

I considered everything that Darcy had told us. The story and her part in it were both bizarre enough to be true. I wished that Adele Gregory had been more forthcoming with this information before I'd left for Paris. Now I glanced at Claude. "How did you manage to get involved in this?"

"Darcy asked questions at the hotel, about the deportations," he said. "Khalid, who works at the hotel, knows me. I am involved with the group that set up the exhibit in Le Marais. So Khalid suggested that Darcy talk with me. I took her with me to Vernon to meet my family. And my *grand-père*, who lives in a small town north of there. He is a hidden child also, helped by Monsieur Vauchon. His experience was similar to that of Madame Gregory."

"Your grandfather is Auguste Rousset," Lindsey said. "That's why I was at the museum this afternoon. Your aunt is supposed to set up an interview."

"He would be happy to speak with you," Claude said. "He believes he must talk about these things, to educate people so they will never forget what happened."

The waiter cleared away the remains of our dinner and asked if we'd like coffee and dessert. After we'd ordered, I turned to Darcy. "Now that you've made your pilgrimage to Paris, it's time to go home."

"But it's not." She finished her wine and her jaw tensed. It made her look particularly stubborn. "There's somewhere else I have to go. Claude was going to take me there tomorrow."

"Where?" I'd been expecting resistance and now steeled myself to counter whatever arguments she was going to throw at me.

"The village near Chartres where Grandma stayed during the war. It's not far. We can do it in a day. Please, Jeri. You can come with us. I just want to see it. I promise, after that I'll go home. But just let me do this one last thing."

Some steel, I told myself, looking at her young, eager face, then at the request that was mirrored in Claude's eyes. Lindsey looked as though she'd like to leave for Chartres that very minute. It sounded like a reasonable request to me. Besides, it would probably take a day for me to arrange transportation back to San Francisco. Some parent I was, folding at the first opportunity.

The waiter appeared again and, with a flourish, delivered our *crème brulée* and *mousse au chocolat*.

"I'll make a deal with you," I said, reaching for my spoon.

CHAPTER 15

AFTER DINNER WE HEADED UP BOULEVARD RASPAIL toward the Sèvres-Babylone Métro stop. As we walked along, Claude pointed across the street at the Hôtel Lutetia, the kind of luxury hotel I'd never be able to afford.

"That was the headquarters of the German army during the Occupation," he said.

We gazed at the hotel's front, flanked by the French tricolor. Darcy stopped and struck a pose. "The Germans wore gray, you wore blue."

I looked at her, amused. *"Casablanca."*

"It's my favorite. I just love Humphrey Bogart."

"I know. I found the Bogart videotapes when I searched your room."

"You searched my room? How tacky."

"I'm a PI, remember. I also found the book you hid under the mattress, *Cheap Sleeps in Paris*. Which led me to the Hôtel Belloc."

Darcy grimaced. "I thought no one would look there. Of course, it's not like I planned to spend the rest of my life in Paris. I was coming home. Eventually."

"Your mother would have canceled the credit card. Eventually."

"Yeah. I guess you're right. But my folks sent you instead. So maybe this is the beginning of a beautiful friendship."

"Here's looking at you, kid." I held out my hand. "If we're such good friends, give me the credit card."

She tossed her head like a skittish filly tossing its mane. "You don't trust me?"

"Let's just say I'm cautious."

Darcy scanned my face, as though she were deciding whether an argument would get her anywhere. Then she shrugged and lifted the hem of the oversized red shirt, unzipping the waist-pack. She pulled out her mother's American Express card and her passport, placing both ceremoniously into my outstretched palm. "See, I trust you. I can't get far without either of those."

"Good, because I don't want you to get much farther than you already have." I zipped both items into my own case. "Now, as agreed, I'll go with you and Claude to his apartment so we can pick up your things."

"I'll go back to the hotel," Lindsey said, "to see if they can switch you from a single room to a double. I'll meet you in the lobby." She set off walking at a quick pace, up boulevard Raspail in the direction of the Seine. Claude, Darcy, and I crossed the street and walked up rue de Sèvres toward Claude's neighborhood.

"And we go to Chartres, perhaps tomorrow or the next day," Claude said.

"I think that will work," I told him. "But I have to talk with Darcy's parents first. Under the circumstances, I don't think they'll have a problem with us staying an extra day or two. But I can't promise anything until we've talked."

It seemed clear that Darcy and Claude had shared the only bed in Claude's tiny flat, which I'd pretty much guessed. Since we appeared to be in *Casablanca*-mode this evening, I wryly told myself, in an internal voice that sounded a lot like Claude Rains as Captain Renault, that I was shocked—shocked!—that Darcy had a sex life.

She was traveling light. It didn't take much time to gather up her belongings and stuff them into her blue nylon case. She gave Claude a kiss that lingered until I cleared my throat. He murmured something about calling in the morning. Then she swung the bag's strap onto her shoulder. We went downstairs and walked up boulevard Saint-Germain toward my hotel.

"How did you get into this private investigating thing?" Darcy asked, as we passed Saint Germain-des-Prés, the oldest church in

Paris, and the three famous cafés that clustered around it. Les Deux Magots, Café de Flore, and Brasserie Lipp were all crowded tonight, customers spilling onto the sidewalks, as usual, watching the world go by. I told her about my years as a legal secretary and paralegal before I went to work for the Errol Seville Agency in Oakland. The boulevard Saint-Germain grew quieter and more residential as we neared its terminus at the Seine. We turned and walked up rue Solférino to rue de Lille.

Lindsey was waiting for us, as planned. We had a quick conversation with the night clerk. The Solférino did have a double, on the second floor at the front. All that was needed was for me to collect my things from the third-floor room I'd been occupying and trundle them downstairs, which was quickly accomplished with help from Darcy and Lindsey. That done, Darcy unpacked her clothes and shoved them into the wardrobe nearest the window. There was more street noise audible from this room than there had been from my other chamber. I'd need my earplugs tonight.

"I'm gonna take a bath," she announced, flinging her white cotton nightshirt over her shoulder and reaching for her toiletry bag. She went into the bathroom and a short time later I heard water running in the tub, followed by splashing sounds. She began singing. I grinned as I recognized the words. I was starting to feel like Ingrid Bergman, leaning over Dooley Wilson's piano at Rick's Café Américain.

I picked up the phone and consulted my watch. Eleven P.M. There was a nine-hour time difference between Paris and the West Coast this time of year. That meant it was two o'clock in the afternoon in Alameda. I got through to the operator, but there was no response at the Stefanos' condo on Harbor Bay Island. Next I tried StefanoWorks. Dan Stefano's secretary told me he wasn't in the office. I left a message for him to call me here in Paris.

The bathroom door opened and Darcy walked out, looking scrubbed, hair piled on top of her head. "So did you talk to my folks?"

"Haven't been able to reach them at the condo or your father's office."

"Mom's probably at The House, hassling the contractors," Darcy offered. "Do you have the number?"

"Yes, I do." But Elaine Stefano wasn't there either, and the work-man who answered the phone didn't know where she was.

Darcy opened the wardrobe and took out a green *Guide Michelin* for France. She flung back the bedspread and sprawled on the twin bed nearest the window. "I'm going to plot our trip to the country-side," she told me.

"My turn in the bathroom, then." I took a bath, soaking in the hot water until it cooled. Then I brushed my teeth and pulled my over-sized T-shirt over my head. Darcy was still humming and leafing through the guidebook when I entered the room. It was a quarter past midnight, three-fifteen in the afternoon in Alameda. I tried the Stefanos' condo again. This time the phone was answered, by a voice that hadn't changed yet.

"Darren?"

"Let me talk to him," Darcy demanded. She tossed the guidebook to the floor and sat up, reaching for the phone.

I waved her hand away from the receiver. "After me. Then you can say hello. Darren, I need to speak with your mother or father."

I heard a big, gusty sigh over the line. "Nobody's here but me. I don't know where they are. I got a ride home from school with a friend of mine."

"Doing your homework?"

"Nah. I'm updating my Web site. Did you find my sister?"

"Yes. She's sitting right here. You can talk with her before we hang up."

"Okay," he said, enthusiasm at a minimum.

"You sound kind of glum, Darren."

"Well . . ." He stretched the word out. "I'm glad you found Darcy, but . . . she's always getting in trouble, you know. I'm the good kid. Not that it does me any good. Everybody pays attention to her and nobody pays attention to me." He sighed again.

I glanced at his more flamboyant sister and felt a flash of sympa-thy. "Your grandmother pays attention to you."

"Yeah," he conceded. "But she's going away." His voice altered, as though he'd just remembered something. "I'll bet that's where they are. They took Grandma to the airport. She's going to Paris, too."

"Adele's coming to Paris?" I repeated, unsure I'd heard him correctly. Darcy echoed the sentiment as she bolted upright and grabbed for the phone. I maintained my hold on the receiver long enough to verify what Darren had told me.

"Yeah, Mom and Grandma had a big fight. There was lots of door-slamming and stuff like that."

I wondered what had precipitated the argument. Perhaps it had something to do with Adele's feeling that her daughter and son-in-law were neglecting their children, not just Darcy the Difficult, but Darren the Good Kid as well.

"Darren, I have to speak with your dad as soon as he gets home. Here's the number. Take it down." Slowly I repeated the phone number of the hotel, preceded by the country code and the city code for Paris.

"Are you gonna let me talk to him?" Darcy demanded again, bouncing impatiently on the edge of her bed.

I gave her custody of the phone and listened with one ear as she greeted him with a cry of "Baby Bro" and launched into a description of her adventures in Paris. It was going to be an expensive phone call, but Dan and Elaine Stefano were paying for it.

They were paying for everything, in more ways than one.

I let Darcy rattle on while I considered this latest development. If Adele Gregory had taken the same Air France flight I had, that meant she'd be arriving in Paris tomorrow afternoon. That put a question mark on my plan to ask the Stefanos if Darcy and I could stay an extra day so that we could make the pilgrimage to the little village near Chartres. I glanced at the *Guide Michelin* on the floor between the beds. It could very well be that Adele had decided to make that trip herself. Which meant that my job was almost complete. I'd found the girl. Now all I had to do was turn her over to her grandmother.

I looked at my watch again, where it lay on the bedside table between us. It was nearly one in the morning. The hot bath had sapped whatever energy I had left. It seemed as though it had been days since I'd followed Darcy and Claude from his apartment this morning. Make that yesterday morning.

"Enough already," I told Darcy, as I repossessed the phone. "We've got to get some sleep."

CHAPTER *16*

I DID MANAGE TO GET SOME REST, COURTESY OF THE EAR-
plugs and the fact that Dan Stefano waited until six Tuesday
morning, Paris time, to call me back.

Gray dawn was visible from the window overlooking rue de Lille
as I swam my way into consciousness. In the next bed, Darcy turned
over onto her side and mumbled in her sleep. I propped myself up
on one elbow and reached for the receiver with my other hand, cutting off the jangle in mid-ring.

"My mother-in-law is on her way to Paris," Dan said.

"Darren told me. What is this all about?"

"She and Elaine got into it over the weekend." He spoke slowly,
as though he were having trouble getting the words out. "On Saturday, when Adele came over here for dinner. It started out as an argument about why hadn't Elaine and I gone to Paris to find Darcy
instead of sending you. Adele's been sniping at us about that since
Darcy took off. Then it all spilled over into this business about
World War II."

"Did you know Adele was a hidden child?"

"No." He sounded subdued, and I pictured him shaking his head.
"Elaine never said anything. Neither did Adele. Oh, I knew Adele
was French, but not that she was Jewish. It just never occurred to me
that my mother-in-law had to hide from the Nazis. Or that she lost
her family in the Holocaust. It never came up. Malcolm, her husband, he was a Protestant and Elaine . . . well, let's just say my wife's
not particularly religious."

I looked over at the sleeping seventeen-year-old. "So Adele told you she thought she was responsible for Darcy's trip to Paris. And she's coming after Darcy."

"Yeah. She says it's her fault. Elaine agrees with her."

"That must have been some argument."

"Oh, yeah." He sighed. "Oh, yeah. I put Adele on the plane last night. She should be there this afternoon. My travel agent made a reservation for her at that hotel where you're staying."

"So my part in this is over when Adele gets here," I said, wanting confirmation.

"Yeah. Elaine wants you to bring Darcy back right away, something about getting her into school as soon as possible. But I think it's okay to let Adele take over when she gets there. She says she's gonna stay a few days. I mean, why fly all that way just to turn right around and fly home? You hand Darcy over to Adele and catch the next available flight. I'll settle with you when you get back."

"Well, there's something Darcy wants to do," I told Dan. "And if Adele is coming, maybe they'll both want to do it."

Darcy stirred and shifted in the bed. "Is that Daddy?" she asked in a sleepy voice. I nodded. "Let me talk to him."

She elevated herself into a sitting position. I handed her the phone and turned on the bedside lamp. Darcy was explaining about the trip to the village as I headed for the bathroom. When I got back, she was still talking, but she looked up at me.

"Daddy says it's okay."

It wasn't okay until I heard Dan Stefano say it was. When he had, we rang off. Darcy stretched her arms above her head and yawned. "What'll we do until Grandma gets here?"

"Have you been to the Marmottan?" I asked her.

She shook her head. "No. But I know what it is. It's that museum where all those Monets are, the paintings that traveled to the de Young in San Francisco."

"It's off the usual Paris tourist track," I said. "Which makes it worth the visit. Let's get dressed and head out there early."

We breakfasted with Lindsey Page, who was delighted to hear that Adele Gregory was on her way to Paris. She hoped to interview Darcy's grandmother as well as Claude's grandfather. She shook her head regretfully when we invited her to accompany us to the Marmottan, begging off because she had some additional interviews to conduct concerning her research on Pierre Vauchon.

It took three Métro trains to get us to the Muette stop on the Right Bank, on the western edge of the Chaillot Quarter, named for a village absorbed into Paris in the nineteenth century. The museum itself was located on rue Louis-Boilly, near the Bois de Boulogne. Darcy and I strolled through the Jardins du Ranelagh to the nineteenth-century mansion housing the collection that included sixty-five paintings by Claude Monet done late in life, bequeathed to the museum by Monet's son, Michel.

These treasures were displayed in a modern, lower-level gallery with three circular connected rooms, the low, round couches in the center of each chamber allowing patrons to sit undisturbed, staring at the weeping willows and the Japanese footbridge I'd seen a few days earlier at Giverny. Here was Monet's *Impression: Sunrise*, the painting that gave Impressionism its name, a study of Rouen Cathedral, and part of Monet's personal art collection, with works by Pissarro, Renoir, and Sisley.

And here were the water lilies, dark and light, ethereal bits of color that seemed to float and drift on canvases as their real counterparts did on the water at Giverny. Darcy and I sat in companionable silence, staring at them, shifting position on the sofas as we moved from painting to painting. At some point, gazing at the blues, greens, and purples of *Water Lilies and Agapanthus*, I felt myself dozing off. I shook myself awake and looked over at Darcy, who was leaning forward with her chin resting on one fist.

"I'm hungry," she said.

"So am I." I glanced at my watch. "Let's head back. I saw several cafés near the Métro stop." We left the museum and retraced our steps through the gardens, heading for the Métro. "I've been meaning to ask you," I said, as we waited for a break in traffic before crossing the street. "About that fight you got into at school, when you got suspended. What was that about?"

"You mean when I punched out Peter Avon?" She gave me a scornful sidelong glance. "That pinhead. We were studying World War II and the Holocaust. Peter said it didn't happen." Her voice turned indignant. "That was right after Grandma told me about her past. And I knew her friend Shoshanna was in a concentration camp. She's got a number tattooed on her arm. If it didn't happen, I sure as hell know a few people who'd like to know just what did happen to their families."

"So you hit him." We paused to look at the culinary possibilities displayed in the window of a café across from the Métro stop.

"I didn't hit him hard enough to knock any sense into him. He's such an idiot. He spends all his time reading all that racist neo-Nazi crap that's on the Internet. Why do they let people put that stuff out there?"

"It's the price we pay for the First Amendment, Darcy. And I wouldn't want to be without that. One of the first things to go in a totalitarian society like the Nazi regime is the right to say or print whatever you like. Of course, that freedom comes with some responsibility as well."

"Like not yelling 'fire' in a crowded theater," she said. "Yeah, you're right. It's just that when people say awful things like that after what my grandmother and Shoshanna went through, it makes me angry."

"I understand. There are more effective ways to deal with that anger, Darcy."

"Like making a pilgrimage to Paris?"

"Well . . . That's not exactly what I had in mind."

The face, reflected in the plate glass, turned impish. "Works for me."

"Only if you swipe your mother's credit card."

Darcy sighed. "I wonder what my folks will do to me when I get home. Pay-the-piper time."

CHAPTER 17

"YOU LOOK TIRED," I TOLD ADELE GREGORY LATER
that afternoon. I examined the lines in the older woman's
face as she presented her own credit card and filled out the registration form at the Hôtel Solférino's front desk.

"I am tired. I've never slept well on airplanes. Is it my imagination, or is there less leg room than there used to be?"

"The latter, I'm afraid."

The registration process complete, we headed up to Adele's room,
on the second floor near the one I'd shared with Darcy last night.
Darcy lifted Adele's suitcase onto the rack provided for that purpose. "D'you want to unpack now, Grandma? Or should we leave
you alone so you can take a nap?"

Adele was shaking her head even before her granddaughter had
finished speaking. "No, no, I want to get out, to walk around. I
haven't been in Paris since 1946. All the way from the airport in the
taxi I kept turning my head this way and that. It doesn't look like the
same city."

"A walk sounds like a good idea," I said. "It's better to fight jet lag
by adjusting to the local time. Where would you like to go?"

Adele smiled. "When I was a little girl, my favorite place to walk
was from the place de la Concorde all the way to the Louvre,
through the Jardin des Tuileries."

We left the hotel and walked along the quai Anatole France to the
Pont de la Concorde, where we crossed to the Right Bank of the
Seine. On our right was the Musée de l'Orangerie, where Monet's

water lily series fills the oval ground-floor rooms. Off to our left the Champs-Elysées stretched westward toward the Arc de Triomphe.

In front of us the obelisk from Luxor in ancient Egypt, more than three millennia old, pointed at the cloudless blue sky. It dominated the place de la Concorde, the huge square that had once been called the place de la Révolution, where Madame la Guillotine claimed her victims. Now the sounds were not the cries of the *sans-culottes*, but the honking of horns and the roar of engines as cars and motorcycles swirled around the obelisk, leaving it stranded like an ancient island in a modern sea.

We angled to the right, leaving pavement for gravel, past vendors hawking everything from soft drinks to film. Darcy stopped to buy a bottle of Evian. Then we strolled into the formal gardens that were once part of the Palais des Tuileries. Here was an octagonal pool surrounded by park benches. The benches themselves were filled with weary tourists as well as Parisians enjoying the fine weather on this late afternoon. In the trees to our right I saw children queuing up for pony rides, and an open-air café where patrons gathered over a plate of *crêpes* or a *café au lait*.

"April in Paris," I sang.

"Chestnuts in blossom." Adele smiled and tilted her head upward and drank in the sight. The trees, in full flower, swayed gently in the breeze. "It's changed so much, I would not have believed it. I've seen pictures of Paris over the years, of course. But to see it again, how it's grown, how busy it is . . ."

"Did you ever have any desire to come back?" I asked her.

Adele took Darcy's arm and we strolled along the central avenue of the Jardin des Tuileries, with chestnuts and plane trees on either side. "No. My husband suggested it once, after our children were grown. But I resisted. Coming to Paris meant remembering. I'd been avoiding those thoughts for a long time."

"Then Grandpa died," Darcy said. "And you met Shoshanna."

"Shoshanna is my friend, the one who lives with me now." Adele glanced at me. "We met at Temple Emanu-El in San Francisco. On her arm she still has the tattoo she got at Bergen-Belsen. She made me see that it was important to remember, to talk about it. Once I began remembering, it was like opening the dam. The images came flooding back. I felt I must talk about them. At first with Shoshanna, then I wanted to share it with my family."

Adele shook her head. "But . . . my children are not interested in the past. Robert does not want to hear anything unpleasant. And learning that his mother's family died in the Holocaust is most unpleasant. Elaine is only interested in what she refers to as 'the here and now.' So I turned to my granddaughter." She squeezed Darcy's arm. "She should know about her family. Besides, Darcy is interested in everything that happens in this world, whether it's past, present, or future. Mind you, I had no idea my memories would make Darcy come to Paris in my place."

"But I got you to come to Paris, didn't I?" Darcy looked pleased with herself.

"Don't tell me that's what you had in mind all the time." Adele regarded her granddaughter with a mixture of fondness and exasperation.

"No, but I figured if you wouldn't go, I had to."

"I'd like to hear your memories," I told her. "If you wouldn't mind."

"I should have told you, that first day we met."

We reached the small, round pond at the end of the avenue of trees. Now formal gardens stretched all around us, bright with flowers. A man with a handcart rented small wooden boats with colored sails to a half dozen children who gathered around him. Other youngsters circled the pond, guiding the boats with long sticks, shouting to each other as they played. A young couple vacated a nearby bench and we sat down, Adele in the middle. She gazed toward the Arc de Triomphe du Carrousel and the Louvre beyond.

"We lived only a few miles from here." She pointed in the direction of the Marais. "My mother, my father. I was the youngest, born in 1934. My brother Robert was oldest. Then came Elaine and Simon. He was just two years older than I." She stopped and shook her head. "I don't know how much Darcy has told you."

"The basics," I said. "Your father had a tailor shop and you lived nearby."

"I was very young," Adele said slowly, "only four years old, but I remember hearing my parents talk about *Kristallnacht*. The night of broken glass. They and my other grown-up relatives spoke quietly among themselves, trying to keep it from the children. But we heard them, talking of what had happened in Germany, wondering if it would happen in France."

She sighed. "I'd never heard the word 'pogrom' before, but I heard it then. That's what it was. The Nazis attacked the Jews. They burned synagogues all over Germany and Austria, ransacked houses and shops. Many people were killed, including a cousin on my father's side in Munich. You see, we still had family in Germany, Poland, Lithuania. My mother's cousins came from Cracow to Paris in the thirties, right before I was born. I remember how strange and foreign they seemed."

She moved her shoulders in a shadow of a Gallic shrug. "You see, Jeri, we were French, not like those other Jews. My father was with the French army in the Great War. He was wounded. But that didn't matter when the Nazis came two years later, in 1940. By the end of the year, they'd confiscated my father's business. He still worked there, but he didn't own it anymore. There were jobs Jews couldn't have and schools we could not go to. They burned synagogues in Paris, too, in October of 1941. By June 1942 all the Jews had to wear the yellow star."

As Adele spoke the colors around us receded. Paris took on a gray pall, the same gray as the uniforms worn by the soldiers of the Third Reich.

"They'd already rounded up the foreign-born Jews in the spring of 1941," Adele continued, her voice tinged with sadness. "My mother's family went to the camps then. In July of 1942 they started rounding up the French Jews. They put them in the Vélodrome d'Hiver, the old cycling stadium. Some went to the Drancy camp, northwest of Paris. The rest were sent straight to Auschwitz. I don't know whether my parents went to one of the transit camps first, but after the war was over I found out they'd died in Auschwitz."

She stopped again. I feared the recitation of memories was taking too much of a toll. "You don't have to continue this right now," I told her.

"No, let me finish." She took a deep breath. "In May of 1942, right before my eighth birthday, my father and mother took us away, separately. Simon and I went with my father, as though for a walk. Elaine and Robert went with my mother, as if to help her shop. That was before the decree about wearing the Star of David, so we looked like everyone else. We went from the Marais across the river to a *fromagerie*, just off the boulevard Saint-Germain." She pointed across the Seine to the Left Bank.

"I remember how nervous my father was, until my mother arrived with Elaine and Robert. My parents told us to be brave, and not to cry. Then they kissed us good-bye and left the shop." She stopped for a moment. On her face I saw the past struggle with the present. "I never saw them again."

A rambunctious boy, about eight, with unruly black curls and huge brown eyes, came tearing toward us with stick in hand. He came to an abrupt stop, spraying up dirt and gravel, and leaned far out over the concrete rim of the pond, aiming at his errant wooden boat. He started to slip into the water. I reached out and grabbed him by the seat of the blue shorts he wore. He snagged the boat with the end of the stick and redirected its path. *"Merci, Madame!"* he said with a grin.

"My brother Simon was like that," Adele said. "Always running here and there." Her eyes followed the boy as he raced off. Then she returned to her story. "That afternoon we waited, for what seemed like hours, though I'm sure it wasn't really that long. The man who owned the *fromagerie* gave us bread and cheese. Then a woman came in, a customer. When she left, Elaine and Robert left with her. I don't know where she took them, only that they were hidden somewhere. After the war I was told that they were discovered and sent to Auschwitz." She stopped, then began again, haltingly. "I learned many years later that sometimes those who agreed to hide Jewish children turned them over to the Nazis. I do not pretend to understand why."

She reached for Darcy's bottle of Evian, unscrewed the cap, and drank. "Another customer came in. I knew who he was, Monsieur Vauchon. I'd seen him in my father's tailor shop. He took us to his house." She handed the bottle back to Darcy.

"I remember Monsieur Vauchon well. He was kind to us," Adele continued. "He cooked omelettes and read us stories and showed us his paintings. He talked about his mother. She was from California, he said, a lovely town near the ocean, called San Luis Obispo. His mother had taken him there for a visit once, when he was a boy. And he said they'd gone to a beautiful place called Monterey, and a wonderful city full of hills, called San Francisco. He made California sound so magical and distant. I never dreamed that one day I would live there, and visit all the places he had."

I thought of Pierre Vauchon and his house on rue de Sèvres, wondering how many Jewish children had gone through that secret transit point until the Gestapo caught up with the young painter. "What happened when you left?"

"Two days after we arrived, my brother Simon went with a man whose accent sounded Breton. The Jewish relief agency never found out what happened to Simon. For years I hoped they would, but that hope died a long time ago. Darren looks like Simon."

"You never told me that." Darcy took a sip from the Evian bottle and passed it to me. The water felt good coursing down my throat.

Adele resumed her story. "On the third day, Monsieur Vauchon sent me away with a big, rough-handed woman. I thought she'd come to clean his house. She didn't say much, just took me to the station. We took a train to Chartres. There she handed me over to a man with a horse-drawn cart. I fell asleep in the cart, amid all the hay. When I woke up it was night. I was in a big kitchen, with a man, a woman, and five children. They stared at me, as though I were an exotic bird they'd found in a sparrow's nest."

Now Adele smiled. "From then on, I was Adele Tresoir, living on a farm south of Chartres."

"Treasure," Darcy said suddenly. "*Trésor* is French for 'treasure.' That's what you are, Grandma." She hugged Adele.

"I suppose being the only one left makes me a *trésor*," Adele continued. "To be a Tresoir, I was given a false baptismal certificate with that name. The Tresoirs taught me stories from the New Testament. I wore a crucifix around my neck and attended a Catholic school, where all the teachers were nuns. Every Sunday I went to mass at the cathedral, with my new parents and my new brothers and sisters. I was very careful, trying to remember that I was supposed to be a Catholic. And shy, so I wouldn't talk and accidentally reveal something."

"That must have felt strange," I said. "To be Jewish and then be told you were Catholic."

"It was." Adele nodded. "The priest and nuns seemed exotic, as different as those Polish Jews in my mother's family. The cathedral at Chartres is so beautiful, though. I loved to see the rose windows every Sunday. It felt even odder to call the Tresoirs 'Maman' and 'Papa,' and to keep the names of the children straight. They were good people, kind people. They didn't have to take in a stray Jewish child, but they did. They could have been arrested for hiding me. As it was, their eldest son, Henri, was in the Resistance. He was killed by the Germans during the Liberation. Papa Tresoir died of a heart attack, not long after the war ended."

"Then what happened?" I asked.

"Maman Tresoir took me to Paris. She said we must try to find my family, so she brought me to the relief agencies. I wound up in the displaced persons system. I didn't see any of the Tresoirs again, but for many years after the war I corresponded with Maman Tresoir. She's dead now. I'm not even sure if any of the family still lives near Chartres."

"That's what I want to find out," Darcy said. "My friend Claude, he said he'd take me to Chartres tomorrow. Grandma, you've got to come with us."

"You take my breath away, Darcy." Adele rolled her eyes heavenward. "Let me come to grips with Paris before you take me to Chartres." She took another sip of Evian. "It was while I was in Paris, late in 1945, that I learned was the only survivor. The only person in my entire family who lived through it all. In the spring of 1946, one of the relief workers told me I was going to live in America. In San Francisco, the city Monsieur Vauchon told me about. With Mom and Dad Wise."

She smiled gently. "I've had three sets of parents, certainly more than most people in one lifetime. There isn't much else to tell. Life became normal, calm. I graduated from high school and took classes at San Francisco State. That's where I met Malcolm, my husband. We married, and we had children who don't want to hear about the Holocaust."

We sat in silence for a while, listening to the children shouting as they splashed in the pond. In the distance I heard traffic noise from the rue de Rivoli, just north of the gardens, filtered by the spring air and the fountain splashing in the middle of the pond as the day faded into evening.

"I'm ravenous," Darcy said finally. "You must be, too, Grandma."

Adele pulled herself out of whatever reverie had occupied her thoughts. "Yes, I am. Let's go have a wonderful meal."

"I know just the place," I said, steering them toward the Pont du Carrousel. "It comes complete with dog."

PART TWO
JULY

CHAPTER *18*

W E WERE IN THE MIDDLE OF A HEAT WAVE. THE MER-
cury had soared for three days, sending Bay Area residents
to beaches or air-conditioned movie theaters. The sweltering temperature gave the lie to that oft-quoted line attributed to Mark
Twain, the one about those chilly San Francisco summers. Right
now the fog was staying outside the Bay, hugging the Pacific coast,
instead of giving us our natural air-conditioning.

My friends Cassie and Eric were married on a bright, sunny Saturday afternoon. I'd served my stint as maid of honor, my lightweight, flowered organdy dress sticking to me in the afternoon heat
that enveloped the church. Afterwards, in the reception hall, I'd
toasted the newlyweds with champagne and danced into the night
with my date, Kaz.

Cassie and her new husband made their exit, escaping to the
bridal suite of the Claremont Hotel before leaving for Paris on their
honeymoon.

Kaz and I slept off the aftereffects of the champagne and woke up
around ten, to find Sunday as hot as the day that preceded it. I
threw on a robe and went into the kitchen to start the coffee. Both
cats, burdened with fur and metabolisms that mandated serious
sleep, were sprawled out on the linoleum in the kitchen because that
was cooler than the wall-to-wall carpet in the rest of my apartment.
Neither of them did more than open their eyes to note my presence.
I made sure they had plenty of fresh water to go with their kitty
crunchies.

Kaz was already in the shower so I joined him under the luke-warm spray. After toweling one another dry, we dressed. I put on a loose-fitting pair of shorts to go with my oversized "Stern Grove Festival" T-shirt, purchased the previous Sunday, when Kaz and I had gone to a free concert at Stern Grove in San Francisco. The Preservation Hall Jazz Band had us dancing in the aisles to "Joe Avery."

We breakfasted on strawberries and bagels. By noon the mercury had passed ninety degrees. I got a call from the real estate agent who was going to help me spend all that money I'd earned from the Stefano case on the down payment and closing costs for a place of my own. She thought I should take another look at that one-bedroom house up in the Oakland hills.

"I don't think so," I told her. "That place is practically on top of the Hayward fault. Looks to me like it would slide right down the hill during the next quake. It's too hot to be traipsing around looking at places that don't ring my chimes."

So far the chimes were definitely silent. All my friends who'd bought houses told me I'd know the right place for me when I saw it.

I hadn't seen it. I'd looked at boxy, prison-like condos with too many restrictions on how many pets I could have and what color my window coverings must be. Then there were those houses and cottages in my price range, but located in neighborhoods that left me edgy about my safety. Houses and cottages in the neighborhoods I liked seemed to be far more expensive than I could afford. At the moment, the great house hunt was a bust.

Besides, there was a double feature of Gene Kelly movies at the U.C. Theatre in Berkeley. I couldn't think of a better place to spend a hot Sunday afternoon than in an air-conditioned theater, sitting in the cool darkness with a huge tub of buttered popcorn and an extra-large soft drink, lots of ice. *Singin' in the Rain* led the parade, followed by *An American in Paris*. Maybe by the time the last popcorn kernel had been crunched and Gene Kelly had won Leslie Caron yet again, the fog would have remembered its environmental duties and come through the Golden Gate to make landfall in Berkeley, spreading itself up and down the eastern shore of the Bay.

No such luck. It seemed just as hot when Kaz and I left the theater. Late afternoon was giving way to evening. My butt was tired from the two-movie marathon, but I still had sufficient energy to whistle "Singin' in the Rain" and tap-dance badly on the sidewalk of Addison Street, where Kaz had parked his car. A young man who looked like a Cal student stared at me as though I'd fallen prey to sunstroke or ingested some mind-altering substance. Large doses of buttered popcorn will do that to you.

Kaz dropped me off at my apartment. The cats were still sacked out on the kitchen linoleum, barely moving their respective whiskers in greeting when I entered and pulled open my refrigerator door. I grabbed a bottle of Calistoga mineral water and opened it, debating whether to drink it or pour it over my head.

Then I noticed the blinking light on my answering machine. I pushed the button and listened.

Just one call, from Darcy.

There was a tremble in her voice. I knew she was in trouble. Big trouble.

"Jeri, it's Darcy. Are you there? If you are, please pick up the phone. Damn."

She sighed. I listened for background noises, hearing the whir of wheels on pavement, the impatient bleat of a horn. A phone booth on a busy street, I guessed. Wait—that tinkling noise. Was that a bell above the door of some business?

"Jeri, I called because . . . you said any time I needed help, just call. Well, I need it now." There was another silence, this time punctuated by the slam of a car door. When she spoke again, Darcy's voice sounded hurried, stretched with anxiety. "I gotta go now, Jeri. I'll call you again. Remember, we'll always have Paris."

My answering machine kept track of when messages were received. This one had been recorded Sunday afternoon at two thirty-three P.M. I played the tape two more times, then I rewound it and removed the cassette from the machine. I reached for my car keys, thinking about that last day in Paris.

I'd felt left out. I was headed for Charles de Gaulle, to catch an Air France flight back to San Francisco. Darcy, Adele, Claude, and Lindsey were all taking the train to Chartres, to visit the Tresoir farm and the Vauchon estate. I wanted to go with them.

But my job was over. Though somehow I knew I hadn't heard the last of Darcy.

"It's been an adventure," I told her, as we stood at the curb in front of the Hôtel Solférino. "Stay out of trouble, okay?"

"Trouble? Me?" She tried hard to look innocent.

"Trouble, you." I scribbled my home number on the back of my business card and gave it to Darcy. "If you ever get into another jam . . ."

"Just whistle?" she said with a grin.

"Wrong movie. Just call me. Tell me we'll always have Paris."

She threw her arms around me in a hug that nearly knocked me off balance. "I told you it was the beginning of a beautiful friendship."

THE STEFANOS' PHONE WAS BUSY THE FIRST TWO TIMES I TRIED ON my cellular phone as I drove through Oakland toward Alameda. On my third try, Darren answered. We'd become frequent e-mail buddies over the past two months. He was trying to convince me to let him design a Web site for J. Howard Investigations. So far I had resisted.

"Hey, Jeri. Where are you?"

"Hey, Darren. I'm on High Street, headed for your place. Are you by any chance having a crisis over there?"

"Aren't we always?" he said, sounding world-weary for a thirteen-year-old. Or maybe I'm just getting old. Thirteen-year-olds are fairly jaded these days. "Grandma's here and she's arguing with Mom and Dad."

I heard raised voices in the background. "Let me talk with your grandmother."

"Sure thing."

A moment later Adele Gregory's voice came over the phone line. "Jeri, have you heard from Darcy? Do you know where she is?"

"She called me around two-thirty this afternoon. She didn't say where she was, but she sounded like she was in trouble. What's going on?"

Adele responded with a ragged sigh. "I don't know where to begin."

"Start with when you got back from Paris." I stopped for a red light and shifted the phone to my other ear.

Adele took a deep breath, then started talking. "A few days after we returned, Dan and Elaine decided that Darcy must go back to school. Not to St. Joseph's. They enrolled her in boarding school. I told them it was a mistake. All she needed was summer school, to finish the work that she missed so she can graduate. I told them it wouldn't work out." In the background I heard Elaine, protesting her mother's remark.

"But they wouldn't listen," Adele said. "The few times she was able to call me I could tell she was miserable. Now it's happened. She ran away, two days ago. She left the school sometime Friday night, and no one has heard from her since."

No one but me. "Where is this school?"

"Just outside Bakersfield."

"Bakersfield?" I repeated. Talk about exile.

"Jeri, it's worse than that," Adele was saying. "There's been a murder. One of the school's employees. The Bakersfield police are looking for Darcy."

CHAPTER 19

Harbor Bay Island in Alameda was close enough to the water that I felt the ghost of the missing fog. I parked the Toyota on Mecartney Drive and walked to the Stefanos' condo. The front door was open, waiting for whatever stray breeze might happen by. When I entered the living room, recrimination crackled in the air. In fact, the atmosphere was decidedly poisonous.

"This isn't doing any good," I said, loud enough so that Dan, Elaine, and Adele would stop quarreling and notice me.

They did. Adele, wilting from stress and heat, sat down wearily in a chair. Elaine, however, paced the living room as though she had energy to burn. Dan perched on the arm of the sofa, worry furrowing his forehead from his eyebrows to his receding hairline.

"Arguing about a decision that's already made is like locking the barn door after the horse is stolen," I said. "She went, she's gone. I assume you want my help locating her." Dan nodded, wiping his hands on his khaki shorts. "Now, what is this about a murder?"

No one responded immediately, except Darren. He slouched in the doorway between the kitchen and the dining area, wearing baggy blue shorts and a T-shirt. Both hung on his thin frame. "Hey, Jeri, you want some cream soda? I put it in the freezer so it gets real cold."

"Thank you, Darren," I told him. "That sounds great."

When he handed me the icy can, I ran the metal surface over my face, then pulled the tab and swallowed a couple of mouthfuls of soda. I took a seat on the sofa. "Okay, let's start with Darcy's disappearance and the murder, then fill in the background."

"I got a phone call this afternoon." Elaine's voice was as crisp as the green cotton shorts and matching blouse she wore. She bit off the words. "From Dr. Perris, the head of the school. He's been calling me every week to discuss Darcy's progress. So I thought this was one of his regular reports. But he told me that she ran away from the school late Friday night. He told me not to worry, that he was taking all possible steps to locate her."

"He didn't say anything about anyone being dead," Dan broke in, looking flummoxed. "I mean, you think he would have mentioned it, but no. Then about an hour later, a couple of Alameda police officers showed up at the door. They said they'd been contacted by the Bakersfield Police Department, and they wanted to know if we'd heard from Darcy. I asked why. That's when they told us some guy who worked at the school had been murdered." He shook his head, stunned, then continued.

"They want to talk with Darcy about it. The Bakersfield cops, I mean. So then I tried to call this cop in Bakersfield, the one whose number the Alameda police gave me." Dan stopped and handed me a sweat-stained slip of paper that bore a name, Sergeant Ray Harmon, and a phone number. "He wasn't in," Dan said. "I left a message but he hasn't called back. Hell, Jeri, it sounds like maybe they think Darcy had something to do with this guy's death."

"You're getting ahead of yourself," I told him. "The police may simply consider Darcy a material witness. Perhaps she has information that will help them catch the killer."

My words seemed to do little to allay the worry on Dan's face. Or my own. Something wasn't right here.

I took another swallow of cream soda and looked at Elaine. "Perris didn't say anything about the employee's death when he called? Why didn't he notify you, or the Bakersfield police, when Darcy disappeared Friday night? Why wait nearly two days to call you?"

Elaine frowned, as though neither of these questions had occurred to her until I brought them up. "I guess I assumed Dr. Perris was trying to handle it himself, without involving the police," she said slowly. "Still . . . you're right, it is odd."

I turned to Dan. "Did the Alameda officers tell you anything at all about the murder? Such as when the body was found? Or why the Bakersfield police think Darcy is a witness?"

He shook his head. "No. They were really closemouthed. Just told me to contact that Sergeant Harmon."

"Who were the Alameda cops?" I asked, wondering if he'd had the presence of mind to get their names.

"They gave me their cards," Dan said. He picked up a couple of business cards from the coffee table and handed them to me. I didn't recognize either name. "I was so unnerved, I hollered for Elaine. Then we called Adele."

"I tried to call Dr. Perris again this afternoon," Elaine said, "but I was told he was out. I left a message, but he hasn't called back."

I finished off the cream soda and set the can on the coffee table. "When you hired me last April, you mentioned a boarding school. Is this school in Bakersfield the one you had in mind then?"

Elaine nodded. "Yes, the Perris School. It's for problem adolescents. My friend Mimi Lattimer sent her son there two years ago and she swears it saved his life."

I supposed Darcy could easily be labeled a problem adolescent, given her behavioral track record. Hopping a plane to Paris in April certainly qualified as impulsive. But she wasn't strung out on drugs or holding up convenience stores, either. I hated to think of her being dumped into some expensive detention hall, when it seemed to me all she needed was love, attention, and limits.

"How did Darcy feel about this?" I asked.

"She didn't want to go." Adele shot an exasperated look at Elaine. "She could have gone to summer school with Darren, right here in Alameda, to make up the work she'd missed."

I glanced at Darren. "You're in summer school? You didn't tell me that."

"Yeah. It's pretty boring, not worth the bandwidth to mention." His brown eyes twinkled impishly. "It keeps me out of Mom's hair while she fools around at The House."

Mom glared at him, unamused. "Darren, go to your room." Given her reaction, I guessed Darren's assessment of why he was in summer school was right on target.

The boy sighed and rolled his eyes. "Guess I'll go cruise the Web."

When Darren had left us for the friendlier frontiers of his computer screen, I turned to Elaine and Dan. "So Darcy didn't want to go to boarding school. How did you persuade her?"

"Elaine handled that," Dan said, passing the buck to his wife. "I was out of town that week. She drove Darcy down to Bakersfield."

"Against her will?" I asked, turning to Elaine.

"Look," she said sharply. "I'm the parent, she's the child. I made the decision and I enrolled her in the school."

"She's not a child anymore," Adele interrupted. "She turned eighteen this month."

"What can you tell me about Dr. Perris and his school?" I asked Elaine.

"He seemed very nice when I first spoke with him on the phone last summer, and again this spring." Elaine folded her arms over her chest. "He sent some information. I looked it over and decided that the Perris School was what Darcy needed." Adele gave a derisive snort and Elaine shot her mother a furious look.

"Did you ever meet him in person? Before you went to Bakersfield, I mean?"

"No." Elaine looked defensive now, in response to my lifted eyebrows. I couldn't believe she'd trundled Darcy off to this school without meeting the head honcho. My opinion must have shown on my face. "I didn't see any need to do so. I took Darcy to Bakersfield the weekend before Memorial Day."

"I'd like to see the information Dr. Perris sent you."

Elaine's mouth tightened. "It's just some brochures about the program."

"Get the folder," Dan told her. "What's the big deal?"

Her lips compressed into a line, Elaine swept from the living room into the condo's dining room, where she sat down at the desk against the wall. She opened a drawer on the lower right and pulled out a file folder. From the corner of my eye I saw her remove something from the folder. It looked like a letter. She slipped the sheet of paper back into the drawer.

When she returned to the living room she handed the folder to me and stood there as though she expected me to leaf through the contents briefly and hand it back. Instead I set the folder next to me on the sofa.

"I'll return this as soon as I review it," I told her. My eyes encompassed both Dan and Elaine. "Now, when are you going to Bakersfield?"

Neither of them responded. Then Dan's eyes slid toward the floor. "I can't," he said slowly. "Not until the end of the week, anyway. I've got these people in from New York, about distributing our latest game."

"Well, I certainly can't leave right now," Elaine protested. "I've got two houses in escrow, and furniture deliveries scheduled all week."

Now Adele turned on her daughter. "Darcy's in trouble and all you can think about is furniture."

The room erupted into a cacophony of angry voices. This is where I'd come in, and this was as good a time as any to leave.

"I'll check with you in the morning," I said to no one in particular as I headed for the door, file folder tucked under my arm. I was tempted to wash my hands of Dan and Elaine Stefano, but I kept hearing that tremble in Darcy's voice when she'd left the message on my answering machine.

As I walked toward my car, I couldn't help feeling like what recovering alcoholics call an enabler. I was doing what Dan and Elaine Stefano should be doing. By doing that, I let them off the hook and allowed them to continue being irresponsible parents.

But bailing out on the Stefanos meant bailing out on Darcy.

I wasn't ready to do that.

CHAPTER *20*

SUNDAY NIGHT THE FOG STOPPED HOVERING OUTSIDE THE Golden Gate and made its welcome way into the Bay. By Monday morning, the temperature had cooled perceptibly from the weekend's onslaught of record-breaking heat. My office, on the third floor of a building on Franklin Street in downtown Oakland, actually felt bearable instead of stifling.

"Who do you know on the Bakersfield force?" I asked my ex-husband, Sid Vernon, when I phoned him at the Oakland Police Department. "I need a contact."

"You're going down to Bakersfield? In the summer?"

In his office, several blocks away, Sid chuckled. I knew why. If it was ninety degrees in the Bay Area, it was probably way over a hundred in Bakersfield. The town was in Kern County, down at the bottom of the San Joaquin Valley, where the southern Sierra Nevada ran into the Tehachapi Mountains. In the summer the Valley was an oven.

"Better you than me," Sid continued. "Yeah, there's a guy in Bakersfield who used to be on the Oakland force. He was in Felony Assault same time I was. His name's Henry Garza. Don't know where he works, but that's a start. Tell him I said hello."

I thanked Sid. He updated me on the adventures of his daughter, Vicki, who had finished her first year at the university in Berkeley in June. She and her housemate Emily were spending July down in San Diego with Vicki's mother and stepfather.

After I'd hung up, I called directory assistance in the appropriate area code and got the number of the Bakersfield Police Department. A brisk female voice answered the phone and asked if this was an emergency.

I asked who was investigating the death at the Perris School. According to the Alameda police officers who'd visited Dan Stefano Sunday afternoon, there was a Sergeant Harmon involved. The woman at the other end of the line said, "That would be Sergeant Harmon and Detective Garza, ma'am, in Crimes Against Persons Detail. But they're not in the office right now. Would you like to leave a message?"

"Is that Detective Henry Garza?" She confirmed that it was. "Yes, I'd like to speak with either of them."

After I'd given her my office number, I hung up the phone and stared into space. So Sid's friend, Henry Garza, was one of the investigators. Whether that would be a negative or a positive I didn't know yet. I didn't have enough information about this business. I didn't even know the name of the murder victim.

That feeling I'd had yesterday returned, doubled. Something about this whole situation didn't jell.

I picked up the file on the Perris School, the one Elaine Stefano had given me the night before. What had she removed? I wondered, replaying last night's scene as I flipped open the manila folder to see what she'd left there.

The first thing that caught my eye was a glossy brochure full of big color photos, an eight-page booklet, about eight by ten inches, that looked as though it had cost a mint to produce. The exteriors showed a bucolic-looking campus spread across low hills, covered with green grass, shrubbery, and trees. The weathered wood-frame buildings had a rustic, summer-camp appearance. It all looked very nice, but I suppose if one didn't want to be there, it didn't matter what kind of amenities the place had.

I turned my attention to the text that decorated the edges of the photographs. Not surprisingly, it sang the school's praises. From what I could tell, the school dedicated its efforts to "problem" adolescents. The treatment appeared to be large doses of classroom time, physical activity, and so-called "tough love." Enrollment ranged from 100 to 120 students, according to the brochure.

The school's director, Dr. Kyle Perris, listed himself as an educator, counselor, and educational consultant, supposedly with twenty-five years' experience in those fields. He had a doctorate in education from some school in Illinois I'd never heard of, and he claimed to have been a major in the United States Army.

The school's mailing address, on the bottom of the last page of the brochure, was a Bakersfield post office box. But the folder also contained a letter from Dr. Perris to Elaine Stefano. The first enclosure was a single sheet containing instructions on how to get to the school, as well as a map showing the school's location on the eastern side of Bakersfield, between the Kern River and state highway 178, in what looked like an undeveloped area inside the city limits. Beneath this I found an agreement signed by Perris and Elaine Stefano, concerning Darcy's enrollment at the school. The program was to last twelve weeks.

The photocopy of the check written on the Stefano bank account made me sit back in my chair. That was a lot of money.

I consulted the phone directory and called the McRae residence in Alameda. "You bet I want to talk with you," Heather declared in an excited voice. "It's about what they did to Darcy."

By "they," I guessed she meant Darcy's parents. "May I come over now?"

"Nah, I'm working this summer. Part-time at a deli on Park Street downtown. I'm, like, on my way out the door. Can you meet me after I get off at two?"

"Sure. I'll be at that coffee place where we talked before. Just one more question, Heather. Do you know of a friend of Darcy's mother, Mimi Lattimer?"

"Sure. Her son was a class ahead of me and Darcy. Mrs. Lattimer works at the same real estate office as Mrs. Stefano. Gotta run, catch you later."

I disconnected the call and looked up the number of the real estate firm. I left a message for Mimi Lattimer, who was out showing a house. My next call was to a friend of mine who worked for the Oakland school system. He told me that an educational consultant was someone who would interview and test a child and would sometimes recommend programs of the sort that Dr. Kyle Perris was evidently running. I thanked him and told him our next lunch was on me, whenever that might be.

Then I switched on my computer and cast the net wider, in this case the Internet, to see if I could pull in more information about Kyle Perris and the Perris School. I spent the next hour or so in cyberspace, doing credit checks and searches and slogging through databases. I learned that the school had been incorporated in Kern County three and a half years earlier. Prior to that, I discovered, Perris had been associated for three years with a school in San Luis Obispo County, called the Coast Academy. Even farther back he'd been on the staff of the Pinewood School, with a post office box in Walsenburg, Colorado. I dug through the map stash I kept on a shelf behind my desk and found one for Colorado. Walsenburg was a dot on the map, on Interstate 25 south of Denver, not far from the northern New Mexico border.

I reached for the phone and called my friend Norm Gerrity in San Jose. "I need someone to do some legwork in Colorado," I said. "Any recommendations?"

"I just worked with a guy in Denver a couple of months ago," Norm said. "Got his card right here. Name's Carl Burnham."

I copied down Burnham's phone number, thanked Norm, and disconnected the call. Then I punched in the Denver number. Burnham was out, so I left a message asking him to call me.

The phone rang as I was pouring myself another cup of coffee. It was Detective Henry Garza in Bakersfield, returning my call. "Your name rings a bell," he told me, sounding friendly. "You're that private eye Sid Vernon was dating. Didn't you two get married?"

"Yeah. Then we got divorced. But we're still friends. Sid gave me your name."

"I figured. You need some information. What's up?"

"You had a homicide this weekend. An employee at the Perris School."

"What do you know about that?" Garza's voice veered from friendly to businesslike.

"Not much. That's why I'm calling you."

I got more silence, as though Henry Garza was considering whether or not he wanted to tell me anything. "Guy named Wayne Talbert. Assistant to the school's maintenance supervisor. He was found dead Friday night, outside the back door of the school's administrative office," he said finally.

"Any suspects?"

"What's your interest in the Talbert homicide, Ms. Howard?"

"Darcy Stefano's a friend of mine. I understand you'd like to talk with her."

"You know where she is?" Garza demanded.

"I don't," I told him truthfully. "But it's possible she might contact me. Last time I saw her, I told her to call if she ever needed help."

"What's your connection with the girl?"

"That's another case, Detective." I could be just as businesslike as he could. "Let's just say I'm planning to drive to Bakersfield tomorrow, at the request of Darcy's parents. I'll do whatever I can to assist you in your inquiries."

Garza had more questions, but I sidestepped them and ended the conversation. Then I called Dan Stefano at his office. He confirmed that he had received an early-morning phone call from Sergeant Harmon in Bakersfield. Harmon urgently wanted to talk to the missing Darcy. The term "material witness" had come up, but Harmon hadn't indicated that Darcy was in even bigger trouble. At least, not yet.

Dan's voice sounded subdued as he shifted direction. "Are you going to Bakersfield? I mean, you left last night, it kinda felt like nothing was settled. Elaine and I . . ."

"I'm doing this for Darcy," I told him. "Let's leave it at that. I'm heading for Bakersfield tomorrow."

"I'll be down there Thursday at the latest." His voice was subdued, sounding guilty. He hesitated. "I know you think we're lousy parents."

"I don't even want to go into that now, Dan. Have you heard from Darcy?"

"Not a word. She hasn't called us, she hasn't called her grandmother. I'm really worried, Jeri."

"She'll call again, I'm sure of it. You've got my numbers, including the cellular phone. Call me if you hear anything."

I disconnected the call and, still holding the receiver, reached for the little plastic box that held business cards. I was looking for a recent addition, one I'd filed upon my return from Paris.

CHAPTER 21

D R. LINDSEY PAGE ANSWERED HER PHONE IN SAN LUIS Obispo on the second ring. "Have you finished that article about Pierre Vauchon?" I asked.

"Jeri Howard, is that you? Yes, as a matter of fact, I have. It's going to be in the *California Historical Quarterly*, sometime next year. Actually, I got so much material on that trip to Paris I may expand it into a book. Have you called to tell me you're coming down the coast?"

"No. But I have a question for you."

"Does it have something to do with a case?" Her voice perked up.

I laughed as I pictured her dark eyes flashing with anticipation. "If you were half as interested in historical research as you are in sleuthing . . ."

"Historical research is sleuthing, my dear. The historian is a detective in search of the truth. Or versions thereof."

"My question deals with recent history. Do you know anything about a school in the San Luis Obispo area, called the Coast Academy?"

"Only what I read in the newspaper and hear on the grapevine. The place closed four years ago, after the owner died. His name was Thomas Shiller."

"How did Shiller die?"

"Officially, an accident. He fell off a cliff out at Montaña de Oro State Park," Lindsey said, naming the rugged headland west of town, full of high cliffs that jutted over the Pacific Ocean.

"You said 'officially.' Was there some doubt?"

"There were rumors he'd committed suicide. According to the grapevine, Shiller had good reason to kill himself. That school of his was under investigation by the SLO district attorney's office. A former student filed a complaint claiming she was abused by the staff and held there against her will. I don't know any details because she was a minor and all the records were sealed. There was a big stink in the local press, of course. Then Shiller turned up dead. Next thing I heard was that the land was up for sale."

"Who had title to the land after Shiller died?"

"I'm not sure," Lindsey said. "But I can find out." I told her how to look for the paper trail in the tax assessor's records and real estate transactions at the San Luis Obispo courthouse. "Okay, I'll do that right away. Now tell me, Jeri, why are you asking questions about the Coast Academy?"

"Shiller had someone working for him, Dr. Kyle Perris. He started his own school in Bakersfield three and a half years ago. Which was not long after Shiller's death, from the sound of it."

"Not working for him. Shiller and Perris were partners. In fact, Perris and his wife were hiking with Shiller when he went over the cliff. Perris tried to climb down to rescue him while Mrs. Perris went for help."

"Interesting."

"I thought so, too," Lindsey said, "especially if you consider the suicide rumor. I'll call you as soon as I get the info."

Carl Burnham called me from Denver just as I was contemplating lunch. When I explained what I wanted him to do, he said, "Pinewood School in Walsenburg? Y'know, that name sounds familiar. I think there was something about that place in the *Rocky Mountain News* a few months back. I'll look for it."

"Just find out whatever you can about the school, Kyle Perris, and his wife. I don't have a name on the wife."

"It may take a few days," he told me. "Walsenburg's in the south part of the state, about four hours from here."

We discussed the details, such as his fee, and how he could contact me, then I went out for a sandwich and brought it back to my office. I caught up on my paperwork while I ate lunch, preparing for my absence. I didn't know how long I'd be in Bakersfield. Mimi

Lattimer returned my call at one o'clock, agreeing to meet me at her real estate office at three. I was just about to leave for my two o'clock appointment with Heather McRae when the phone rang.

"You'll find this very interesting, I'm sure," Lindsey Page reported. "According to the real estate transaction that was filed when the Coast Academy property was sold, the land was owned jointly by Thomas Shiller and Kyle Perris. About six months after Shiller died, Perris and his wife, Martina, sold the property to a developer. They're building condominiums on it as we speak."

"How much did he sell it for?" She named a figure and I whistled. "Not too shabby. Certainly gave him plenty of money to start his school in Bakersfield."

Lindsey's voice turned serious. "Say, Jeri, does this have anything to do with Darcy Stefano?"

"I'm afraid it does."

I called Burnham back and let him know Mrs. Perris's first name. Then I headed for Alameda.

Heather McRae sat on the curb outside the java joint on Park Street, wearing what looked like a long lime-green T-shirt that showed a lot of leg between the hem and her clunky sandals. She nursed an iced mocha as she flirted with a couple of cocky adolescents who were into baggy pants and skateboards.

"You're late," she told me. "I've got to be home by three. I'm supposed to ride herd on my kid brother this summer. Boring. I'll be so glad when I go away to college in the fall."

She got to her feet, exposing more thigh, and glared at the two boys who were quite happy with the view. We left them on the sidewalk and went into the espresso bar, where I ordered an iced latte. Heather and I sat down at a table.

"Tell me what happened when Darcy got back from Paris," I said. "Did the words 'boarding school' come up?"

"Yeah. I only saw her twice. The first time was a couple of days after she got back. She was grounded forever, but I went over to see her. She told me all about her trip to Paris. It was so cool. Right before I left, I asked if she was gonna go to summer school to make up the work she'd missed so she could graduate from high school. She said there was some problem with St. Joseph's, and she thought they didn't want her to come back. Then she told me her mother wanted to send her away to school."

"Did Darcy want to go?"

"God, no." Heather shook her head so vigorously that her yellow hair flew around. "She said, no way was she going. She said she'd run away again, that they'd have to haul her off. And they did!"

"Her parents?"

"No. These guys came and took her away."

But Elaine Stefano had said last night that she herself had driven Darcy to Bakersfield. I must have looked doubtful, because Heather now looked indignant.

"I know it sounds crazy, Jeri, but they did. I saw it. It was the Saturday before Memorial Day. Darcy and I had arranged to meet that morning on the path by the lagoon, near the complex where the Stefanos live. When she didn't show up, I walked to the condo and I saw Darcy. There were these two guys on either side of her and she was struggling. They put her in a big black car and drove away."

"What did they look like?"

"One of them was a big blond guy with a gut," Heather said. "He looked like a football player. But he was an old guy, like he hadn't played for a while. The other guy didn't have any hair. He was a skinhead."

My eyebrows went up. "You mean, steel-toed boots and swastika tattoos?"

"Well, I didn't see any tattoos. But his head was shaved and he was wearing boots. He was real skinny, with a pointy nose."

"Did you tell anyone about this?"

"I told my mom. She didn't believe me. I thought about calling the police, but I knew they wouldn't believe me either. Then I called a couple of days later and talked to Darren. He said his mother drove Darcy down to some school in Bakersfield. He acted like everything was okay. By then I was starting to think maybe I'd imagined it. But I know what I saw."

I had a feeling I knew what Heather had seen as well. I didn't like that feeling. I had some hard questions for Elaine Stefano. But they'd have to wait. It was nearly three, time for my meeting with

Mimi Lattimer. I wrote my cellular phone number on the back of one of my business cards and gave it to Heather.

"Darcy's run away from that school. I think she's in a lot of trouble. I'm going down there tomorrow. If she should call you, tell her to get in touch with me as soon as possible."

CHAPTER 22

"I MADE THE SUGGESTION LAST SUMMER," MIMI LAT-timer told me, her long, pink-tipped fingers wrapped around a can of diet cola. She'd offered me one, but I'd declined. Now she took a sip and settled back into her chair, crossing her legs. She was a tall, slender woman in her late forties, with short gray-blond hair, wearing a summer suit of pink linen, the kind that wrinkles if you look at it cross-eyed.

"It was after Darcy pulled that Carmel stunt," she continued. "I knew Elaine was interested. I mean, she was desperate for a solution, but Dan wanted to try St. Joseph's. Obviously, it didn't work. Things just got worse. First New York, then Paris. Elaine was at the end of her rope. She said as much when she and I were picking out furniture at Showplace Square."

"When was that? Recently?" I had taken a seat on a straight-backed chair next to her desk and I couldn't get comfortable.

"No, I believe it was the same weekend Darcy went away to school."

Now I shifted on the unpadded seat and looked at her more closely. "Really? You're sure about that?"

"Yes. It must have been . . ." Mimi Lattimer leaned forward and flipped through the pages of the calendar on her desk. "The Satur-day before Memorial Day. See, I made a note that I was spending the day with Elaine. Dan was out of town and Darren was with his grandmother. Anyway, I told her it was the right decision. I just hope Dr. Perris can turn Darcy around the way he did my son Tommy."

"I see. Your son was a real problem, I take it."

"God, you have no idea." She shuddered and ran a hand through her short hair. "I couldn't handle him. He'd been difficult ever since the divorce six years ago. His father doesn't take any interest in him. I was terrified that I was going to lose my boy."

"When was this?" I asked.

"About two years ago. Tommy was sixteen. He'd just started driving, and he'd take my car and stay out all night. He was involved with a crowd of older guys. When Tommy got into drugs, he started stealing from me. And he ran away from home a couple of times."

"How did you hear about the Perris School?" I asked her.

"Tommy was about to flunk out of Alameda High, which is ridiculous because he's an intelligent kid, he really is. So I went to see an educational consultant."

"Who was this consultant?" I interrupted.

She looked curious but answered the question. "I don't recall. Someone I picked out of the Oakland phone book. Anyway, he recommended Dr. Perris down in Bakersfield. I arranged for Tommy to go through the program. He stayed four months. It was expensive, but it was worth it. Tommy stayed out of trouble when he came home, and he graduated last year. He just finished his first term at Humboldt State up in Arcata, and he's in summer school now."

"Was Tommy agreeable to going to the Perris School?"

"Oh, no. He said he wouldn't go. Which is just what Dr. Perris predicted. So we arranged to have him taken down there."

"You hired a child transport service," I said.

"I certainly did. Valley Security, out of L.A. Dr. Perris recommended the firm. They took care of everything. So when Elaine asked me how to get Darcy down to Bakersfield, I told her who to call." She beamed at me.

"Thank you," I told her as I pushed back my chair. "You've been a big help."

I boiled with anger as I drove to Harbor Bay Island. Elaine Stefano had lied to me when she claimed she had taken her daughter down to Bakersfield. She'd spent the day shopping with Mimi Lattimer instead, and hired someone to do her dirty work for her.

That wasn't the only thing that made me fighting mad. It was what had been done to Darcy. Out of control or not, she didn't deserve that kind of treatment.

There is money in the child transport business. Big money. It pays well, but it isn't something I want to get involved with, though I've been actively recruited twice by such an outfit. Some services are small and others large, and they often employ private investigators and ex-police officers.

Got a "problem kid" like Darcy? If you've got the money to pay the fee, a child transport service will haul her off for you, to a special school or camp. And if your kid doesn't want to go, well, that's too damn bad. You're the parent, she's a kid, and she doesn't have any rights.

Over the past few years there had been plenty of controversy and a couple of court battles on both sides of the issue, arguing about whose rights were paramount, those of the parent or those of the child. Whose story did you believe, frantic parents trying to turn around out-of-control kids? Or kids snatched suddenly and without warning from homes or schools and taken miles away, sometimes out of state, to a special school or a wilderness camp?

If this was the kind of place Perris was running in Bakersfield, he was operating on the edge. California law states that community facilities such as schools can't lock up or restrain kids. But a lot of times the law gets overlooked when it comes to a debate about children's rights.

I'd already made up my mind which side of the issue this private investigator was on. Transporting kids to where they didn't want to go was, in my opinion, dancing on a thin felonious line with kidnapping, false imprisonment, and child abuse. But the child transport business was booming in California. All those recalcitrant teenagers.

I found Elaine Stefano where I thought I would, at The House.

Work at the stucco palace had progressed since my last visit, three months earlier. In the huge living room vertical blinds hung from the oversized windows that looked out onto the Bay, shining in the afternoon sun. Both the living room and the stairs that curved to the upper floor were carpeted in a thick, cream-colored Berber that looked as though it would be hell to keep clean. A refrigerator that would not have been out of place in my mother's restaurant now gleamed alongside the white tile and bleached pine cabinets in the kitchen. The dining area held a modern-looking oval table, its glass surface balanced on two thick pedestals. I didn't see any other furniture, except in the living room, where a vast sectional sofa upholstered in mauve resembled an island marooned in front of the stone fireplace.

Elaine perched on one end of the sofa, talking on her cordless phone as she had been the first time I'd seen her. From her end of the conversation it sounded as though she was arranging for delivery of some additional furniture. She looked annoyed when she saw me, but she quickly hid it. She finished the call and punched the disconnect button, setting the phone on the sofa cushion as she stood. I felt a distinct lack of welcome in her greeting.

"Your file on the Perris School seems to be incomplete," I said with no preamble, my voice chilly.

"Was it?" She raised her eyebrows. "What's missing?"

"Suppose you tell me. You took something out of the folder last night, before you gave it to me."

She didn't answer.

"All right, Elaine. I can guess what it was. Some paperwork about the transport service. Does Valley Security ring a bell?" The look on her face confirmed my guess.

"I just had an interesting chat with your friend Mimi Lattimer. She told me a couple of things. First, she not only recommended the school, she recommended the transport service. Second, that Saturday in May when you supposedly drove Darcy down to school, you were shopping with Mimi. She's sure of the date; it's on her calendar. And if that weren't enough, Heather McRae saw two men hustle Darcy out of the condo that Saturday morning. Were you even there to watch them do it? Or had you already gone shopping? Were you planning to tell Dan about this, or is he still buying your story?"

Her face darkened with anger. "All right, I didn't take her to Bakersfield. I hired somebody else to do it. That's what busy people do these days, they hire people like you to do things they don't have time to do."

"Don't compare me to a transport service," I said with distaste, uncomfortable and angry at the analogy. "I don't abduct children.

You hired me to locate your daughter in Paris. I did and I turned her over to your mother. As for what you don't have time to do, your eighteen-year-old daughter has disappeared. The police want to talk with her about a murder. Yet you don't seem to be the least bit interested in finding out what happened."

"My eighteen-year-old daughter is now an adult," Elaine snapped. "Maybe it's time she learned to take responsibility and face the consequences of her actions."

"Let's talk about your responsibility." I glared at her. "You're the one who had her hauled off to that overpriced reform school, taken against her will by two strangers. You must have known she'd run away. Just how thoroughly did you look into that place? Or did you simply grab the first opportunity to ship Darcy off so you wouldn't have to deal with her?"

"What the hell do you know about it?" Whatever gloves Elaine had been wearing in our previous encounters were now off. She put her hands on her hips and glowered at me. "Have you ever had children? Have you ever had to deal with a problem teenager? I didn't think so. Don't make pronouncements at me. Darcy's been a pain in the ass since she learned how to talk back, and believe me, that was at an early age. I just can't handle it anymore."

I wasn't sure she'd ever handled it. I watched as she stalked away from me, toward the glass wall that looked out on the Bay. Then she turned as the phone began to ring.

"If she's committed a crime, I wash my hands of it." Her voice was cold as she reached for the cordless. "If you're so damned concerned about Darcy, you go down to Bakersfield."

"I plan to. On my own. I'm not going to be your hired gun again."

CHAPTER 23

I T MUST HAVE BEEN A HUNDRED AND TEN IN THE SHADE when I arrived in Bakersfield on Tuesday afternoon.

As it happened, I was there as Adele Gregory's hired gun. Or more accurately, as an investigator employed by a Bakersfield attorney named Cecilia Bromley.

I'd never met Ms. Bromley, but when I returned to my office Monday afternoon, there was a message from her on my answering machine, along with one from Adele. I called Adele first.

"I've hired someone to represent Darcy," she told me. "Just in case she needs representing."

"Would that be Cecilia Bromley?" I asked.

"Ah, she's called you, then. My attorney in San Francisco recommended her and retained her on the condition that you act as her investigator."

"If she doesn't have a problem with it, neither do I."

Adele told me she was driving down to Bakersfield later in the week with Dan Stefano. As soon as we finished our conversation, I punched in the number the attorney had left. Ms. Bromley had a crisp, no-nonsense voice that gave me no clue as to her age. I gave her some background about my connection with Darcy Stefano, both past and present, and added the information I'd found out so far about Perris and his school.

"I don't have many details of this Talbert homicide yet," she said, "other than what Mrs. Gregory told me today. And what was in the newspaper. I do know Ray Harmon, one of the cops who's investigating. I'll talk with him tomorrow and brief you when you get into town. By the way, I made a reservation for you at the Holiday Inn on Truxtun Avenue. It's not far from my office. Call me after you check in."

Before going home to pack, I did some research on Valley Security. As Mimi Lattimer had told me, the firm had an office in the L.A. Basin, on Lankershim in North Hollywood. Another branch was located on West Shaw Avenue in Fresno. The company's ads indicated that it specialized in corporate security and background investigations, but said nothing about child transport. Guess that was a dirty little secret.

According to the Secretary of State's office in Sacramento, Valley Security was owned and operated by George Larsen, who had a California private investigator's license. I called Norm Gerrity in San Jose and another fellow investigator, Rita Lydecker in San Rafael. Neither had heard of Larsen or his firm.

Tuesday morning I took my cats to the vet to be boarded, much to their dismay. My gray nylon overnight bag and my laptop were already stashed in the trunk of the Toyota. Beside me on the passenger seat were my cellular phone, a large bottle of water, and some munchies. Darcy hadn't called again. Just in case she did, I'd left a message on my home answering machine giving her the numbers of my cell phone and the hotel in Bakersfield where I'd be staying.

The Bay Area's usual excruciating rush hour traffic had thinned by the time I left. I drove east on Interstate 580, climbing past the windmills on Altamont Pass, then down the slope toward Tracy. Farther south, the freeway joined Interstate 5, the long, straight highway that runs down the spine of California's vast Central Valley. I headed south, singing along with the soundtrack to *American Graffiti*, which I'd popped into the cassette player. I sang along with Chuck Berry and the Big Bopper, sharing the road with big rigs and vacationers in recreational vehicles.

After stopping for lunch at Pea Soup Andersen's in Santa Nella, I switched to Elvis and pushed on, accompanied by "All Shook Up" and "Jailhouse Rock." It got hotter as I drove further south, and I was glad the sun was on my right, rather than beating down on the driver's side of the car. I took restorative swigs from my water bottle and swore, as I always did on trips into California's interior, that my next car would have air-conditioning.

I took the exit for Highway 58 and headed east, rolling into Bakersfield at two-thirty, wailing along with Patsy Cline as she belted out "I Fall to Pieces." The switch from rock to country was most appropriate, given my surroundings. Country music is big in Bakersfield. It's Okie country, where many Dust Bowl refugees wound up in their search for California's golden promise.

I drove south on Highway 99 and took the Truxtun Avenue exit. I maneuvered the Toyota into a parking place at the Holiday Inn and cut Patsy off in the middle of "Crazy." When I got out of the car it was like stepping into an oven. I made a beeline for the air-conditioned lobby of the hotel, where I checked in.

My room was on the second floor, the window facing the street. It was a generic room with a double bed covered by a muted pink floral spread. Opposite the bed a big TV sat on a credenza. In the bathroom, which featured white tile and fixtures, I splashed cold water on my face and dried off with a scratchy white towel. It took me all of five minutes to unpack and stash my clothing in the top drawer of the credenza. I picked up the phone and called Oakland, checking messages on my answering machines, both at the office and at home. Still nothing from Darcy.

Then I called Cecilia Bromley. Her office was in the Haberfelde Building, an older structure at the corner of 17th Street and Chester Avenue. I parked at a meter on 17th and entered through the double glass doors that led to a first-floor arcade. There was a bookstore on my left, and, opposite that, a shop featuring cat paraphernalia. I located the elevator and punched the button for the third floor. The law office was on the side of the building overlooking 17th. When I identified myself to the receptionist, she ushered me through an interior door.

Ms. Bromley turned out to be a short, buxom woman in her late thirties with wide blue eyes and an unruly mop of curly golden hair that looked as though she was in the habit of running her hands through it. She wore a severe gray lawyer suit in what seemed to be an effort not to be mistaken for a dumb blonde.

I had no trouble taking her seriously, however. She had plenty of ammo on the wall of her office. I saw a diploma from UCLA, a photograph taken during her stint as a public defender here in Kern County, and a certificate that said she'd been a vice president of the California Trial Lawyers Association. I suspected she was a real scrapper in the courtroom. On her desk I spotted a framed photo of two boys who looked enough like her to be her sons, but there was no wedding ring on her left hand.

"Call me Cece," she told me after she rose to greet me. "Everybody does. Want something cool to drink?"

"I certainly do."

"Let's go down to the espresso bar on the first floor. They've got this frozen cappuccino mocha and I'm addicted to it."

I grinned. "Espresso in Bakersfield?"

She rolled her blue eyes in exasperation. "Hey, we're not totally out here in the boonies."

Cece led the way downstairs, carrying a file folder under one arm. "Interesting old building," I said, looking at the architectural details and the metal grillwork. Piped-in music echoed from speakers as we stepped up to the counter of Espresso Etcetera.

"Yeah. It used to be the old Stock Exchange. And it's supposed to have a ghost. But I've never seen it, though I've pulled plenty of late-nighters preparing for trial."

After we had our frosty concoctions in hand we settled at a corner table away from the foot traffic. I took a pull on my straw. The frozen cappuccino mocha was quite good.

"What have you got so far?" I asked.

"The people who run this school, Kyle and Martina Perris, say Darcy has been a problem since she arrived, nearly two months ago. Now, I haven't talked with them myself. I got this information from Ray Harmon, one of the investigating officers. He says the Perrises claim Darcy's had arguments and altercations with several teachers and counselors, and with the victim."

I frowned. Not good. "What do we know about the victim? All I've got is a name, no details on what happened."

Cece handed me the file folder. Its contents were slim, consisting of several pages of handwritten notes on yellow lined paper, a folded letter-sized sheet containing a pencil sketch, and clippings from the Bakersfield *Californian*. I read the newspaper articles first, starting with the front-page story about the murder which had appeared in the Sunday edition. Accompanying the article was a black-and-white photo of Wayne Talbert, a straight-ahead, eyes-front pose. He had a pleasant, squarish face bisected by a neatly trimmed mustache. His hair looked brown, and it was long enough to touch his collar. His eyes were light-colored. Average handsome, I thought, totally unremarkable.

"Looks like a driver's license photo," I said.

Cece nodded. "An old one. He'd shaved off the mustache and cut his hair. Funny . . . Harmon said Talbert had blond hair and blue eyes. But this newspaper reproduction makes his hair look darker." She consulted her notes and continued.

"His name was Wayne Nicholas Talbert, age thirty-two, according to his driver's license. Which also has an old L.A. address on it. He moved up here in May, got a job at the school a couple of weeks later. From what I can tell he was pretty much a loner. Lived by himself in an apartment on Monterey Street, on the east side of town. Harmon told me that Dr. Perris says Darcy had a run-in with Talbert last month. And threatened him. I don't know the details of that incident, at least not yet."

"Time of death?"

"The body was found about midnight," Cece said. "Talbert was last seen alive at eleven o'clock. So sometime between eleven and twelve."

"Had he been inside the administrative office?"

"Sergeant Harmon told me they don't know. It looks like Talbert was attacked from behind as he was walking toward the building. They found the body near the back door. The autopsy was Monday. Talbert had been hit on the head. He bled to death. No murder weapon was found at the scene."

"Could it have been an accident? Maybe he fell and hit his head on something."

"Possible," Cece conceded. "But Harmon was pretty close-mouthed about the evidence. We'll know more when we get a copy of that autopsy report."

"And when we go over the crime scene, to see if there's anything Talbert could have hit his head on." I sipped my drink. "Speaking of the crime scene, what was Talbert doing outside the school's office after hours?"

"Good question," Cece said. "I don't have the answer to that one yet."

"I'd certainly like to see the layout of that school."

"I have a sketch. I took a look at the plat over at the county offices, and Sergeant Harmon filled in some details." Cece unfolded the sheet of paper that contained the drawing, and I studied it.

The Perris School property was rectangular, with the short ends of the rectangle facing east and west. It was located east of town but within the city limits, accessed by a lane that led from a county road running between Highway 178 to the south and the Kern River to the north. Cece's sketch of the school itself showed a circular drive within the rectangle, with buildings arrayed around the ring. The first of these, at the end of the lane, was the administrative office, at three o'clock on Cece's drawing. Moving roughly clockwise from this was a classroom building, a gymnasium, five cottages, a dining hall, five more cottages, the maintenance building, and a small parking lot. The space behind the dining hall held playing fields and another cottage.

"The place used to be a church retreat," Cece said, "but it went out of business. After the Perrises bought the place, they converted the church into classrooms."

"What's that?" I pointed at a double line running along the western perimeter of the property.

"An irrigation canal. The whole town's crisscrossed with them."

"This helps," I told Cece, looking up from the sketch. "But I need to see the actual crime scene."

"So do I. It's time we paid an unannounced visit to the Perris School. Let's rattle a few cages and see if we shake loose some information." As she finished the slushy remains of her cappuccino mocha, a wicked grin spread over her face.

I had a feeling Cece Bromley and I were going to work well together.

CHAPTER 24

W E TOOK CECE'S CAR, A LATE-MODEL LEXUS WITH AIR-conditioning, which was both fortunate and necessary because Bakersfield was still baking in the late afternoon sun. We headed east on Truxtun and north on Union, then took the ramp onto eastbound Highway 178.

If we'd kept going, we would have driven into the southern Sierra Nevada, shimmering ahead in the heat haze. But Cece turned left onto the narrow asphalt county road leading north over gently rolling terrain toward the Kern River. I almost missed the small white sign on our left, with discreet lettering that read THE PERRIS SCHOOL. Cece made another left turn onto the gravel lane that continued for a half mile.

"So much for unannounced," I said, when I saw the gate. It was metal, rolling on a track, set in a high wire and post fence that surrounded the school. There was shrubbery on the other side, hiding the buildings. Near the gate, on the driver's side, I saw a black metal pole topped by an intercom and a box that would allow insertion of an electronic key card.

Cece pressed the intercom button and spoke into the mesh-covered speaker, identifying herself as an attorney hired by the Stefano family, here to see Dr. Perris. There was a short silence, then the intercom buzzed and the gate moved slowly to the right, stopping when the gap was wide enough to admit a vehicle.

Inside, the gravel lane was lined with low shrubs I couldn't iden-

tify. We connected with the circular drive just to the north of the admin building, where the small parking lot held about a dozen cars,
probably belonging to staff members. Cece parked her Lexus at the
end of a row and we got out. I glanced around. The campus didn't
look as it had in the photographs in the school's brochure. The lawn,
bright green in the photos, was dun-colored and dry as tinder, like
the rest of the California summer landscape. Here and there valley
oaks offered pools of shady respite from the bright, blistering sun.
The maintenance building was a boxy gray square with metal siding
and high windows hugging the roof line, its front door facing east. A
dark green Chevy Blazer was parked here, and I guessed it belonged
to the maintenance supervisor. The cottages beyond this were plain,
with small front porches.

The administrative office was the size of a small suburban house.
Windows on either side of the front door faced the mountains to the
east. As we reached the door of the admin office, I heard young
voices buzzing through the open windows of the onetime church
that was now the classroom building. I heard shouts emanating from
the gymnasium behind it, indicating some game in progress.

Suddenly a bell sounded, then kids poured through the doors
of the classroom building. I couldn't tell how many there were, but
they were all teenagers. Male and female alike, they were attired in
khaki camp shirts and shorts, with white socks and sturdy sneakers.
Most of them wore brown baseball caps with the letter *P* embroi-
dered in gold on the front. They looked as though they'd signed on
for some sort of scouting program, without the merit badges and the
S'Mores. They were accompanied by a scattering of adults. Teachers or counselors, maybe. Or guards.

Most of them headed in the direction of the bungalows. Cece and
I got a few curious glances, but for the most part the kids ignored us.

Then I felt a prickling sensation on the back of my neck. I was being watched.

I turned quickly. A girl of about sixteen stood ten feet away, staring at me with almost colorless blue eyes. She had pale, translucent
skin that stretched tight on her skinny frame and looked as though it
would burn if exposed to the pitiless sun too long. Her shirt was
much too large for her. Its tail had pulled free of the waistband of

the khaki shorts, and she had a scab on one bony knee. Short, uneven yellow hair straggled from beneath the cap she wore. She looked like one of Peter Pan's Lost Boys.

She opened her pale mouth as though to speak. Then a male voice cut through the oppressively hot afternoon air. "Gillie, aren't you supposed to be working in the dining hall this afternoon?"

Gillie jumped like a startled jackrabbit. A man had just come out the front door of the admin building. He was forty-five or thereabouts, about six feet tall, slender in a lightweight gray suit. He had short brown hair with a dusting of gray at his temples, a narrow face and light hazel eyes.

Gillie stared at him for a moment. Then she ducked her head and hared off to the left, trotting in the direction of the dormitories. The man turned to us.

"May I help you?" His voice was somewhat more solicitous than it had been when he'd been speaking to Gillie.

"That depends," I said, "on whether you're Dr. Perris."

"I am. And who are you?"

Whoever had buzzed us through the gate hadn't notified Perris we were coming. Before we could answer, the door behind him opened and two other men walked out. Unless I missed another guess, these were two Bakersfield police officers in charge of the Talbert homicide, Sergeant Ray Harmon and Detective Henry Garza.

I faced all three of them. "This is Cecilia Bromley, an attorney retained by the Stefano family," I said. "I'm Jeri Howard, an investigator assisting Ms. Bromley."

Ray Harmon was pushing fifty, tall and broad-shouldered, with a weary slump in his blue suit. His hair was a gray crew cut and he wore bags under his blue eyes. "You the PI Henry told me about?" he asked, raising one eyebrow.

"I am."

I gave him my card. He narrowed his eyes as he read it, then raised them to survey me, pursing his lips as though he were chewing on this prior to commenting. Detective Henry Garza greeted me with a nod. He was younger than his partner by about ten years, short with a wiry build. His thick black hair was slicked back from an angular face.

"Why do you need a PI? From Oakland, no less." Harmon's question was aimed at Cece, and he spoke in a low voice that sounded more personal than professional. "You don't trust me to do my job?"

When Cece answered, she sounded slightly annoyed. "I told you yesterday. I was hired by Darcy Stefano's grandmother."

"I just want to talk with the girl," Harmon said. He glanced at me. "So where do you come in? You know the girl? You know where she is?"

"I'm her friend. No, I don't know where she is."

I didn't see any need to tell them about the Paris caper. Besides, I had a feeling all that was in Darcy's record here at the school, a record Dr. Perris had no doubt shared with the detectives.

"She called you, though, didn't she? I mean, since you're such good friends." Harmon's voice took on an edge of sarcasm.

"She left a message on my answering machine Sunday afternoon." I kept my voice level. "I haven't heard from her since."

My answer didn't satisfy Harmon, who obviously thought I knew more about Darcy's whereabouts than I was letting on. If he wanted to play hard guy it was okay by me. He couldn't get any more answers. I didn't have any.

Besides, I'd been busy watching Dr. Perris from the corner of my eye, as he registered the news that Cece Bromley was Darcy's attorney and that I was a private investigator. The good doctor didn't like our being here one bit. But he didn't want to make the situation worse by objecting to our presence.

He smoothed the alarm from his face. In its place was polite concern. "If there's anything I can do to help," he told Cece. "To find Darcy, I mean. She's a very troubled girl. I feel as though we here at the school have failed her."

I cut him off. "I understand Darcy had some sort of altercation with Talbert in the past. What was that about?"

"Darcy tried to run away, the third Friday in June." Perris looked at the two cops but they didn't seem inclined to stop my questioning. "She persuaded another student to go with her. Both girls were caught outside their bungalow by Mr. Talbert, who alerted Mr. Fosby. He's in charge of our physical plant, and he lives here on the grounds. I'm afraid Darcy became quite angry at being thwarted. She threatened both men. Threatened to 'get' them. I'm not sure what she meant by that."

He may not have been sure, as he claimed, but there were implications in his regretful tone. Implications that "get" may have meant "kill."

"Who told you this? Fosby? Or Talbert?"

"No one told me, Ms. Howard," Perris said, with a slight smile. "I was there. Mr. Fosby notified me of the incident as soon as the girls were discovered. I returned to the school immediately. I don't live far away. When I took charge of Darcy on my arrival, I brought her into my office for a talk. She made the threat then, in my hearing."

"But not in Fosby's hearing, or Talbert's," I said. "So we only have your word that Darcy threatened them."

"Yes," Perris said. "I suppose so. Nevertheless, my recall of the conversation is correct."

"This escape attempt," I said. "How did it happen?"

Perris gave the detectives another look. He'd no doubt gone over these details with them, and it pained him to do it again, especially for me. But Harmon and Garza had stepped to one side of the door, talking in low whispers. Perris frowned and answered my question. "Mr. Talbert saw the two girls slip out the window of their bungalow around ten o'clock that evening. He alerted Mr. Fosby, and they stopped the girls before they got very far."

"Who was the other student?" I asked.

"Gillie Cooper," Perris said reluctantly.

"The blond girl we saw when we got here?" Perris nodded. "I'd like to talk with Gillie."

Perris shook his head regretfully. "I can't let you do that."

"Why not? It's possible she knows where Darcy's gone."

Perris glanced at Harmon and Garza. "As I told the officers, interviewing Gillie won't help. She has trouble telling the truth. Her own parents refer to her as a congenital liar. Much as I dislike that term, I'm afraid it's rather accurate in Gillie's case."

Fine, I thought. I'll get to Gillie on my own, somehow. "What did you do to Darcy and Gillie after they tried to run away?"

"They were each placed in discipline rooms, where they were kept for the next twenty-four hours."

"Solitary confinement, in other words."

"Oh, hardly that, Ms. Howard." He gave me a deprecating smile. "Each discipline room has a bed and a sink, toilet, and shower. The girls were given meals, the same food the other students get, not bread and water. When a student misbehaves, as Darcy did, we keep the individual isolated for a time. We gave Darcy time to contemplate, as it were, the consequences of her actions. It's usually quite effective. I'm sorry to say this was not Darcy's first sojourn in a discipline room." Perris shook his head. "She's been quite disruptive since she arrived, one of the most difficult students I've ever had. If you're familiar with her history of running away I'm sure you're not surprised."

He looked at me for confirmation but I gave him none. "I'm curious, Dr. Perris. About the night Darcy and Gillie tried to run away. It's odd that Talbert would be here at that hour."

"He was visiting Mr. Fosby, who lives in a cottage near our dining hall. It was as he left that Mr. Talbert saw the girls."

His answer sounded a bit too pat and too rehearsed to me. "Is that why Talbert was here this past Friday night?"

"Yes. He was playing cards with Mr. Fosby. Evidently they did so regularly." Perris was getting tired of my questions, but I wasn't quite finished.

"How well did you know Talbert?"

"Not well." Perris shrugged. His manner shifted again, into professional detachment, as though the school's underlings were unworthy of his consideration. "Mr. Fosby needed an assistant. He knew Mr. Talbert was looking for work and that he'd fit the bill. Mr. Talbert seemed to be a clean-cut young man, prompt, did a full day's work."

"How did Fosby meet Talbert?"

"You'll have to ask him that." Perris smiled again.

"I intend to," I said, and Perris's smile dimmed.

"I'd like to talk with Fosby, too." As she spoke, Cece looked past Perris at Sergeant Harmon. "And we'd like to see the crime scene."

He looked at her for a few seconds before speaking and I saw something pass between them, though I wasn't quite sure what it was. Then he shrugged. "Be my guest. We're finished with it. The crime lab did their work over the weekend."

"We'll want a copy of the report, of course," she told him.

"Of course," he repeated, giving her the same look. Then he looked at his watch. He and Garza moved toward their car.

"Talbert's car," I said. "What was he driving? Was it here when the body was found?"

Harmon and Garza traded looks. "Blue Ford Escort sedan," Harmon said. "It wasn't here when the body was found."

Which meant that whoever killed Talbert quite possibly took his car.

CHAPTER 25

"THERE ISN'T MUCH TO SEE," DR. PERRIS TOLD CECE and me after the two detectives had gone.

"Nevertheless, I'd like to take a look at the scene," I told him.

"Certainly. I'll cooperate in any way that I can." His pleasant, noncommittal tone belied his earlier unspoken concern at our presence.

He extended his hand, indicating that we should follow him. We walked around the side of the building. An elevated square of concrete served as the back porch. A sidewalk led from the porch to the rest of the campus. About ten feet from the porch, a few inches from the brown summer grass, I saw a dark stain discoloring the walk.

"Blood?" I inquired, looking at Perris's face.

His lips tightened, and he nodded. "Yes. Mr. Talbert was found here. It looked as though he'd tried to reach the door, and fell backwards. He was lying on his back."

"How do you know that?"

"I saw the body. When I arrived the police were here, and he was covered, of course. The officers asked if I could identify him, so I did." He gave a slight shudder at the memory.

"Did Talbert have a key to the admin office?" I asked.

"Yes." Perris nodded. "He had keys to all the buildings on campus. But if your question is, was he inside the office before he was killed, I'll tell you what I told the police. No, I saw nothing to indicate that he had been."

I always wonder when people give me more information than I ask for. And Perris just had.

I looked carefully at the porch and the back door, looking for any sharp edges that might explain the head injury that supposedly killed Talbert. But I didn't see anything except the stain on the sidewalk. Had Talbert sustained his injury elsewhere and made his way to the rear of the admin office on his own? Or had the body been dumped here? If Harmon and Garza were good cops, and I figured they were until they proved otherwise, they'd already asked those questions and looked for evidence to support those theories.

Either way, I couldn't believe Darcy had anything to do with the man's death.

I turned to the east, following with my eyes the sidewalk's path some fifty yards away, where it terminated at the dining hall, a large building with a wide porch and a plank railing. Students clustered on the porch. It was almost five, no doubt nearing the time for the evening meal. Arrayed between this building and the admin office were the cottages, five each on the north and the south. Walkways branched off the main one like twigs from a tree limb, each leading to a student residence. Here and there, next to the sidewalks, were short poles with lights on them to provide some nighttime illumination.

I pointed west, beyond the dining hall, toward Bakersfield and the afternoon sun that was inching down in the sky. "What's over that hill?"

"A housing development," Perris told me.

I squinted. There appeared to be a road threading down this side of the hill. "But there's no access to the school from the west?"

Perris shook his head. "The only road is the one you came in on."

"Which cottage did Darcy live in?" I asked.

"Number ten. It's actually the first one on the right." He pointed in a northwesterly direction, at the nearest cottage. "They're numbered clockwise, starting with the boys' cottages on the south, then the girls' cottages on the north."

I examined the building, which was about thirty feet ahead and to my right. It was the size of a suburban tract home, a plain, one-story wood-frame, with Venetian blinds in the windows. On further questioning, Perris told me that each cottage had a common room, plus four bedrooms, one for the resident counselor, and three for the students. Normally there were four students living in each room. I did the math. That meant that the Perris School had the capacity for 120 students. Even if Perris wasn't full all the time, if I multiplied what Elaine Stefano was paying him for a twelve-week program by a hundred students, Perris was making money hand over fist.

Perris seemed to know what I was thinking. "We're by no means at capacity," he said. "It being summer, of course. Darcy only had one other student in her room—"

"Gillie," I interrupted.

"Yes. Since Gillie was the only other person in Darcy's room, that may explain how she was able to get out without being detected."

Behind us I heard the back door open. We turned. The man who stepped out onto the porch wore khaki slacks and a short-sleeved blue work shirt. A large key ring attached to his belt jingled as he walked. He was in his late forties, medium height, with blue eyes and short, sandy hair which held a hint of gray. His face was tanned and square-jawed.

"Here's Mr. Fosby now," Perris said. Fosby stopped abruptly and gave both Cece and me a measuring stare. "Bennett Fosby, head of maintenance. Let me introduce Ms. Bromley, an attorney, and Ms. Howard, a private detective."

"Private detective?" Fosby echoed. "What for?"

"Ms. Bromley and Ms. Howard are looking into the circumstances surrounding Mr. Talbert's death." Perris's voice held a note of caution, as though he were warning Fosby not to say anything.

"Should think you'd let the police handle that." Fosby's words were as sharp as his blue eyes.

"I'd like to ask you some questions about Friday night," I said.

He folded his arms across his chest and looked at me steadily. "What do you want to know?"

"Start with the sequence of events, when Talbert came to visit you."

"He got there about seven. We played cards until eleven."

"Who buzzed him through the gate?"

"Nobody. He had his own key card. So do the other members of the staff."

"He left at eleven? That's the last time you saw him?"

"Alive," Fosby said. "About a quarter to twelve, Mrs. Perris called. She told me Darcy was gone."

"Why Mrs. Perris?" I asked, looking from Fosby to Perris. "What was she doing here?"

"The resident counselor for Darcy's cottage is Ms. Lincoln," Perris explained. "But she'd taken the weekend off. So my wife was substituting for her."

"After Mrs. Perris called me, I got out some flashlights and came over to the cottage. Mrs. Perris said we should look around the campus, to see if we saw any trace of the girl. I headed back toward the dining hall and she came toward the admin office. That's when she found the body."

"Lying here on the sidewalk?" I indicated the dark stain on the pavement, which was about six feet from one of the exterior lights. The area was marginally visible from the porch of the cottage where Darcy had lived, but it would have been in full view of the side windows.

"That's right. I heard Mrs. Perris call out," Fosby said. "I came running. There was Wayne, on the sidewalk. I could tell right away he was dead. The whole left side of his head was caved in, and there was blood on the pavement underneath him."

"But nothing that looked like a murder weapon."

Fosby shook his head. "Not that I could see. Mrs. Perris went into the admin office and called the police, and Dr. Perris, too. That's about all I can tell you."

"Thanks for your cooperation," I told him. He nodded again, and stepped off the porch, walking briskly down the sidewalk toward the dining hall.

Perris smiled. "Now, if that's all . . ."

"Not quite," I said, mulling over the odd coincidence that Mrs. Perris was on the scene Friday night. "I'd like to speak with your wife. Is she in the office?" I stepped up onto the porch and reached for the handle of the back door.

Perris looked nonplussed, but just for a second. "We do have to be somewhere this evening. But I'm sure she wouldn't mind speaking with you. Briefly, of course."

"Of course."

We followed him into the back hallway of the administrative office. The air-conditioning felt good after the superheated air outside.

Perris led us past the restrooms and a small room with a sink and a refrigerator. Another room held banks of filing cabinets on three walls and shelves of supplies on the fourth. The front half of the building was large and open, separated from the main door by a counter. As we entered this area, I saw a conference room to my left, an oval table and several upholstered chairs visible through the open door.

In the area in the middle were two desks, each with a computer on the extension, sharing a laser printer on a stand in between. At each desk was a woman. The first was nearing sixty, if not past it. Her short hair was done in tight head-hugging gray curls.

"No, I haven't seen the big stapler," she was saying in a voice with a twang I associated with the South. "Did you look in the supply room?"

"Yes, but it's not there. It was here on my desk the last time I saw it. Oh, well, it'll turn up." The second woman shrugged. She was Hispanic, in her late twenties, I guessed. She was quite pretty, wearing a rose-colored seersucker dress, her black hair shoulder-length.

"Did you ask . . . ?" The older woman didn't finish but nodded to the left, toward the closed door of an office in the back corner of the building.

The younger woman frowned and shook her head. She glanced at her watch. It was now five o'clock, so she switched off her computer and covered it with a plastic hood.

As she pushed back her chair and stood up, the door to the corner office opened. A woman walked out, heels clicking against the tile floor, a file folder open in her right hand. She was in her early forties, attractive in a glacial way, with a thin, angular body in a chic blue suit, her hair done in stylish blond waves. Gold circles decorated each earlobe and a gold chain was visible around her neck.

I'd never seen her before in my life. Why, then, did she look vaguely familiar?

"Mrs. Webber, did you finish that report?" the newcomer barked at the younger woman.

Ah, management by intimidation, I thought. Not something I cared to experience, now or in my days as a paralegal.

Mrs. Webber had the same reaction. Her lips thinned and she

narrowed her dark eyes, but she answered in crisp, neutral tones. "I put it in your in-basket ten minutes ago."

"Well, let me take a look at it before you go," the woman said. "In case I have any changes."

"Sorry, Mrs. Perris." Mrs. Webber didn't look sorry at all. She glanced at her watch again. "It's five o'clock. I have to pick up my children at day care."

She stepped around her desk, heading for the front door. The older woman looked from Mrs. Webber to Mrs. Perris, as though wondering what would happen next. Martina Perris scowled at Mrs. Webber's departing back as though she were used to giving orders and having them obeyed without question. She opened her mouth as if to breathe fire, but she was forestalled by her husband.

"Martina, my dear, a word with you." Perris turned his gaze to encompass the remaining office employee. He spoke with a tone of polite dismissal. "Good night, Mrs. Johnson. We'll see you tomorrow."

Before Mrs. Webber opened the front door and stepped outside, her brown eyes raked over Cece Bromley and me, almost as though she knew who we were and why we were there.

Mrs. Johnson, on the other hand, didn't let any grass grow under her feet. She covered her computer, gathered up her handbag, and left the office in record time.

Martina Perris sighed and stepped back into her office, followed by her husband. I watched her slam the file folder onto the surface of her desk. "Really, Kyle, I can't imagine why you hired her. Her performance is unacceptable." Perris shut the door, cutting off his wife's tirade about Mrs. Webber.

I glanced over at Cece. "I've seen her somewhere before. But I can't place her."

Cece shrugged. "The face doesn't ring any bells with me."

The office door opened. Perris and his wife stepped out. Now Martina Perris had smoothed the frown off her narrow face. She smiled as she offered one elegant, long-fingered hand.

"I'm sorry to sound so crabby," she said. "It's been a long day and I'm getting one of my headaches. I understand you represent Darcy's family." Her voice left a question mark at the end of the words.

Neither Cece nor I answered her directly. "Tell us what happened Friday night," I said.

"It's all my fault," Mrs. Perris said, shaking her head. "That Darcy got away, I mean. I was tired after lights-out, and I felt one of my migraines coming on. So I took some medication. Next thing I knew, it was eleven-thirty. One of the girls was shaking me. She said Darcy was gone."

"How did she know that?" Cece asked.

"She got up to go to the bathroom. As she passed Darcy's room, she saw that the bunk was empty. When I confirmed this, I alerted Mr. Fosby in his cottage. I think that was about a quarter to twelve.

"We took flashlights and started looking for Darcy." Now her smile disappeared as Mrs. Perris toyed with the lapel of her tailored suit. "Poor Mr. Talbert was lying on the sidewalk near the back door of this building. I left Mr. Fosby with him and I came in here to call the police. And my husband."

"Did Talbert say anything to you and Fosby when you found him?"

She shook her head. "Oh, no. I think he was already dead. There was a lot of blood. It was really awful."

Her left hand, the one with the big diamond and the wide gold wedding band, sought her husband's. Perris took it in both of his and squeezed gently.

"Do you have any idea what Talbert was doing outside the admin building?"

Mrs. Perris shook her head. "No, I'm completely mystified."

Perris intervened, with a pointed glance at his watch. "As I told you earlier, my wife and I have a dinner engagement this evening." He looked at her. "Unless you're not feeling up to it, Martina. Your headache . . . ?"

"Oh, I'll be fine, Kyle." Martina's smile was back. "I'll just take one of my pills."

"Just one more question," I said. "For you, Dr. Perris. You called Darcy's mother Sunday afternoon, to let her know Darcy was missing. Why did you wait more than twenty-four hours to call her? And why didn't you mention that Talbert had been killed?"

"The police were here most of the day on Saturday," Perris said smoothly. Again he sounded as though he'd rehearsed his answer. "I must confess that calling Darcy's family slipped my mind until Sunday morning. I drove over here to the school and made the call to Mrs. Stefano. As for Mr. Talbert's death, it . . ."

"Slipped your mind?"

"Certainly not." He favored me with a tight smile. "It just didn't seem like the time to mention it. After all, Mrs. Stefano's primary concern is her daughter. As is ours."

I returned his smile. "Yes, I'm sure it is."

C H A P T E R *26*

"**S**OMETHING DOESN'T FIT," I SAID. "ABOUT THE school, about the Perrises, about Talbert's death. I can't put my finger on it, but I know it's hinky."

"I agree." Cece piloted her Lexus back down the lane toward the gate. From this side I could see a sensor that opened the gate at the approach of a departing vehicle. Once we were through, the gate closed again and we headed west, toward the county road. Cece stopped at the intersection and scanned the oncoming traffic, then turned right and hit the accelerator.

"I wish I could remember where I've seen Martina Perris."

"Maybe you met her before, a long time ago."

"Formally introduced?" I shook my head. "Not that I recall. Maybe on the street somewhere, in a crowd. Or maybe I've seen a photograph of her. But I can't imagine when or where."

"It'll come to you," Cece said. "Any impressions about the school and its layout?"

"The school's in an isolated location at the edge of town. There is only one road in. So how did Darcy get away from the campus?"

"She could have taken Talbert's car. In fact, I'll bet that's what Ray Harmon thinks."

"Or she had help getting away," I said. "Darcy's pretty savvy. I expect she could stay out of sight in an unfamiliar town. But it's also possible she's with someone. When she took off for Paris, she hooked up with a young man. So maybe she's done the same thing here."

"Another employee?" Cece speculated. "I think we can eliminate teachers and counselors from that column, but there must be additional support staff. We know the school has clerical help in the office, and they've got to have kitchen help. People making food deliveries, people picking up garbage. I wonder if Wayne Talbert was the only maintenance employee they had. Someone has to do the cleaning and landscaping. Of course, they've got the students working in the dining hall, so they may also be doing some of the scut work. I'll see if I can come up with some employees' names, other than Mrs. Webber and Mrs. Johnson."

"The other line of investigation is the murder victim," I said. "Let's see what kind of friends Talbert had, or what sort of enemies he made."

"I know Harmon's already looked at Talbert's apartment," Cece said. "And talked with his neighbors. But he certainly hasn't told me what he found out."

I looked at my watch. "Now that it's after five, Talbert's neighbors are likely to be home. I'll go over there and nose around, see if I can turn up a talkative tenant."

"Good idea." She gave me Talbert's address on Monterey Street. "Come over to my place afterwards, and I'll order a pizza. I live in the Westchester part of town, on Pine Street above Twenty-fourth."

After providing some directions to her house, Cece pulled up to the curb near the Haberfelde Building. I got out and retrieved my Toyota, heading east again. Monterey Street was a busy thoroughfare bisecting a working-class neighborhood that looked tough around the edges. I stayed in the right lane, looking at numbers as I sought the place where Wayne Talbert had lived in the brief time between his arrival in Bakersfield last May and his death at the Perris School Friday night.

I found the apartment building just past Robinson Street, one of those generic stucco boxes so common to California, slotted into a narrow lot with the side of the building facing the street. The exterior was painted a depressingly dull green that loudly proclaimed the cheapness of the rent. I pulled into the narrow drive and parked at the edge of the paved lot, where the lines denoting spaces had faded to the point that the half dozen or so vehicles were parked any which way.

I got out of my car, looking at the building's uninspiring facade. It was two stories, four units on each, with metal walkways on the front and stairs at either end of the building. Each unit had a screen door as well as a hollow-core door, and the windows were covered with cheap plastic mini-blinds, also brown.

A check of the mailboxes near the stairs at the front of the building netted me the information that Talbert had lived in number four, at the back of the first level. I didn't see any mail visible in the slot, but according to Cece, the Bakersfield police had already searched Talbert's apartment. No doubt they'd collected whatever mail had been in the box as well.

I headed toward the rear of the building. The first two apartments were shut tight, as though the residents weren't home from work yet. The door of the third was open on this hot summer evening. As I walked past, I smelled someone's supper, a skilletful of hamburger and onions. The evening news flickered on the large-screen TV I glimpsed through the screen door.

The next apartment had been Talbert's. It, too, had a closed-up look, but someone had left the mini-blinds partly open. I leaned toward the window and squinted, trying to peer inside.

"You lookin' for Wayne?"

I glanced to my right. Talbert's next-door neighbor stood holding her screen door open with one hand, a can of beer in the other. She was a frowzy-looking woman with curly gray hair that hadn't seen a comb lately, at least not since this morning. Fifty-plus, I guessed, medium height and built like a barrel, her torso covered with a big, baggy white T-shirt. The hems of her orange shorts stopped just above her saggy knees, and her feet were jammed into a pair of black rubber sandals with bright pink straps. Her eyes resembled a couple of dark brown dates stuck into her pale pink skin.

"He ain't there, hon. Ain't gonna be, either." Her expression was sympathetic and curious at the same time. "He's dead, hon. Didn't you know that? There was a story in the Sunday paper. You been out of town or something?"

"You could say that. What did he die of?"

"Somebody bopped him on the noggin," she declared. "Not here, though. It was out where he worked. The cops were here, looking around. Doesn't surprise me in the least. None of it."

I left Talbert's window and stepped toward my newfound source. "I'm Jeri."

"I'm Stevie. Short for Stephanie." She grimaced. "But I'm not a Stephanie. Is yours short for Geraldine?"

"Jerusha. But I'm not a Jerusha, or a Geraldine." I smiled. "Since I didn't see the Sunday paper, could you give me some more details about what happened?"

"You ain't his girlfriend or anything?" She wrinkled her pink forehead and looked me up and down.

"Well, no."

"Didn't think so." She took a healthy swig from her beer can. "You look like you got better taste in men than to take up with a guy like Wayne. So why are you casing the joint?"

"Tell me about Wayne," I said, "and I'll tell you why I'm here."

She sniffed the air. "Just a sec, hon. I gotta turn off the heat under that skillet. Come on in."

She turned and headed deeper into her apartment, which seemed to be ten degrees hotter. I followed, shutting the screen door behind me. Everything she'd said so far had stimulated my curiosity, and I wasn't leaving until I got some information.

"You want something to drink?" she called in her wake. "I got beer, iced tea, Coke."

"Iced tea would be fine."

Stevie's apartment was small, with windows on either side of the only door, and she wasn't the most organized housekeeper. The kitchen where she was tending to her skillet was to my right, entered through a small dining nook with a round table and four chairs. The table's surface held a couple of plastic placemats and a scattered assortment of magazines and mail.

The living room to the left was dominated by the huge TV set, which perched on a stand against the wall at the end. A couple of low bookcases had been placed under the front window, containing paperback books: mysteries, westerns, and science fiction. It also held a portable CD player and an untidy pile of discs. In front of the shelves was a floor lamp and an old recliner upholstered in green fabric and covered with a daisy afghan. A threadbare sofa occupied the opposite wall, with a framed floral print hanging above it. Magazines were strewn on the coffee table. Directly in front of me a doorway led to a short hall presumably joining the bathroom and bedroom.

A huge orange tomcat ambled into the living room, tail stuck straight up into the air. He sauntered toward me as though he owned the place, and he probably did. After he'd inspected me and shed cat hair on the legs of my slacks, he headed for the tiny kitchen. I followed him and saw him drinking water from a big ceramic bowl.

"Nice-looking cat," I commented as Stevie handed me a bottle of lemon-flavored iced tea.

"That's Booger. Had him since he was a little fluff-ball. Now look at him. Twenty pounds, I'll bet."

"I've got two," I said, unscrewing the lid. "Abigail's a gray and brown tabby, and I've got a kitten named Black Bart."

"After the outlaw?" Stevie grinned. "Good name for a cat. They always tell you what their names are, don't they? I took a gander at this guy and said, he's a booger." She took another swallow from her beer can and then looked at me through narrowed eyes. "Now, about Wayne. Didn't know the guy all that well. Hell, he only lived here a coupla months. Like I said, I didn't think you were his girl-friend. From what I could see, he kept to himself, or hung out with some lowlifes."

"How did you know they were lowlifes?"

Stevie tilted her unruly head to one side and gave her best world-weary expression. "Hon, I been around the block a few times. I know a lowlife when I see one. I own a café over on Union Street, and I get all kinds comin' through the door. Now suppose you tell me why you're peeking through the window of the place next door. Specially since I figure you didn't know Wayne at all."

I slipped one of my business cards from my purse and handed it to her. "I didn't. I'm a private investigator."

"All the way from Oakland?" Stevie held the card between thumb and forefinger. "You working with the cops?" she asked. I shook my head. "Who, then?"

"I can't tell you who my client is, Stevie. But I'd certainly like to hear more about Wayne Talbert and the people he associated with. Tell me about those lowlifes."

"Don't know if he was one of them or a wannabe. But I saw him with these guys in my café, a coupla weeks ago. And they were sure as hell looking for him Friday night. They broke into his place, right after the girl was here."

The girl? I leaned forward. "Who broke in? And who was the girl?"

"Never saw her before, but she had a key."

"Did you get a good look at her?"

"Not really," Stevie admitted. "I heard a car drive up. Then someone got out. I heard Wayne's screen door open, so I looked out the window to see if it was him. But it was this girl. That surprised me, because I'd never seen Wayne with a girl, just those weird guys. Nice-looking kid, maybe eighteen or nineteen. Didn't look like a hooker. And believe me, I know. My café's right in the middle of Hooker Row. This one was real pretty, fresh-faced, not hard. Dark hair, shoulder-length. She looked like one of those college students from out at Cal State. Like I said, she had a key. Unlocked the door, went inside, and was back out again in less than ten minutes. She left in his car."

That brought me upright. "His car? You're sure?"

"Yeah. Wayne drove one of those little Ford Escorts, blue. It had a dent in the right front fender. That's how I knew it was his car. She'd pulled it right up in front of his door. She was driving, 'cause when she came out, she went around to the left side. Did a tight turn in the parking lot and took off, real fast."

Stevie's description sounded very much like Darcy. And it didn't sound good. I pulled the snapshot from my purse. "Is this the girl you saw?"

"Sure looks like her," Stevie said. "Hair was shorter, though."

"What time did she get here?" I asked.

"Maybe eleven-thirty. The lowlifes showed up around midnight."

"What did they look like?"

"All in black. Wearing steel-toed boots and swastika tattoos." Stevie made a face and took a swig of beer, as though she had to wash the taste of the words from her mouth. "Skinheads."

CHAPTER *27*

HIS WAS THE SECOND TIME IN TWO DAYS I'D HEARD THE
word "skinhead."

Heather had described one of the two men who took Darcy from
her Alameda condo as a skinhead. I thought about some articles on
hate crimes I'd read recently. One described American skinheads,
with their overt racism and ready violence, as a terrorist youth
subculture.

Skinheads were responsible for an escalating number of racist at-
tacks over the past few years, in California and all over the United
States. One of the worst incidents occurred in Portland, Oregon,
when several skinheads associated with Tom Metzger of the California Knights of the Ku Klux Klan, who'd formed a group called the
White Aryan Resistance, had battered an Ethiopian immigrant to
death. In a closely watched wrongful death lawsuit, the Southern
Poverty Law Center went after Metzger and WAR, who were found
liable for ten million dollars in punitive damages.

Skinheads in Bakersfield?

Why should I be surprised? There had been incidents in Bay Area
communities as well as in Sacramento. And other groups, the Klan
included, had pockets of activity all up and down California.

"There were three of 'em," Stevie was saying. We were on her
lumpy sofa. She had kicked off her rubber sandals and had propped
her feet on the pile of magazines that covered her messy coffee table.
In her left hand she still held a beer can. With her right, she stroked
her big orange cat, who had settled into her lap.

"Midnight, you said?" I thought about the timeline. According to Martina Perris, she'd been awakened by another student around eleven-thirty, and discovered that Darcy was missing. This was about the time Stevie had seen a girl entering the apartment next door. Bennett Fosby said Martina had called him about a quarter to twelve. Then Martina had found Talbert's body around midnight. The same time the skinheads showed up at Talbert's apartment. How long would it take Darcy—if the girl Stevie had seen *were* Darcy—to get here from the school?

"Midnight," Stevie said. "I heard them pounding on Wayne's door. I looked out my window and saw them in the light from one of the outside fixtures. Just in time to see them kick in the door. That's when I called the cops. But they were long gone, time the patrol car got here."

"Can you give me more of a description, Stevie? Were all three of them skinheads?"

"Two of 'em were. Young guys, you know, nineteen, twenty, with those creepy shaved heads. Looked like they was cut from the same bolt of cloth. Or bought their clothes at the same place, anyway. Black jeans, black T-shirts, those big, ugly boots. One had a chain around his waist and both of 'em had swastikas tattooed on their arms." She grimaced as her right hand ruffled the fur on Booger's back. "To think he had friends like that. Disgusting."

I would agree with disgusting, if in fact Talbert had chosen the skinheads as his buddies. Since they'd kicked in his front door, it was likely that their reason for seeking him had been less than friendly. A possibility worth considering, now that Talbert was in the Kern County morgue. Had the skinheads helped put him there?

"What about the third one? He wasn't a skinhead? Did you get a look at him?"

"Not a good one. He was hanging back, out of the light. He was wearing slacks and a shirt, looked older than the other two. Brown hair, blue eyes, fortyish. More like a regular person."

Stevie's description sounded a lot like Bennett Fosby, I realized. But Fosby couldn't have been at Talbert's apartment at midnight. He'd been at the Perris School then, when Martina found Talbert's body. Unless someone was wrong about the timing.

"What else can you tell me about Talbert?"

Stevie shook her head. "Not a whole lot, hon. He only lived here a couple of months. We'd say hello now and then at the mailbox or out in the parking lot, but for all he lived next door, I never saw the guy much. He kept to himself."

"Yes, but you strike me as the observant type. Let's go back to when he moved in. Were you here that day?"

"Yeah, I was. And you're right, I keep my eyes open." Stevie massaged her left foot with her right hand and thought about it for a moment. "It was a Sunday, middle of May. He backed one of those rental trucks up to the door and unloaded his stuff. He didn't have a lot, and it all looked brand-new."

"As in, right out of the store?" I asked. Not what I'd expect from someone who didn't have a job in Bakersfield until after he moved into the Monterey Street apartment.

Stevie nodded. "Yep. Like it still had the price tag on it. One of those futons on a frame, the kind you can use as a sofa and a bed. A table, a coupla chairs. TV and a portable CD player. A microwave oven. A few cardboard boxes, and that was it. He did have one of those little portable computers. I went over to introduce myself once he got settled in, and he had the thing out on the table, like he was working on something. I don't think he even had a bed, just that futon. His place has the same floor plan as mine and it looked like he'd only furnished the living room and dining room. He ate a lot of take-out. Pizza, burgers, deli stuff. The time I was in his place, I didn't even see any dishes, just paper plates and plastic spoons and forks."

How very transitory. Talbert's impermanence might be an important piece of information, but at the moment I didn't know how that piece fit into the puzzle. "Sounds like he wasn't much of a homebody. Or maybe he didn't plan on staying long."

"Yeah," Stevie said. "Kinda like this was just a place he slept. Or maybe he was starting over, got rid of all his old things before he moved to Bakersfield and was planning to buy new when he could."

"I understand he got the job at the school after he moved here. Did you know where he worked?"

"Not till I read that article about the murder in Sunday's paper. If he was out of work, I guess that explains why he didn't pick a nicer apartment. I mean, this place is okay and I live here because it's close to my café. But it ain't exactly the Ritz."

She stopped talking and took a swallow of beer. Booger decided he'd had enough lap time and jumped down to the brown carpet, stretching and sharpening his claws on its tattered nap. I thought about what she'd told me. I had a feeling Talbert hadn't cared where he lived, as long as it was cheap and convenient.

"You told the police about the girl?" I asked, knowing the answer.

"Sure did. Told 'em everything I saw that night, from the girl going in, to the skinheads kicking in Wayne's door."

But Sergeant Harmon hadn't said anything about the girl or the skinheads when we'd seen him and his partner out at the Perris School. All he'd given us was that Talbert's car hadn't been found yet. And the information certainly hadn't appeared in the newspaper article about Talbert's death. If the sergeant had told Cece about the break-in at Talbert's apartment, or the fact that a witness had seen a young woman resembling Darcy enter the dead man's apartment, surely the attorney would have told me. I had a feeling Cece was in the dark concerning this facet of the investigation. Harmon and Garza were keeping a few details to themselves.

"Anything else you can tell me about him?" I asked, as I got to my feet, ready to leave.

Stevie shrugged. "Well, he dyed his hair. Or had it done. I thought that was kinda weird for a guy."

It wasn't all that strange for the Bay Area, but Bakersfield might be a different matter. "You're sure?"

"Yeah. It was brown when he moved in, and sorta long. Next day it was real short and dirty blond. Looked natural, like he'd been to a beauty parlor instead of doin' it himself. But the last few weeks I noticed the roots growing out."

Interesting, I thought, as I made my way back to my car. But what did it all mean? One thing I knew for certain. I'd have to do more research about Wayne Talbert to unravel the reasons for his death.

CHAPTER *28*

CECE BROMLEY'S NEIGHBORHOOD WAS A PLEASANT ENclave of winding, tree-shaded streets, located northwest of downtown and southeast of the Kern River. I found the address easily enough. An older, two-story wood-frame with a double garage, the house was painted white with green shutters. It wouldn't have looked out of place back in the Midwest.

I parked my Toyota on one side of the double driveway next to Cece's Lexus, and headed for the front door. Although it was now evening, the heat still felt oppressive. I rang the bell. A moment later the door opened. Cece stood there barefoot, wearing a pair of pale blue shorts and a sleeveless white T-shirt.

"I've ordered pizza." She admitted me to the air-conditioned sanctuary of her living room and shut the door on the exterior heat. "About ten minutes ago. I'm so hungry I couldn't wait any longer. Want a beer?"

"Yes. The colder the better."

The living room was big and comfortable, carpeted in beige plush and furnished with lots of oak and neutral upholstery. We went through a wide doorway into the den, separated from the kitchen by a work island that was the current resting place for Cece's purse and briefcase, as well as a stack of mail. The den was carpeted in the same beige, while the kitchen featured white vinyl flooring to go with the white-tiled surfaces of the counters. Beyond the work island, a sliding glass door led onto a covered patio, visible through the open vertical blinds.

On the floor in front of the glass door a middle-sized brindle mutt with beagle somewhere in his ancestry sprawled flat on his side, stretched out on the floor next to his water dish. He was curious enough about me to raise his head for a look and bang his tail a couple of times on the floor. I knelt, let him sniff my hand, then scratched his ears. He gave a pleasure-filled groan.

"That's Woofer Dog," Cece said. "He loves it if you rub his belly."

I took her suggestion. Woofer Dog moaned in ecstasy and thumped his tail even faster. Cece had opened the refrigerator and was eyeing a row of beer bottles. "You want domestic light or Mexican dark?"

"Dark sounds good to me."

She handed me a bottle. A sofa and an armchair were grouped around a coffee table in the den, all more or less facing a wide-screen TV. Cece sat down in the chair and propped her bare feet on the coffee table. I sat on the sofa and took a long pull from the bottle. The beer tasted great.

I heard the front door open and close, and voices approach. Woofer Dog hauled himself up to greet two teenaged boys, older versions of the photographs I'd seen earlier in the office. Both had Cece's blond hair and fair complexion, reddened by the sun. They trooped into the kitchen carrying skateboards, helmets, and knee and elbow pads, which they dropped onto the floor next to the work island. Then they headed for the refrigerator.

"Man, it's hot," one of them exclaimed, the smaller of the two. He stuck his head into the appliance as though he were trying to cool it off. A few seconds later he straightened, holding a can of soda in one hand.

The taller boy snatched the soda. "Gimme that, squirt."

"Hey!" The first boy grabbed for the can, missing it by an inch or so as the other backed away, laughing.

"Guys," Cece said in a no-nonsense mother voice as she glanced at them over her shoulder. "There's plenty of soda in there and no need to fight over who gets what. Besides, we have company. I want you yahoos to be on your best behavior. This is Jeri Howard. She's a private investigator from Oakland. She'll be working with me on a case. Jeri, these are my sons, Kevin and Chad."

The boys greeted me with polite mumbles. Kevin was the older of the two, about sixteen I guessed. He popped the top on the can and tilted it back. Chad, who was thirteen or fourteen, grabbed another soda from the refrigerator and slammed the door. Then he knelt to roughhouse with the dog.

"What's for dinner?" Kevin asked.

"I ordered a couple of pizzas," Cece told him. "They should be here any minute. Go wash up. And take that skateboard stuff with you."

The two gathered up their gear and thumped up the stairs, accompanied by Woofer Dog. "Divorced?" I guessed.

"Oh, yeah." She paused for a swallow of beer. "Four years now. He's a lawyer, too. Don't you just love it? Two attorneys divorcing one another. It was a bitch."

"He lives here?"

She nodded. "We both used to work at this big law firm over on Eye Street. I found out he was a little friendlier than he should have been with one of the summer interns. I left him, left the firm, started my own practice."

"But you didn't leave town."

"Born here, grew up here, my folks still live here. Where am I gonna go?" She shrugged. "Besides, it's not the boys' fault. They need to see their dad on a regular basis."

The doorbell rang and Cece got up to answer it, grabbing her purse. She returned a moment later with two pizza boxes. The boys had heard the bell. Now they thundered down the stairs to claim one of the pizzas.

"Cholesterol special for the guys," Cece announced. "Pepperoni, sausage, and black olives. Their favorite." She handed over the box. "For the ladies, a veggie deluxe. Guys, you can eat this upstairs. Jeri and I have to talk business."

When they'd gone, I cleared a spot on the coffee table for the box. Cece got a couple of plates and napkins. Once she'd resumed her seat in the armchair we each took a slice of pizza, then settled back to eat and talk.

"Did you find out anything at Talbert's apartment?" she asked.

"Indeed I did. He's got a talkative neighbor, a woman named Stevie Kay. She told me a couple of interesting things. First, you were right about Talbert having blond hair. The neighbor says he dyed it, right after he moved in."

"Change in hair color," Cece said. "And he loses the mustache. An attempt to disguise himself?"

"Sounds like it. More importantly, the neighbor says a young woman with dark hair showed up at Talbert's place Friday night, around eleven-thirty. She was driving Talbert's car and she had the key to the apartment. She went in, stayed about ten minutes, then left again."

"Damnation," Cece said around a mouthful of pizza. She grabbed a napkin and mopped some tomato sauce from her chin. "It sounds like Darcy. Is the neighbor sure it was Talbert's car?"

"Very sure. Blue Ford Escort with a dent in the right front fender. It gets more interesting. Half an hour after the girl left, three guys showed up and kicked in Talbert's door. Stevie called the cops. Did Sergeant Harmon mention any of this when he talked with you?"

"He did not. He's holding out on me, which is just like him. So who were these guys who broke into the apartment? Did the neighbor give you a description?"

"Yes, and she says she thinks she'd seen Talbert with two of them before. All three were white. One an older man, brown hair, blue eyes, fortyish. The other ones were late teens, early twenties. Black jeans, black T-shirts, steel-toed boots, and shaved heads. One had a chain around his waist. Both had swastika tattoos."

"Skinheads? My, my." Cece cocked her head to one side as she finished her pizza slice and chased it with some beer.

"You don't seem surprised," I said.

"We have whatever the big city's got. I'd heard there were some skinheads up in Oildale." She jerked her head in a northerly direction. Oildale is just the other side of the Kern River, close to the oil fields, a landscape of sere hills dotted with oil pumps and storage tanks.

"What about the Klan?"

"The Klan's alive and well in California, even if people don't want to talk about it." She reached for another slice of pizza. "I haven't heard anything about them locally, though."

"What about militia activity in this area?"

Cece nodded. "Not only Kern County, but Tulare, Kings, and

Fresno counties as well. And it was Stanislaus County where some extremist group attacked the assessor."

"People tend to be conservative here in the Valley," I said.

"You bet. Conservative politics and fundamentalist religion. Some of them are my relatives."

"Just how conservative?" I helped myself to another slice. "Do they stick with writing and talking their politics? Or do they act? Any hate crimes lately?"

"Hate crimes," Cece repeated. "There's a lot of anti-immigrant sentiment recently, but it's not confined to Kern County. It's all over the state. We have a large Hispanic population, because of our agricultural base. I've heard of some skinhead stuff going on at the high school in Lancaster. But that's L.A. County. As far as I know, we haven't had any incidents here. Or if we have, people aren't talking about it. I'll put a few feelers out, see if any local law enforcement has information about these skinheads. And if there's any information on militias. I know people over at the Sheriff's Department. And, of course, the Bakersfield Police Department."

"Like Sergeant Harmon." She looked blank. "You and Ray Harmon. I thought I felt a little undercurrent there. Or am I seeing things where they don't exist?"

Cece didn't say anything as she reached into the pizza box for another slice. "You have excellent powers of observation," she said finally. "Yeah, Ray and I had a thing about a year ago. He was coming down after his divorce. Which is not the best time to get involved with a guy. My kids started being real needy. They didn't like me going out with anyone. So we broke it off. And now Ray's bending over backward to be a real hard-ass whenever we encounter each other. Like that bad-cop routine today." She sighed. "Sometimes I wish it had worked out. But being involved with a cop . . ."

"I was married to a cop. It didn't work out for us, either."

"Well, that water went under the bridge a long time ago," Cece said. She wiped her hands on a napkin. "Did the neighbor give you anything else?"

"Just that he didn't have much in the way of furniture, and it was all new." I told her what Stevie had said about Talbert's possessions, or lack of them.

Cece shook her head. "There's something fishy about this guy.

He just appears in town in May, gets a job at the Perris School, nobody knows much about him. I don't like it. I'm also pissed at Ray Harmon for not telling me about that break-in."

"While you're prying more information out of the sergeant," I said, "I'll dig a little deeper into Wayne Talbert's past. We need to find out more about him, especially if he's got skinheads kicking in his door the night he gets killed."

The phone rang as we were finishing the pizza, then stopped. One of Cece's boys had answered. Then I heard an adolescent male voice bellowing down the stairs. "Mom! It's for you."

Cece got up to fetch a cordless phone from its nest on the kitchen counter. After she'd said hello, she listened for a moment, then she cupped her hand over the mouthpiece and looked at me.

"It's Mrs. Webber. From the Perris School."

" **I** TOOK THAT JOB," CONSUELA WEBBER TOLD ME, "BE-
cause I needed it. The pay was good and the commute was
short. But I don't know how much longer I can work for the Bitch of
Bakersfield."

As I'd suspected earlier, Mrs. Webber had recognized Cece
Bromley when we were at the school earlier that afternoon. The attorney had handled a case for Mrs. Webber's cousin a year or so
ago. Presumably she'd called Cece because she had some information she wanted to convey to us, either about Wayne Talbert or
Darcy Stefano. She hadn't done so yet. First she needed to ventilate
about her job.

When I arrived at the older tract house, in a neighborhood east of
Highway 99 and north of Wilson Avenue, Consuela's husband,
Zach, answered the door. Blond, in his early thirties, he wore jeans
and a T-shirt. He let me in, explaining that his wife was putting the
kids to bed. Consuela joined us in the living room as we were making polite conversation. Zach retired to the den behind the kitchen
to watch TV as Consuela offered me a soft drink, which I declined.

The living room was small, and it looked as though it were used
only for company. It was furnished with a sofa and matching chair
covered in a muted floral pattern, mostly peach and green. The
same colors were repeated in an arrangement of silk flowers on the
coffee table in front of us.

The end tables on either side were crowded with framed pictures.
Most of them showed Consuela and Zach with their two children, a

boy and a girl, three and six years old she told me. The rest of the photos were of family members on both sides. I took the armchair. Consuela sat on the nearest end of the sofa, sipping from the glass she held. The lamplight reflected off her glossy black hair.

"Part of me wants to stick it out," she said. "Just to irritate the woman, since she so obviously hates Hispanics. The other part of me says, hey, it's not worth the aggravation. That's what Zach says, too. We really do need the money, but I'm sure I could find another job."

"How long have you worked at the Perris School?" I asked.

"Since April. I got laid off from my last job in February and I'd been looking since then. I saw an ad in the paper for the Perris School. I called and went out to interview that same morning. They needed someone right away. The previous secretary quit without notice, and I was the first person to walk through the door. Dr. Perris hired me on the spot."

"So he doesn't share his wife's prejudice?"

"Not that I've noticed. Mrs. Perris was out of town when I interviewed. At least that's what Emma Johnson, the other secretary, told me." Now her mouth curved down in a frown. "A week later she got back from wherever she'd gone. I'll never forget the look on her face when she realized the name Webber didn't actually mean she was getting an Anglo."

"Mrs. Perris looks as though she'd be difficult to work for." I recalled the scene I'd witnessed that afternoon in the school's admin office.

"Difficult doesn't cover it," Consuela said. "She's always on my case. Pick, pick, pick. I can't do anything right. And I know she complains about me to her husband. It's like she wants me to quit, but she doesn't want to fire me. She knows if she did that, I'd march right down to the Department of Fair Employment and Housing, and file a claim."

"You're sure it's because you're Hispanic?"

She shot me an indignant look that told me she'd been down that road before, too many times. "Believe me, I know what I'm talking about. My family's lived in this area for three generations. Still I get called 'wetback' and 'spic.' Not that she's ever said those words or been out in the open about it. She's too slick for that. But I know people like Martina Perris and Bennett Fosby. I can read the signs. I've had to, all my life."

I tilted my head to one side. "Fosby, too?"

"Well, he's never come right out with any slurs," she admitted. "But when my brother worked at the school earlier this summer, he didn't get along with Fosby at all. Fosby made some wild accusation about Miguel messing around with his keys. That's nonsense. Miguel wouldn't do that. I think Fosby just didn't like him. He's so antisocial. No wonder he lives at the school, so he doesn't have to be with anyone he doesn't like."

She pointed at one of the framed pictures clustered on the end table between us. "That's Miguel, on the left, next to my grandmother. He's a junior at Cal State."

I picked up the photograph and examined it. Miguel was about twenty, lean, dark, and quite handsome. He had one arm around the shoulder of a gray-haired woman, and both were grinning at the camera.

"What was Miguel doing at the school?"

"Athletic counselor, but he only lasted two weeks." She shook her head. "He didn't like the way the teachers and counselors treated the students. So he quit."

"When was that?"

She considered for a moment. "He started in the middle of June. And he was gone by the end of the month."

So Miguel had barely begun his summer employment at the school when Darcy and Gillie tried to run away. "Do you have much contact with the students?"

She took a sip of her soft drink before answering. "Not really. Emma Johnson and I are just there to type, file, and answer the phone. I stick pretty close to the admin office. Most of the time I only see the kids walking around the campus. Now and then a few of them get called into Dr. Perris's office."

"What's your impression of the school itself? Particularly after what your brother told you?"

"You know," she said thoughtfully, "when I went to work there I thought that it was just a fancy private school for rich kids. But I have to say, after Miguel told me why he quit, I started keeping a closer eye on things. They treat those kids like they're in some kind of boot camp. Oh, I know the students are supposed to have behavior problems. That's why they got sent to the school, according to Emma. So they'll shape up. But still . . ." Her voice trailed off.

"How well did you know Wayne Talbert?" I asked.

She looked startled. "Wayne? Not well. He seemed like a nice guy. The only person he was friendly with was Fosby. I think they met in some bar in Oildale where Fosby likes to drink. Wayne started working there in May, about a month after I did. We didn't see him in the admin office that often, unless there was something that needed fixing."

"Did Wayne have access to the whole school?" I asked.

"Sure," she told me. "He knew the place inside and out, had keys and everything."

"So he could have been inside the admin office before he was killed Friday night." She didn't say anything. "Why did you ask me to come over here, Consuela? Is there something you wanted to tell me?"

She finished her drink and carefully placed the glass on the little woven coaster next to the lamp. Then she folded her hands in her lap and looked over at me. "I'm not sure Dr. Perris is giving you—or the police—the whole story."

"Why do you say that?"

"Call it a hunch," Consuela said slowly. "You were there when I asked Emma about the stapler."

"I remember. It's missing from your desk. You said, a big stapler. How big?"

"Really big." She held her hands about twenty inches apart. "The heavy-duty kind, for stapling thick stacks of pages."

I nodded. I knew what she was talking about. Such staplers were standard equipment around the law offices where I'd worked as a legal secretary and paralegal before becoming a private investigator. A stapler like that was a heavy piece of metal. It would make an effective bludgeon.

"When was the last time you saw it?"

"Friday, at five, when I left the office," Consuela said. "It wasn't there when I got to work Monday morning. Somebody took it. I've been looking for it ever since. It's just vanished. And the building isn't that big. Now, I know the police were in and out this past week-end. But . . ."

"Have you mentioned this to anyone?"

"Just Emma. It seems so silly, now that I tell you. A stapler. Probably got misplaced."

Maybe. Maybe not. Was the stapler part of the evidence collected at the school? But Cece told me Sergeant Harmon had said there was no murder weapon at the scene. Unless he was holding out on her again. And if Talbert hadn't been in the office before he was killed, as Kyle Perris claimed, why would the evidence techs take the stapler? Why would Perris lie about Talbert being in the office?

"You think someone was in the building on Friday?"

"Wayne," Consuela said with a shrug. "Who else? It makes as much sense for him to be inside as outside. But Dr. Perris says no."

It was tempting to view the stapler as the murder weapon. But there was little to back up that theory. I filed it away for further con-sideration. "Did you ever see Darcy Stefano in the admin office, or on the campus?"

"I didn't see her, except at a distance. But I heard them talking about her, Dr. and Mrs. Perris, and one of the teachers. They said she'd be a hard nut to crack."

Darcy was tough, I thought, but she was outnumbered. I hoped they hadn't cracked her.

"When she and Gillie Cooper made a break for it, and Fosby and Wayne caught them, there was quite a fuss. I heard all about it from Miguel. He was upset that Dr. Perris put them in isolation. Solitary, he called it. He said they shouldn't be treated like that. That they were troubled, not troublemakers."

"I agree," I said. What Dr. Perris had earlier called a discipline room, I'd called solitary confinement. It sounded as though Miguel and I were in agreement. "Where can I find your brother?"

Consuela shifted her eyes to one side, as though she didn't want to meet mine. "Well, he's working for my uncle now, driving a truck. He goes from place to place all over the county. I'm not sure where he'll be until school starts again in the fall."

So Consuela didn't want me talking to Miguel. Why was that? Maybe the young man really had been messing around with Fosby's keys. I'd have to look him up on my own. But it would help if I had a last name.

"I'd certainly like to talk with Gillie," I said, shifting my focus from Miguel back to the school. "Since she tried to escape with Darcy that first time back in June, it's possible she knows something."

"Good luck with that," Consuela said. "Dr. Perris isn't going to let you near her."

"I've already asked him. He refused. But I'm going to go out there tomorrow and give it a try. He also said talking to her wouldn't gain me any information, because she's a liar."

"He said that about her?" Consuela seemed bothered by the word. "I'd think Gillie would want to help Darcy."

"I think she does, too. When Cece Bromley and I arrived at the school this afternoon, Gillie was watching us. I had a feeling she wanted to talk with us, but then Dr. Perris came out of the office and told her she was supposed to be working in the dining hall."

"A lot of the students work in the dining hall," she told me. "They rotate through, different schedules, different meals, different jobs, too. This is the week for Gillie's cottage."

An idea was percolating in my mind. "Where do you eat lunch, Consuela?"

"Me? Sometimes I take a lunch. Or I drive over to East Hills Mall and shop. Or I eat in the dining hall." She stopped, realizing where I was headed. "You want me to talk to Gillie, don't you?"

"If I can't manage to get the girl alone, I'll need to go to Plan B." I took one of my cards from my purse and wrote down the number of my cell phone and my hotel.

"And I'm Plan B?" Consuela shook her head. "That's crazy."

"All you have to do is go to lunch in the dining hall. You walk up to Gillie, give her this card, with my phone numbers on it." I thought of a possible stumbling block, a big one. "Can Gillie get to a phone?"

Consuela looked doubtful. "There are phones in all the buildings, including the dining hall, but the staff members are the only ones who are supposed to use them. I think the students get to call home on weekends. If Gillie's working there, she might be able to use it. But if she got caught, she'd be in a lot of trouble. If I got caught, I would be in trouble, too."

She shook her head again. "Better you should talk to her tomorrow. The best time for you to come to the school is in the morning. Dr. Perris makes his rounds of the classes then, usually between nine-thirty and eleven-thirty. The kids who work in the dining hall are supposed to report half an hour before the meal. Lunch starts at eleven forty-five."

"So I could catch Gillie at eleven-fifteen. But if I can't, I need to know what Gillie wanted to tell me and Cece." I looked at her, mentally applying the pressure.

Consuela sighed and held out her hand. "All right, give me the card. I'll try. But I can't promise anything."

CHAPTER 30

THE PHONE WOKE ME AT SEVEN-THIRTY WEDNESDAY MORN-
ing. It was Cece Bromley, sounding as though she hadn't had
enough coffee yet.

"I've got a lead," I told her as I propped myself up in bed and
gave her a quick rundown of last night's conversation.

"We need all the leads we can find," Cece said. "I just got off the
phone with Ray Harmon. They found Wayne Talbert's car."

"The blue Ford Escort?"

"With the dented front right fender. It was abandoned in the
parking lot over at Valley Plaza Mall. Jeri, it's got Darcy's prints on
the steering wheel."

She quickly gave me the details. A security guard at the shopping
mall had noticed Talbert's car early Monday morning, before the
stores opened, parked by itself at the end of a row near the Sears
store. When it was still there Monday night, he figured it had been
abandoned. He had the vehicle towed Tuesday morning.

By Tuesday afternoon someone made the connection between the
plates on the dusty blue sedan and Talbert's missing Ford Escort.
The fact that Darcy Stefano's fingerprints were all over the car's interior looked bad indeed. But I'd figured it was coming, after what
Stevie Kay said about the girl entering Talbert's apartment the night
of the murder.

I'd brought the answering machine tape with me, the one with
Darcy's message on it. After Cece and I ended our conversation, I

got out of bed and played the tape again on my portable cassette player. Listening, I filtered out the frightened tremble in her voice, focusing on the background sounds.

Wheels on pavement, a car horn. On my first few hearings I'd thought that she'd been near a busy street. Did the sounds fit in with a shopping mall parking lot on a Sunday afternoon? Or did they indicate cars moving faster, at a steadier pace than vehicles cruising a parking lot looking for a space? The tinkling bell sounded like the signal many businesses use to announce the arrival of customers. The slam of a car door. Was that a random noise from some vehicle near the phone booth?

Or did it have a darker implication? Someone after her, someone besides the Bakersfield police?

Maybe that's why she'd made no further attempt to get in touch with me. Lying low, afraid to come up for air. But the sound of the car door could mean that someone had arrived to pick her up.

I knew—and so did the police—how Darcy had left the Perris School. She'd taken Talbert's car and gone to Talbert's apartment, why I didn't yet know. But that was Friday. Where had she slept that night and Saturday night? Had she spent the next forty-eight hours driving around Bakersfield before ditching Talbert's car at the mall? And from there, where? Cece had told me Bakersfield had reliable bus service. But Darcy was a stranger who'd been held prisoner at that school for nearly two months. If she'd caught a bus from the mall, where would she go?

I was convinced someone was helping her stay out of sight. But who could that be? Someone she'd met at the school? She hadn't had the opportunity to meet anyone else.

My favorite candidate was Miguel, Consuela's brother. I recalled her reluctance to talk about him last night, as well as her statement that he'd left the school not long after he started his summer job, because he didn't like the way the students were treated.

I needed a last name for Miguel. Maybe I could get it out at the Perris School.

At ten o'clock I headed east on Highway 178. I wanted to waylay Gillie Cooper on her way from the classroom building to the dining hall at eleven-fifteen. But I also wanted to talk with Bennett Fosby.

When I reached the front gate of the Perris School I rolled down the window and pushed the intercom button. I heard Fosby's voice answer. "Perris School. Who is it, please?"

"Jeri Howard to see Bennett Fosby," I said.

"What do you want?" His voice sounded gruff.

"I have some more questions I'd like to ask you."

"Does Dr. Perris know you're coming?"

"No."

There was a long silence, as though Fosby were deciding whether or not to let me in. Or maybe he was calling Perris to alert him to my presence. Finally I heard the intercom buzz. The gate clanked and moved rightward on its track. I drove through the opening. The gate shut behind me as I headed up the short lane, then turned right onto the drive that circled the school's buildings.

I drove past the parking area next to the administration building, heading for the maintenance building. The same dark green Blazer I'd seen yesterday was parked near the building's front door. I pulled in next to it and got out of my Toyota. Sunlight bounced off the Blazer's dusty finish. It was already hot, the mercury edging toward a hundred degrees, though it was only mid-morning. Light and dust shimmered together against the hard blue sky.

I saw something I hadn't noticed yesterday. Just past an oak tree some forty or fifty feet to my right was a gate, built into the fence on the school's northern perimeter. I walked toward the gate, crossing the gravel drive. There didn't appear to be a road on either side of the gate. Just beyond I saw the furrows of a field, something growing there that looked like wheat or alfalfa. I turned to my left and looked to the west, at the narrow track I'd seen yesterday, snaking up the side of the low hill between the school and Bakersfield.

Now I heard a door open and glanced back. Fosby had come out of the building and was walking toward me, ramrod-straight. He was dressed as he had been Tuesday, in a pair of khaki slacks and a short-sleeved shirt. His attire gave him a vaguely military appearance. As before, the large key ring at his belt jingled as he walked.

"Where does that road go?" I asked, pointing west.

"Nowhere," he said, hands on his hips.

Now I turned to face him. "Dr. Perris says there's a subdivision over that hill."

"There is. But you can't get to it from here."

"Why not?"

"That path over the hill isn't much more than a dirt track. I sure as hell wouldn't want to take a car over it. Besides, there's an irrigation canal just past the west boundary of the school. That path dead-ends at the canal."

Fosby narrowed his blue eyes. "I know what you're thinking. But you're wrong. There's only one way in or out of this place. That gravel road you came in on, the one that connects with the county road."

"What about this gate?" I pointed at the opening in the fence that I'd spotted. "It opens onto that field, and I'll bet there's some sort of road that links the field to the county road."

"No, there isn't. It's fenced all the way north. The guy who owns that acreage has a road up by his house, which is near the river. This gate's never used. It's kept locked. The Perrises didn't see any need to replace it. This was already a school, you see, one that went belly-up. The Perrises just made some improvements when they bought the place. Put in the intercom system that opens the front gate, did some landscaping on the grounds."

He gestured at the bushes that paralleled the fence, then turned to me as he continued. "You and I both know Darcy took Wayne's car. Drove right out the front gate with it. That's the only way she could have gotten out of here."

"Perhaps," I said, not willing to concede the point just yet.

"I overheard Dr. Perris this morning," Fosby said, "telling Mrs. Perris the cops found Wayne's car over at the mall. I'll bet that girl's prints are all over the steering wheel."

He was correct about that, I admitted to myself, but not to him. "Do you think Darcy killed Wayne Talbert?"

He hesitated. "I don't know what happened. All I know is what I saw, what I told the police. What I told you yesterday."

"I'd appreciate it if you'd tell me again."

He gazed at me for a moment, then waved one hand at the door. "Come on into my office. It's too hot to stand out here talking."

I followed him into the building. Fosby's office was on the left, through an open door. Beyond this door was another, open slightly, through which I glimpsed a toilet and a sink. On my right and in front of me I saw work tables and cabinets, their doors secured with padlocks. The interior space didn't seem to match the size of the building, however, and when I looked again I saw that one of the cabinets was actually a door leading to the rear half of the building.

"What's back there?" I asked, pausing in the doorway of Fosby's office.

"The Perrises have some furniture stored there," Fosby said.

"For the school?"

"Personal stuff." He stepped past me into his office. His desk faced the door. There were some filing cabinets lined up against the interior wall. On the wall was a plain, utilitarian clock with a second hand. At the moment it read ten-forty. Under the window on the opposite wall a long table held some tool catalogs, several brown mugs on a round tray, and a shiny metal percolator.

"You want some coffee?" Fosby asked.

"No, thanks."

He poured himself a mugful and sat down at his desk. I looked around for something to sit on. I saw a plain ladderback chair stuck in one corner, under a metal key box affixed to the wall. It wasn't locked at the moment, however. The door was open, and as I reached for the chair I could see neat rows of keys, all labeled. The bungalows, the dining hall, the admin office, even one marked "side gate." I wondered if the key box was left unlocked during the day. If so, anyone might have access.

"What is it you wanted to ask me?" Fosby said behind me. "I thought I covered everything yesterday when you and that lawyer were here."

I turned, moved the chair closer to Fosby's desk, and sat down. "I wanted to get a clearer picture of the layout of the school, and your routine as well. And get some more information on Wayne Talbert." I looked at the elaborate electronics panel next to his telephone. "Does this control the front gate?"

"Yes. If I'm not here I switch it to the admin office and at night to my cottage. It also controls the exterior lights."

"How long have you worked at the school?"

"Since it opened." He permitted himself a tight little smile. "I thought you were only going to ask questions about the layout and my routine. And Wayne."

"I have a roundabout way of doing it," I said.

"Humph." He sipped his coffee, blue eyes surveying me over the rim of the mug. "I retired from the Navy four years ago, after twenty years. Master chief petty officer, electrician's mate."

"You're a long way from blue water."

"I grew up here. My folks are gone, but my sister and her husband live in Oildale. Seemed natural to come back here. But I wasn't interested in working in the oil business like my brother-in-law. Dr. Perris was looking for someone to keep an eye on things. The pay's decent and I've got a place to live, rent-free. So that's how I wound up here, if that's what you wanted to know."

"What I want to know is how Wayne Talbert wound up here."

"I needed an assistant. I ran it past Dr. Perris, he approved hiring the additional help. We ran an ad and Wayne applied."

"I heard you met Wayne at a bar up in Oildale."

Fosby looked at me steadily before he answered. "Yes, I did. He said he was looking for a job. I told him about the opening and suggested he apply."

"Did that have any influence on your ultimate decision to hire him?"

"He was the most qualified," Fosby said. "And Dr. Perris made the final decision. Based on my recommendation."

"Did Wayne say why he'd relocated to Bakersfield?"

"He wanted to get out of L.A. It's not a very pleasant place to live these days."

"Why is that?"

"Overcrowding, crime. We don't have as much of that in Bakersfield."

"I suppose no place is immune to crime," I said. "Witness Wayne's murder. You told the police that you and Wayne were playing cards Friday night in your cottage. Was that a regular routine?"

He nodded. "Most Fridays, yes."

"Do you make nightly rounds?"

"Yes. I do a walking tour of the perimeter after supper, about six-thirty, seven o'clock, just looking for anything unusual, out of the ordinary. Didn't see anything then that caught my eye. By that time the students are supposed to be in their bungalows with their counselors, studying. Lights-out is at nine-thirty."

"You didn't eat dinner in the dining hall."

"No. Wayne was bringing a pizza. As I told you yesterday, he got to my place about seven. We ate dinner, played poker, talked. Then Wayne left, about eleven o'clock."

"What did you do then?"

"Cleaned up the kitchen," Fosby said. "Then I switched on the TV. I was watching some movie on cable."

"You never heard or saw anything out of the ordinary?"

"No, I didn't." He gazed at me, his blue eyes revealing little. "Had no idea anything was wrong until Mrs. Perris called at a quarter to twelve."

"You didn't see Talbert's car anywhere?"

Fosby shook his head. "Didn't see it, wasn't looking for it. I was looking for some sign of the girl."

"Yesterday you said that Mrs. Perris said the two of you should look around the campus, to see if you could find Darcy." He nodded. "But surely she was long gone."

"We didn't know for certain what time the girl had gotten out. But I figure it was sometime after lights-out."

"Then Mrs. Perris found Wayne's body, went into the admin office, and called the police. And Dr. Perris. When did he arrive?"

"About ten minutes after we found the body. They live close by, up on Panorama Drive. The police got there just a few minutes after that. By then all the kids were awake. The counselors had to ride herd on them."

"So the convenient theory is," I said, "that Wayne encountered Darcy as she was escaping, that he tried to stop her, and that she hit him over the head with something and took his car. Do you believe she did?"

He took his time answering. "I don't know what to think. Wayne was a good-sized young man, in the prime of life. Darcy's a girl of eighteen. Doesn't make sense to me that she should be able to get the jump on him. Don't know why she would, either. That business about her threatening him—if she did—that's just talk."

I noticed the "if." "What do you think happened?"

"Hell, I don't know." He glanced at the clock on his wall, as though he had somewhere he needed to be.

I'd been keeping an eye on the clock as well. It was ten after eleven, and soon Gillie would be reporting for her duties in the dining hall. "Just one more question, Mr. Fosby. I understand there was a young man working here the latter half of June, Mrs. Webber's brother. I believe his name was Miguel."

"Hidalgo." Fosby snorted. "The Mexican kid. Yes, the athletic director, Mr. Kelvin, took him on as summer help. He lasted about two weeks."

"Was there a problem?"

"Caught him prowling around areas where he shouldn't be." Fosby shot a quick glance in the direction of the key box. "His job was in the gym or on the playing fields, not coming and going as he pleased." He sniffed. "Besides, he was getting a little too chummy with the female students, if you know what I mean."

I knew what he was implying. It lent some weight to my theory that Miguel may have helped Darcy after she got away from the school. "Chummy with all the female students, or just Darcy?" I asked.

"All I know is, he was plenty upset with me and Wayne that Friday when we caught Darcy and Gillie trying to get out of their bungalow. And he was shooting off his mouth about it to his sister. I told him he'd better button his lip and not interfere with school routine. He quit at the end of the week. That didn't surprise me. That kind's got no initiative."

"What kind is that, Mr. Fosby? Mexicans?"

He tightened his mouth as though he didn't like what I was implying. "Loudmouth punks, Ms. Howard. Now if that's all, I've got work to do."

CHAPTER 31

I LEFT THE MAINTENANCE BUILDING JUST AS THE STUDENTS were emptying out of the classrooms. Dressed as I'd seen them yesterday, in khaki shorts, shirts, and baseball caps, they hurried in groups or alone, across the grassy lawn toward their bungalows or the dining hall. Some of them talked among themselves but I had to say, as I watched them, that they were far more subdued than their counterparts at Alameda High School.

I spotted Gillie, her clothes baggy on her thin frame. She had her head down, the brown baseball cap stuck on over her short blond hair, both cap and hair askew. I caught up with her on the sidewalk leading from the admin office to the dining hall.

"Hello, Gillie."

She looked up, her pale eyes startled, her white skin reddening with a flush of embarrassment or fear.

"I think you wanted to tell me something yesterday," I said quietly, afraid the girl would bolt. "About Darcy, and what happened Friday night. Why don't you tell me now?"

Gillie glanced quickly from side to side, to see if anyone was watching us. Then she looked down at the sidewalk and began to stutter. "I . . . I . . ." She looked into my eyes, then somewhere over my shoulder. Panic was etched on her features as she spun and fled in the direction of the dining hall.

I turned around, to see who had come out the back door of the office. This time it was Martina Perris who had interrupted Gillie's attempt to communicate with me.

"I had no idea you were on the campus, Ms. Howard," she said, as though my presence did not exactly fill her with unrestrained joy. "This is private property. Unless you've got a reason to be here . . ."

"I was just asking Mr. Fosby some questions," I said, walking toward her.

"Really? He should have cleared that with me."

"Why is that, Mrs. Perris?" She didn't answer. "By the way, I do have some additional questions for you and Dr. Perris."

"Dr. Perris is busy over in the educational building." Her voice had a we-can't-be-bothered edge as she gestured in that direction. Then we both saw Perris step through the door. He caught sight of us and crossed the grass. "Here he is now," she said reluctantly.

Kyle Perris didn't looked thrilled to see me either, but he masked his dismay and gave me a chilly professional smile. "Well, look who's here."

"Ms. Howard has some additional questions, Kyle," his wife told him.

Perris opened the rear door of the admin building and ushered me into the back hallway. "I'm afraid it will have to be brief, Ms. Howard. I have some business to attend to and I'll have to leave shortly."

"Ms. Howard was attempting to talk with one of the students." Martina kept her voice low as we walked through the open area where Consuela Webber and Emma Johnson sat at their desks.

Consuela heard her, though, and looked up at me. I shook my head slightly, indicating that I'd failed to talk with Gillie. Consuela frowned, then she dipped her chin slightly, the briefest of nods indicating that she'd go to lunch at the dining hall and try to slip my card to Gillie.

"I really must ask you not to communicate with the students, Ms. Howard," Dr. Perris said as he led the way into his office. He shut the door firmly. "It disrupts the school's routine. As to your questions, I don't know what else we can tell you, that we didn't cover yesterday when you and Ms. Bromley were here."

I kept him waiting while I examined the office. It was heavy on big, dark furniture, with a wide mahogany desk to my immediate right, and a matching credenza behind that held a computer and printer. The window opposite the desk afforded Dr. Perris a view of the southern Sierra Nevada to the east, dark blue mountains rising in the heat-hazed morning sky. Between the desk and the window was a low square table bracketed by two chairs upholstered in a dark plum.

Directly in front of me was a pair of lateral filing cabinets, also mahogany, both with shiny brass locks that looked new. I stepped closer, under the guise of examining the large reprint of Ansel Adams's *Half Dome* that hung on the wall above the cabinets. Were those scratch marks in the wood just around those locks? Had someone been tampering with the locks on Kyle's filing cabinets?

I kept thinking it might have been Wayne Talbert. But Perris insisted that no one had been inside the office Friday night.

I sat down in one of the plum chairs, aware of the impatience radiating from Kyle and Martina Perris. He had taken a seat in the wide gray leather chair behind his desk and she stood to his left, one hand resting on his shoulder. I took them through their stories again, as I had Fosby, asking questions, but getting the same version I had yesterday.

Perris kept looking at his watch and finally, just before noon, told me he had to go. When I left the administrative office, I didn't see Consuela Webber and I guessed she'd gone up to the dining hall for lunch. I walked back toward the maintenance building, where I'd left my car. Fosby's green Blazer was gone.

I headed back toward Bakersfield, but I took the Fairfax Avenue exit off Highway 178 and drove north into a subdivision full of fairly new tract homes. I checked my odometer as I drove, until I figured I was about due west of the Perris School. Then I turned east on one of the side streets. I was looking for the other end of that dirt road I'd seen winding down the hill.

I found it where a street dead-ended just past an elementary school, deserted now in the middle of summer. The sun was high as I parked my car at the curb in front of a white stucco house that didn't even have a lawn yet. I retrieved the pair of binoculars I keep stashed in the glove compartment and started walking. There was no fence or barricade to keep me from the lane that was rutted with tire tracks. The ground sloped upward in a gradual rise for about thirty yards.

When I reached the crest of this hill I raised the binoculars to my eyes and looked down, focusing first on the Perris School. The bushes and trees planted along the fence made it easy to spot. I picked out the buildings ranged around the circular drive. Then I swept the binoculars along the route of the concrete-lined irrigation canal at the western boundary of the school. It ran at a diagonal, cutting through the low hills from northeast to southwest.

Fosby—and Perris—had both told me that the dirt road ended at the canal. It meandered down the slope in a northeasterly direction from where I stood, perhaps a mile, to the edge of the canal.

But there was a bridge. Did Fosby and Perris know about it?

Maybe not. The bridge crossed the canal, about half a mile from the northwest corner of the school's property. Through the lenses of my binoculars, it looked as though that section of the canal was hidden from view by the trees behind Fosby's cottage, which was between the dining hall and the playing field.

The bridge itself looked new. It was made of wooden beams and had no rails. Narrow, about the width of a truck, it seemed perfectly serviceable. It also meant there was another way to get to—or away from—the school.

I turned and walked back to my car, pondering Fosby's omission. Then I looked at my watch. It was time to go trolling elsewhere for information, namely Valley Plaza Mall.

I drove around the perimeter of the mall's parking lot, winding up near the entrance to Sears, at the northwest corner of the shopping center. Wayne Talbert's Escort had been found somewhere in this vicinity. I parked my car and consulted my map. Ming Avenue was to the north, and the street on the west was Wible Road, which paralleled Highway 99. The streets to the east and south weren't as busy as these two.

In my head I replayed the recording of Darcy's phone call. Those sounds in the background indicated cars nearby, moving constantly, and at a faster speed than they would through a parking lot. I stuck to my guess that she'd been near a busy street. Besides, on my circuit of the lot I hadn't seen any outdoor phone booths near the mall. Stands to reason, I figured. The phones were probably inside the mall.

If I were Darcy, I theorized, I'd have gone to either Wible Road or Ming Avenue, looking for a phone. And I wouldn't have crossed the freeway. I started my car and exited the parking lot. Nothing on Wible caught my eye, although the freeway running beside the road provided a steady overlay of noise. I cruised eastward on Ming, eyeing bus stops and pay phones on the south side of the street. Then I turned around and did the same for the north side.

When I got back to the vicinity of the mall I spotted a bus stop near a deli. There was a pay phone just outside, on the corner of the stucco building between the front window and the strip of parking lot it shared with a shoe repair shop. I pulled into the lot, parked, and walked around to the door. Next to it was a newspaper rack containing today's edition of the Bakersfield *Californian*. According to the sign in the corner of the window, Marino's Deli was open every day of the week. And there was a bell above the door.

It was past twelve, time for lunch. Inside the deli, pastrami, sharp mustard, and the perfume of onion rolls called to me. The storefront was long and narrow, with a counter to my right and several small tables crowded into the space along the window. The place was packed with customers, eating lunch at the tables or waiting patiently at the counter. I saw two employees, a man and a woman, behind the counter making sandwiches. Both wore red-and-white striped aprons over their clothes.

I took a number from the dispenser on the counter, then went to the cooler at the rear of the deli and selected a bottle of mineral water. When my turn at the counter came I stepped up and faced a short man about my age, with brown eyes and curly dark hair. "May I help you?" he asked.

"Pastrami on rye with mustard, the spicier the better."

"Got you covered. Anything else?"

"Were you working here Sunday afternoon?"

He looked up from the construction of my sandwich, curiosity in his eyes as he slathered mustard on the rye bread. "Yeah. Why?"

"I'm looking for someone who may have made a telephone call from that pay phone out there, around two-thirty Sunday afternoon. A girl, eighteen, with dark hair."

"That's a tall order," he said with a short laugh. He reached for the pastrami.

"You can see the phone from here." I glanced to my right to confirm this.

"If I'm looking. But no guarantee I'm gonna be looking. We get a lot of people in and out of here." He gestured at the lunchtime crowd, then wrapped my sandwich in paper and handed it to me. "We get a lot of foot traffic, too, since we're close to the bus stop and all." He moved toward the cash register and rang up my sandwich and the mineral water.

"Two-thirty would have been after the lunch rush," I said, handing him a twenty. "You sure you didn't notice her?"

"I didn't. But maybe my sister did." He handed me my change and jerked his head in the direction of the young woman behind the counter. She was discussing the merits of smoked versus unsmoked provolone with a white-haired man. "What's your name, and why are you asking about this girl?"

"Jeri Howard." I gave him one of my business cards. He looked at it and raised one eyebrow. "I'm asking because the girl's missing."

"I'm Sal Marino." He stuck out his hand and I shook it. "My sister's name is Ellie. Tell you what, you eat your sandwich, I'll send her over once things get less hectic."

"Thanks," I told him.

All of the little round tables at the front of the deli were occupied. But a guy in painter's coveralls told me he was just leaving, so I set my sandwich and drink on the table as he obligingly cleared away the rubbish left over from his lunch. I settled in and made short work of the pastrami, washing down every last scrap with swigs from the bottle of mineral water. I was transferring mustard from my hands to a paper napkin when Ellie pulled up a chair and sat down, sighing as though she were glad to be off her feet for a while.

"My brother says you're looking for someone who made a phone call Sunday afternoon," she said. "Girl about nineteen, twenty, with dark hair?"

I reached for my purse and took out the old snapshot of Darcy that I'd kept from the spring. "Is that her?"

Ellie took the photo and looked it over, nodding slowly. "The girl who was here Sunday had shorter hair, about shoulder-length. But the face looks the same."

"Tell me why you remember her. Was it her clothes, the way she acted?"

"Clothes . . . she was wearing a big red shirt. And she had her money in a little black waist-pack." Ellie handed back the photo. "Before she came in she bought a Sunday paper from the rack outside."

"What did she do next?"

"She came up to the counter, looking at the front page of the paper. She seemed real preoccupied, maybe even upset. I had to ask her twice what she wanted. She sat at that corner table and ate while she read the paper." Ellie jerked her chin at the table in question. "She stayed awhile. Usually people come in, buy something, and leave. Even if they eat lunch here, they just stay long enough to consume whatever it is. This girl, she came in around one, right at the tail end of our busy time."

The Sunday paper had been the one with the front-page account of Wayne Talbert's murder. That would have been enough to account for Darcy's being upset, particularly if she'd just abandoned Talbert's car across the street at the mall. Where had she been since Friday night, when she left the school and showed up briefly at Talbert's apartment?

"Did she only make one phone call?"

Ellie shook her head. "No, she used the phone more than once. At least I remember seeing her go outside and come back in. That was when she looked upset, like whoever she was trying to call wasn't there. Or maybe the conversation didn't go the way she wanted."

"When she left," I asked, "did she catch a bus? Hitch a ride? Or did someone pick her up?"

Ellie thought about it for a moment. "I was waiting on a customer and I saw her go out to the phone, but she didn't come back that time. I can't be sure, but I think someone picked her up. I saw her wave to someone."

"Did you see who it was?"

"A guy, I think. He was driving a red pickup truck."

I probed Ellie's memory further, but she couldn't come up with a description of the driver, or a more detailed description of the truck. "Do you remember anything else?"

"She seemed really interested in that newspaper," Ellie said, "but just the first section. She left the rest of it on the table when she went outside, but she had that front part under her arm."

CHAPTER 32

JUST AS I ANGLED MY TOYOTA INTO A PARKING SPACE near the Haberfelde Building, my cellular phone rang. I threw the car into Park and dug into my purse for the phone, hitting the button that would allow me to pick up the call.

"I gave Gillie the card," Consuela Webber said, her voice low and tight, as though she were trying not to be overheard by her office-mate. "I had lunch in the dining hall. She was bussing tables. She didn't say anything when I gave it to her, but she stuck it in her pocket."

"Thanks," I told her, meaning it. Now if Gillie would just call me.

"I just hope she doesn't get caught. Or me, either." Consuela sighed and hung up.

I stuck the phone back into my purse and got out of the car, feeding coins into the parking meter. Then I headed into the building, where I bought a couple of iced cappuccino mochas before taking the elevator up to Cece's office. She was on the phone. I was nearly done with my concoction before I could deliver hers.

"Oh, thank you," she said, taking it from my hands. "I was just craving one of these."

She told her secretary to hold her calls, then kicked off her shoes and leaned back in her chair to drink her mocha while I gave her a report of my day's activities.

"I think you're right," Cece said when I'd finished. "Sounds like Darcy called someone and he came to that deli to pick her up."

"Miguel Hidalgo. Call it a hunch. But he may have helped

himself to a key, and he didn't like the way Darcy and the other kids were treated. So he's my prime candidate."

"Okay, but why didn't she connect with him Friday night after she'd been to Talbert's apartment?"

"Maybe she tried, but he wasn't available. Remember, Consuela told me her brother was out of the area, driving a truck for an uncle. Assuming she's telling me the truth, which I'll have to assume for lack of a better alternative, that would leave Darcy on her own for thirty-six hours plus."

I pictured her alone, driving around Bakersfield in Talbert's car, knowing that the police were looking for it, not knowing what to do other than to keep moving. Why hadn't she called me sooner?

I shook my head. That line of thought got me nowhere. I had to focus on what was happening now. "I need to find Miguel. If he's the same person who picked up Darcy at that deli, he drives a red pickup truck, model unknown. Got any friends at the local DMV office?"

"Yeah," Cece said slowly. "And she owes me one. But not enough to lose her job over it. I'll have to approach this delicately. In the meantime, I've got a client due in five minutes."

I asked Cece's secretary for the Bakersfield area phone directory. There were an even dozen Hidalgos listed, but only one Miguel, at an address on Gosford Road. I used the phone on the secretary's desk. When I called Miguel's number I got an answering machine. I didn't leave a message.

After leaving Cece's office, I headed for the Bakersfield Police Department, a two-story redbrick and glass structure just a few blocks from my hotel. I had to wait about ten minutes for Detective Henry Garza, in a reception area outside the locked door that led back to the Criminal Investigations Division. I spent the time examining the glass cases arrayed around the room, which held police uniforms from cities all over the world.

"Ms. Howard?"

I turned. He stood holding the door open.

"Why so formal, Detective Garza? When we were on the phone the other day it was Jeri and Henry."

He shrugged. "Yeah, well . . . gotta keep up appearances. Come back to my office and we'll get informal."

He led the way down the corridor and preceded me into a small office, where we sat down. "Let me guess. Sergeant Harmon doesn't like getting familiar with the lawyer and the private investigator on this case."

Garza smiled. "Sergeant Harmon and the lawyer used to be an item. But they're not anymore. So Ray's feeling uncomfortable. Wants to keep you and the counselor at arm's length."

"I tend not to stay at arm's length," I said. "Even if that's where the police want to keep me. I know you found Talbert's car, over at Valley Plaza Mall."

Garza drummed his fingers on his desk. "Officially, there are certain aspects of this case I can't discuss with you."

"And unofficially?"

Garza sighed. "What do you want to know? Within reason. And if you've got any information, I want to hear it."

"Was Talbert inside the admin building before he was killed?"

He shrugged. "We're not sure. We found his prints, but of course, he was the hired help. He had keys and he was in and out of the place all the time. Dr. Perris says nothing was missing."

Except the stapler Consuela had told me about. "He could be lying."

"Maybe. So far I don't see a reason why the good doctor should keep anything from us. Besides, the blood spatter analysis indicates Talbert was hit from behind while he was facing the building. It also looks like he lived long enough to crawl a few feet toward the building."

"Why would he be walking toward the building in the first place? He left Fosby's cottage at eleven, supposedly heading for home. Why did he stop at the admin building?"

"Maybe he noticed something out of the ordinary," Garza said. "A window open, a light burning."

"But you don't know for sure."

"No, we don't," he conceded. "Mrs. Perris went into the building after she and Fosby found the body. She called 911, then her husband. So the lights were on when the officers arrived on the scene."

"And the gate?"

"Fosby had already opened it."

"Anything in Talbert's wound to give a clue as to the murder weapon?"

"That's one of the things I won't discuss."

Which meant they had found something, I guessed, something that didn't show up in the autopsy report. "Got any skinhead activity in Bakersfield?"

Garza narrowed his eyes, then leaned back in his chair. "I hear they got some skinheads hanging out at a bar up in Oildale. But that's not our problem. It's the county's problem."

"It's your problem if they're committing crimes in Bakersfield. Like kicking in the front door of the late Wayne Talbert the night he was murdered."

"You talked to Talbert's neighbor."

"You knew I would. Have you had any luck locating these particular skinheads? Or the third man, the guy who was with them?"

"No. And neither has the Kern County Sheriff's Department."

"None of them left any prints?"

"They were wearing gloves," Garza admitted.

"How very organized of them. So which bar in Oildale is the skinhead hangout?"

He shot me a look from his dark brown eyes. "You don't want to know."

"I can take care of myself. Which means I'm cautious. I've been a PI for a long time, Henry. I don't take chances unless I have to."

Of course, being cautious and not taking chances didn't always guarantee that I wasn't going to be taken by surprise. It had happened before and I figured it would happen again. But that was part of the risk associated with the job.

"It's called the Rust Bucket," he said reluctantly. "It's on North Chester. A fairly ordinary neighborhood bar, for Oildale. But I strongly recommend you don't go near the back room."

"I'll keep that in mind. Did you find any other prints in Talbert's place?"

"You mean besides Darcy Stefano's? You talked with the neighbor. You know damn well Darcy was there, right before the skinheads arrived."

"Did she take anything?"

"I don't know what she took or what the skinheads took," Garza said. "All I know is that Talbert's neighbor said he had a computer and it's gone. As far as we can tell, that's the only thing that's missing."

"Did she also tell you Talbert dyed his hair?"

"So did the medical examiner. What of it?"

"He deliberately changed his appearance. It strikes me that Mr. Talbert was not your usual handyman." Henry didn't take the bait so I dangled it a little closer. "I assume you're checking his previous life in Los Angeles."

"We've got LAPD looking into it," he said finally. The intercom on Garza's phone buzzed insistently, but he made no move to pick up the call. "Sharing information works both ways, you know. Seems to me I've been doing most of the sharing."

"And I had to pry it out of you." I wasn't ready to give him Miguel Hidalgo. Not until I'd had a chance to find him first.

When I left the Bakersfield Police Department, I headed west over the freeway. Miguel's address on Gosford Road turned out to be an apartment complex located near the intersection of Stockdale Highway. Four buildings, two on either side, were grouped around a central area which contained carports with numbered slots for the tenants, a laundry room, and a swimming pool. The buildings themselves were three stories high, brown stucco with darker brown trim on the balconies and windows.

I pulled into the parking lot and found a vacant slot marked VISITOR. Once out of my car, I walked toward the bank of mailboxes in front of the first building on the south side of the complex. Miguel's name wasn't there, so I headed for the mailboxes in front of the second building. I peered at the box marked HIDALGO but couldn't tell whether he'd picked up his mail recently. His parking slot was empty, save for an oil stain on the pavement. When I rang the bell of his first-floor apartment, there was no answer. I knocked on a few other doors but struck out all around. No one was home. It was three-thirty, too early for most people to be coming home from work.

I headed up Gosford Road to Stockdale Highway and turned west again, this time to the campus of California State University at Bakersfield. It was mid-July, so the school should be in summer session. Consuela had told me her brother was out of the area, driving a truck for his uncle. But I didn't want to take her word for it, since she seemed reluctant for me to speak with Miguel. There was an outside chance he was taking some classes, or that I might run into a friend of his who was a bit more forthcoming with information.

But I struck out at the university as well. At a quarter to five I returned to Miguel's apartment building, hoping to unearth someone who had an idea where he was. This time I had more luck.

He was about twenty-five, looking uncomfortable in a blue suit that seemed to wilt in the late afternoon heat as he collected bills and catalogs from the mailbox next to Miguel's. I looked at the identifying name and asked Mr. Lemuel if he knew his neighbor, Miguel Hidalgo.

"Sure," Lemuel told me. "Not well, though. Just to speak to. We see each other in the laundry room, at the mailbox, that kind of thing. I mean, the guy's hardly ever here. He goes to school full-time and works part-time."

"What sort of jobs?" I asked.

"He had this evening and weekend gig at a sporting goods store, but it was cutting into his study time. Then there was a full-time job earlier in the summer that didn't work out." The Perris School, I thought, as Lemuel sifted through the envelopes in his hand and frowned at one of them. He looked up at me. "I think right now he's doing some work for one of his relatives. An uncle or a cousin."

"Any idea where I could find this uncle or cousin? Here in Bakersfield?"

The young man shook his head. "Somewhere out in the county. Sorry, I don't remember for sure."

The cellular phone in my purse started ringing. The young man looked startled as I reached for it, then grinned as he realized what it was. "Thanks for your help," I told him, and he walked away. I hit the button on the phone and said hello.

"Is this Jeri?" The voice was a hoarse whisper.

I said yes and listened for a reply. I heard noises in the background. It sounded like clattering pans and sizzling stoves in my mother's restaurant in Monterey, but I didn't think Mother had called on a whim to say hello. "Gillie. Is that you?"

"Yeah. I can't talk long. If they catch me using the phone . . ."

"Do you know where Darcy is?"

"Maybe with . . ." She stopped and I feared she'd gone.

"Miguel?" I asked.

"Maybe. I dunno. You gotta find her before they do."

"Who are they?" I tried to keep the urgency from my voice. I had a feeling Gillie didn't mean the cops.

"Y'know, he's not who he said he was." Now she'd gone off in a completely different direction. It was like following a child through a maze.

"You mean Miguel?" She didn't respond. There were a lot of "hes" to choose from, if we wanted to play twenty questions. "Dr. Perris? Mr. Fosby? Or Wayne Talbert?"

"The dead guy," she said.

So it was Talbert, I thought, who wasn't what he seemed. Gillie's statement confirmed what I'd already suspected. In the back of my mind I heard Dr. Perris saying that the girl was a liar. Maybe that was true. Or maybe he'd been trying to steer me away from her.

"He had a mustache then," Gillie said. "And his hair was dark."

"Tell me more about Talbert, Gillie. I need to know."

She didn't answer right away. When her voice came over the wire, it sounded faint and thin. "I met him in Hollywood. Last year."

Then she gasped. After that I heard only the clatter of pans in the school's kitchen. I had the feeling someone else was listening to that receiver on the other end, to see if I'd say something. Then I heard a loud bang as the phone was plunked back into its cradle.

CHAPTER 33

WHOEVER HAD INTERRUPTED GILLIE'S PHONE CALL TO
me now had the card Consuela had given her. Which meant
that person now knew I was looking in places where people didn't
want me to look. Well, I'd been down that road before. It hadn't de-
terred me yet.

I tucked the cellular phone back into my purse and headed for
the lot where I'd left my Toyota. By now it was six. My stomach
growled, reminding me that I like to eat on a regular schedule. Besides, I needed some time to think about my next move.

I drove back toward downtown Bakersfield, stopping at a Mexi-
can restaurant. After downing a fajita platter, I headed north on
Chester Avenue, past the county museum and recreation center.
Once I crossed the Kern River, I was in Oildale.

The town was unincorporated. It had grown up between Bakersfield, which began as an agricultural community, and the Kern
County oil fields, among the oldest in the nation. Pumping rigs and
storage tanks were a familiar sight on the surrounding landscape,
dotting the bluffs to the north and east.

Oildale had a blue-collar feel to it, I thought as I stopped for a
traffic light. And it wasn't just the array of thrift shops, used furniture stores, and bars on this particular block. There was a run-down
look to the whole business district, a town with its rough edges showing, at least along its main drag.

Up ahead and on the left of the four-lane street, I saw a small, unlit neon sign jutting over the sidewalk. I made a U-turn at the next intersection and headed back along Chester.

The Rust Bucket was as rusty as its name, occupying a low, flat-topped stucco building that looked as though it hadn't been painted since World War II. I parked the Toyota a block farther down the street and got out, walking toward the bar. I was mindful of Henry Garza's warning about staying out of the place, or at least the back room. I told myself I just wanted to look around, to get the lay of the land. I'd have a beer and check out the clientele.

The interior of the bar looked about as low-rent as the outside, glimpsed through a miasma of cigarette smoke. I paused for a moment, letting my eyes adjust to the dimness overlaid with haze.

The bar ran along the wall to my left, and it was crowded with customers. Mostly men, and a lot of them looked like oil field workers, from the way they were dressed. They were off the clock and getting rowdy over their beers. A TV set was suspended on a shelf over the bar, tuned to a sports channel, but if any of them were paying attention to what was being broadcast, they wouldn't have been able to hear anything. A jukebox back in the corner was pounding out rock 'n' roll, nearly obliterating any other sound in the room and making conversation next to impossible.

The few women in the place were scattered among the men, mostly in booths on the other side of the room. In my slacks and cotton shirt, I was way overdressed for this place, I thought. All I saw around me were blue jeans, most of them faded. I watched one harried-looking woman, waiting tables. She was attired in sneakers, tight jeans, and a white T-shirt with a beer company logo on the front.

At the back, near the jukebox, I saw a pool table. Gathered there was a trio of tough-looking bikers in leather, racking up balls and chalking cues. They appeared to be the most colorful guys in the joint.

What I didn't see were any skinheads.

I wondered if Garza's information about this particular bar was bogus. Or whether it was disinformation, designed to steer me away from another location. Of course, I hadn't checked out that back room.

I elbowed my way to the bar and took the only empty stool, conscious of the looks I was getting. I ignored the appraising stare of the man next to me and scanned the offerings behind the bar. The bartender took his time walking over to me and when he got there he didn't crack a smile. "What'll it be?" he growled.

"Bud." I barely moved my lips as I laid some folding money on the scarred wooden surface. The bartender slammed a brown bottle down in front of me and swept the bills off the bar. He returned a moment later and deposited my change in a puddle.

"New in town?" the man next to me asked. He was an average kind of a fellow with brown hair and a round face, about thirty. Like many of the patrons I'd seen so far, he looked as though he'd just gotten off work and stopped in for a brew before going home.

"Passing through." I raised the bottle to my lips and drank.

"Planning to stay long?"

"Not if I can help it." I meant the bar but he figured I meant Oildale. I let him talk, nodding my head at the appropriate moments, while I swiveled the stool around so I could survey the bar's denizens. The rock music on the jukebox gave way to a country tune. The guy next to me invited me to dance, but I shook my head. Before the music had changed there had been a brief lull in the noise level. In that short space of time I'd heard more music, loud rock again, but coming from somewhere at the rear of the bar. There was an open door back there, by the pool table where the bikers were going at their game with single-minded concentration. I saw an exit sign over the door and a corridor beyond that. It must lead to the restrooms, the bar's rear exit, and that back room Garza had warned me about.

Then I saw what I'd come looking for.

He walked through the back door and stood for a moment, looking around, a young guy, maybe twenty. Then he approached the bar with a tough-guy swagger, feet moving in steel-toed boots, a chain looped around the waist of his tight black jeans. The short sleeves of his black T-shirt were rolled up, the better to display the swastika tattoos decorating both stringy biceps. His eyes were so pale they almost weren't there, hovering in his narrow face below his shaved scalp. He was skinny and he had a pointed nose, which fit

Heather McRae's description of one of the two men who had abducted Darcy from Alameda.

I heard the bartender call him Brick. When he'd collected a couple of bottles of beer, he turned and went back the way he'd come. Then I slipped off the stool and told the guy who was trying to pick me up that I had to use the restroom.

The corridor I'd glimpsed from the bar was inadequately lit by a flickering fluorescent fixture on the ceiling. It was about fifteen feet long, and it ended in another door with an EXIT sign over it. I saw a pay phone on my right, between two doors. The first was marked MEN. I dodged a guy exiting the john and walked up even with the phone. The second door was the women's restroom.

Beyond this was another door, partly closed, but not enough to keep the raucous music from filtering into the hallway. I picked up the receiver of the pay phone, pretending I had to make a call. I held the instrument away from my ear so I wouldn't hear the buzz of the dial tone. As I listened to the music I could make out the lyrics. This was "Reich 'n' Roll," a kind of rock used to relay messages full of violence and racism.

I flashed back to the first time I'd heard of this music. That was a few years back, when an extremist group had scheduled a so-called "Aryan Woodstock" up near Napa, in Northern California. The ensuing outcry caused cancellation of the event, but I'd heard that a similar festival had in fact been held somewhere in Oklahoma.

Someone came out of the back room, a young woman in jeans and a sleeveless red T-shirt that looked painted onto her busty, braless torso. She had short, bleached blond hair, and the dark eye shadow outlining her eyes made her look like a raccoon in the dim overhead light. She barely glanced at me as I kept up my pretense of talking on the phone, and pushed open the door marked WOMEN.

She hadn't closed the door to the back room where the music was playing. Now I edged as close as I dared. There were about a half dozen people in the room, another woman and the rest men, all young. Beyond them I saw the red and black Nazi flag tacked up on the wall, flanked by racist posters.

I heard a toilet flush in the women's restroom and moved back to the phone. Then running water, and the young woman came out of the john, wiping her hands on the legs of her jeans. This time she looked me over.

"Yeah, well, you know where you can stick it," I shouted into the receiver. I slammed the phone back into the cradle, then looked at her and shrugged. "Men."

Her eyes moved over me. Then one of the skinheads, a beefy, red-faced guy, stuck his head out the door. "Hey, Lori, get your ass back in here."

"Yeah," she said with a crooked smile. "Know what you mean."

She went back into the room and shut the door, all the way this time. That was okay. I'd seen enough.

Or I thought I had. As I left the bar and walked toward my car, I glanced back at the Rust Bucket and saw two men walking toward the bar from the opposite direction. I didn't recognize the short, gray-haired guy.

But the other man was Bennett Fosby.

CHAPTER *34*

I HEADED BACK TO MY TEMPORARY HOME IN BAKERSFIELD,
eager to wash the stink of cigarette smoke and hatred out of my
clothes and hair. After a long soak in the tub, I toweled myself dry
and put on the T-shirt I sleep in and my robe.

I noticed the blinking message light on the phone. I dialed into
the hotel's voice mail system and listened to two recorded messages.
The first was from Kaz, just calling to say hello. The next message
was from Adele Gregory. She hadn't received any phone calls from
Darcy and was still planning to drive to Bakersfield later in the week
with her son-in-law.

I decided to return her call in the morning. The only report I
could give Adele at this point was that Darcy was somehow en-
meshed in Wayne Talbert's death and still among the missing.

I called my answering machines in Oakland, both at home and at
my office. The messages I copied onto the pad were mostly routine,
and either needed no response or could be handled with a quick
phone call later. There was nothing from Darcy.

This done, I opened my laptop computer and plugged the mo-
dem into the phone jack. I dialed into my Internet provider and
checked my e-mail. There was a message from Darren Stefano in-
forming me that Darcy hadn't checked in with him or his parents.
He added that Dan and Elaine were fighting, presumably over
Darcy.

Damn it, why didn't she call? It was Wednesday night. Had

something happened to her since that phone message she'd left on my machine Sunday afternoon?

If she were with Miguel, maybe they'd left town. But where would they go? I recalled what Miguel's neighbor had said about relatives somewhere in the county. Kern County was one of the biggest in the state, however, covering a lot of territory. Or was it possible they were on the move, trying to get back to the Bay Area? But Darcy had called me, wanting and needing my assistance. I felt sure I'd hear from her again, but I wished it would be sooner rather than later.

I logged onto one of the databases I used regularly for research and went looking in cyberspace for Bennett Fosby. I didn't find much, other than what he'd already told me. His current address was the Perris School and I verified the time he'd spent in the Navy. His credit rating was good and he didn't own any other vehicles besides the green Blazer I'd seen.

Fine upstanding citizen, I told myself. With lousy taste in bars?

I opened the file folder Cece had given me and switched my focus to the murder victim. According to the address on his driver's license, Wayne Talbert had lived on Martell Avenue in Los Angeles. My map for metropolitan L.A. showed the street running north and south, intersecting the West Hollywood city limit. The number placed Talbert's residence somewhere between Melrose Avenue and Santa Monica Boulevard.

What I found in cyberspace left me with more questions. Such as why it looked as though Wayne Talbert still lived in L.A.

Was this the same Talbert? He drove a blue Ford Escort. He had a decent credit rating, a couple of credit cards, and a bank account at Glendale Federal Savings. He worked for something called Blake Enterprises, no address, just a post office box and a phone number.

There was no indication that the Talbert who'd lived in L.A. had quit his job or given up his apartment. In fact, it appeared that he was still paying rent on the place. He hadn't moved his bank account, nor had he canceled his phone and utilities at the same time he'd started paying for those services here in Bakersfield.

Why? If Wayne Talbert already had a decent job in Los Angeles, why disguise his appearance and move up to Bakersfield to work as an assistant maintenance man at a boarding school? It wasn't exactly a leap up the employment ladder, even if Talbert had gotten his fill of the Southern California megalopolis.

I remembered what Gillie had told me on the phone, before our conversation had been abruptly terminated. The dead guy, meaning Talbert, wasn't who he'd said he was. But who was he?

The computer was plugged into the only phone jack. So I saved the information I'd found on Talbert onto the hard drive, then logged off the Internet. I plugged the phone back into the jack, then picked up the receiver and punched in the number of the Martell Avenue address. The phone rang once, then an answering machine picked up the call. I heard a recorded message in a pleasant tenor, saying, "This is Nick. Can't take your call right now. Leave a message, I'll get back to you."

Nick, not Wayne. But it had to be the same person. This was the address on the driver's license found on the dead man. His middle name was Nicholas. He'd preferred Nick, I guessed, and had opted to use Wayne, his first name, when he'd moved to Bakersfield. A convenient alias. For what purpose?

I went back to the computer and the Internet, this time onto the World Wide Web. I sent one of the popular Internet search engines trolling for Nick Talbert's name. I got more than a hundred hits for Web sites featuring that name somewhere in the text. I began checking them out, working my way down the list.

The first few sites led me to a Dr. Nick Talbert who was affiliated with the University of Michigan in Ann Arbor. His chosen field was physics. He was prolific, published both on the Web and, no doubt, in the vast paper fields of academia as well. The next few instances of the name told me more than I wanted to know about a Nick Talbert in Manchester, England. He played rugby and was considered quite a tasty specimen of male pulchritude. After looking at his picture I decided I wouldn't kick him out of bed.

I was about two-thirds of the way through all those Talberts when I found myself looking at an article dated December of the previous year. The Nick Talbert of the byline had written a lengthy feature about teenaged runaways living on the streets of Hollywood.

I read the article, slowly and carefully. The author had written at the outset that he was using pseudonyms for the kids he'd interviewed, kids scrounging for themselves on the streets. One of them he called Ginger, but it was clear from his description that he was talking about Gillie Cooper.

Had she gone home, I wondered, beaten down and defeated by her experience as a runaway? Or maybe she'd been picked up by the cops and returned home.

Either way, Gillie's homecoming had been short-lived. She'd been trundled off to Kyle and Martina Perris's spooky school for "problem adolescents." There she'd recognized Wayne Talbert, the handyman, as Nick Talbert, investigative reporter. Poor Gillie. Had she let something slip to the wrong person? And who might the wrong person be?

I scrolled down to the bottom of the article and clicked on the symbol that read "Return to Home Page." That netted me the colorful graphic masthead of a magazine called *On the Rag*. A cursory read confirmed my guess that this was the cyberspace edition of an alternative publication, like the *East Bay Express* or the *San Francisco Bay Guardian*, back on my home turf. At the bottom of this page I saw a copyright notice for Blake Enterprises.

"What were you working on, Nick?" I said out loud. "Something to do with the Perris School? Or skinheads, maybe?"

At the bottom of the page I also found *On the Rag*'s post office box, the same one as Blake Enterprises, though the phone number was different from the one I'd found earlier. There was also an e-mail address and a fax number.

I saved the information to the hard drive, then I sent the magazine a brief message asking that Nick Talbert get in touch with me, either by e-mail or by phone here at the Holiday Inn in Bakersfield. If he did, I'd know I was wrong, he wasn't the same Talbert, and the database had some bogus information.

But I had a feeling the Nick Talbert who'd written the article was the same Talbert, the one who now lay on a slab in the Bakersfield morgue. Maybe his coworkers were beginning to wonder where he was.

I turned off the computer and went to bed. Thursday morning, I rose at seven, got dressed, and went downstairs in search of breakfast. When I returned to my room, the message light was blinking.

Someone named Simon Blake had called. He'd identified himself as the editor of *On the Rag.* He wanted me to call him as soon as possible.

I picked up the phone and punched in the number Blake had left. The phone rang four times before it was answered by a female voice that sounded hostile even as it offered assistance. "*On the Rag,* may I help you?"

"Simon Blake, please."

"He's in a meeting."

"I'd like to leave a message."

"Yeah, what is it?" she asked, as though taking the message would be a monumental pain.

"My name is Jeri Howard." I spelled my name for her. "I'm returning his call and the matter is urgent." I gave her my room number as well as the hotel number. "Have you got that?"

"Yeah, I got that," she snapped and hung up before I could ask her to repeat it back to me.

They must be hard up for office staff, I thought, replacing the receiver. Or they didn't care about the niceties of phone manners. Alternative publications were sometimes like that.

I was just getting ready to leave the room when the phone rang. When I answered it, I heard a brisk, no-nonsense male voice. "Jeri Howard? Simon Blake, *On the Rag.* You sent me an e-mail about Nick Talbert. Why?"

Blake evidently believed in cutting to the chase. So did I. "I'm a private investigator from Oakland."

"Yeah? But you're in Bakersfield."

"Is Nick Talbert on the staff of your magazine?"

There was a suspicious silence on the other end of the phone. I could cut to the chase as well as Blake could.

"I'll take that as a yes, Mr. Blake. I'll also assume he was on some sort of assignment. When did you last hear from him?"

Blake hesitated. I guessed I was getting warm. "He was supposed to check in with me Friday night. I haven't heard from him. There's no answer at his apartment. Just what is this about?"

"Mr. Blake, a man named Wayne Nicholas Talbert was murdered in Bakersfield Friday night. I really would like to know if it was your Nick Talbert."

"Oh, my God," Simon Blake said. His voice made several false starts. "Are you sure? What did this Talbert look like?"

"I've only seen a newspaper photograph, from the story about the murder in Sunday's Bakersfield *Californian*. Thirty-two, six feet tall, blue eyes, and brown hair, which he'd dyed blond. He drove a blue Ford Escort and he lived in an apartment on Monterey Street. His driver's license lists an address on Martell Avenue in L.A. He moved to Bakersfield in May and was working as a maintenance man at the Perris School."

"Oh, my God," Blake said again.

Warmer still. Practically hot.

"It sounds like your Nick Talbert is the one in the morgue. You should contact Sergeant Ray Harmon at the Bakersfield Police Department. But before you do, I have some questions. What sort of story was Talbert working on?"

"You said you're a PI. What's your connection with all this?"

"My client is considered a material witness, though I don't think my client had anything to do with the murder. It would certainly assist my investigation if I knew why he was in Bakersfield."

I heard voices in the background. "I'm late for a production meeting," Blake said, hedging.

I looked at my watch. It was just after nine. "I can be in L.A. in two hours, Mr. Blake. Let's do this face-to-face rather than on the phone. Besides, that will give you an opportunity to check me out. I've done work for several law firms down there."

I gave him names of firms and attorneys. "Where is your office located?"

He thought about it for a moment. Then he gave me a street address on Melrose Avenue. "Near the corner of La Brea. I'll expect you at noon."

CHAPTER 35

I CALLED CECE AT HER OFFICE. "I'M HEADING FOR L.A. THAT lead I told you about last night just got hotter." I gave her a quick rundown of my conversation with Simon Blake.

"Go for it," she said. "Call me after you've talked with him."

I didn't know how long I'd be in Los Angeles, so I quickly jammed all my belongings into my gray overnight bag and headed downstairs for the parking lot. I filled my gas tank at a station on Truxtun, then got onto Highway 99, heading south toward its rendezvous with Interstate 5 at the base of the Tehachapis.

From that point the interstate is called the Grapevine, because it twists up through canyons until it goes over the mountains and finally descends into the San Fernando Valley on the other side. Once in the L.A. Basin, I left I-5 for U.S. 101, heading southeast. I took the exit near the Hollywood Bowl and drove south on Highland Avenue, which intersected Melrose. I made a right, heading west, and once I crossed La Brea Avenue I started looking for a parking place.

The neighborhood was trendy, the shops and restaurants full of Angelenos who ranged in age from high school students on the loose from Fairfax High to young adults in their twenties. I found a parking spot on a side street and doubled back to Melrose.

The building that housed the offices of *On the Rag* was an unremarkable three-story stucco and glass structure on the north side of the street. Once through the front door I saw a signboard telling the location of the office I sought, on the second floor. When I came out of the stairwell, I headed down the corridor on my left, until I spotted a wooden door with ON THE RAG printed in white block letters on a red sign.

The small reception area was about eight by ten feet, with yellow walls. The carpet was a particularly unpleasant shade of orange with a nap that had long since departed. Directly in front of me, a wooden desk stood before a narrow frosted window. This evidently looked down on a courtyard or airshaft, since the amount of light coming through the window didn't accurately reflect the bright July sunshine out on the street. To the left of the desk I saw a hallway that I assumed led back to the magazine's offices. The wall at the right held a row of uncomfortable-looking chairs, with a table on which sat the latest issue of *On the Rag*. It was a thick tabloid-sized newspaper with the same red, black, and white graphics I'd seen on the cyberspace edition.

At the far end of the chairs was a ficus that should have been closer to the window. Judging from its sparse and anemic leaves, the tree suffered from a lack of sunshine or water or both. On either side of me, the walls were decorated with arty-looking black-and-white photographs, all of them hanging slightly askew, as though they hadn't been straightened since the last earthquake.

The desk was staffed by a twentysomething woman with earrings in every available bit of ear cartilage. She also had a pierced nose and an anorexic frame displayed in green Spandex. Her eye shadow was grape-soda purple, the same flavor as her hair, which looked as though it had been styled in a wind tunnel with an eggbeater. It didn't go well with the green Spandex.

If this was the same ditz I'd spoken with on the phone earlier, she was passing for a receptionist, but didn't quite have her act together. I stood in front of her desk and asked for Simon Blake. She gave me an utterly bored look and tugged on one of her purple locks. Rings weighted the fingers of both her hands and her wrists were heavy with bangles that made a racket every time she moved.

"It's lunchtime," she said, as though that were that. I gave her a steady look that indicated it wasn't. She elaborated. "Like, I don't know if he's here."

"I suggest you find out," I told her. "My name is Jeri Howard.

Mr. Blake's expecting me at noon. It's eight minutes to twelve. He can't have gone far."

She shot me a poisonous look through improbably black lashes, bracelets jangling as she reached for the phone. Punching in a number, she made an impatient moue as the phone rang on the other end.

Someone must have answered. "Simon. There's somebody here to see you." She looked up at me. "What'd you say your name was?" I told her and she repeated it into the receiver as though the words tasted sour. "He'll be right out," she told me, hanging up the phone. "Have a seat or something."

I opted for something, taking a look at the framed photos on the yellow walls. The phone rang and I heard the girl answer it, sounding as hostile and put-upon as she had when I'd called this morning. "*On the Rag,* may I help you?"

Footsteps approached. I turned to see a young man in his late twenties entering the reception area from the hallway. He had creamy brown skin and curly dark hair. His slender frame did justice to a pair of loose-fitting black jeans and a tight yellow T-shirt. He wore loafers with no socks, and a gold stud in his left earlobe.

"Jeri Howard?" he asked in the same brisk voice I'd heard on the phone this morning. He smiled and extended his right hand. I took it, confirming my identity. "I'm Simon Blake. I checked you out."

"Good. Let's talk."

Simon glanced at the receptionist and another staffer who'd wandered into the room, then he gestured toward the door. "Let's do lunch, as they say down here."

"I'm afraid they say it everywhere. Actually, lunch sounds good to me."

Green Spandex seemed to be having a verbal tussle with whoever was on the other end of the phone. "Yeah, well, stuff it in your shirt," she growled, and hung up the phone with a bang, setting her bracelets all a-tinkle.

"Some receptionist," I commented, once Simon and I were outside in the hallway, heading for the stairs. "She's very L.A."

He gave me an amused look. "Hey, don't give me that. She'd fit into San Francisco easy, admit it."

"Bike messenger, maybe. Office help, I don't think so. Her people skills are interesting, to say the least."

Simon laughed. "She doesn't have any people skills, but that's okay. We're an in-your-face kind of place. Besides, she's someone's kid sister. Comes cheap."

"Did you ever hear the one about you get what you pay for?"

"Nah, I'm too young for homilies." We'd reached the ground floor and he opened the door leading out onto Melrose.

"Now just a minute. You're not that much younger than I am."

"Maybe not." He stopped and pointed up the street. "Thai or Mexican that way, Italian the other direction."

"Mexican."

"Let's do it."

"You didn't want to talk about Nick in the office," I said, as Simon Blake and I walked west along Melrose Avenue.

His brown eyes flickered. "Figured that out, did you? Hey, you're good."

"It's how I make my living. Did you call Harmon?"

"Yeah. I didn't tell him you and I had talked. Just said I'd heard about someone named Talbert being killed in Bakersfield. Someone from LAPD is going to show up to interview me. Am I right in guessing that Harmon might not be thrilled to learn that you're beating his time?"

"I don't suppose he would be. Tell me about *On the Rag.* And Nick Talbert."

"I started the magazine three years ago," Simon told me as we walked. "We were monthly at first, then switched to biweekly. We cover the usual beats. Music, art, city politics, stuff like that. I met Nick when we were both freelancing for another alternative. I liked his stuff, I asked him to join us."

We stopped, waiting for a light to change. "What can you tell me about his personal life?"

Simon shrugged. The signal changed and we stepped into the crosswalk. "Nick? Not a whole lot. I knew him on a professional basis. We got into personal stuff only peripherally. He went to journalism school back in the Midwest, I think. Came to California after he graduated. Worked for a couple of dailies around the state before coming to L.A. to try freelancing."

"Do you recall where?"

"Y'know, he told me, but I'm drawing a blank right now. Some town up the coast, and before that, the San Joaquin Valley. He's got an ex-wife and kid somewhere."

"Would anyone else on your staff have more details about Talbert's background?"

He shrugged. "Could be. I'll ask around when we get back to the office."

The place Simon had in mind for lunch was a crowded taquería painted red, white, and green, the colors of the Mexican flag. We queued at the counter and I scanned the menu board. When our turn came, I ordered a chicken *mole* burrito and a bottle of mineral water. Simon opted for beer and *carne asada*.

While the guy in the white apron constructed our lunches, I picked up our beverages and laid claim to a recently vacated table near the window. I swiped a napkin across the table to mop up a stray puddle of salsa, then unscrewed the cap from my mineral water and drank. By that time Simon had threaded his way through the narrow passage between tables, carrying both our plates on a tray. My burrito looked like a knife-and-forker rather than something I should attempt to pick up with my hands. When I'd tamed the beast in my stomach, I set my cutlery on the plate and looked at Simon.

"Okay, Nick was up in Bakersfield pretending to be a maintenance man named Wayne Talbert, which is an easy alias. You're acting very cloak-and-dagger about this story. What was he working on? Could it have gotten him killed?"

"Quite possibly." Simon picked up his knife and fork and hacked off a section of his *carne asada*. "With people like that anything can happen. And usually does."

"People like who?" I had a feeling I already knew. Probably the same people who'd kicked in the door to Talbert's apartment the night he died.

Simon didn't answer right away. He raised the bottle to his lips and drank, then wiped his mouth with a napkin.

"Let me tell you about my grandma," he said. "Bella Epstein. She's something else. You'd like her."

"I'm sure I would," I agreed, letting him tell it in his own way.

Simon shook his head. "Bella was born in Poland, in a town not far from a city called Lublin. That's southeast of Warsaw. When the Nazis invaded in 1939, she was eight years old. These Polish Catholics in the neighborhood agreed to hide the whole family, mother, father, three children. For money. Instead they turned them over to the Nazis. For more money."

He picked up his beer again, to wash the taste of those words from his mouth. "They shot Bella's parents on the spot. She, her brother, and sister were shipped to a labor camp called Majdanek. Later it became a death camp. Bella's sister was gassed."

I pushed the remains of my burrito aside. I no longer had an appetite. "What happened to her brother?"

"The guards in this camp thought it was a lot of fun to play target practice with the prisoners. Especially the children. So one day Bella's brother wound up being a target. The other thing these guards would do for the hell of it was set their dogs on the kids. That's what happened to my grandma, Jeri. Some fucking Nazi sicced a German shepherd on her."

He took another swallow of beer, his knuckles white in contrast with the amber glass. "Some of the other prisoners got her away before the damn dog tore her to pieces. It's a wonder she didn't die from the wounds. As it is, she's still got scars on her legs."

And her psyche, I imagined. I waited for the rest of Simon's story—Bella's, actually. "When I was little, I'd ask Bella about those scars," he said. "She didn't want to talk about it. Then some jerk-off, neo-Nazi scumbag here in L.A. published some revisionist crapola book saying that the Holocaust never happened. Funny how all those Jews just accidentally dropped dead between 1933 and 1945." He smiled, but none of what he was talking about was the least bit amusing.

"Bella got mad. She went down to the Museum of Tolerance at the Wiesenthal Center on Pico and volunteered, two days a week. Now she talks about it. She tells people there's no such thing as being just a little bit prejudiced, and shows them the results of bigotry. She shows people those ugly scars from the dog's fangs and tells how they got there. She says she owes it to her family, since she's the only one who survived. And I owe my grandma."

"So Nick Talbert was in Bakersfield researching neo-Nazis."

"Neo-Nazis, the Klan, Christian Identity." Simon used his fingers

WITNESS TO EVIL 205

to tick off the names. "Militias, Freemen, jural societies, skinheads. Aryan this and patriot that. Lump it all under the heading of extremist groups," he said. "They're all in the same stinking stew. The white supremacists and the anti-Semites have tapped into that pool of people who are perennially pissed off at the government or at anyone who doesn't look like them or think like them. They're recruiting people every day, here in L.A., up in the Bay Area, all over the state."

"But Nick decided to focus on the San Joaquin Valley? Or specifically on Kern County or Bakersfield?"

"He didn't have to go to Bakersfield. We've got plenty of these clowns running around greater Los Angeles. But we concentrate on L.A. all the time, so Nick figured it would be better if he went somewhere else to do the research. And since he'd worked in the Valley I guess he knew the area. Heartland stuff, y'know. Where people are supposed to retain those good old bedrock American values." Simon's mouth quirked. "Like narrow-mindedness and intolerance."

"How did he start the process?" I asked.

"He did some preliminary research at the Wiesenthal Center. He also interviewed a professor up at Cal State Fresno. The guy's name is Ira Blum, and he's supposed to be an expert on extremist groups. I've got some of Nick's early notes back in the office. Anyway, his idea was to go up to Bakersfield, get some disaffected-white-guy kind of job, and just hang out in bars, mouthing off about minorities and pretending to be a right-winger. He figured it would be easy enough to attract some real ones."

Evidently he'd been successful, I thought. Too successful. "Where was he with this article?"

"That's what he and I were arguing about the last time we talked, Wednesday of last week. Usually we'd communicate by e-mail. But he called me that night and said he wanted more time for the story."

"So he was coming up on a deadline."

"He was past it. The original due date was mid-July, for an August pub-date. I wanted him to wrap it up and get back down here to L.A. because I had something else I wanted him to work on."

"But he felt he needed more time?"

"Something like that. He said the story had taken an unexpected turn. He wanted to follow that lead. We argued about it. He said he had to go and he'd call me Friday night. I didn't hear from him. I called the apartment in Bakersfield. Zip city." He paused. "Harmon told me he was killed Friday night. What was he doing there at night?"

"Until eleven, he was supposedly playing cards with his supervisor, a man named Bennett Fosby. Instead he wound up dead on the sidewalk outside the back door of the school's administration building. Did Harmon tell you someone had broken into Nick's apartment that same night?"

Simon frowned. "No, he didn't."

"A neighbor saw three men kick in Nick's door and called the police. She described two of them as skinheads. The only thing they took was his computer and probably the disks that went with it." Simon swore under his breath. "Nick may have picked up the wrong rock, particularly since he told you he had an unexpected lead he wanted to investigate before turning in his article. Someone must have discovered he was a reporter and decided to kill the story— permanently."

"I was afraid of that, when you told me he was dead."

I finished off my mineral water. "I got into this because of my client, and the school. I'm curious. Why did he get a job at the Perris School?"

"He told me he was going to look for a nothing job, a low-paying one. Later he told me he'd talked to someone who knew about the handyman job at the school."

"That was Fosby," I said. "It all comes back to the same question. What was Nick doing outside the school admin office Friday night? Did this new lead he was so hot to investigate involve that school?"

"Anything's possible. But if the school figured into the story, Nick never said anything about it."

"Had he sent you any drafts? More research notes?"

Simon shook his head. "Just the occasional e-mail to let me know how it was going. He probably deleted those from his computer. He wouldn't want anyone finding anything on his hard drive. The story would have been on a disk, and the notes on another."

Someone else probably had those disks. It was a good bet that those were what the two skinheads and their companion were looking for when they broke into Talbert's apartment. Maybe they'd found them.

Maybe not. Maybe Darcy got there first. If that's why she was there.

"Did you save the e-mails Nick sent you?" I asked Simon.

He shifted in the chair and dug into the pocket of his black jeans. He took out a white square and unfolded several sheets of paper.

"I thought you'd ask that question," he said. "So I printed them out."

CHAPTER 36

HE HANDED ME SIX SHEETS OF PAPER. EACH CONTAINED the printout of an e-mail message Talbert had sent to Simon at *On the Rag*. The first was dated May 14. Talbert began by telling Simon his visit to his ex-wife and son had "gone as well as expected."

"What does that mean?" I looked up, indicating the phrase with my forefinger.

"My guess is, it means he didn't get along with his ex. But he wanted to see his kid, so he gritted his teeth and got on with it."

"You know the ex-wife's name?" He shook his head. "Well, let me know if you remember where she lives."

"Sorry to sound like I haven't got a clue," he said. "But Nick didn't talk much about his marriage. I got the feeling it had ended badly, and he just didn't want to discuss it. I don't pry into my coworkers' personal lives."

"In the context of a coworker, then, would there be anything about Talbert in your personnel files?"

Simon grinned. "Do we look that organized? Well, I suppose we are, in our own fashion. IRS forms, of course. But we're a shoe-string operation. None of those fancy benefits like health insurance or profit sharing. So there wouldn't be a beneficiary form." He thought for a moment. "There may be something floating around the office. On paper, on computer, or in people's heads. Like the name of a person to contact in case of an emergency, which I guess would be the ex. I'll check when we get back to the office."

I bent my head again, reading the words the dead man had typed into a computer two months earlier. "Moved into a cheap apartment on Monterey Street," Talbert had written, adding that he'd chosen that part of Bakersfield because it was a lower-income, working-class neighborhood. "My next-door neighbor's a hoot." Stevie was indeed, I thought with a smile.

Talbert ended by giving Simon his Bakersfield phone number, cautioning, "Use it sparingly."

I turned to the next sheet, dated May 18. Talbert wrote Simon that he'd been hanging out at bars in Bakersfield and Oildale, where he loudly claimed he was having a hard time finding a job because he was a white male. After all, those uppity women had it all wired.

Talbert was trolling for information for his story. He figured that by punching the usual buttons of gender and race, he would draw the kind of people he sought. Talbert didn't indicate which bars he'd gone to, and there were a lot of them in Bakersfield and Oildale. Would I have to take the same route he had, to find the same people? I felt my throat close up at the thought of all that cigarette smoke mixed with the stench of spilled beer. Maybe it was just the summer L.A. smog. Or the thought of boozing it up with the people I'd glimpsed in the back room of the Rust Bucket.

On May 29, Talbert reported that he'd found work at the Perris School. He'd gotten a line on the job through a conversation with Bennett Fosby, whom he'd met at one of those unnamed bars, no doubt the Rust Bucket, since that seemed to be where Fosby did his drinking.

"I'll be working as a maintenance man. Doesn't pay much, but it'll do." The school, he explained, was "one of those private holding cells where rich people get rid of their problem children." An apt description, I thought, seconding Nick's characterization of Dr. Perris's enterprise.

Talbert had gone to work there just a few days after Darcy Stefano's arrival. But he didn't mention Fosby again, other than a short comment about the Friday-night poker games, which were of the low-stakes, nickel-dime-quarter variety.

The only other time Talbert mentioned the school in his e-mails to Simon was in mid-June. He wrote that he'd caught two kids trying to run away from the place. "Hated like hell to stop them," he wrote. "God knows they had good reason to split. But I couldn't afford to blow my cover."

This had to be the night when Darcy and Gillie tried to leave the Perris School. What about Gillie, I wondered? She'd recognized Talbert, but it seemed he hadn't recognized her. I supposed he must have talked with dozens of kids for his story on Hollywood's runaways. But why did it matter to Talbert if the two girls had gotten away? From what I'd read thus far, it looked as though Talbert's employment at the school was just a coincidence, a means to his end. Yet, according to Perris, Darcy had threatened Talbert and this was the reason why. It didn't make sense.

Talbert's last two e-mails related to the story he was researching, the reason he'd gone undercover in Bakersfield. By late June he'd found the contact he was looking for, someone who had ties to a militia, and was working to gain that person's trust. Another message written in early July referred to a proposed meeting and pay dirt.

Was the contact, taken in by Talbert's guise, trying to recruit him? More important, was the contact the third man Stevie Kay had seen breaking into her neighbor's apartment, with the two skinheads, the night Talbert was murdered? Perhaps the proposed meeting had gone awry and Nick had somehow alerted the contact to his real reason for being in Bakersfield. Pay dirt had ultimately led to murder.

I looked up at Simon. He was staring out the window as he toyed with his beer bottle. Then I saw him take a surreptitious glance at his watch. Time to get back to the office.

"Tell me again about your last phone conversation with Nick," I said, wanting to go over it one more time in case either of us had missed something.

"Wednesday evening last week. He called me at home. I'd just gotten there, so it must have been about seven. I asked him when he was going to deliver the story. He said he needed two more weeks, because of this new angle." Simon shook his head as he remembered the conversation. "I asked Nick if he had enough material to do the story as we'd originally planned, and he said yes. I told him in that case, we had to go with what he had. That story was originally scheduled to run in the first August issue. When Nick didn't turn it in on his original deadline, we moved the pub-date to mid-August."

"He tried to convince you to give him more time."

Simon nodded. "Full-court press. He said this new angle was hot. But he wouldn't tell me what it was, like he was afraid that would jinx it. I told him we couldn't change the schedule again. We went back and forth for a couple of minutes, and he asked me to give him till the weekend and said he'd call Friday night. I hope I didn't push him into doing something foolhardy, just to get the damn story."

There was a chance of that, but some things are better left unsaid. Simon was already chewing on that one, and Nick Talbert had made his own choices.

Back in the *On the Rag* office, Green Spandex was snarling into the telephone, as though someone had dared to interrupt her own lunch, which was spread out on the desk blotter. Simon led me back to his office, barely more than a cubicle, and dug out the file containing Nick's preliminary research. In addition to computer printouts of what he'd learned at the Wiesenthal Center, there were some handwritten scribbles of a telephone interview with Dr. Ira Blum at Cal State Fresno, and a notation of an appointment for a face-to-face interview. Simon made copies of these for me.

I stayed another thirty minutes or so while Simon polled the rest of the staff to see if any of them knew anything about Nick Talbert. Back in the darkroom, he turned up a spaced-out photographer with long gray hair and a battered Leica draped around his neck. The guy was about fifty, wearing Birkenstocks, a pair of patched Levi's, and a black Grateful Dead T-shirt stretched tight over his beer belly. Wire-rimmed glasses held together with tape perched on his nose. I could have sworn his eyes were spinning. Inhaling developer fumes, I figured, or something more herbal.

The photographer swore on a stack of Ansel Adamses that Nick Talbert's ex-wife was a bodacious brunette named Peggy. "He showed me her picture once, man." He winked at me lasciviously through his bifocals. "I'm here to tell you, that woman had legs."

"Most of us do," I said. "If you were to go looking for Peggy, man, where would you look?"

The lensman blinked like a drunken owl and scratched the likeness of Jerry Garcia on his Dead T-shirt. "Raisins," he said suddenly.

"Raisins?"

"Fresno, man. They got raisins in Fresno."

"Last time I looked," I told him solemnly. "Is Peggy in Fresno?"

So was Ira Blum. If Nick's ex was there as well, that was all the more reason to add Fresno to my itinerary.

"Fresno, Modesto, one of those Valley towns. They're all alike. Drove through one, you drove through 'em all. Hey, maybe it was Lodi." Suddenly the photographer bellowed the lyrics to the Creedence Clearwater Revival song about being stuck in Lodi again. He was still bellowing as Simon steered him back toward his darkroom. It was all I could do to keep from laughing.

"He's a great photographer," Simon told me, his mouth twitching. "A little burned out, wouldn't you say?"

"He's been in the toaster way too long. Very L.A., but we get them in Berkeley, too." I shook Simon's hand. "Thanks for the information. I'll let you know if I find out anything."

CHAPTER 37

NICK TALBERT'S ADDRESS ON MARTELL AVENUE PROVED
to be a fourplex on the left side of the street, in the middle
of a pleasant-looking neighborhood above Waring Avenue. The two
one-story stucco buildings, painted blue with white trim, faced each
other across a concrete sidewalk lined with borders of succulents,
and a couple of date palms towered above the buildings, which
looked as though they'd been constructed in the forties.

Talbert had lived in the first unit on the left. All the windows were
shut tight and covered with drawn mini-blinds, so I couldn't peer in.
The mailbox next to the door was locked and I couldn't tell if there
was anything inside. Nick must have had his mail stopped or picked
up. Since he'd kept paying rent on the place, expecting to return to
it when he'd completed his story, he had to be receiving some mail,
if only bills for phone and utilities.

The unit opposite Nick's had a sign indicating that the apartment manager lived there. I knocked on the door. The woman who
opened it was my age or a little younger. Through the screen door I
saw that she was barefoot, wearing a white, paint-stained T-shirt
over a pair of mulberry-colored cotton shorts. Her black hair was
thick and curly, held back with a scarf. She looked at me with
opaque brown eyes.

"You're the manager?" I asked.

"That's what the sign on the door says," she told me, her voice
crisp. "We don't have any vacancies."

"I'm not looking for an apartment. I'm here about Nick Talbert."

"He's not in."

"I'm aware of that."

She put one long-fingered hand on her hip and narrowed her eyes, staring at me as though I had an Uzi behind my back. "You a bill collector or process server or something like that?"

"I'm a private investigator." I showed her my license.

She scraped her eyes over it scornfully. "That and a buck will get you a cup of coffee, if you're lucky. Just what is it you want?"

She seemed like the straightforward type, so I decided to hit her with the truth. "A look at his apartment."

"What the hell makes you think I'm going to let you into Nick's apartment?" she snapped. "That license, or my good nature?"

"I'll hope for your good nature. Nick was murdered Friday night in Bakersfield."

"Fuck." The word exploded from her mouth. I wasn't sure whether it was directed at me or a reaction to the news of Nick's death. Her face sagged a little, so I guessed it might be the latter. "Why should I believe you? You could be running some scam."

"I could," I admitted. "But you can call the Bakersfield Police Department and ask for Sergeant Harmon or Detective Garza." Which would, of course, tip both detectives off to my activities. But she needed convincing. "You can contact the attorney I'm working for, Cecilia Bromley. I have her card right here. Or you can call the office of *On the Rag*, that magazine Nick worked for. I just had lunch with Simon Blake, his editor."

She stood as though rooted in the doorway of her apartment. A tortoiseshell cat appeared and wound itself around her bare legs, then disappeared again into the interior. Finally the woman opened the screen door, snatched Cece's business card from my fingers, and shut the door in my face. I heard the bolt click. I waited. Five minutes later the door opened again.

"The attorney vouches for you," she said abruptly.

"Is that enough to convince you?"

"Not entirely. But I called the Bakersfield cop shop, too. Those detectives you mentioned are out of the office, but the cop who answered the phone confirmed they had a murder victim named Talbert. Are they going to come down here and search his place?"

"More likely they'll send someone from LAPD," I told her. "But that might take a couple of days. I'd like to get a head start."

"What is it you want to know?"

"For starters, I'd like to find out where to locate his ex-wife. I understand her name is Peggy and she lives in the San Joaquin Valley."

"Fresno."

Raisins indeed, I thought. Score one for the Deadhead.

"How well did you know him?"

She stared past me at the closed door to Nick's unit. "We were sleeping together, if that means anything," she said, and was silent for a moment as though she were trying to decide if it did. "I've been watering his plants and taking in his mail."

"What is your name, by the way?"

"Soledad," she said, stingy with the word, even at three syllables.

"Did Nick tell you why he was going to Bakersfield?"

"Something about a story. He was a writer. I paint." She glanced down at her stained T-shirt and smiled so briefly I might have missed it, if I hadn't been looking at her face then. "When he moved in, I recognized his byline from *On the Rag*. He did a wonderful piece on runaways in Hollywood. Went undercover as a street person to do it. What did he get himself into this time, to wind up good and dead?"

"Something about extremist groups," I said, not wanting to go into details.

Her eyes widened. "Those people are dangerous."

"I'm afraid so. Nick was undercover on this story, too. I have a feeling someone pegged him as a reporter. I'm looking for any information I can find. His ex-wife's address and phone number. And maybe a crack at his answering machine and computer."

I thought I saw the glimmer of tears in her eyes. Then her face hardened. "I'll get the key," she said.

Soledad disappeared from view, returning almost immediately with a set of keys. She stepped outside and closed her own door behind her. I followed her as she strode across the walkway to Nick's front door. She selected a brass key and turned it in the lock, then opened the door and shoved it wide. She turned to me and held out her hand. "Be my guest."

Nick's place had a musty, shut-up feel, as though the premises knew the occupant wasn't coming back. He'd left everything neat in anticipation of his absence and eventual return, but the surfaces were coated with dust.

Soledad shut the door behind us and stood there, as though reluctant to move any further into the space Nick had once occupied. I looked around the apartment. It had a light brown carpet to go with the ivory plastic mini-blinds. The kitchen to my right was small, separated from the living room by a counter. Beyond this was a dining area that held a round table and two wooden folding chairs.

The living room was on my left. I saw a few framed posters on the wall, nothing remarkable or particularly colorful. Other than that, the only decoration was provided by several large potted plants, the kind that are hard to kill. They were still green, due to Soledad's diligence in watering them. The furniture was utilitarian. Three sets of pine shelves stood against one wall. One held a large-screen television, a VCR, and a portable CD player. The other two were crammed with an eclectic assortment of books.

On one shelf I saw an eight-by-ten framed photograph of a little boy with blue eyes, freckles, and sandy hair. I had a feeling he was going to miss his dad. Maybe Nick's ex would, too.

There were no end tables or coffee table, just brass torchère lamps at either side of a futon on a frame that served as a sofa. It was covered with sheets and a quilted comforter in a vaguely southwestern pattern. A wicker basket at the far end held a couple of pillows.

"He slept in here?" I asked Soledad.

She nodded. "He'd turned his bedroom into an office."

On the counter between the living room and kitchen, I saw that Soledad had sorted Nick's mail into orderly stacks, separating it by category. Here were several mail-order catalogs, three bills, and a letter with a Phoenix postmark.

"Who did he know in Phoenix?" I asked Soledad.

"His parents. They're retired."

Two more people who'd miss Nick Talbert. "Did he come down to see you? To check on things and get his mail?"

"Twice in June. Once in July. He wanted to make sure the bills were paid. He was up to date on his rent, through the end of July."

Her face looked hard and set as she surveyed the living room, as though she were already trying to forget him. "Last time I saw him was right before the Fourth. I asked when he was coming back. He said he was almost done with the story and that he thought another couple of weeks would do it."

"Did he say anything at all about the story, the people he was talking with?"

She shook her head. "No. He never would. Always played it close to the chest."

"Where did he live before?"

She ran a hand through her black hair. "Some town up north, on the coast. He didn't like to talk about it. All I knew was, his marriage went sour and something went wrong with the job, about the same time. I got the impression the breakup was his wife's idea. He was really bummed about it, and he missed his kid. His ex-wife moved to Fresno after the divorce. Her family is there."

I walked back past the bathroom and into the bedroom, with Soledad following closely behind me. Here I found more shelves and more books. On the far wall was a large particleboard desk loaded with computer, monitor, and a keyboard drawer. To the left of this was a fax machine complete with a telephone receiver. It was the kind with lots of bells and whistles, which could be used as a copier and an answering machine. For all I knew, it could boil a three-minute egg as well. A little green light was blinking, indicating that Nick has received some messages.

I sat down in the padded gray chair in front of the desk and looked more closely at the items on it. Tucked behind the fax machine were a black Rolodex, which would surely have the phone number of Nick's ex, and a lacquer tray full of business cards Nick had collected from other people. To the right of the computer monitor I saw some empty plastic trays and a locked plastic box with an assortment of computer disks visible through its clear lid. A ceramic beer mug bristled with pens and pencils.

Nick's laser printer was in the corner, perched on top of a two-drawer filing cabinet on casters. The closet door was open and inside, below Nick's clothes hanging from the bar, I saw two plastic file boxes.

I dug into my purse for the latex gloves I carry with me. I slipped them onto my hands, then I powered up Nick's computer. I didn't get very far with that. He'd installed a password and I couldn't get past the DOS prompt. Considering that someone more officially sanctioned than I would be searching the apartment soon, I fought down the impulse to pick the lock on the box of disks. Instead, I pulled a pencil from the ceramic cup and used the eraser end to push the button on the fax/answering machine that would let me access his messages.

Nick had probably called in from Bakersfield on a regular basis to get his messages, so I was guessing these had been left since his last call. There were five. The first was from a guy named Sam over at *LA Weekly*. He'd called July 6, wanting to talk with Nick about doing a story. The second message was from Peggy, the ex-wife herself, on July 10. Next was a man who identified himself as Joe. He hadn't left a date, but he told Nick he'd rented a cabin up at Big Bear Lake and Nick was welcome to come up any time. The last two calls were hang-ups.

I flipped open the Rolodex and quickly found that there wasn't a card for Peggy Talbert. I did a more thorough search and located Peggy Rostrow, with a Fresno address and phone number. I wrote it in my notebook, then sifted through the rest of the cards in the Rolodex, hoping that something important might leap out at me. It didn't.

I pulled open the top drawer of the filing cabinet to the right of the computer desk, and saw the paper trail we all leave, an array of folders that contained paid bills and tax receipts. Behind this, in some personal papers, I found Nick's birth certificate and résumé. The former told me he'd been born in Oklahoma City. The latter had more details. He'd graduated from the University of Oklahoma School of Journalism eleven years ago. While he was in school, he'd worked on the *Oklahoma Daily*, the campus newspaper, and as a stringer for the Norman *Transcript*, the newspaper in O.U.'s hometown.

After graduation he'd headed for California, taking a job as a general reporter on the Fresno *Bee*. He'd worked there five years, and during this time had presumably wed Peggy, the mother of his son. What I found most interesting was that when he left Fresno five years ago, he'd moved on to a job at the San Luis Obispo *Telegram-Tribune.*

Nick Talbert had been in SLO the same time the Coast Academy had been under investigation by the district attorney's office. He'd been in SLO when Kyle Perris's former partner, Thomas Shiller, fell off that cliff at Montaña de Oro. Then Nick left San Luis Obispo for L.A. a couple of months after Shiller's death.

I'd been wondering if Nick's presence at the Perris School was co-incidence or design. Now I was almost sure that no coincidence was involved. But how did the Perrises tie in with Nick's subject, extrem-ist groups? Or maybe that wasn't the story he was after at all. Could he have an agenda other than the article he was doing for *On the Rag?* In other words, finishing a story he'd begun in SLO?

Take it easy, Jeri, I told myself. You're getting ahead of yourself. You don't even know if Nick ever covered the DA's investigation or Shiller's death. For all I knew those two stories could have been some other reporter's beat while Nick covered city council meetings and demonstrations out at the Diablo Canyon nuclear power plant.

I turned my attention to the filing cabinet. Most reporters keep a clip file, a record of their work published over the years. I was sure Nick Talbert was no exception. His wasn't in the filing cabinet, but in one of the plastic file boxes in the closet. I sat cross-legged on the floor with the file in my lap and leafed through yellowing newsprint. The stories were arranged in a roughly chronological fashion, the most recent items first. Item by item, I dug down in the file until I found some copies of the front section of the SLO *Telegram-Tribune,* dated three-plus years ago. As I scanned the headlines on the front pages, I got that panning-gold feeling. Nick wrote the initial story about Shiller's death.

There were a lot of copies of the newspaper from that time pe-riod. Shiller's death had occurred shortly after the DA launched the investigation. The Coast Academy story, according to the byline, had been covered by a reporter named Teresa Bosk.

I shut the file and replaced it in the box. Then I stood up and crossed to the desk. I flipped through the *B* section of the Rolodex, past Simon Blake, until I found a card for Teresa Bosk, with a phone number and home address on West Foothill Boulevard in San Luis Obispo. But the office number at the *Telegram-Tribune* had been crossed out. Did that mean she was no longer on the newspaper's staff?

"Are you finding what you need?" Soledad asked, coming up behind me. "I mean, I can't let you stay here indefinitely, even if I do have the key."

I removed the gloves and stashed them in my purse. "I'm done. I got what I came for. And more."

CHAPTER 38

I HEADED FOR NORTH HOLLYWOOD, IN THE SAN FERNANDO Valley. Valley Security, the firm Elaine Stefano had hired to transport Darcy from Alameda to the Perris School, had an office on Lankershim, just north of Victory Boulevard. The address proved to be a two-story, gray stucco office building, set on a scrap of land abutting a strip mall anchored by a chain drugstore. I didn't see any other parking except that at the mall, so I slotted my Toyota into a space and walked past a storefront housing a dog grooming service, the clientele in full bark. Once inside the office building, I located Valley Security on the second floor. But the office door was shut and locked.

The suite next door held an accountant's office, where the receptionist told me Valley Security had been closed for several days. "He's not here half the time," she said. "I think he's got another office somewhere else."

Fresno, I recalled from my earlier research. Which was where Peggy Rostrow, Nick Talbert's ex, lived.

"Do you know any of his employees?" I asked. When George Larsen took Darcy from the Stefanos' condo, he'd had help, a skinhead who looked a lot like the one I'd seen at the Rust Bucket in Oildale on Wednesday night.

The receptionist shook her head. "As far as I know it's a one-man operation. I've never seen anyone but the guy who owns it, and I don't even know his name."

I asked if she could describe the owner. What she gave me was a repeat of Heather McRae's description. Larsen was blond, with short hair and a gut.

I went back outside, consulting my watch. It was nearly five o'clock in the afternoon. No way was I going to attempt to fight my way out of Los Angeles during the evening rush hour. I may be crazy, but not that crazy.

I spotted a coffee shop at the other end of the strip mall and walked toward it. Once inside, I stashed myself in a corner booth. A tired-looking woman in a black and white uniform brought a glass of water and a menu. I glanced at the laminated pages, then ordered a salad.

When the server had gone I pulled my cellular phone and my notebook from my purse. I called the first of the numbers I'd copied from Nick Talbert's Rolodex. Peggy Rostrow's Fresno exchange rang and rang, but there was no answer.

A call to the San Luis Obispo *Telegram-Tribune* confirmed that Teresa Bosk no longer worked there. She'd left to have a baby, one of her former coworkers told me. Now she was freelancing in public relations, working from her home. I called the home number. This time I got an answering machine. A woman's voice advised me that I'd reached the Bosk residence and invited me to leave a message. I didn't.

My next call was to Cece Bromley's Bakersfield office. "Are you still in L.A.?" she demanded when she answered the phone, her voice strung tight. "When are you coming back?"

"I'm in a coffee shop on Lankershim near Victory. I'm going to have some dinner before I put myself on the freeway."

"Sounds sensible."

"You sound harried," I told her. "Is something going on? Has Darcy called or turned up?"

"No, she hasn't. There's nothing happening on the Stefano front. I've just been on the phone, reassuring Mrs. Gregory. She says she and her son-in-law had planned to drive down here today, but they're coming tomorrow instead. She's very worried about Darcy. As for the something going on, it's a client who missed a hearing today because he got picked up for drunk driving last night."

She groaned, and I pictured her at her desk, running her fingers through her blond mop as she had the first day we'd met. "When are you coming back to Bakersfield?"

"Not tonight, Cece. I need to go to San Luis Obispo. And after that, Fresno."

"You must have found out something useful in L.A."

"Yes. And the trail leads to those two cities." I gave her the complete rundown, from Talbert's e-mails to Simon Blake, all the way to what I'd found in Talbert's apartment.

"San Luis Obispo and Perris's old school? That can't be a coincidence," she declared. "I don't believe in coincidences."

"Well, I do. I've encountered too many of them in this life. But not this time. That's why I need to talk to the reporter who worked with Talbert at the *Telegram-Tribune*. Maybe Teresa Bosk has more details on the Perris angle."

"How do you think it fits with what Talbert was doing in Bakersfield?"

"Try this on," I said. "Talbert gets the story assignment from *On the Rag*, goes to Bakersfield to do his undercover number, and discovers that the Perrises, formerly the big story in San Luis Obispo, are now operating in Kern County. He decides to take a look at their operation at the same time he's trolling for information about extremist groups. Are the two connected? Could be."

The server brought my salad and set it on the table. When I finished my conversation with Cece, I called the hotel in Bakersfield to check my messages. Nothing from Darcy, or from Carl Burnham, the investigator in Denver whom I'd sent to Walsenburg to dig up information on the Pinewood School, where Kyle Perris had worked before he came to California. Then I set the phone to one side and picked up my fork. When I'd finished my dinner, I took my address book from my purse and leafed through the pages, looking for a number in San Luis Obispo.

"Does your offer of a bed for the night still stand?" I asked Lindsey Page when she answered the phone.

"Of course it does. Where are you?"

"North Hollywood. I'm in a coffee shop having dinner. I'll explain when I get there."

I lingered a while longer over pie and coffee, then I paid my check and visited the restroom before heading out to my car. It was about a quarter to seven Thursday evening, still light, though the sun was edging toward the Pacific to the west. I'd missed the worst of the traffic, but U.S. 101 was still thick with commuters going home to the outlying suburbs. The freeway cut northwest along the southern edge of the San Fernando Valley, into Ventura County. Two hours later I stopped for coffee in Santa Barbara. It was another two hours before I got off the freeway again.

I drove through the darkened streets of San Luis Obispo, following the directions Lindsey had given me. She lived in a small house on Mill Street, not far from her job at Cal Poly. It was just after eleven P.M. when I parked the Toyota at the curb, grabbed my overnighter from the backseat, and stumbled toward the welcoming light streaming from the porch.

"You must be exhausted," Lindsey said, opening the door to my knock. She wore a blue seersucker robe over her nightgown. "The extra bed's all made up. This way." She steered me through the living room, where I saw a fluffy white cat sleeping on the sofa next to a stack of books. We walked down the hall to her back bedroom, where she relieved me of my bag and handed me a red robe. "Bathroom's across the hall, fresh towels on the counter. Take a long, hot shower and get some sleep. You can tell me what this is about in the morning."

"It's quite a story," I said.

"I'll bet." She grinned in anticipation and headed back to the living room. I was vaguely aware of her checking the lock on the front door and turning off the light in the living room before she headed for her own bedroom.

I stripped off my clothes and fell into bed, bone-tired. I didn't surface until nine on Friday morning, far later than I'd intended, groggy, raspy-throated, and in dire need of coffee. I headed for the bathroom, where I showered. When I returned to the bedroom, a delicate green and white china cup and saucer had miraculously appeared on the nightstand. The cup was brimful of strong, black coffee. I took a restorative sip and got dressed.

Lindsey had the kind of house I was looking for and probably couldn't afford, at least not in the Bay Area. It was an older home with three bedrooms and two baths. Lindsey had taken the largest bedroom for herself, turning the smallest into the guest room where

I'd slept. The middle-sized bedroom had become her office, which was crowded with bookshelves, desk, and computer equipment.

I wandered into the living room. A large glass-fronted cabinet along one wall held an assortment of compacts, ranging in appearance from Victorian to Art Deco to pure 1950s modern. I'd never realized there were so many ways to store powder and rouge.

A barrister's bookcase next to this held the sort of books I might well find in my father's office. I remembered what Lindsey had said in Paris, about the passion she and my father shared. Cowboys, Indians, and outlaws, with one particular outlaw predominating.

"You're a Billy the Kid buff," I said to Lindsey as I went through a doorway into the kitchen. My host was seated at a round oak table, drinking coffee from another china cup and reading the morning paper. She looked up at me and grinned, brown eyes twinkling.

"Absolutely," she said. "I read Walter Noble Burns at an impressionable age. One of these days I'm going to write the ultimate Billy the Kid book. Of course, I'll have to disguise it as a scholarly work on the Lincoln County War to get it published. More coffee?"

"Please. It's delicious."

She reached for a white carafe in the center of the table, unscrewed the knob at the top and poured. "It's SLO Roast Morning Foglifter. Guaranteed to make you bright-eyed and bushy-tailed."

"I don't know about bright eyes," I said, "but talk about bushy tails . . ."

The cat I'd seen last night was perched on the sill of Lindsey's kitchen window, twitching a thick tail as it stared intently at a sparrow. The bird hopped unconcerned among the purple blossoms that littered the grass under the huge jacaranda tree in the front yard. The cat's fur was mostly white, with a few pale brown streaks on its back, dark brown ears, and a tabby mask over its slightly crossed blue eyes.

"She flaunts that tail like a feather boa," Lindsey said. "That's Lola." The white cat paid us no mind, just continued staring at the bird, twitching her elegant tail and making that chittering sound cats make when they see birds. "Sometimes she gets so excited about the birds she falls off the sill. Then she glares at me, as though it's my fault."

I pulled out a chair and sat down opposite Lindsey, sipping coffee.

The pleated placemats on the oak table were the same shade of purple as the blossoms that thickly covered the tree outside. I looked at the white floral pattern on the rim of the green cup I held. "This is lovely. So delicate. Reminds me of some china my grandmother had."

"They're all different," she said, indicating a cup rack on the kitchen wall, just above a work table that held an assortment of spice jars and a small wooden wine rack containing several bottles. The shelves were oak, divided into little compartments, and each compartment contained a different cup and saucer. "I collect them. And books, and cats, and compacts."

"I saw the compacts. That's quite a collection."

"One of these days I'll have to buy a bigger house, just to contain the clutter. Let's face it, I'm a pack rat. Would you like some breakfast? I have cereal, English muffins, and fruit."

"An English muffin will do. No, don't get up. Just point me in the right direction and I'll get it."

"In the basket next to the toaster. The butter's in that glass dish with the blue cover. There are strawberries and blueberries in the refrigerator."

The basket yielded a choice of whole wheat or sourdough. I opted for the latter. I split one of the muffins and put it into the toaster, then took the berries from the refrigerator and filled a bowl, adding a couple of spoonfuls of vanilla yogurt for good measure. When the muffin popped up, I buttered both halves, then rejoined Lindsey at the table.

"Thanks again for the hospitality," I told her between mouthfuls.

She poured both of us another cup of coffee. "The door's always open. I do expect a full report on just why you needed to come to San Luis Obispo."

"I have to talk with a woman named Teresa Bosk who used to work at the *Telegram-Tribune*. She's freelancing now."

"What's this all about?"

"It's about a murder in Bakersfield. The trail led to L.A., then up here."

I gave her as much information as I felt comfortable disclosing. "By the way, do you know a professor at Cal State Fresno named Ira Blum?"

"Why, yes, I do. I'll bet your father does, too. Ira's quite a character. In fact, he was a hidden child, like Adele Gregory. How does he figure into this?"

"The murder victim contacted him for information, prior to going to Bakersfield. Do you have a number for Dr. Blum?"

"Sure." Lindsey got up and went to her office, returning a moment later with an address book. I copied Blum's home and office numbers. Then another cat ambled into the kitchen, a calico with equal distribution of orange, black, and white fur. The newcomer fixed the white cat in the window with a rancorous stare and made the same chittering noise that Lola had made at the bird.

"Clementine," Lindsey explained, indicating the calico. "She's the oldest. She was quite sure she was the only cat in the world and thus was bent out of shape when I brought Lola home. She doesn't much care for Lola and considers it her mission in life to put Lola in her place. Of course, Lola is scared of her. We've had some interesting altercations. Nothing like a cat fight on the bed at four A.M."

"I acquired a kitten last December and my tabby had quite an adjustment. But the two of them are getting along fine now."

"This has been going on for two years, ever since Lola was a kitten," Lindsey said, carrying the dishes to the sink. "I don't think either of them is going to adjust."

Clementine left off chittering at Lola and went to the set of cat bowls on the floor near a door that I guessed led out to the garage at the side of the house. While the calico was drinking water, the white cat took advantage of this diversion to jump from the window sill. Quick as lightning, the calico wheeled and pounced. For a split second I had the impression of cats flying through the air, then they streaked from kitchen to living room. I got up and stepped to the doorway in time to see Clementine chase Lola under an end table. She growled at her rival. Lola, her fluffy white fur on end to make her look bigger, spat a reply.

"See what I mean?" Lindsey asked. "I keep telling myself when they get older they'll tolerate each other, but I'm not so sure."

"Maybe Lola will finally have enough, and bop Clementine. I'll be rooting for her."

CHAPTER 39

ICALLED TERESA BOSK FROM LINDSEY'S HOUSE. THE PHONE was busy, so I guessed she was home. I drove to west San Luis Obispo and located her Foothill Drive address, a fairly new one-story house of white stucco.

The woman who answered the door was about thirty, medium height, with fair skin and a snub nose, her oval face framed by straight brown hair that fell to her shoulders, with bangs almost to her eyebrows. She was dressed casually in a short-sleeved blouse and a long denim skirt, her feet bare.

"Ms. Bosk, my name is Jeri Howard." I handed her one of my business cards. "I'm a private investigator from Oakland."

She frowned. "What's this about?"

"Nick Talbert."

"Nick Talbert?" she repeated. "I haven't talked with him in a year, maybe more. Is this a background investigation for a job?"

"No, it isn't. I'm sorry to tell you this, Ms. Bosk. Nick's dead. He was murdered Friday night in Bakersfield."

I watched the shock move over her face. When words came, they tumbled from her mouth, disjointed. "What . . . ? How . . . ? Why . . . ? I don't understand." She stepped back, gripping the edge of her front door. "How did he die? What was he doing in Bakersfield? He moved to L.A. after he lost . . . after he left here."

"Sounds like you started to say he lost his job. Was he fired? Why?"

She didn't say anything, then she nodded slowly. "Yes, he was fired. His work started to slip when his wife filed for divorce. He missed a few deadlines, had a few warnings, got into a fight with the managing editor. Finally they let him go. So he went to L.A. and he was writing features for some alternative magazine. I don't recall the name."

"*On the Rag,*" I said. "He was working on a story that led him to Bakersfield. As to how he died, he was hit over the head with a blunt instrument. At the time of his death he was on the campus of a private school where he worked as a handyman. The owners and operators of that school are Kyle and Martina Perris."

Teresa Bosk's eyes widened. "My God," she said.

I smiled. "That's how I thought you'd react."

"I guess you'd better come in and tell me."

I followed her into the living room, which was furnished in a contemporary style and had lots of pictures of her husband and a baby with very little hair, but enough frilly outfits to tell me the child was a girl. She offered coffee and went into the kitchen, returning with two mugs. When we were settled on the sofa, I gave her an overview of what had happened to Nick Talbert, and why I was involved.

"Nick was sure Tom Shiller's death was neither an accident nor a suicide," Teresa told me.

"That leaves murder."

"Yes, it does. But he couldn't prove that Kyle or Martina Perris helped Shiller fall off that cliff. And Nick had a conflict of interest. One that led to him being taken off the story. Nick was married to a woman named Peggy Rostrow. She and Shiller were lovers."

More complications by the minute, I thought. "When was this? And when did Nick find out?"

"The affair began a year before Shiller's death. Peggy Rostrow worked as a secretary in the office up at Coast Academy. That's when she started seeing Shiller on the sly. She left that job for another one, about six months before Shiller died, and filed for divorce. Nick was devastated. He cried on my shoulder a lot. But it appeared to me that the marriage had always been rocky."

"Was Shiller the reason Peggy filed for divorce? Did they have plans to get married?"

Teresa shrugged and shook her head. "I don't know. You'll have to ask her."

"I intend to. How did Peggy react to Shiller's death?"

"Very upset, from what I heard. She left SLO shortly after his funeral. Packed up the little boy and went home to Fresno, where her family lives."

"What information did Nick have that convinced him Shiller's death wasn't suicide or an accident? And that the Perrises might be involved?"

"Nothing but a hunch, really, and that may have been colored by his dislike of the Perrises. He felt that Martina in particular had encouraged Peggy's affair with Shiller."

"Why would she do that?"

"I have no idea, other than that the two women became friends. In fact, when Peggy left the school, she went to work for Martina, who was self-employed as an educational consultant. You know what that is?"

I nodded. "Someone who recommends to unsuspecting parents that they send their children to places like the Coast Academy. What motive for murder did Nick ascribe to the Perrises?"

"The obvious reason is that they benefited from Shiller's death," she said. "Both they and Shiller owned the land where the Coast Academy was located. When Shiller died, they sold out to a developer as soon as they could, and left town. I happen to know they made some serious bucks out of that one."

"Which they used to start their own school in Bakersfield, evidently using the same model as the Coast Academy."

"I didn't know where they went after they left here, until now."

"Did Nick know?"

"That I can't tell you," Teresa said. "After Peggy left, Nick got canned, packed up his stuff, and moved to L.A. He'd call me now and then, but we didn't have much contact."

"Was he upset about being taken off the Shiller story?"

She nodded. "Very much so. He felt he could maintain his objectivity, but our editor felt otherwise. There was another reason. Nick seemed to be veering away from simply being a reporter. He'd decided all on his own that Shiller was murdered, and he was going to solve the case."

"Would you say he was obsessed?" I asked.

She narrowed her eyes. "What are you getting at?"

"Nick Talbert was in Bakersfield working on a story for *On the Rag*. But I'm wondering if he might have had another agenda, such as building evidence against Kyle and Martina Perris."

"I don't know if I'd call it obsessed," Teresa said slowly. "Whenever someone would speculate whether Shiller died by accident or killed himself, Nick would grin at me and say, 'Remember, we'll always have Paris.' But he didn't mean it the way Bogart meant it. He was talking about the Perrises. He always came back to them as suspects in Shiller's murder."

There was some irony in Bogie's famous line from *Casablanca* coming from Nick as well as Darcy. "If Nick had known the Perrises were in Bakersfield, he might have gone after them."

"Maybe. But I can't say for sure. Did he get a job at the school because the Perrises run it? Or is there some connection between the school and Nick's story?"

"That's what I'm trying to find out. Maybe he didn't know the Perrises were in Bakersfield until he got this job as a handyman at their school. It's called the Perris School, so he would have recognized the name. On the other hand, it's possible that someone connected to the school is also connected with some group that Nick encountered while researching his story. May I look at your clip file about the DA's investigation of the Coast Academy?"

"Sure. I've got clips about Shiller's death, too." I followed her to the bedroom she'd converted into an office. As we passed an open door I peered into a nursery, where a curly dark head was visible in a white crib. The baby had acquired some hair since the photos.

As Lindsey Page had told me, the investigation had been triggered when a female student, a juvenile who was identified only as Jane Doe in the court proceedings, had filed a complaint against the Perris School, and individually against Thomas Shiller and Kyle Perris. Jane Doe alleged that she had been abused physically and emotionally while attending the school. The complaint had been filed six weeks before Shiller took his header off the cliff at Montaña de Oro.

I read some of Teresa's sidebars for background on the Coast Academy. The school had been in operation for three years before its troubles began. Like its successor, the Perris School, it had a year-round schedule of classes and activities. It targeted parents with problem adolescents, those who would pay big bucks for a twelve-, sixteen-, or twenty-week program designed to turn those trouble-makers into model citizens. Teresa had dug up the same stats on Kyle Perris that I had. He was supposedly an educational consultant and he'd been affiliated with the Pinewood School in Walsenburg, Colorado before coming to California. What was new information for me was that Thomas Shiller had been affiliated with the same school.

"What do you know about this Pinewood School?" I asked her, mindful that I still hadn't heard from Carl Burnham.

"When I called the school to get some background on Shiller and Perris, they wouldn't tell me anything. What little information I got was from someone I know at the *Rocky Mountain News* in Denver. It's a combination school and wilderness program."

"What was the end result of the DA's investigation?" I asked.

"It didn't really go anywhere, since Shiller died," Teresa told me. "But the girl who filed the complaint is an adult now. Two months ago she filed a civil lawsuit against Perris and Shiller's estate."

CHAPTER 40

KYLE AND MARTINA PERRIS WERE GOING TO HAVE SOME serious financial problems if Carly Nason prevailed in her lawsuit against them. The young woman was asking for general, special, and punitive damages. Added to that were attorney's fees and any other costs she could squeeze out of the defendants.

If half of what I read about the general allegations was true, I thought she and her lawyers would have no trouble convincing a jury to get out the checkbook. That would probably mean economic ruin for the Perrises and their school.

The complaint listed causes of action, ranging from false imprisonment, assault and battery, and intentional infliction of emotional distress, to invasion of privacy, sexual harassment, and fraud, deceit, and concealment. It also listed several other defendants besides Kyle and Martina Perris. I only recognized two other names—Valley Security and George Larsen.

"Heavy-duty stuff. With lots of zeros after the dollar signs." I looked up from the complaint, which had been filed in San Mateo County, just south of San Francisco. I didn't recognize the name of the law firm, but three attorneys were listed and they had a San Mateo address. "Where did you get this?"

"A friend of mine works at the courthouse in Redwood City. He saw the court filing, recognized the names, and got a copy of the complaint. Would you like one?"

"I certainly would."

Teresa had a plain-paper fax machine that doubled as a copier.

She unclipped the pages and set them into the paper feeder. "I did a follow-up story mentioning the lawsuit," Teresa told me as the pages fed through the machine. "Carly Nason's not talking to reporters. She must be saving it for the trial, though a date hasn't been set. I did talk with one of her lawyers, though. He told me all the parties had been served."

Which meant Dr. Perris had a close encounter with a process server some time in the past two months.

Much as I would have liked my own interview with Carly Nason, I figured the best course of action would be to let Cece Bromley talk with her attorneys. They might be more forthcoming if they heard from another lawyer. Especially if they thought it would help their case against the Perrises.

Teresa gave me some additional copies, pertinent information from her files on the police investigation into Tom Shiller's death. I went back to Lindsey's house, to collect my things and eat lunch. Before we ate, I called Cece to tell her about Carly Nason's lawsuit against the Perrises and everyone else who'd had a hand in her sojourn at the Coast Academy. Lindsey had a fax machine in her office, so I told Cece I'd fax the complaint to her after we ended our conversation.

"I'll contact Nason's attorneys to see if I can pry some additional information out of them," Cece said. "Are you coming back to Bakersfield today?"

"Fresno first," I told her. "I've got to talk with Peggy Rostrow, Nick's ex. Somehow she's tied up in all of this."

"Get back here as soon as you can," Cece told me. "Dan Stefano and Adele Gregory are arriving at the end of the day."

After lunch I called Dr. Ira Blum in Fresno. When he heard why I was calling, he invited me to dinner at his home. I headed for my car. An hour later my Toyota left U.S. 101 North and I drove east on Highway 46. It was here, near Cholame in rural eastern San Luis Obispo County, that James Dean had wrapped his silver Porsche around a tree on September 30, 1955. Past Cholame I took Highway 41, angling northeast through Kettleman City and Lemoore toward Fresno.

It was late Friday afternoon when I entered the city limits. I pulled into a grocery store parking lot, dug out the notebook where I'd written Peggy Rostrow's address and phone number, and consulted my Fresno map.

Peggy lived on Maroa Avenue in the Tower District, a pleasant neighborhood featuring a mix of older homes as well as restaurants and shops. I drove east on Olive Avenue, past the old movie theater which gave the area its name, and turned left at Lauck's Bakery, a red and white building that anchored the corner of Olive and Maroa.

I parked my car at the curb and got out, leaving the Toyota's stuffiness for the dry baked air of the Valley summer. The neighborhood's background music included an underlay of nearby traffic noise, punctuated here and there by shouts from a group of children playing in a front yard across the street.

The one-story stucco bungalow where Peggy Rostrow lived looked as though it had been built in the thirties. The front yard was shaded by a huge camphor tree. A late-model Chevy station wagon was parked in the driveway. I stepped onto the small porch and rang the bell.

At first there was no response. Then I heard a voice call, "Just a minute." A moment later the front door opened.

She was in her late twenties, I guessed, barefoot, looking as though I'd awakened her from a nap. Brown hair fell in untidy waves to her shoulders and a pair of pale blue eyes seemed a bit fuzzy as she stared out at me. She wore wrinkled blue cotton shorts with a ribbed sleeveless knit shirt cut low enough to reveal the tops of her small, round breasts.

"Peggy Rostrow?"

"Yeah." She ran one hand through her hair, disarranging it further. "Who're you? What do you want?"

"My name's Jeri Howard. I'm a private investigator. I'd like to talk with you about your ex-husband, Nick Talbert."

She narrowed her eyes and when she spoke, her voice held a hint of exasperation. "A private investigator? What about Nick? Is he in some kind of trouble?"

As though she expected him to be, I thought. But she didn't know Nick was dead yet. "It's a little more complicated than that. You know, it's really hot out here. May I come in?"

"It's not much cooler in here," she said with a wry smile.

She was right, I discovered when I pulled open the screen door
and stepped inside. The small, rectangular living room to my right
didn't seem perceptibly cooler. A ceiling fan making lazy rotations
above did little more than stir the air. It certainly did nothing to
lower the temperature.

I looked around me. A woven rug covered most of the scuffed
wooden floor. In the far corner was a large TV on a stand and below
this, a shelf holding a VCR and several Disney videos. Resting on
a table at the end of the sofa nearest me was a framed photo of a little boy, the same child whose picture I'd seen in Talbert's L.A.
apartment.

"That's my little boy, Danny," she said.

"Nice-looking kid."

Nubby beige fabric covered the sofa, and several flowered pillows
were heaped at one end. The coffee table in front of the sofa held an
assortment of magazines. Resting atop these I saw a glass with melt-
ing ice cubes at the bottom and a plate, empty except for a few
crumbs of cracker and cheese.

"Had a snack after I got home from work," Peggy said, seeing the
direction of my gaze. She picked up the dishes. "I'm gonna get a refill on this iced tea. You want some?"

"Yes, thanks."

She carried the plate and glass toward the back of the house,
where a doorway led to the kitchen. To the left of this was another
opening, leading to a hallway. A glance inside showed me the
arrangement of the rest of the house, one bedroom in front, another
in back, and a bathroom in between.

I sat down on the sofa and sifted through the magazines that covered the coffee table. Most were aimed at women, and a couple were
of the gossipy, celebrity-oriented variety. Two others caught my eye
and I leafed through them. One I'd heard of. It looked like a glossy-
paged news magazine, but when I opened it I found articles and ad-
vertisements that trumpeted extremist views, hitting all the bases
from survivalism to conspiracy theories, militias to tax protests. The
second looked more like a newsletter and spewed forth more of
the same.

"Those aren't mine," Peggy said, a bit defensively, when she returned to the living room and saw what I was reading. She bore

glasses of iced tea in either hand. "My cousin Cliff brought them over. He's into that kind of stuff."

"Really?" I took one of the glasses and sipped the cold liquid gratefully. "How much is he into it?"

"Cliff's in some militia," she said, sitting cross-legged on the sofa.

"There's a lot of that going on these days," I said. "All over the country."

"Around here it's just a bunch of guys who like to drink beer, dress up in camouflage, and go play war in the foothills." She shrugged. "It's pretty harmless, right?"

"Some people don't think it's harmless."

"You sound like Nick." She raised her glass and took a sip. "It's like I told him, everyone gets pissed off at the government at one time or another. Whether it's the IRS or some environmental regulation. Like that farmer who got in trouble doing something on his own land, just because of some rat that was on the endangered species list. I mean, people are more important than rats, right?"

I didn't comment, just smiled politely and let her fill the ensuing silence.

"Cliff's big on the Second Amendment," she continued, glancing at the magazines. "He and Nick used to argue for hours about gun control and the government. To tell you the truth, I mostly ignore it. Cliff always has a mad on about something, and Nick always likes a good argument."

Her use of the present tense underscored the need for someone to tell her Nick was dead. It looked like that would be me.

"When was the last time you saw Nick?"

She thought for a moment. "Early May. He was here for a couple of days to see Danny." She gestured toward the photograph I'd seen earlier. "Nick didn't say why he'd suddenly decided to grace us with his presence. It was the middle of the week, and he hadn't called to let me know he was coming. I assumed he was on some sort of free-lance assignment and we were en route."

"Where is your little boy now?" I asked.

"Over at my mother's. She takes care of him while I'm at work, when he's not in school, that is." She glanced at her watch. It was just after six. Then she frowned. "Say, you never did tell me why you wanted to talk about Nick."

I used one of the magazines for a coaster and set down my glass. "Peggy, I'm sorry to be the one to tell you this. Nick's dead."

She'd been about to take a sip of tea. Now she sat stunned and open-mouthed. I reached over and took her glass just as it started to slip from her fingers.

"How?" she said when she found her voice. "When?"

"He was murdered last Friday night in Bakersfield."

"Bakersfield? What the hell was he doing in Bakersfield?"

"Working on a story. One that may have gotten him killed."

"Story about what?" Her face held a mixture of grief and anger. Though she and Nick had been divorced, and despite the circumstances that led to their breakup, I guessed that Peggy still had some residue of feeling for her ex-husband.

"He didn't tell you?"

"No. When he was writing something he'd get into this investigative-reporter mode. Everything's a secret, to protect the source, to make sure you don't get scooped."

"Nick was working on a story about extremist groups," I said. "Like the people who beat up the Stanislaus County assessor. Or the ones who planned to blow up the IRS office in Reno." I glanced down at the publications on the coffee table. "You said your cousin Cliff is involved with a militia."

"You're talking about people who blow things up." Disbelief was etched on her face. "I told you, these are just guys who putz around the woods on the weekends."

"Maybe that's true. But there are a lot of people right here in the San Joaquin Valley who espouse some radical views and seem willing to back them up with violence."

"But not Cliff. I can't believe he'd . . . Cliff's not an extremist," she said stubbornly. "He's just . . . well, he's vocal about a lot of things."

If Cliff was passing out literature like that on the coffee table, he seemed extreme to me. I backtracked a bit, trying to stay on the subject of Nick.

"You said Nick and Cliff used to argue a lot about politics. Did Nick see Cliff while he was here in May?"

"No. He asked about him. But he asked about the whole family. I fixed dinner and Nick asked about Mom, Dad, everyone. He didn't zero in on Cliff, if that's what you're driving at."

I sat back, wondering if it might be as simple as this, just Nick visiting his ex-wife and his son because he was in the Valley. But he'd also been here to interview Ira Blum. I took another sip of tea.

"Peggy, I want you to tell me exactly what happened when Nick visited. In as much detail as you can remember."

She took a deep breath. "Okay. It was a Tuesday. He showed up just as I was getting home from work. I'd stopped at my mother's to pick up Danny. So it must have been about six, like now. I fixed dinner, we talked, he read to Danny and put him to bed. I let Nick sleep on the sofa, because he hadn't made arrangements to stay anywhere."

"What did you talk about?"

"Like I said, he asked about Mom and Dad, my brothers and sisters, Cliff."

"Did he ask about any of your other cousins?"

"No, just Cliff. Said something about how he liked to argue with Cliff, and asked what he was doing now."

"What did you tell him?"

"That Cliff had joined this militia. When I told Nick that, he asked me all sorts of questions about it. Like he was interviewing me, but he was always like that."

"What did you tell Nick?"

"Just what I told you. That's all I know. Then Nick asked me about my job. I told him that we'd been busy. George has been out of town a lot."

"George?" I asked, trying to hide the fact that the name triggered a reaction.

"George Larsen, my boss. He's a security consultant. Does a lot of work for big firms up and down the Valley."

T HAT WASN'T ALL GEORGE LARSEN DID.
I wondered if Peggy Rostrow knew about her employer's lucrative sideline. Or maybe he kept the details of the child transport business to himself.

It had to be the same George Larsen and Valley Security listed as named defendants in Carly Nason's lawsuit, who had, four years earlier, snatched Nason from her parents' house in San Mateo and transported her to the Coast Academy. It was certainly the same firm that two months ago abducted Darcy Stefano from her home in Alameda and transported her to the Perris School in Bakersfield.

No more interesting coincidences. There were too many of them running around this case to be just happenstance.

"Does your firm have another office?" I asked, just to be sure. "In Southern California?"

Peggy looked surprised as she confirmed what I already knew. "In L.A. Actually it's in North Hollywood, on Lankershim Boulevard. George spends about half his time down there."

"Does he have clients in Bakersfield?"

"Yes, I told you he worked all up and down the Valley. And no," she added, looking annoyed, "I'm not going to tell you who his clients are."

I shifted gears, in the direction of Peggy's past employment. "You used to work at the Coast Academy in San Luis Obispo. You met a man there named Thomas Shiller."

Her face reddened. "Look, that was all over a long time ago."

"Your marriage? Or your affair with Shiller?"

"You've been talking to someone," she fired back. "Let me guess. Little Miss Perfect, Teresa Bosk, Nick's old friend from the SLO paper. I always thought there was something between those two."

"Why did you get involved with Shiller?" I asked.

"Because he was a kind and decent man," Peggy said. "The rest is my business."

"Even his death?"

"It was a horrible accident. Tom . . ." Her mouth tightened. "Tom was hiking with some friends of ours, Kyle and Martina Perris. He stumbled over a cliff. Kyle tried to climb down to Tom while Martina ran for help, but it was too late." Emotions struggled on her face, as though she were trying to convince herself that was in fact the case, and had been trying to ever since he died.

"I understand Nick thought otherwise. That he even thought Kyle and Martina Perris had something to do with Shiller's death."

"Nick's as bad as Cliff, looking for conspiracies where they don't exist." Peggy shook her head. "Look, my marriage to Nick was on the rocks a long time before Tom and I connected. I'd been planning to file for divorce before Nick found out about Tom."

"How did Nick react?"

"He was angry." She bit her lip, then continued. "I suppose that was to be expected, that he'd be angry with me. He was angry with Tom as well. And when Tom died, that didn't make Nick feel any better. He couldn't let go of his anger, so he turned it on Kyle and Martina."

"Why? Because they were Shiller's partners? Or were they friends with Shiller as well?"

"I don't know how close they were. Just that Kyle and Tom had known each other for a while. They'd worked together at some school in Colorado before they decided to start their own in California."

That much I knew, from the information Teresa Bosk had given me. "I understand you and Martina were friends. You went to work for her after you left the Coast Academy, six months before Shiller died."

Peggy shrugged that off, but the movement of her shoulders looked forced rather than casual. "That just happened. Martina's secretary quit about the time I decided it wasn't a good idea for me to continue working at the school. So I went to work for Martina. It was better money and a shorter commute."

"Teresa Bosk told me Nick thought Martina encouraged your relationship with Shiller."

"Oh, that's ridiculous," Peggy declared. "She did no such thing. It's just that she was very supportive when I told her I was seeing Tom, when I needed to talk, or cry on someone's shoulder."

I wondered what they'd talked about during those emotional sessions, especially if Martina was simply pretending to be a friend. It's easy to let too much slip when you're crying on someone's shoulder.

"What was Shiller's state of mind right before he died? I know the school was the target of some sort of DA's probe."

"I know what you're getting at, but Tom didn't kill himself." Peggy's mouth was set in a stubborn line. "It was an accident. Kyle and Martina saw him fall. Besides, he had nothing to fear from that investigation. I worked at that school for a year, and I never saw anything out of the ordinary."

Or maybe she didn't want to see. "Surely he was concerned about the investigation. Something like that could have put the school out of business."

"Of course he was concerned, about that, and the . . ." She shook her head vigorously. "But Tom wouldn't have committed suicide."

"There was something else bothering him, though." I'd picked up on her unspoken words. "What was it? Something to do with the school?"

"Nothing, really. Tom mentioned he thought there were some financial irregularities. He was going to have someone audit the books. But Martina said at the time he was being overly cautious."

"You told Martina about Shiller's plan to audit Coast Academy's books," I said slowly. "Was this before or after his death?"

"A few days before. It's not like I planned to tell her. It just came up in conversation one day while I was at work."

I'll bet it did. What better way to keep tabs on your husband's partner than to become good friends with the man's latest girlfriend? In fact, if Nick had been correct in his belief that the Perrises had encouraged Peggy's relationship with Shiller, what better way of keeping Shiller distracted?

"Have you and Martina stayed in touch?" I asked.

"Oh, yes," Peggy said. "We talk on the phone a lot. I've even been down to Bakersfield to visit them. They have a lovely place off Panorama Drive. Martina and Kyle loaned me money when I wanted to leave San Luis Obispo and move back to Fresno. Martina grew up here in Fresno, just like I did. In fact, it was Martina who helped me get this job."

"How did she manage that?"

"George is Martina's brother." Peggy took a sip from her iced tea.

Now that was an interesting piece of the puzzle. But there were still a few missing. "Did George do any other favors for his sister, besides giving you a job? Such as work for Martina or Kyle?"

"Not Martina. Not then, anyway. George did some work for the Coast Academy, though. Now he does the same for the Perris School, the place Kyle and Martina started down in Bakersfield. He calls it deliveries, but I'm not sure what he's delivering."

He's delivering people, I thought, usually against their will. Was Peggy really as clueless as she seemed about what kind of work George Larsen was doing, and her relationship with the Perrises?

"Did Nick know the Perrises were living in Bakersfield? That they'd started another school?"

She shrugged again, and looked at the clock. It was six-thirty. She may have been interested in the time. Probably she was more interested in nudging me toward the front door. "I may have said something, when he was here in May."

I mulled over what she'd told me. It muddied the waters some when I considered Nick Talbert's state of mind and his reasons for going to Bakersfield. Granted, he was working on the article about extremist groups. I was sure that was why he'd quizzed Peggy about her cousin Cliff. But I was less sure of his motivation for getting a job at the Perris School. Was there a tie-in to the story?

Or was it more personal? Both Teresa and Peggy had mentioned Nick's obsession with Tom Shiller's death and his conviction that the Perrises had something to do with it. It was quite possible he'd been sidetracked by that when he learned that they'd set up shop in Bakersfield.

What better way to keep an eye on them than to get a job at their school? But what if either Kyle or Martina had recognized him as Nick Talbert, Peggy's ex, from their days in San Luis Obispo? Since Peggy had worked for Martina then, I was willing to bet she had at least seen a photograph of Nick, at some time or another.

A car door slammed outside. Then I heard two voices, one adult, the other the higher piping sound of a child. I looked out the front window and saw a man and a little boy coming up the walk toward the house.

"Oh, my God," Peggy said. "It's Danny."

I glanced at her face, stricken with the realization that there was no easy way to tell her little boy his father was dead. She got to her feet, moving toward the door.

"Who's the man with him?" I asked.

She peered through the glass and looked even more worried, given the earlier direction of our conversation. "That's my cousin Cliff."

Clifford Rostrow didn't look like someone who liked to dress up in camouflage and play war in the Sierra Nevada foothills. He looked perfectly normal, which made his belief in the extremist views of the magazines he'd left with his cousin all the more disturbing.

He was in his late thirties, with short, brown hair and light blue eyes in a round, fair face. He stood politely in the living room, dressed in a pair of jeans and a blue short-sleeved cotton knit shirt. He held a plate covered with aluminum foil. He nodded in my direction as Peggy introduced me as Jeri Howard, with no mention of my occupation or why I was here.

"Have you eaten dinner?" Peggy knelt and hugged her son. In person Danny Talbert looked more like his father than he had in the photograph on the end table. He'd probably resemble him even more as he grew older. Right now he had a tanned, wiry body, dressed for summertime play in shorts, T-shirt, and sneakers.

"Yeah. Grandma fixed chicken. And peach pie. It was dee-lish." He looked at me curiously, then shifted his eyes away shyly when he saw me watching him. "She sent some pie home with us so we can have it later."

"I was coming this way," Clifford said in a pleasant tenor. He handed Peggy the foil-wrapped dish. "So I thought I'd bring Danny home and save your mom the trip. Can't stay long. Got a meeting to go to."

"What sort of meeting?" I asked him.

Something flickered in Clifford's eyes, as though he were gauging the reason for my question. He didn't answer.

"Peggy was showing me some of the magazines you'd brought over," I said, priming the pump.

"Are you interested in those magazines?" he asked.

"Curious," I said, which was always the truth.

"I belong to a jural society."

I wasn't sure what a jural society was. I'd have to ask Ira Blum. "I thought Peggy said you belonged to a militia." Might as well see what sort of response that got.

Clifford scowled at Peggy. She glared back.

Then she took Danny by the arm. "You're looking grubby, son of mine. Time you had a bath." He set up a chorus of protest. "Bath first. Then we'll watch a video and eat peach pie."

And somehow, I thought, Peggy would tell the boy his father was dead.

Peggy detoured through the kitchen, setting the pie on the counter, then led Danny to the back of the house. In the ensuing silence I heard water running into the bathtub.

By that time Clifford had smoothed the frown from his face. "Are you interested in militias?" he asked.

I shrugged. "I've read about them in the newspapers, seen some stuff on TV."

"The liberal media exaggerates," he said.

"Does it?" I wondered which combination of buttons I had to push to get Clifford Rostrow started. It was obvious he didn't trust me. But he wanted to tell me his side of the story anyway. "Peggy tells me you and your friends play soldier."

"Peggy doesn't know anything about it." There was an edge to his voice. "That's Nick's influence. Do you know Nick?"

"Never met him," I said truthfully. "He's a reporter, right?" That he was one of the liberal media Clifford Rostrow disliked so much went without saying. "You and he must have had some interesting discussions the last time he was here. May, wasn't it?"

"How did you know that?" Clifford looked at me with suspicion.

"Peggy mentioned it."

"Peggy mentioned what?" she asked, coming into the living room from the back of the house.

"That Nick was here in May. And that he and Clifford used to argue about politics," I said.

Peggy didn't want to go down that road. Instead she set her mouth in a thin line. "You're still here?" she asked pointedly, all but ushering me out the door.

"I'll be in touch," I told her as I made my exit, wondering what she and her cousin Clifford would talk about when I was gone.

CHAPTER 42

IRA BLUM LIVED ON ACACIA DRIVE, OFF NORTH PALM AVE-nue below West Shaw Avenue, near the Fig Garden Shopping Center. My stomach was growling by the time I parked the Toyota in front of a large, two-story house in the pleasant wooded neighbor-hood. It was after seven and the summer sun was edging toward the horizon in the west.

"I'm later than I'd planned," I said, when the professor answered his front door.

"Not a problem," he assured me.

Blum looked as though he'd navigated through sixty-plus years of life with pugnacious resolve, and he wasn't letting his age slow him down any. His face was square-jawed and clean-shaven, mapped with networks of tiny wrinkles. He was shorter than I, about five-feet-six, with a tiny patch of white hair embellishing his mostly bald head. He wore sandals and his stocky frame was clad in comfortable brown slacks and a Cal State Fresno T-shirt.

He led me through a comfortable living room decorated with books and family photographs. A big golden retriever came to greet me with a friendly wag of its tail and a curious nose. Past the living room was a formal dining room, with an oval table set for three. A moment later Mrs. Blum entered from the kitchen, carrying a large pottery bowl filled to the brim with vegetables. She was short, too, with a generous figure and curly gray hair.

"Hi, I'm Carol," she told me. "It's too hot to cook, so I fixed a salad."

"That sounds wonderful," I said. By now I was really hungry. Blum offered wine, but I declined, since I was planning to drive back to Bakersfield after I talked with him. Instead I opted for mineral water.

"I've met your father, Timothy Howard, at one conference or another," he said, when we were seated at the table. He passed me the salad bowl. "And Lindsey Page told me all about your adventures in France."

"Who knew it would lead to this," I said, helping myself. I gave him the highlights of my current investigation as we ate dinner.

Afterwards, Blum steered me back to his office, a room off the den cluttered with a computer, fax, printer, and copier, plus several filing cabinets. "I often work at home," he said, waving me toward an overstuffed sofa covered in faded plaid. He sat down on one end and I took the other.

"Lindsey tells me you were a hidden child."

Blum nodded. "Yes, like your friend Mrs. Gregory. Lindsey told me all about her when she returned from Paris. My experience is similar, in some respects. I was born in Germany, though my parents left in the thirties and moved to Amsterdam. I was seven years old when the Germans invaded the Netherlands in 1940. When they started rounding up Jews for the forced labor camps in 1942, we went into hiding. My parents found a place in Amsterdam, and my brother and I went to live with a family out in the country. Unfortunately my parents were discovered the next year. They were shipped to Westerbork transit camp, and later Auschwitz, where they were killed." He stopped and took a deep breath before continuing. "After the war my brother and I lived with relatives who later immigrated to the States."

"I'm sure these memories are painful, even after all these years." I recalled Adele's response to her experience. She'd avoided thinking about it, until her husband's death and her friendship with Shoshanna had forced her to acknowledge the past. And I remembered what Simon Blake had told me of his grandmother, giving testimony at the Museum of Tolerance.

"Painful, yes," Blum said. "The passage of time doesn't dim what I . . . what we went through. But if I—and others like me—don't talk about what it was like to experience the Holocaust, others will not learn. Of course, some people, like the ones Nick Talbert was researching, will never learn. I was sorry to learn he'd been killed. I warned him to be careful. These people he was proposing to infiltrate are very dangerous."

"How dangerous? I met someone earlier this evening who supposedly belongs to a militia. He talks the talk, but certainly looks perfectly average."

"Not everyone who puts on a set of cammies and goes out to crawl around the woods with his buddies on militia days is an extremist," Blum said. "But many are."

"Are they being co-opted?"

"That's exactly what's happening," Blum said. "The old-line white supremacists and neo-Nazis have moved in and are consolidating power. They've found a fertile field of recruits. Let me put it this way. If a racist walks down the street wearing a robe and a hood, he'll turn off a lot of people. But if he talks a line of antigovernment rhetoric . . ."

"He'll win more converts," I finished. "Like David Duke in Louisiana."

"Of course," Blum said. "The message is obscured, therefore more palatable. The militias may have started out as a bunch of average guys. There are hunters angry about antigun legislation; farmers, ranchers, and loggers angry about environmental laws; anyone with a beef about regulations, whether they're federal, state, or local. Who among us hasn't been upset with some governmental entity?"

I nodded, remembering some of the unkind things I'd said about the IRS around tax time. "So the extremists view this disaffection as a way to tap into the middle class. People they haven't had access to before."

"Exactly. That angry white male may be a stereotype, but in many ways the stereotype fits. He—and she—are feeling squeezed, economically and politically, and they're fodder for the extremists. We've become a fractious nation, Jeri. Instead of viewing ourselves simply as Americans, we're dividing ourselves with hyphens."

"So who's in charge, among the old-line racists?"

"The Klan is ever present. And these days if you scratch some of the militia leaders, you'll find people associated with Christian Identity or the Aryan movement. The Weavers are a classic example," Blum added, invoking memories of the events of a few years ago at Ruby Ridge in Idaho.

"Weaver was a neo-Nazi associated with the Militia of Montana," he continued, "which has long been associated with the Aryan Nations Congress, which advocates the establishment of a white racist state. Both Weavers were heavily into Christian Identity. You know what that is?"

"I've heard of it. Give me some details."

"It's a perversion of everything Christianity professes to be," Blum said. "The so-called Identity movement is a loosely affiliated collection of 'churches,' run by white Christian extremists, a millennialist sect with visions of impending apocalypse. Their theology teaches that the Jews are the seed of Satan, anyone whose skin is black or brown is inferior, so-called mud people. In their view, 'Euro-Americans,' specifically northern Europeans, are God's chosen people."

"Aryans," I said. "This sounds a lot like the Know-Nothing movement in the nineteenth century. I know they targeted Catholics and immigrants."

"Very similar," Blum agreed. "CI also has roots in 'Anglo-Israelism.' An obscure movement, also nineteenth-century, that believed Europeans were descendants of the ten lost tribes of Israel."

"How can anyone buy into this stuff?" I shook my head.

"But you see, these groups have become quite adept at packaging their message. They've softened the virulent racist stuff and hidden it behind the antigovernment feeling that's sprung up over the past few years." Blum shook his head. "Mainstream politicians made the Weavers—and David Koresh—into their poster children. Some of those politicians may be reexamining that position, however, after the Oklahoma City bombing and the Freemen standoff in Montana."

"I agree with your assessment. They're dangerous."

Blum nodded. "True believers are usually dangerous. You can't reason with them. They're always right, everyone else is always wrong." He paused, gathering steam. "Pragmatists believe in considering the other person's point of view and working things out.

Ideologues don't. I'd say the most dangerous ones are those who buy into the Identity movement. They claim to be 'Christian patriots,' and they're frequently violent. In fact, many CI adherents believe specific passages in the Bible give them an excuse for violence. The Phineas Priesthood, for example, uses a story in the Old Testament book of Numbers to justify bank robbery and murder."

"Let's backtrack to some specifics," I said. "Namely your conversation with Nick Talbert in May. How did he contact you?"

"Someone at the Wiesenthal Center gave him my name and he called me at the university." Blum shifted position on the sofa. "I've been tracking Klan and neo-Nazi activity in the Valley for years. After Talbert did his initial research in L.A. he figured I was the next person to interview. I agreed to meet with him when he arrived in Fresno. We had a long talk and he looked at some of the materials I've collected."

"I'm trying to figure out why he went to Bakersfield. He had plenty of material to work with in L.A., or right here in Fresno. But he worked for the Fresno *Bee* some years ago, so I suppose he thought he might be recognized if he went undercover."

"He may have been recognized anyway," Blum said. "While he was here, he mentioned that his ex-wife's birth name is Rostrow. I asked if she was related to a man named Clifford Rostrow. He said yes, and that he planned to talk with Rostrow. I advised him against it."

I leaned forward. "That's the average-looking guy I met tonight. I was at Peggy Rostrow's place before I came over here."

"I hope you didn't let Rostrow know you were a private investigator."

I shook my head. "Peggy didn't tell him, either, at least not while I was there. She probably will, though. He seemed suspicious of me anyway. Why did you tell Nick not to approach him?"

"I've had my eye on Rostrow for quite a while," Blum said. "He got sucked into the extremist movement the way I described earlier, after a run-in with the IRS a few years back. He became a tax protester and stopped paying taxes altogether."

"He told me he was a member of a jural society. What exactly is that?"

"Jural societies are similar to the Freemen," Blum said. "They don't believe in government above the county level. Here in California, such groups don't recognize the state constitution beyond the original, written in 1849. They've declared, all on their own, that any amendments are null, void, and had no foundation in law. In other words, they pick and choose what aspects of the constitution, both federal and state, they think are valid. It was members of a group called the Juris Christian Associates who assaulted the Stanislaus County assessor, triggered by her refusal to file some bogus liens."

"I've read of some monetary scams by these outfits," I said.

"Yes, and Rostrow's in the thick of it. He's part of a group that's counterfeiting government pay warrants. I've seen some of these. They look like perfectly legitimate government checks. Rostrow and his buddies are passing them out all over the Valley. They've defrauded the government of millions."

"So there's a lot of money flowing through these organizations." Where there was money, in my experience, there was trouble.

"Absolutely," Blum declared. "Not only from bogus warrants, but that average guy we're talking about, the one who has joined a militia, is contributing part of his paycheck as well."

"What are they doing with it?"

"Buying weapons." He got up from the sofa and went to a four-drawer lateral filing cabinet behind his cluttered desk. "Here's an article that was in *Klanwatch*, which is published by the Southern Poverty Law Center. When the feds raided the Viper Militia in Arizona, they found a huge cache of weapons, ammunition, and explosives. The militias have to get that money from somewhere."

I glanced through the article, noting that the raid had netted surveillance videos of federal buildings in Phoenix as well as lists of government targets that included police stations and communications centers. The specter of the bombed-out federal building in Oklahoma City rose before my eyes as I handed the copy of *Klanwatch* back to Blum. He stuck it back into the file folder, which he dropped onto his desk.

"You think Rostrow found out what Nick was up to, and tipped someone that he was a reporter?"

"It's quite possible. There's a lot of movement up and down the Valley, people attending meetings of one sort or another. There's a

right-wing radio station in Delano, in northern Kern County. Rostrow turns up on the talk shows now and then. I know there are militias down there as well, but I don't know much about them. So far
whoever is at the helm is keeping a very low profile. Someone's got
to be funding this activity. I have a feeling Rostrow's group is
involved."

"What else did Talbert ask about?"

"Skinheads and Klan activity. These days the skinheads are taking their marching orders from various arms of the Klan."

"What would you say if I told you a couple of skinheads and an
older man tossed Talbert's apartment the night he was killed?"

"I'd say Talbert most definitely pushed the wrong buttons while
he was down in Bakersfield. Find those skinheads and you'll find
who killed him. What did the older man look like?"

"Brown hair, fair. A lot like a man who works at the Perris
School. And a lot like Clifford Rostrow. While Nick was looking at
the files, did you notice if anything made a particular impression on
him?"

Blum thought for a moment. "Come to think of it, he did seem
quite interested in one photograph. I'm damned if I can remember
which one. But it was in the Klan files."

"I'd like to take a look at those files, then. Maybe something will
click."

Blum dug the files out of the cabinet. There were several fat ac-
cordion folders in roughly chronological order, dating from the
Klan's political heyday in the 1920s to the present day. "I'll go make
some coffee," he said. "Decaf or high-test?"

The drive to Bakersfield that awaited me was easily another two
hours. "I need all the caffeine I can get."

He laughed. "High-test it is. I'll bring some of Carol's double
fudge cake, too. You'll really be wired."

I pulled materials from the first folder and spread them out on the
coffee table in front of the sofa, paying particular attention to the
photographs of men and women, fellow Californians from the 1920s
and 1930s, dressed in the white sheets and hoods of the Ku Klux
Klan. I looked at the earlier photographs with distaste tempered by
a historian's detachment. It was a long time ago, but the race hatred
of that era played a part in the 1940s removal and internment of

Japanese American citizens all over the state. I moved to the second folder, then the third, marveling at the persistence of hatred.

Blum came back into his office carrying a tray with coffee and cake for both of us. I took a break to sample some of Mrs. Blum's cooking, then turned back to the photographs.

Midway through the fourth folder, something clicked.

CHAPTER 43

THE PHOTOGRAPH LOOKED AS THOUGH IT HAD BEEN TAKEN about twenty-five years ago, judging from the hairstyle of the young woman in it. She was perhaps sixteen, with light brown hair and blue eyes that looked right into the camera as she smiled. Her fingernails gleamed with iridescent pink as she held a platter containing a birthday cake, tipped slightly forward so the photographer could record the decoration on top.

It was what she wore that caught my eye and made the image stick. It was a photograph I'd seen somewhere before in a magazine or a book. A white Klan robe fell from her shoulders to the floor and a matching hood perched in bizarre jauntiness atop her head.

The cake decoration was memorable on its own. A burning cross was etched obscenely in red and yellow atop the white icing.

"Who is this?" I demanded, the urgency in my voice bringing Ira Blum to attention. He leaned toward me and glanced at the photograph. Then I flipped it over to see if there was anything written on the back. A few lines had been scribbled with a black felt tip pen, what looked like a couple of names and a date.

"Martina Larsen," Blum said, squinting as he deciphered his own handwriting. "Her father, John Larsen, was a Grand Dragon of the California Klan, about thirty years ago. That was taken at his birthday party."

"Did Larsen have a son named George?"

"Yes. He still lives here in Fresno. And he's still active in the Klan. As for Martina Larsen, she married a man named Earl Waller. He was active in the Order, which was a violent offshoot of Aryan Nations. Those in the Order financed their activities by robbing banks, which was justified, according to them, because all the banks are owned by Jews."

"And they killed that talk show host in Denver," I added.

"Alan Berg, yes. Waller and some of his buddies wound up on the losing side of a shoot-out with the police during a robbery in Colorado Springs. I don't know what happened to Martina after Waller died."

"I do," I said, getting to my feet. "She married a man named Kyle Perris. They run the school in Bakersfield where Talbert was killed. Before that they lived in San Luis Obispo. Nick must have recognized her when he saw this picture."

"That picture's been reproduced many times in books and magazines," Blum said. "There's even a copy in a slide show down at the Museum of Tolerance. Talbert could have seen it there as well as here. Of course, this copy has the identifying information."

"This picture connects the Perrises to the story Nick was working on," I said, my mind trying out the possibilities. "So it's no accident he took a job at that school. I thought maybe it was because he was convinced the Perrises had something to do with the death of Kyle's partner in San Luis Obispo. That may have started it, but this . . ."

I looked at the picture of Martina's younger but still recognizable self, decked out in her Klan regalia. "This was what Nick was after. This is the bigger story. If Martina was brought up in a Klan family and her brother's still active, I'll give you odds she's got ties to some extremist group. That's why Nick was trying to talk his editor into more time to do the story. But something went wrong." And I thought I knew what. Gillie recognized Talbert. Had she said something that tipped off the Perrises?

I fortified myself for the two-hour drive to Bakersfield with another cup of coffee, sipping the strong brew while I used Ira Blum's copier to duplicate the photograph as well as some of his files on Martina Larsen Perris, her father, her brother, and Clifford Rostrow, for good measure. Before I left, I called Cece and told her I had plenty to report.

"Come right to my house as soon as you get here," she said.

I glanced at my watch. It was after nine. "It'll be past eleven."

"It's okay. I'm a night owl. Besides, now that Darcy's father and grandmother are here, we need to plot some strategy. They got in this afternoon and I'm meeting them in my office tomorrow at noon."

Blum and the golden retriever walked me to the door. He and I watched the dog sniff around the bushes. "Thanks for all your help," I said. "Not only to me, but what you're doing to alert people to the dangers of extremism."

"I'd like to think these people can't exist in the cold light of day," Blum said. "I think the more these groups are held up to public scrutiny, the more people will reject such ideology. But it won't be a comfortable transition. We have a long way to go to work through our racism."

"I keep thinking of a quote I read once," I told him. "I don't remember where or who said it, but the substance has stuck with me. Something about democracy being like a raft. It manages to stay afloat, but our feet are always wet."

He laughed and held out his hand. "Let's keep bailing."

Blum had given me the call numbers of the right-wing radio station in Delano. I tuned it in to my car radio as I drove south on Highway 99, out of Fresno's lights and into the dark night that enveloped the Valley. But once I found the radio station I couldn't listen to it for very long. I couldn't stomach the virulent racism, the malignant hatred that spewed over the airwaves. I turned the dial and found another station, one playing oldies.

For the umpteenth time I turned the case over in my mind. Surely Gillie told Darcy that Talbert wasn't who he professed to be. And Darcy must have seen Talbert, right before he was killed. My guess was that he'd given her his keys and told her how to get to his apartment from the school, one step ahead of the three men who'd broken in later that night. Those men had taken Talbert's computer, but there was a good chance Darcy had what they'd been looking for—Talbert's computer disks. Then, I theorized, she'd hooked up with Miguel Hidalgo. But where had she gone after that?

What had happened to Gillie after she'd been intercepted while making that phone call to me? As soon as I got back, I'd call Consuela Webber. Maybe she would know, and maybe I could pressure her into telling me where to find Miguel. If she'd talk with me at all.

I pushed the Toyota up a hair past the speed limit and the truckers still streamed past me like I was standing still. It was after eleven Friday night when I got back to Bakersfield, less than forty-eight hours since I'd left. But it felt like weeks. The caffeine I'd consumed at the Blums' house had long since worn off, and I felt tired and grubby. All I could think about as I parked in Cece's driveway was bed. But first we had to talk.

Cece opened the door to my knock and led me back to the den, where Woofer Dog was dreaming about rabbits, twitching and whining as he lay stretched out on the rug. I stretched out myself, on the sofa, while Cece curled up in the armchair. She sifted through the materials I'd brought with me, obtained from Simon Blake, Teresa Bosk, and Ira Blum.

"Sure as hell puts a different twist on Martina's obvious distaste for Mrs. Webber," she said finally.

"Right. Martina doesn't like having a Hispanic cluttering up her pristine office. She makes it plain, according to what Consuela Webber told us the other day."

Cece put the papers in order and shook her head. "My grandparents came out here during the Depression. They got foreclosed out of their place in Oklahoma and headed for California looking for work. They picked crops all up and down this Valley. Lived in a labor camp for a while, just like the ones Steinbeck wrote about in *The Grapes of Wrath*. Then they moved into a little house on the east side of Bakersfield. It was a settlement of migrant workers. The locals called it Little Oklahoma or Okieville."

She laughed briefly, shaking her head again. "Did you know, in 1936 the L.A. police chief sent a bunch of cops outside his jurisdiction to patrol the state line? Or that in 1938, right here in Bakersfield, they formed a citizens' association to deal with what they called the 'migrant threat.' They meant my grandma and grandpa, those damned Okies."

I nodded. "I've read some of the stuff they wrote about them back then. Steinbeck was right on target."

"They said those damned Okies were white trash, dirty and ignorant, backward and uneducated, lazy scum. They were all going to wind up on relief or take jobs away from regular Californians. The good citizens of the San Joaquin Valley talked about those damned

Okies as though they were some inferior subspecies, just because they were poor and didn't fit in." Cece smiled, but there wasn't much humor in it.

"You know, Jeri, those damned Okies had the last laugh. They were the 'others' back then. Now they're the ones running things here in the Valley. But I hear the grandchildren of those same 'inferior, dirty, ignorant Okies' saying the same old things about blacks, Hispanics, and Asians. It makes my skin crawl. So does the stuff in these files."

Wearily I pulled myself into a sitting position, remembering my earlier conversation with Ira Blum.

"We seem to have some compulsion to consider people who are different from us the 'others,' " I said, "to divide ourselves into little increments of them and us. Sooner or later we'll have to realize we're all in this together. I only hope we don't tear ourselves apart before we figure it out." I paused. "Did you talk with Carly Nason's attorney?"

"Tried calling him this afternoon," she said. "He wasn't available and his assistant seemed reluctant to discuss the case. I left a message. We'll see if he calls me back. Have you heard from that PI in Denver, the one who was digging up information on Perris and that school he worked at in Colorado?"

"Not yet. If I don't have a message from him at the hotel, I'll call him first thing tomorrow morning."

"I asked Ray Harmon if he'd heard any rumors about paramilitary activity in this area. He said he'd check with a friend of his out at the sheriff's department. So far he hasn't gotten back to me."

"You're meeting Dan and Adele at noon tomorrow?"

"Yeah. I'd like you to be there. I can't do it any earlier, because I've got to get my kids to a Boy Scout thing in the morning."

I left Cece's house and drove through the darkened streets of Bakersfield to my hotel on Truxtun. I carried my things up to my room and looked longingly at the bed, noticing at the same time that the message light on the phone was flashing.

I sat down on the bed, unbuttoning the shirt I'd been wearing, and punched in the number to retrieve the messages. There were three of them. The first was from Adele Gregory, calling earlier Friday afternoon to let me know that she and Dan had arrived.

Carl Burnham had finally called, at four o'clock Friday afternoon, Denver time. His voice was cheerful as he told me he'd dug up plenty of background information on Kyle Perris. And his wife, he added. Burnham left his office number and told me he'd await a callback Saturday morning.

There was another message after Burnham's, one that made me sit upright, my ears straining to hear the voice. Darcy had called. At last.

"I know you've been trying to track me down," she said, sounding better than she had in her earlier message. "But I'm in a safe place and I'm trying to figure out what to do. I know the police think I had something to do with killing that man, but it didn't happen that way. I'll explain it all when I see you. Listen, Jeri, I'm worried about my friend Gillie Cooper. You gotta see if you can get her out of that place. I have to go now. I'll see you soon, I promise."

The message ended with a click. Damn it, where was she? I saved the message, then pushed the buttons so that I could hear it again. On the second round, I listened for background noise. I heard music, so low that I couldn't distinguish what kind. But that was all. And there wasn't much I could do until morning. I called Cece, who was just going to bed, to tell her I'd heard from Darcy and Burnham. She told me she was leaving her house at nine the next morning, and to call her on her cellular phone after I'd talked with Burnham.

I was so tired I slept past nine Saturday morning, awakened only by a phone call from Adele Gregory. She apologized when she realized this and I hastened to tell her it was all right. "I did have a message from Darcy. She said she's okay. No, I didn't talk with her directly. It was on the hotel voice mail. Give me an hour to shower and get some breakfast. You and Dan can come listen to it."

I called Burnham in Denver as soon as I got out of the shower. Sipping the coffee from the room service breakfast I'd ordered, I sat on the unmade bed in my bathrobe. "You said you got the goods on Kyle Perris," I told him. "Hope they're nice and juicy."

He laughed. "So juicy it'll be running down your chin. How does a felony conviction for embezzlement sound?"

"Tell me more."

"After I talked with you on Monday I did some digging to see what else I could find out about Pinewood School. Like I said, that article in the *Rocky Mountain News* stuck in my mind. Seems the place was mentioned when there was all that coverage about the wilderness program here in Colorado that got shut down by the authorities. Tuesday I drove down to Walsenburg. Said I was doing a background check on Perris, for employment purposes."

"Did you get much from the school?" I asked, refilling my coffee cup from the carafe on the tray.

"Not from the school. Real closemouthed. Seems they've had a lot of reporters on their tail and they're suspicious of strangers. But when I started nosing around town, I heard plenty. You see, I always look for the disgruntled employee. Or ex-employee. And I found her. She used to work in the office at Pinewood but she claims Perris got her fired. It seems she started asking questions about that college where Perris supposedly got his doctorate."

"A college which doesn't exist?"

"Oh, the college is real enough. She knows, because she grew up in that town. Trouble is, she says the college only offers a four-year degree."

"Meaning no graduate program. I suppose they could have started one after she left town." But I had a feeling the college hadn't. Burnham's next words confirmed it.

"I followed that little bit of information up with a phone call. She's right. They don't have graduate students and they never heard of Kyle Perris."

"If his education credentials are phony, I'll bet his military record is, too."

"I'm way ahead of you," Burnham said. "Called an old Army buddy of mine who's stationed at the Pentagon. Perris didn't have a commission. As far as he could determine, Perris has never served as an enlisted man or an officer in any of the armed forces."

"So how did you track down the felony?" I asked.

"I figured he was from Illinois, since he knew there was a college in that town, even if he didn't check it too closely. That's when I found out he did a stretch in Joliet, about fifteen years ago. He'd been working for a company in Chicago that owned a chain of dry cleaning stores. He was supposed to keep track of the receipts but he couldn't keep his hand out of the till. He started skimming money.

Didn't get caught right away, since he was keeping two sets of books. But he got greedy and his boss finally noticed the shortages. When he got out of the joint, he left Illinois. No one had a hint of him until he turned up in Denver, claiming to be an educational consultant."

"So he reinvented himself. Or reinvented his scam."

"Right on both counts," Burnham said. "He moved to Denver nine years ago. He hooked up with the Pinewood School shortly after that, and moved down to Walsenburg. He was there nearly two years, then he and one of the teachers, Thomas Shiller, left. That's when they went to California to start their own school."

"Were you able to find out anything about Shiller?" Shiller, I thought, who'd happened to mention to his girlfriend, Peggy Rostrow, that there were some financial irregularities in the school's books, such that he was thinking of having those books audited. And Peggy let it slip to her very good friend Martina Perris, right before Shiller wound up dead.

"Straight arrow, from what little I could dig up. Now Mrs. Perris, she's in a class by herself."

"One marked bank robbery."

"You know about that business in Colorado Springs?" he asked. "When her husband got killed?"

"Just found out about it yesterday, and I don't know much. Give me the details."

"I'll do better than that," Burnham said. "I'll send you copies of the clips from the newspaper. Her name was Martina Waller back then. Her husband was Earl Waller and involved with Aryan Nations. They had a cell of these looney tunes down in Colorado Springs, passing out hate literature, that kind of thing. They decided they'd fund some of their activities by hitting a bank in downtown Colorado Springs. Claimed it was owned by a Jewish conspiracy, the usual neo-Nazi line."

That much I'd gotten from Ira Blum. "I know her husband and one of his accomplices were killed in a shoot-out with Colorado Springs police. At what level did Martina participate?"

"As near as I can figure out, she wasn't involved in the execution of the robbery. I have a feeling she was involved in the planning. But the district attorney wasn't able to make an accessory charge stick.

So while the rest of her husband's merry band, the ones that survived, are doing time in Canon City, Martina walked."

"How did she wind up in Walsenburg married to Kyle Perris?"

"After the bank robbery business died down, Martina moved to Pueblo, south of Colorado Springs. That's where she hooked up with Perris. You see, the bogus doctor got involved in right-wing politics after he got out of the joint. Started hanging out with some militia types in Pueblo."

"So that's where he met Martina," I said.

"Yeah. But from what I can find out, Martina's the true believer in the Perris family," Burnham said. "With Kyle, it's only skin-deep. First and foremost, the guy's a con man."

WHILE I DRESSED AND FINISHED BREAKFAST, I CALLED Cece on her cellular phone as she'd asked me to do last night. I heard the sound of boys' voices in the background as I gave her a report on my conversation with Carl Burnham.

"Burnham is going to fax his report and some copies of documents to your office," I told her. "You'd better let Harmon and Garza know that we may have the answer to our questions about militia activity. Given the fact that Martina Perris has a history of involvement, I suspect they're up to something out at that school."

"I'll track down the detectives," Cece said. "Change of plans. Skip the meeting in my office with Dan and Adele. Go twist Consuela's arm. We've got to find Miguel."

"Dan and Adele are on their way to my room now. In fact, that's them now," I added as an urgent knock rattled my door. "After I talk with them, I'll head over to Consuela's house. I'll check in with you from there."

I hung up the phone and went to admit Dan and Adele. Dark circles showed under Adele's eyes. Dan appeared to have a few more lines in his face, and he seemed subdued as he stood quietly, hands stuck in the pockets of his slacks. I didn't ask about Elaine. I guessed from my earlier e-mails from Darren that the battle among the three of them had raged all week.

"She said she was all right?" Adele asked. She sat down in the chair next to my bed and leaned forward, smoothing her restless hands over the blue cotton fabric of her skirt. "I know it was just a voice mail message, but it's the only word we've had from her in days."

"You can listen to it yourselves." I lifted the phone, punching in the numbers to retrieve the message from Darcy that I'd saved. Then I handed the receiver to Adele, who leaned forward eagerly as she strained to catch every nuance of Darcy's words. Then I took the receiver from her and replayed the message for Dan, who now stood over his mother-in-law, one hand tugging at the collar of his checked shirt while he listened.

"She didn't say where she was," he said, handing the receiver back to me. "Do you have any idea?"

I nodded as I replaced the phone in the cradle. "I think she's with a young man named Miguel Hidalgo, someone who worked briefly at the school in June. I'm taking steps to locate him. In fact, I'm going over to his sister's house while you meet with Cece Bromley at noon."

"That Sergeant Harmon told me earlier in the week that the cops found that murdered man's car with Darcy's prints on the steering wheel." Dan looked worried and ran a hand through the dark curls receding from his forehead. "That looks bad, but I just can't believe my daughter had anything to do with killing that guy. She's wild and she drives me crazy most of the time, but she wouldn't kill anyone."

"Of course she didn't kill anyone. But I think she saw who did. Don't worry, we'll find Darcy and bring her home."

"Like you did before?" Adele smiled. "I hope it turns out better this time."

I took Adele's hands in mine. "You know, I wish I'd gone to Chartres with all of you, back in April. I've been meaning to ask you. How did that trip go?"

"It was strange, and familiar, all at once," Adele said. "The village and the Tresoir farmhouse were both smaller than I remembered. A bittersweet homecoming, to these people who saved my life by hiding me from the Nazis. I told you Maman and Papa Tresoir were dead. But their children greeted me like a long-lost sister. And they took to Darcy immediately, of course. Everyone takes to Darcy."

Except her own mother, I thought.

I spent some more time reassuring Dan and Adele, though my words weren't doing much good. By now it was nearly eleven-thirty.

I eased them out of my room, telling them I'd show them how to get to Cece's office. Dan followed me over to the Haberfelde Building. I left them at the 17th Street entrance and pointed my Toyota toward Consuela Webber's house.

But the Webbers weren't home. After ringing the bell and checking their backyard, I walked to the house next door, where a woman in shorts was deadheading her roses. "I think they went shopping," she told me. "I saw them leave, must have been about eleven. I'm sure they'll be back, in an hour or so."

Frustrated, I walked back to where I'd left my car, parked at the curb in the inadequate shade provided by an ornamental plum tree on the Webbers' front lawn. There was nothing for me to do but wait.

Staking out a house in a hot car in the middle of a summer day in Bakersfield is not my idea of a good time. I was glad that I always carry a bottle of water in the Toyota, even if the water was the same temperature as the car's interior. I sipped sparingly, though. Drinking liquids while on stakeout results in another problem.

It was past two when I saw a dark blue Plymouth Voyager pull into the driveway of the Webbers' house and the automatic opener lift the garage door. Zach slowly moved the Voyager forward into the garage and he and Consuela got out, each with a child in tow. Zach opened the rear door of the vehicle and hoisted a couple of gallon jugs of milk. It looked like they'd hit a hardware store or a home improvement warehouse before buying groceries. Or maybe they'd visited one of those cavernous club stores with everything under one huge roof. I saw a case of motor oil in the depths of the Voyager, next to a coiled garden hose and some extra-large containers of toilet tissue, paper towels, and laundry detergent.

The children looked at me as I approached, the little boy with curiosity, the younger girl ducking shyly behind her mother. Both had Consuela's dark eyes and Zach's fair hair. Zach greeted me as though he wasn't sure what my visit presaged.

"What are you doing here?" Consuela asked as she picked up a grocery sack. She handed the little girl a box of cereal and told her to go with Daddy. Zach shepherded both kids ahead of him, going into the house.

"I have to talk with you. It's important." I reached for a sack, figuring I'd either help her carry the stuff into the house or hold the groceries hostage for information.

"Well, I have an earful for you." Consuela tightened her mouth. "The Bitch of Bakersfield fired me."

"You sound indignant for someone who didn't like the job to begin with," I said.

She stared at me, then gave a snort of laughter. "You're right. I'm better off not working at that place, for that awful woman. But my pride's hurt. I've never been sent packing like that before."

"Tell me what happened. From the beginning."

"Help me get these groceries into the house and I'll give you the whole story."

"If you'll let me use your bathroom and give me something cool to drink."

By that time Zach and the children had come back for another load. With all that help it took us five minutes to empty the back of the Voyager. Consuela directed me to the bathroom. When I returned to the kitchen, they were emptying sacks, but Zach handed Consuela a bottle of soda and two plastic glasses full of ice.

"You go and talk," he said. "I'll finish this."

Consuela led the way out to the patio, which had a slatted wooden roof covered with vines and a round table covered with a vinyl cloth. I pulled out one of the matching lawn chairs grouped around the table and sat down. Consuela unscrewed the top of the bottle and poured us each a glass of soda.

"After you were at the school on Wednesday," she said, as she set the bottle on the table and sat down next to me, "I went to lunch at the dining hall. I managed to slip the card to Gillie. Then I called you later that afternoon."

"Right. And Gillie called me Wednesday during the evening meal. But someone interrupted on her end. Do you know what happened?"

Consuela nodded. "I don't know who caught her. I didn't see her at all on Thursday. So on my way to lunch, I asked one of the teachers about her. He said she'd committed some infraction and was confined to her bungalow. Friday morning I had to walk some papers over to Mr. Fosby in the maintenance building. On my way over there, I saw the counselor in charge of the bungalow. I asked about Gillie, since by then I hadn't seen her in almost two days. She told me Gillie was in that discipline room they use."

Bad news, I thought, taking a swallow of soda. "Has she been there since Wednesday night?"

"Probably. When I started the job, Dr. Perris told me that they kept kids in isolation for only twenty-four hours. But if Gillie's been locked up since she made that phone call, that's almost three days."

"When did Martina fire you? And what reason did she give?"

"Friday, right before lunch. Which was maybe an hour after I'd talked with the counselor. I'm sure she was the one who told Martina I was asking questions about Gillie. So Martina called me into her office and shut the door, then she told me I had a bad attitude and my work performance was substandard." Consuela's tone of voice indicated how much credence she gave Martina's reasons for terminating her employment.

"She said I was hard to get along with and that my work wasn't up to her standards. Then she handed me a check, two weeks' pay in lieu of notice, and she told me to clear out my desk and leave. So I did just that. But there's something else, Jeri. Those papers I took over to Fosby. There was an invoice that I asked him about. He must have told Martina."

"An invoice for what?"

"A locksmith. They had a locksmith in there on Sunday, changing the locks on Dr. Perris's filing cabinets. It was all on the invoice, the date, the time, and who requested the work. That's why I noticed it. I mentioned it to Fosby. He's usually the one who takes care of things like that."

I thought those locks looked new when I was in Perris's office on Wednesday. And there had been scratches on the wood around them. I set the glass down and leaned toward Consuela. "Did Fosby act as though he knew about the locksmith?"

"It was hard to tell. But I don't think he did. And I'll bet the police don't, either."

I knew Harmon and Garza had checked the admin building, but from what Garza had told me Wednesday afternoon, it looked as though Talbert hadn't been inside. But Consuela's information about the locksmith's invoice confirmed what I'd guessed. Talbert had been inside. He'd gone looking in Perris's files, and he'd gotten caught.

"Consuela, you've got to tell me where Miguel is. I know Darcy's with him. She called me last night."

"Did she say she was with Miguel?"

"Not in so many words. But I'm fairly sure he picked her up after she abandoned Talbert's car last weekend. My guess is she's been with him ever since. You've known that, too. That's why you've been steering me away from him."

She was silent for a moment. Then she sighed and stood up. "All right. He's at my grandmother's place, in the west part of the county. Let's call him now."

CHAPTER 45

ONSUELA DIALED HER GRANDMOTHER'S NUMBER FROM the bedroom while I listened on the kitchen extension. The phone rang, then a woman's voice answered.

"*Abuelita, Consuela aquí. ¿Dónde está Miguel?*"

"*Momentito,*" the old woman said. I heard a thunk on the other end as the phone was set down on some hard surface. A few minutes later the receiver was picked up again.

"*Hermana,*" Miguel said, his voice deep and rich. "*¿Qué pasa?*"

"Is Darcy with you?" Consuela asked.

Miguel hesitated. "Yeah. She's outside in the barn. What's goin' on?"

"This is Jeri Howard. The private investigator Darcy called last night. I need to speak with both of you."

"Just a minute," he said. He set the phone down and I heard him say something to his grandmother in Spanish, but I couldn't make out the words. A screen door slammed, and I heard voices in the distance. Finally Darcy picked up the phone.

"Jeri? Oh, I'm so glad to hear your voice."

"I'm glad to hear yours. I've been worried about you. So are your parents."

"Yeah, right," she said bitterly. "They're the ones who sent me to that place."

"I don't think they knew what kind of a place it was. Your father's here in town with your grandmother."

"But not my mother?" I didn't answer. But Darcy guessed

anyway. When she spoke, her voice was tinged with regret under her customary bravado. "Well, that cause is lost. To hell with her, anyway."

"Darcy, we have to talk about what happened at the school." She started to blurt it out but I stopped her. I wanted to see her face while she told me rather than just listen to it. "Not on the phone. Better we do it in person. I want you and Miguel to come into Bakersfield."

"But the police . . ."

"Your grandmother has retained a lawyer named Cecilia Bromley. I've been working with her to get to the bottom of this. After Cece and I have heard what you have to say, we'll bring the police into it. But first we need to get together."

Now Miguel's voice came over the line. "Consuela?"

"I'm here," his sister said.

"What do you think?"

"I think you're in over your head, *hermano*. You'd better get back here and let these people sort it out."

"Okay. I gotta finish a couple of things I promised Grandma I'd do, then we'll head for town. Jeri, we'll meet you at six. At my sister's."

"Your apartment." It was on the west side of town and he'd be coming from the west. "We'll go to Cece Bromley's from there."

I hung up the phone and glanced at my watch. It was nearly three-thirty. A few more hours, and we'd be home free.

I called Cece. "Making progress," I said, and brought her up to date.

"Great," she said. "Come to my house. I've got the materials that investigator from Denver faxed to my office."

Consuela walked me to the door. "Just don't let anything happen to my kid brother."

"I'll try not to."

When I got to Cece's house, I parked in the double drive and headed for the front door. Her sons were romping on the lawn with Woofer Dog, who was loath to return the battered Frisbee they'd tossed for him. They waved at me, then tried to corner the dog, who dodged them and flopped down near a hedge, tail wagging as he gnawed on the plastic disk.

"He goes through those Frisbees at the rate of one a month," Cece said when she answered the door. "Just chews the hell out of them. Want something to drink?"

"I could use something to eat. I didn't get any lunch, since I was waiting for the Webbers to come home. Got any food?"

She rolled her eyes. "I have teenage boys. I have food. *If* they left any."

We went back to the kitchen and raided the refrigerator. I settled for cheese, crackers, and leftover salad, consumed while I examined the documents Carl Burnham had faxed, spread out before me on the kitchen table. First was his report detailing his trip to Walsenburg and what he'd found out about Pinewood School, Kyle Perris, and Martina Perris. He'd also included clips of newspaper articles about the shoot-out with police in Colorado Springs, in which Martina Perris's first husband had died. That had occurred eight years ago. More recent was the article from the *Rocky Mountain News* that Burnham had mentioned in our initial phone conversation. It concerned the wilderness program shut down in Colorado and mentioned Pinewood School.

"Were you able to get in touch with Sergeant Harmon?" I asked when I'd finished with the report and my late lunch.

"Yeah. I had him paged." She frowned. "As far as he's concerned, the stuff you found out about Martina Perris is hearsay, since she was never charged with anything. He said he'd look into Kyle's felony conviction and get back to me. Which he hasn't yet. Maybe you'd have better luck with Garza."

"At this point I want to talk with Darcy first, before bringing the cops into it." I carried my dishes to the sink.

"I agree. But we'd better let her father and grandmother know that she's okay and she's on her way to Bakersfield. I'll have them come over here."

Cece called the hotel and spoke with Dan, giving him directions to her house. He and Adele arrived just before five. Once they were settled in Cece's den, I headed over to Miguel's apartment building. I wanted to get there before he did.

This time I parked at the end of the row of carports closest to the building where Miguel lived, at the southeast corner of the complex. I got out of my car and made a circuit of the parking area, keeping my eyes open for potential trouble. On this hot afternoon there weren't many people outside. I heard a splash from the complex's swimming pool. Someone exited the nearby building that held the laundry facilities. It was Mr. Lemuel, the young man I'd talked with on Wednesday afternoon, this time attired less formally in shorts, T-shirt, and sandals. On one hip he carried an oval plastic basket containing his neatly folded sheets and towels, a plastic bottle of liquid laundry detergent swinging from his free hand.

As he neared me, recognition swept over his face. "Hey, you were here the other day, looking for Miguel. Did you two ever connect?"

"Yes." I consulted my watch again.

"Good. He's a popular guy." He kept walking toward the southwest building, but I touched his arm and he stopped.

"What do you mean by that?"

"Someone else was here, looking for Miguel. Thursday, no, Friday afternoon, as I was coming home from work."

"Can you describe this person?"

Lemuel pondered this for a moment. "Well . . . a man, fortyish, medium height. Brown hair and blue eyes, looked average. Asked if this was where Miguel lived and if I knew where he was."

The third man, I thought, and he knew about Miguel and Darcy. "Did you see what he was driving?"

"No, sorry. Didn't think it was important."

I thanked him. He looked curious, but seeing that I wasn't going to tell him anything else, he shifted the laundry basket on his hip and headed for the building. I unzipped my purse. I'd call Cece to give her a heads-up. But before I put my hand on my cell phone, a dusty red pickup truck turned into the parking lot and drove toward me, then turned left into one of the vacant numbered slots.

Darcy had unhooked her shoulder belt and had the passenger door open almost before Miguel had shifted the pickup into Park. She ran toward me and flung her arms around me. I hugged her as fiercely as she hugged me, then stepped back and surveyed her. She'd cut her hair to shoulder-length, as the deli clerk had described. Right now it was windblown and tousled. She was wearing disreputable sneakers, faded blue jeans, and a T-shirt with a Highway 99 symbol on it. Around her neck I saw a plain gold chain.

"Borrowed some clothes from Miguel, I see." I looked past her at

Miguel Hidalgo and he grinned at me. He was about five-ten, with the muscled physique of an athlete, wearing equally faded jeans with a leather belt looped at the waist and work boots. There was a red bandanna tied around his neck and he wore a Western-cut shirt. His coarse black hair fell onto his forehead and curled around his ears. I saw some resemblance to his sister in the planes of his face and his warm brown eyes, but he was darker, looking as though he'd been working outside all summer.

"I don't know what I would have done without him," Darcy said, putting an arm around Miguel's waist.

"Let's go," I said. "You can follow me over to Cece's."

I walked with them toward the pickup. Then I heard a motor roar, somewhere behind us. A black Chevy van streaked around the rear corner of the parking lot and screeched to a halt in back of Miguel's pickup. Simultaneously the side door slammed open and two men jumped out.

Skinheads.

They were dressed as they had been the night they'd kicked open Talbert's door. One of them was Brick, the skinny guy I'd seen at the Rust Bucket Wednesday night. Darcy gasped, and I knew she'd recognized him as one of the men who'd abducted her from Alameda.

Brick brandished what looked like an automatic weapon. His companion, swastika tattoos visible on both forearms, held a length of pipe in his left hand and brass knuckles gleamed on his right. I looked past them, trying to see who was driving the van. It was Lori, the little blonde I'd seen the other night at the bar, in the hallway outside the restrooms.

My hand inched toward the cell phone in my purse. But the one with the gun noticed the movement.

"Don't even think about it, bitch." Brick ripped the bag from my shoulder and tossed it toward Lori in the driver's seat. She jammed it down between the seats.

The guy with the brass knuckles focused on Darcy. "Here's the little kike. And her spic mudboy. Where's the computer disk?"

Darcy's eyes blazed defiance and bravado. "Go to hell, you Nazi creep."

She had guts, but this wasn't the kid at school she had fought earlier this year. The punk with the gun backhanded her, leaving a scratch that trailed blood. "Search her, Trog," he ordered.

His beefier companion stuck the pipe into his back pocket and grabbed Darcy. He shoved up the T-shirt she wore and started fumbling with the zipper on her black waist-pack. Miguel lunged toward him. Trog shoved Darcy to his right and pulled the pipe from his pocket. As he raised it over Miguel's head, I pushed Miguel out of range. He fell to his knees and I felt the pipe whiz by, inches from my head. Before Miguel could scramble to his feet, Trog wheeled and kicked him hard in the stomach. He drew his foot back for another blow.

"Back off, Trog," Lori shouted. "We gotta take 'em back to base camp. Come on, let's get out of here."

Brick looked at me with cold, dead eyes. He raised his weapon and pointed the end of the barrel at the middle of my forehead.

"In the van," he ordered.

I DIDN'T FEEL DISPOSED TO ARGUE. I NEVER DO WHEN SOME-one is pointing a gun at me.

We got into the van, Darcy and I helping Miguel, who winced with pain at every movement. The seats in the back had been removed and we had to sit on the carpeted floor, bracing ourselves with our hands. "You okay?" I asked Miguel. He nodded quickly, but I could tell he was hurting. Broken ribs, maybe. But he'd just missed getting a broken skull.

The guy with the gun jumped into the passenger seat next to Lori, while his brass-knuckled companion slammed the door shut and sat facing the rear, leering at us as he clenched his right hand around the pipe.

"Hit it," Brick said, slapping the dash.

Lori floored the accelerator and screamed out of the parking lot, narrowly missing a couple of residents who'd just left the pool. I hoped they'd call the police to complain. I knew Cece would when I didn't return to her house with Darcy and Miguel. But the whole thing had happened so quickly I wasn't sure anyone had seen us.

I figured base camp was the Perris School. The black van had no side windows, and the rear window was covered with black mesh. From my position, sitting cross-legged on the floor with Darcy on my left and Miguel on my right, I could see past Trog, through the gap between the front seats. As we drove through Bakersfield, I couldn't get my bearings. I saw Brick pawing through my purse, looking for the computer disk and whatever else he could find. He kept the cellular phone, my money and credit cards, then tossed the bag onto the floor.

The hazy southern Sierra Nevada mountains loomed in the front windshield, which meant we were headed east. Then the mountains shifted from view as we turned north off Highway 178. Lori made another left, off asphalt and onto gravel. Then she hit the brakes. We stopped abruptly at the gate of the Perris School, engine idling.

"Brick!" She snapped her fingers at the skinhead in the passenger seat, the one with the gun. "The card, where's the card?"

"Trog has the fucking card," he snarled.

"Don't have a heart attack." Trog pulled the key card from his rear pocket and passed it to Lori. She shoved it into the electronic box mounted on the pole outside the gate. It cranked open. Lori hit the accelerator again and we lurched forward, then angled to the right past the admin building and the parking lot.

I saw the corrugated gray metal siding of the maintenance building as Lori swung the van around a curve and hit the brakes. Brick opened the passenger door and jumped out. Trog flung open the side door and waggled the pipe at us, indicating we should get out. I got to my feet and stepped out of the van, looking around. We weren't parked near the front door of the maintenance building, the one I'd gone through when I'd visited Fosby on Wednesday. This was the back half of the building, where Fosby told me the Perrises were storing some furniture. The door, about ten feet wide, was open.

I almost expected to see Fosby standing there. But it was Clifford Rostrow.

"You're the third man," I told him. "The one who helped these two ransack Talbert's apartment the night of the murder. But you didn't find what you were looking for."

His mouth tightened. "You talk too much. And you poke your nose in too many places. As for finding what we were looking for . . ." He turned wintry eyes on Brick and Trog. "Got the disk?"

"Not yet," Brick told him, hedging.

"Did you search her?"

"Things started getting dicey," Lori said, slamming the driver's-side door as she walked toward us. "We had to blow."

Not finding the disk hadn't made Rostrow particularly happy, nor did Lori's excuse. His exasperation showed on his face. "Lock them up. We'll deal with this later."

He turned and walked into the dimly lit interior of the back half of the maintenance building. Trog grabbed my arm and hauled me forward. Brick did the same for Miguel, while Lori brought up the rear with Darcy.

Inside it was hot and stuffy, as though the room had been closed up for a long time. The space appeared to be about thirty by forty feet. I didn't see any furniture. Instead I saw rectangular wooden crates stacked against the wall to my left. Our captors marched us toward a storage unit built into the far right-hand corner of the room. The door was held shut by a large shiny bolt that looked like a recent addition. Rostrow shot the bolt to the left and pulled open the door.

Trog shoved me into the fetid, dark closet. I stumbled forward and down, banging my knee against the concrete floor. I looked back the way I'd come in time to see Miguel fly toward me. He landed hard. I heard him cry out. Then Darcy tumbled against us.

The door slammed shut. I heard the bolt slide into place. All I could see now were slivers of light at the edges of the door, where it didn't join tightly with the frame holding it in place. I got to my feet slowly, as my eyes adjusted to the dimness. It was even hotter in here, and it stank. I pivoted, getting my bearings, noting that it wasn't as dark as I'd thought. There was a small window high on the wall opposite me, the exterior wall of the maintenance building. But it was covered so thickly with grime that very little light penetrated.

"Talk to me," I said.

"I'm over here," Darcy said, her voice somewhere to the right of the door.

"Are you okay, Miguel?"

"Hurts like hell. I think I've got some broken ribs where that asshole kicked me."

"I was afraid of that," I said. "Try not to move too much."

I moved toward the door, guided by the thin strips of illumination that outlined the rectangle. My outstretched hands encountered the door. I felt it, knocked my knuckles against it. It seemed to be a typical hollow-core door, the kind you can buy in any hardware store or lumberyard. Not very strong. Maybe we could force our way through it. But there was no guarantee what might be on the other side.

I ran my fingers along the inner edge of the frame, feeling the hinges on my right. On my left was a handle, about waist level. I knelt and focused my eyes just above the handle, gauging the thickness of the bolt on the other side that was holding the door shut. It glinted in the light bleeding in from the larger room. Solid steel, I guessed and damned thick.

The unpleasant odor was stronger now. Maybe the three of us could get that window open, if only to admit some fresh air. Then my nose sorted out the smells. That was human waste I was smelling. There was someone else in here.

"Stay where you are," I said, to Darcy and Miguel and whoever else was with us.

Then I heard a whimper, coming from one of the far corners. I felt my way around the perimeter of the room, going from the storage closets' wooden walls to the metal exterior wall. I moved toward the sound, somewhere to my right. My foot encountered a bucket, source of the stench. Then my hand brushed against flesh. I smelled fear and the acrid scent of a body that had been kept locked up for too long.

"Gillie?"

"They're gonna kill us," she sobbed, leaning into me.

"Not if I can help it."

I put my arm around her and led her across the storage room to the door, where Darcy and Miguel were huddled together. Now my eyes were used to the dimness. I could see forms and faces, though not clearly. Darcy grabbed Gillie and hugged her, then we all huddled together, in the corner nearest the door.

"How long have you been in here?" I asked Gillie. "Since Wednesday?"

"Since last night," she whispered. "They put me in detention Wednesday, after I called you. Then last night after Mr. Fosby left his office, they took me out of detention. I thought they were taking me back to my cottage but they put me in here."

"Who put you in here?" I asked.

"Dr. and Mrs. Perris."

"With just a bucket to pee in?" Anger heated my voice.

"And a sleeping bag. But I couldn't sleep. I'm afraid of the dark."

"Have you had anything to eat?"

"That blond girl brought me some food this morning, and emptied the bucket."

I wasn't surprised that the Perrises had used Lori for this task. I couldn't imagine Martina Perris soiling her hands by emptying a bucket full of urine and excrement.

"I think it was this morning." Gillie's voice was stronger now that she had some company in her dark prison. "For all I know, it was this afternoon. There was some light coming through the window, so I knew it was day."

"I should have come back for you," Darcy said. "I should have made you come with me."

Gillie ducked her head. "You didn't have time. Besides, I was scared. I would have just slowed you down." Tears thickened her voice. "It's my fault Mr. Talbert's dead. A couple of days before it happened, I said something about recognizing him to one of the girls in our cottage. She must have told Dr. and Mrs. Perris."

"Never mind that now," I said. "I want to know what you both saw the night Talbert was murdered."

"I didn't actually see who killed him," Darcy said.

"That doesn't matter. Just tell me what happened."

"Well, Gillie and I were going to run away." Darcy looked at me. "You know, we tried it in June, but Mr. Talbert caught us and told Mr. Fosby. I was really angry with him then, but I realize now . . ." She stopped, then continued. "We were going to get out that side gate. The one just beyond the maintenance building."

"I thought it was kept locked," I said.

"I have the key. Miguel gave it to me. It's on this chain around my neck."

I looked at Miguel. He grinned through the pain. "After the girls got caught the first time, I sneaked that key out of the lock box in Fosby's office and had a copy made. Don't think Fosby ever noticed."

"Miguel told me about the bridge over the irrigation canal,"

Darcy continued, "and the dirt road on the other side. He said if
Gillie and I could get to that subdivision that's over the hill, there
was a pay phone near a school."

"All they had to do was call me, and I'd come pick them up,"
Miguel added.

"Why?" I asked. "What reason did you have to help Darcy and
Gillie?"

"You've seen the way they treat these kids," Miguel said. "This
isn't a school, it's a jail."

"I agree with you. Darcy, Friday night you and Gillie were making a run for it."

"We waited until after lights-out," she said. "I didn't expect Ms.
Lincoln, our counselor, to be out of town. We were stuck with Mrs.
Perris, so we had to be extra-careful. About eleven o'clock, we got
up and put on our clothes. Then we opened the window and started
to climb out."

"That's when we saw it." Now Gillie joined in, her voice subdued.
"Behind the admin building. Two . . . people, men, because they
were both wearing pants."

"I couldn't tell who they were, not right then," Darcy said. "Of
course, the one who got killed was Mr. Talbert. Anyway, when we
first saw them, they were struggling. Then Mr. Talbert broke away.
But the other one caught up with him and grabbed him. He had
something in his hand, something metal. I saw it shining in the
porch light above the back door. He hit Mr. Talbert a couple of
times, real hard." She shuddered. "Then he stopped. He went into
the office, carrying that metal thing."

"What did this metal thing look like?"

"Kind of like a *V*, but not exactly." Darcy sketched a shape with
her hands.

"Like one of those oversized staplers," I said. "What did you do
then?"

"He just left Mr. Talbert lying there," Gillie said. "We thought he
was dead. But I knew whoever killed him would come back soon.
That's when I lost my nerve. So I told Darcy to go without me."

"I tried to get her to come with me." Darcy put her hand on
Gillie's shoulder and squeezed. "I was just going out the window

when I saw the body on the ground. He wasn't dead after all. He . . . he was trying to crawl away."

She swallowed hard and when she spoke again, her voice sounded ragged. "I couldn't just leave him without seeing if there was something I could do. So I ran over to him. That's when I recognized Mr. Talbert. He was all bloody. But his eyes were open, and he was trying to talk."

"What did he say?"

"To get the hell out of there," Darcy said. "But he had something for me to do first. He had this computer disk stuck down in his pants. He told me to take the disk and his keys out of his pocket. His car was parked over by the side gate and he already had the gate opened. He said to go to his apartment, and told me where it was. There were two other disks there, hidden in the kitchen."

She took a deep breath. "So that's what I did. I took his car and went the back way Miguel told me about, across the canal and through the subdivision. I went to his place and got the other disks. After that I drove around. I went to a grocery store on the west side of town and called Miguel, but he wasn't there."

"I've been driving a truck for my uncle," he said. "I spent Friday night down in Tehachapi."

I turned to Gillie. "What happened after Darcy left? Did you see or hear anything else?"

She nodded, her face pale in the dim light. "I heard the phone ringing in the cottage, and I heard Mrs. Perris answer it. But I didn't hear what she was saying."

That was interesting. According to Martina Perris, she'd dozed off until one of the other residents of the cottage had told her Darcy was missing.

"I was going to get back into bed, to hide under the covers," Gillie said. "Then I saw the other man came out of the admin office. He had a black bag, like a trash bag, in his hand."

"With the murder weapon inside," I guessed.

"I think so," Gillie said. "But when he saw Mr. Talbert had moved, he hit him a couple more times, with the bag and whatever was inside it. I was shaking so bad I got into bed and pulled the covers up over my head. I pretended to be asleep. I just lay there until they came looking for Darcy."

Now I glanced at Darcy. "What did you do for the next thirty-six hours?"

"I thought about going over to Miguel's to spend the night in the parking lot, but I decided it wasn't safe. So I found a really nice neighborhood and slept in the car. As soon as it got light I kept moving, and kept calling Miguel. Saturday I hung around a bunch of shopping malls, including that one where I left the car. In the afternoon I went to one of those multiplexes and saw about four movies, until they closed the place down and kicked me out." She laughed at the memory.

"So I sat in an all-night coffee shop for a while. Then I was so tired I found another nice neighborhood. Sunday morning some old guy knocked on the window of the car and told me I couldn't sleep there. So I drove back to that mall and just walked around. Finally I went to a deli to get something to eat and make some phone calls. That's when I saw the Sunday paper about Mr. Talbert's murder. Called you, but you weren't home either. But the next time I called Miguel, he was at his apartment. He came and got me."

"We spent the night at my place," Miguel said. "And Monday I took her to my grandma's farm."

"Do you have a computer, Miguel?"

"Yeah, he does," Darcy said. "We looked at all three disks before we hid them."

"Don't tell me where the disks are," I said. "Just tell me what was on them."

CHAPTER 47

Miguel was hurting, the pain in his ribs worse as time dragged on. Darcy and Gillie gave me a leg up so that I could reach the window in the exterior wall. It was about seven feet from the concrete floor of the storage room to the bottom edge of the window. The opening itself was perhaps a foot high and eighteen inches wide. If I could get it open, or break it, there was a chance we might get through it. In my examination, however, I didn't see a latch. I wrapped my fist in Miguel's bandanna, but my initial attempts to break the window netted me sore knuckles and a lot of frustration.

"Someone's coming," Miguel warned from his station near the door.

I jumped down, my bones jarring as I landed. I stuffed the bandanna in my pocket and swiftly crossed to the door, listening at one of the cracks. I heard several voices, all male. No, there was one female voice, and it belonged to Martina Perris. The voices moved closer. Now I could make out a few words of what they were saying.

Not that I liked what I heard. "Federal building" and "grenade launcher" in the same sentence made me decidedly apprehensive. It was time for some action.

"Hey," I bellowed. "We could use some air in here."

The voices stopped. I motioned to the others. We were all in the corner to the left of the door when it opened, admitting a slanting square of light.

Clifford Rostrow stepped inside. He held a gun in his right hand and a large flashlight in his left. He played the beam around the storeroom, lighting first on the corner where Gillie had been, with the bucket and the sleeping bag. Then he followed the wall counter-clockwise until he found us, facing out of the corner. He shone the light on each face, then stopped at Darcy's, causing her to blink her eyes.

"You. Outside."

I put my hand on Darcy's shoulder. She froze.

"We all come out," I said, "or we all stay in."

Rostrow favored me with an unpleasant smile. "Last time I looked, you were in no position to bargain."

I returned his smile, with the same degree of warmth. "Last time I looked, we still had something you wanted."

Rostrow glanced to his left, out the door, as though asking for an okay from one of his cohorts. Presumably he got it. He turned his head toward me and nodded. "All right. All of you."

I didn't want to take a chance that whoever else was outside would grab Darcy the minute she came out and slam the door on the rest of us. Maybe they wouldn't, if Rostrow was included in the rest of us.

"First you back into that corner, Clifford," I told him. "You stand there nice and quiet, where I can see you."

He complied reluctantly. I directed Miguel through the door first, followed by Darcy and Gillie. Then I brought up the rear, keeping one eye on Rostrow and the other on the door.

When we were all out in the larger room, I moved so that the outer door was to my right. Darcy was to my left, with her arm around Gillie, who was shaking. Miguel was on Gillie's left, face im-passive. The wooden crates I'd seen earlier were behind me. From the corner of my eye I spotted a closed brown leather briefcase lying on top of the crates nearest the door.

Rostrow came out of the storage room, leaving the door open. Martina stood between him and the outer door, dressed in trim slacks with a striped blouse, a leather shoulder bag dangling from her left shoulder. Next to her, I saw Kyle Perris. He was wearing slacks, but he still held himself as though he had on the expensive suit he'd worn when I'd last seen him. There were tight lines around his mouth. The strain was starting to show.

"I want that disk," he demanded.

"Disks." I smiled as I corrected him. "There's more than one. Surely you knew that. After all, you didn't find anything on Talbert's computer when Clifford and his pals broke into the apartment."

Martina greeted this news with a smirk of her own. "Just how many disks are there?"

"I think I'll leave that to your imagination," I said.

The outer door was open and the summer sun hung low in the west. A quick glance at my watch told me it was seven-thirty, an hour and a half past the time I was supposed to meet Miguel and Darcy at his apartment. Cece had probably started to worry long ago. Surely she'd guessed we'd been brought to the school.

But it was Saturday. It might take her some time to locate Harmon and Garza and convince them that a rescue operation was urgently needed.

In the meantime, I glanced to my right, at the outer door, and gauged how far it was. Twenty feet. How many seconds would it take to cross that distance? Or how long before Clifford Rostrow shot me and my companions?

Someone at the school would hear the shots, though. As I looked out the door I saw the back of several cottages and, in the distance, the little house where Bennett Fosby lived. But it was strangely quiet for a Saturday evening at a boarding school with students and counselors in those cottages.

"Where's the rest of the student body?" I asked.

"They've gone on a field trip, to Lake Isabella," Martina said. "Students, counselors, every one of them. It's quite a treat for them to get off campus."

"And Fosby? I thought he was part of your merry band."

"Fosby doesn't know anything about this," Kyle said. "He spends most weekends with his sister. I want those disks, all of them."

I heard an engine, a vehicle approaching. Then the black van backed up to the door, blocking my view of the sun. The driver cut the engine as the rear door opened. Brick and Trog jumped out. Together they hauled out a metal ramp. Once they had it in place, they lifted a dolly from the bed of the van. Through the door I could see Lori at the wheel.

I folded my arms across my chest. "I see. Something's about to happen and you couldn't take any chances of being observed. Not after last weekend, and all those cops and technicians swarming around the grounds. Looks like you're going to move whatever is in these crates to a safer place."

As I spoke, someone came into view from behind the stacked wooden crates. He was a burly blond man with a gut straining his shirt. His head was tilted to one side as he examined the crates, and he seemed preoccupied. Then he looked up. I heard Darcy's sharp intake of breath. This was George Larsen, the other man who had snatched her from Alameda, bringing her here to this hellhole of a school.

"Hey, Cliff," Larsen called. "Come over here."

Rostrow handed the gun to Martina, then crossed to where Larsen stood near the door. The two men conferred with Trog and Brick. Then the skinheads began stacking cartons on the dolly and rolling them to the van, starting with the crates near the rear wall.

"Sure it's all there, George?" I asked, as the burly man unsnapped the fasteners and opened the briefcase.

He looked up, seeing me for the first time. I didn't see much resemblance between him and Martina, except for the icy blue eyes and the fair coloring. He directed his comments to his sister. "What's she talking about?"

"I have no idea," Martina said. Her hand shifted on the handle of the gun.

I laughed. The sound startled all of them, and the skinheads stopped for a moment, then continued loading their crates. "You really don't, do you?"

Martina stepped closer and fixed me with her glare. "Suppose you explain it to me."

"Looks like I'll have to." My eyes moved from Martina to Kyle. "The true believer and the con man."

"What's that supposed to mean?" Kyle could barely force the words out through his tightened jaw.

"Martina's the true believer." I looked at her. The cold light in her eyes was matched by that in her brother's and Rostrow's. But Kyle didn't have it. "So are Clifford and George. They think they've got the one true path to righteousness. Or salvation, or patriotism. Anyone else who doesn't want to live in that constricted mindset where the three of you live, or believe what you believe, is the enemy."

I turned to her husband. "Now Kyle, here, he's a different matter. He doesn't give a damn about politics. Just feathering his own comfortable nest. Kyle's a con man."

"It's pointless to prolong this." Kyle glared at me, then looked at his wife. "They're not going to tell us where those disks are. Kill them."

"You're worried that they'll get a look at those disks before you have a chance to destroy them," I said. "Or at least the one Talbert had with him."

"What the hell are you talking about?" Rostrow demanded. He crossed to where we were standing. Larsen followed him, moving slowly.

I let them stew for a moment. By then the skinheads had the first load, about half the crates, jammed into the back of the van. Trog slammed the door shut, then he and Brick looked toward Larsen, who waved them on. They got into the van and Lori cranked the engine. I waited until the van had disappeared from view and I could see the sun again.

"I'm talking about what's in the crates. Automatic weapons, right? Plenty of ammo, maybe some explosives. Some grenades and launchers. Sounds like you're planning an assault on something big. Is it all there, George? Everything you ordered?"

He met my gaze with his own. George didn't look stupid. In fact, at the moment he looked as though what I was saying was getting through to him. "Kyle bought the stuff, didn't he? How much was he supposed to buy?"

Larsen shifted his gaze from me to his brother-in-law. "I thought it looked a little light. Did you buy everything on the list?"

"Of course I did." Kyle walked toward Larsen, standing near the crates, and laid a hand on the other man's arm. "I told you, it was expensive. More expensive than you thought it would be."

"He's feeding you a line," I broke in. "There's a very good reason you don't have as many supplies as you expected. Talbert found out why, so Kyle here killed him."

"Don't pay any attention to her," Kyle said. "She's trying the old divide-and-conquer routine."

I shook my head. "I'm telling the truth, George. I'll lay it out for you, step by step. Talbert's one of those investigative reporters. He comes to Bakersfield to do his big story on extremist groups, like your little operation here. He's done his research beforehand, and he knows that you and Martina come from an old Klan family. Talbert's suspicious of Kyle and Martina anyway, since he thinks they helped Tom Shiller fall off that cliff over in San Luis Obispo. An 'accident' which conveniently occurred about the same time Shiller had decided to let an auditor look at the books of the Coast Academy."

At the look on Kyle's face, I chuckled. "Oh, yes, I know about that. Wayne Talbert got a job here. You didn't recognize him as Nick Talbert, the reporter from SLO. Then Gillie let it slip that she knew who he was. Before you could neutralize him, Talbert broke into your office that Friday, after his poker game with Fosby. He was looking for anything he could get on you and Martina. He jimmied your filing cabinets. I don't know what he found there, but the next place he looked was your hard drive and your disk file. And he found the financial records for your little paramilitary operation here."

I looked him in the eye and dropped the bomb, the one I figured his cohorts didn't know anything about. "Only you were keeping two sets of books, just like you did when you got caught embezzling from that dry cleaning firm back in Illinois, fifteen years ago. One set for the true believers like Martina and George and Clifford, who are funneling all their cash into the organization. And one set for yourself, that shows how much money you're skimming off the top."

I laughed again. "Greed wins out over ideology every time."

"She's lying," Kyle insisted.

But right now the other three were looking at him instead of me. And they looked like they believed me.

The gun in Martina's hand wavered. The barrel moved. Then she pulled the trigger. The sound was deafening. Darcy and Gillie screamed. Out of the corner of my eye, I saw Miguel move to encircle them with his arms.

But the bullet missed Kyle Perris and buried itself in the wooden side of one of the crates. She hadn't intended to shoot him, but she'd sure as hell scared him.

And her brother. George Larsen's face had drained of color. "Damn it, you could have set something off. Give me that gun."

"We'll deal with this later," Martina said, echoing Rostrow's earlier words. She placed the gun in her brother's outstretched hand. "How soon will they be back? We've got to get the rest of these crates out of here."

"Get your car," Larsen told Rostrow. "We can load some of it into your trunk."

Rostrow started for the outer door. But I thought I'd heard the van, back when the true believers had been staring at the con man, before Martina fired a shot across Kyle's brow. I must have been mistaken. I didn't hear anything now.

Then Bennett Fosby appeared in the doorway, minus his jingling keys, hands wrapped around what looked like his old service revolver. "What the hell's going on here?" he barked indignantly, taking in the scene and the participants. "I heard a shot. You, with that gun. Drop it."

"It's all right, Bennett," Martina said, in the same saccharine voice she'd first used on me. "There's been a misunderstanding."

"Everything's under control, Fosby." Kyle Perris sounded a little shaky on the first word but by the time he'd finished the sentence, he'd regained his old smooth confidence.

"No, it's not, Fosby," I said. "Call the police."

Fosby glanced at Rostrow, on his right, who'd taken a step forward. Then I saw George Larsen, on Fosby's left, raise the gun. I sprinted forward and hit Larsen's torso as he fired. He stumbled. I hit him again, kicking the backs of his knees. As he fell forward, the gun flew from his hand.

Miguel had moved, too, shoving Kyle Perris to the floor, as Darcy and Gillie darted between the crates. I turned, catching a glimpse of Rostrow struggling with Fosby. Then I saw Martina reaching for the gun I'd knocked from her brother's hand. I caught up with her a split second before she could grab it. I swung her around and my balled-up fist connected with her jaw. It made a most satisfying crack. She staggered backward and fell.

I scooped up the gun and pointed it at Rostrow, who was still try-ing to overpower Fosby. "Back off," I shouted.

Rostrow moved away from Fosby. By now Larsen was on his feet again, scowling. Kyle Perris opted for staying on the concrete floor near his wife, who lay there moaning.

Fosby's right hand tightened on the grip of his revolver as Miguel joined us. The three of us consolidated our hold on the outer door. I noticed that Fosby was sweating, not because of the heat, though. Larsen's shot had hit him after all. Blood oozed from a wound on his upper left arm.

"Where's your Blazer?" I asked him.

"In front of my office. Key's in my right back pocket." He tried a grin. "Mind telling me what's going on?"

"After we get out of here. Miguel, get the key. Let's go."

Miguel reached behind Fosby and gently lifted the key from his pocket. Darcy and Gillie appeared from the shadows. They ran out the door, followed by Miguel. Fosby and I backed away from the building, holding our weapons on the Perrises, Larsen, and Rostrow.

I saw a flash of movement as Larsen reached for the briefcase he'd left on top of the crates. I saw his hand close on something and real-ized it was a gun. I shot him.

I shouted at Fosby as Larsen fell. We ran for the corner of the building. Fosby's Blazer was backing toward us at an alarming rate of speed. It screeched to a halt in the gravel and the passenger-side door was flung open. Darcy was at the wheel, Miguel and Gillie in the back. I piled into the backseat and Fosby jumped into the pas-senger seat. Darcy spun the Blazer around as Rostrow came out of the maintenance building with Larsen's gun. Darcy was headed for the front gate, then I saw headlights, moving fast up the short lane that led to the circular drive. It was still light enough, on this long midsummer evening, for me to see that it was the black van with the skinheads, back for a second load of weapons.

"The side gate," I said.

Darcy altered course before the words were out of my mouth. At the side gate she leapt from the driver's seat, pulling the chain with the key over her head. I slipped between the two front seats and moved behind the wheel as Darcy unlocked the gate. Rostrow was using the side of the maintenance building for cover. He fired at us, then the van moved into view. Darcy had the gate open now. She ran for the Blazer, leaping through the passenger-side door into Fosby's lap. He shut the door and I gunned the Blazer through the gap in the fence.

"Are you crazy?" Fosby said as I turned left, heading for the canal. "You can't get out that way."

"Bennett, there's a bridge over the canal. That's how Darcy got out."

"Where'd you get the key to that gate?" he bellowed as I fishtailed the van over the sod of the furrowed field. Darcy braced both hands on the dash while Fosby held her with his injured arm. He still had the gun in his right hand.

"I gave it to her," Miguel said. "Jeri, they're following us."

I glanced in the rearview mirror, and saw the van. Then I heard a sharp crack and a spiderweb pattern appeared in the back window of the Blazer. Gillie screamed.

"Now they're shooting at us," I said as I floored the accelerator.

In front of me I saw the concrete rim of the canal. The bridge was somewhere to the right. I turned and we were paralleling the canal. The van changed direction, bouncing over the field, trying to get ahead of us. Brick was driving this time, steering with his right hand and holding the gun in his left. I heard another crack, more gunfire. Next to me Fosby told Darcy to duck down toward the floorboard, then he hit the electronic button that lowered the window. He fired once, twice at the van, which veered away.

Now I saw the bridge over the canal. I sped up, bumped over the concrete edge, and made a hard left. The Blazer jolted over the narrow bridge, then onto the dirt road that led to the subdivision. I started to climb the hill, glancing into the rearview mirror.

The van was on the bridge now, but Brick was going too fast. He'd misjudged the narrowness of the bridge, or the fact that it had no rails. The front left wheel of the van slipped off the edge. Then the van spun slowly and fell into the canal.

CHAPTER *48*

"**S**EMIAUTOMATIC ASSAULT RIFLES, PISTOLS, SHOTGUNS," I said, "and ammo for all three."

Cece and I were having breakfast at her house on Monday morning. I was reading aloud from the front-page article in the Bakersfield *Californian*, where a sidebar listed the items seized by the Bakersfield Police Department, Kern County Sheriff's Department, and agents from the Bureau of Alcohol, Tobacco and Firearms.

After descending on the Perris School, the authorities had searched the Perrises' house on Panorama Drive and the Oildale house rented by Clifford Rostrow, which was where the skinheads had been taking the weapons on Saturday night. Fresno city and county authorities had done the same at George Larsen's house and office, as well as Rostrow's apartment.

"Blasting caps, fuses, detonation cord," I continued. "Grenades and grenade launchers. And explosives, including ammonium nitrate and nitromethane. Body armor, gas masks, and two booby traps. They found bomb-making handbooks, guerrilla manuals, and some fairly incriminating documents. Also lots of racist and anti-Semitic hate literature. Pamphlets, posters, magazines, books."

I looked up from the newspaper. "Of course, there's all that data on Talbert's disks, which Miguel and Darcy hid in three separate places out on Grandma's west county farm. One disk had all his research, one had his article, and the third was the financial information from Kyle's computer. That's really why Talbert was killed. Kyle had driven over to the school to do a little late-night tinkering with the books. He'd made a lot of money disappear that way. He saw Talbert going in the back way and surprised him. He did use that big stapler as a bludgeon. Afterwards, he tossed it in the river and told Martina and the others he'd done it because Talbert was on to them. But having the cops, and me, running around asking questions about the murder led them to move the weapons."

Cece shook her head in disbelief and poured herself another cup of coffee. "What the hell were they planning to do with all that stuff?"

"I'm not sure. Neither are the authorities. Everyone who was arrested has links to a whole network of white supremacist and neo-Nazi groups. Garza tells me they found surveillance videos of the federal building over on Truxtun Avenue, the Bakersfield Police Department, and the Kern County Sheriff's Department up on Norris road, all with voice-over describing the best places to plant bombs."

"Are these people crazy?" Cece asked rhetorically.

"It would certainly be convenient to think so." I recalled what Ira Blum had said about true believers.

"But people like Martina, Rostrow, and Larsen really believe that they're the anointed of God, the only true patriots. They believe other people are inferior because of religion or race or sexual orientation. They really believe that the Holocaust didn't happen, and that the federal government is tyrannical and they have to do something about it. A great many of them believe they have a perfect right to kill anyone who doesn't agree with them. They're sane. That's what makes them so frightening."

I'd been in Bakersfield nearly a week now. I was eager to get home, cuddle my cats, and sleep in my own bed. It looked like most of the sorting out was over, at least as far as I was concerned. I'd have to come back to Bakersfield to testify in some trials, but that was months away.

I sipped my coffee and recalled the chaotic scene Saturday night. By the time I'd driven Fosby's Blazer up the hill, Sergeant Harmon and Detective Garza were already on their way to the school, alerted by a worried Cece. A homeowner whose backyard overlooked the school had seen the black van pursuing the Blazer. When the van fell into the irrigation canal, he called 911. So did I, from the pay phone near the school in the subdivision.

I was all right, just a few scratches, bruises, and strained muscles, but the night had taken its toll, physically and mentally. By the time we got to the hospital Gillie Cooper was shaking and crying so hard that she couldn't stop. She was thoroughly traumatized, and under the care of a psychologist.

Miguel had two broken ribs. "Not too bad," he told me later. "I hurt worse when one of Grandma's horses threw me."

Bennett Fosby had taken a bullet in the arm, but he was in fairly good spirits. On the way to the hospital I apologized to him for suspecting he was part of the group of conspirators.

"I may be a conservative," he said. "Maybe prejudiced, too. But I'm not an extremist. I've got no truck with that kind."

Fosby explained that he'd been coming home to get a book he'd promised, but forgotten, to take to his sister. He was concerned when he saw the black van and the skinheads leaving the school, because they had no business being there. Then he spotted both the Perrises' cars in the lot and wondered what they were doing there on a Saturday evening, especially since they'd sent the students off to Lake Isabella. Just as he'd reached the maintenance building, he'd heard the shot Martina had fired at Kyle. He'd left the Blazer there and set out on foot for his house, circling in front of the cottages so he wouldn't be seen. Once he'd reached his house he'd retrieved his own gun and gone to investigate.

I'd shot George Larsen in the shoulder, but he'd live to face the law's scrutiny, as would Kyle Perris. He admitted killing Nick Talbert with the stapler that Consuela Webber had told me was missing from the office. Garza told me later that a fragment of a staple had been found in Talbert's head wound. The police hadn't found the murder weapon, though. Perris had thrown the stapler into the Kern River, and it wasn't likely that they'd ever locate it.

Martina had a big bruise on her face where I'd hit her, and from that I derived a certain satisfaction. The skinhead Brick had drowned when the van went into the canal, but the others, Lori, Trog, and Rostrow, had made it out of the swiftly flowing water in time to be arrested.

But Darcy was going to be okay. I thought. I hoped.

I recalled the scene late that night in the hospital emergency room, when Dan and Adele showed up. There were plenty of tears and hugs all around. The other scene came much later, when we all went back to the Holiday Inn on Truxtun Avenue.

I preceded them into the lobby, then stopped. Elaine Stefano sat on a sofa near the registration desk, a container of coffee in one hand. Darren was stretched out beside her, his head on her lap, sound asleep. She was frowning and staring into space, as though the coffee was cold and she was wondering why she'd driven down to Bakersfield to sit in a hotel lobby at midnight.

"Elaine?" I spoke gently and she blinked. Dan, Adele, and Darcy were about twenty feet behind me and I didn't think she'd seen them yet.

"Where have you been?" Elaine set the coffee down and ran a hand through her hair. "I've been sitting here for hours. You weren't here. I called that lawyer Mother hired and she wasn't home. I called the police and that detective wasn't there. I was starting to worry." She nudged Darren. "Wake up, kiddo."

Darren stirred, sat up, swung his legs to the floor, and yawned elaborately. "Oh, hi, Jeri. What time is it?" He squinted at his watch. "Midnight? Wow. I told Mom we needed to come down here, so we left this afternoon and we got here about eight. But nobody was around." Then he caught sight of his father, grandmother, and sister.

"Hey, Darcy." He bounced off the sofa and ran to her. The two Stefano kids bear-hugged each other with fierce affection. Then Darcy looked over her brother's shoulder, at her mother, no emotion on her face.

Elaine stood up. "Darcy? Are you all right?"

"Yes, I'm all right." Darcy released Darren. She folded her arms and glared at her mother. "No thanks to you."

Elaine took a deep breath. "Okay. I was wrong. About a lot of things. I'm sorry."

"It's a little late for that," Darcy said.

"I suppose it is." Elaine's words came awkwardly. "But I'm here, and I said it. I hope that means something."

I didn't know if that would be enough for Darcy, or her mother. But it was a start.

It was Tuesday before Harmon and Garza decreed that we could all leave Bakersfield, still baking in midsummer heat, and go home to the Bay Area, where I hoped it was cooler. And less eventful. Darcy walked with me out to my car and watched as I loaded my things into the Toyota.

"Do me a favor," I told her, standing there with the driver's-side door open. "Stay out of trouble." This sounded like a repeat of our parting in Paris. But we'd been through a lot more this time around.

"Trouble just seems to find me," she said.

"That's because you wave your arms to attract it," I admonished. "You know, if you need to talk, you can always call me."

She grinned. "You mean you're not going to change your phone number?"

"I considered it. Give your mother a chance." Her smile dimmed and she didn't answer. "I don't get along with my mother either, Darcy. Haven't for years. But at some point you have to open a dialogue. Either now, or when you're older, like me."

"I'll think about it." The grin returned and she threw her arms around me. "Y'know, Jeri, I'm gonna miss you. We've had such an adventure."

"Adventure? Is that what you call it? I call it one doozy of a case." I hugged her, then laughed. "Well, here's looking at you, kid. We'll always have Bakersfield."

THE INFORMATION ON CHILDREN WHO SURVIVED THE Holocaust after being hidden from the Nazis comes from *Hidden Children* by Andre Stein (Penguin) and *The Hidden Children* by Jane Marks (Bantam). Sources for France and World War II include *Vichy France and the Jews* by Michael R. Marrus and Robert O. Paxton (Stanford University Press) and *The War Against the Jews, 1933–1945,* by Lucy S. Dawidowicz (Bantam).

There is much information available on the Internet concerning extremist groups. Also consulted were *Klanwatch Intelligence Report,* August 1996, from the Southern Poverty Law Center; *Gathering Storm: America's Militia Threat* by Morris Dees and James Corcoran (HarperCollins); and *The Limits of Dissent* by Thomas Halpern and Brian Levine.

American Exodus: The Dust Bowl Migration and Okie Culture in California by James N. Gregory (Oxford University Press) provides a fascinating study of the 1930s immigrants and their effect on California, particularly the San Joaquin Valley.